THE CURIOUS READER

A LITERARY MISCELLANY OF NOVELS & NOVELISTS

EDITED BY **ERIN McCARTHY** AND THE TEAM AT **MENTAL FLOSS**

MENTAL FLOSS

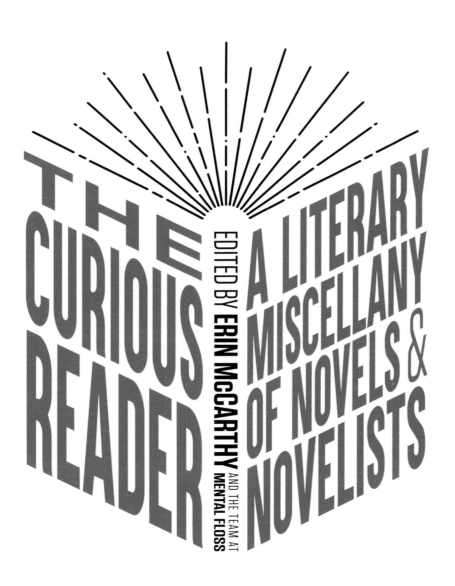

THE CURIOUS READER

EDITED BY **ERIN McCARTHY** AND THE TEAM AT **MENTAL FLOSS**

A LITERARY MISCELLANY OF NOVELS & NOVELISTS

weldon**owen**

CEO Raoul Goff
PUBLISHER Roger Shaw
ASSOCIATE PUBLISHER Mariah Bear
CREATIVE DIRECTOR Chrissy Kwasnik
SENIOR EDITOR Ian Cannon

weldon**owen**

PO Box 3088
San Rafael, CA 94912
www.weldonowen.com

© 2021 Sportority Inc.

ISBN 978-1-68188-755-5

Produced by Indelible Editions

INDELIBLE
EDITIONS

Printed in Italy
10 9 8 7 6 5 4 3 2 1
2021 2022 2023 2024

Weldon Owen would like to thank
Katie Moore for editorial assistance.

CONTENTS

INTRODUCTION ERIN McCARTHY

I f there's one thing that drives both the Mental Floss team and the Mental Floss reader, it's curiosity—the desire to discover strange stories and fun facts about every facet of the world, including the books we have on our shelves.

Books have been a huge part of Mental Floss's coverage since Will Pearson and Mangesh Hattikudur launched the magazine from their Duke University dorm room twenty years ago, not to mention one of our most popular topics on MentalFloss.com, which launched in 2006. Since then, we've featured stories by librarians and rare book dealers and authors like John Green, Jenn Doll, Ransom Riggs, and A.J. Jacobs. We've revealed the tales behind iconic cover designs and little-known facts about authors (did you know that Dr. Seuss dabbled in taxidermy sculptures, or that Agatha Christie came up with plots in the bathtub?).

In *The Curious Reader*, we've compiled decades of Mental Floss articles on all things literary, from how to distinguish between a novella and a short story to what word to use when you can't stop buying books. We've sought out tales strange and obscure, inspiring and funny. You'll find out about the savage rejections received by beloved authors, weird writing tricks involving index cards and pushpins, and even which dishes famous writers might bring to a potluck.

This is my kind of collection. I've been a voracious reader ever since I was little, when I could often be found with my nose quite literally in a book late into the night, even though my parents told me that reading in the dark would ruin my eyes (that's a myth, by the way)—and not much has changed as I've gotten older. And whenever I finish a book, I always want to know *more*: What inspired the author? How did the time period in which the book was written influence the work? What was the writer's process, and what hiccups did they experience along the way to publication? Were their characters based on any real people? How did they settle on a title, and did they agree with how readers interpreted their book? These are the kind of questions I've been able to answer during my many years at Mental Floss, making me one of the luckiest readers on the planet.

We hope that *The Curious Reader* will teach you things you never knew—and inspire you to pick up a book, whether it's revisiting one you've read a thousand times before or a new classic that's been sitting in your to-be-read pile forever. Happy reading!

GEORGE ORWELL

June 25, 1903–January 21, 1950

BORN: Motihari, Bihar, India

OTHER NOTABLE WORKS:
Down and Out in Paris and London (1933)
Animal Farm (1945)

E ric Arthur Blair, better known as George Orwell, came of age in the revolutionary atmosphere of the early twentieth century and quickly became disillusioned with Britain's oppressive imperialism. Orwell didn't just observe the class divides and rising fascism of the era from afar—he lived them. He worked as a British imperial police officer in Burma; he fought in the Spanish Civil War; he washed dishes in Paris; he traipsed through England with vagabonds. These experiences shaped his socialist ideology and inspired such novels as *Animal Farm* and *1984*, which continue to reflect certain unshakeable injustices in today's society.

Orwell's 1949 novel *1984* has given us a whole slew of shorthand phrases for dystopian or oppressive governments and surveillance, but even if you've already read about Winston Smith's struggle against Big Brother, there are a few facts, stories, and theories about the novel that are worth a closer look.

IT NEARLY WASN'T CALLED *1984*.

Before *1984* was published, Orwell was wracked with indecision about it. For a while, he considered the title *The Last Man in Europe* and based the novel in both 1980 and 1982 before settling on 1984.

BEFORE CRITICIZING PROPAGANDA IN *1984*, ORWELL WORKED AS A PROPAGANDIST.

During World War II, Orwell worked for the British Broadcasting Corporation. His role with the BBC Empire Service involved creating and supervising programming that the nation would feed to Indian networks to encourage a pro-Allies sentiment and spark volunteering.

THE AUTHOR MODELED ROOM 101 AFTER AN OFFICE AT THE BBC.

The most horrifying setting in *1984* is Room 101, the Ministry of Love's torture chamber in which victims are exposed to their worst nightmares—a chilling setting that Orwell modeled on an actual room.

As a propagandist, Orwell knew that much of what the BBC said had to be approved by the Ministry of Information, possibly in the BBC's Room 101. He likely drew the name of his nightmare room from there. Room 101 was later demolished during building renovations.

ORWELL WAS BEING WATCHED WHILE HE WROTE *1984*.

Twelve years before he published *1984*, Orwell released the nonfiction piece *The Road to Wigan Pier*, an exploration of poverty and class oppression in England during the 1930s. Thanks to the investigative research he had conducted for *Wigan Pier*, which included the documentation of labor conditions in coal mines, and because he attended Communist Party meetings, Orwell was placed on a watch list by the government's Special Branch and kept under tight surveillance for over a decade. His official file noted Orwell's "advanced communist views" and that he "dresse[d] in a bohemian fashion."

BIG BROTHER'S REGIME BORROWED PRACTICES FROM WORLD GOVERNMENTS.

Orwell didn't limit his sights to a single tyrannical power when designing the oppressive regime in *1984*. The author borrowed a number of elements from the Soviet Union, including the "2 + 2 = 5" slogan from the so-called "five-year plan" for national development beginning in 1928 (though the phrase had been used for decades before that), and the NKVD police force likely provided the model for most of the Thought Police and Ministry of Love's activity. Additionally, *1984*'s treatment of Thought Crimes resembled how the Special Higher Police, a Japanese policing service active during World War II, condemned unpatriotic thoughts during their self-styled "thought war."

JULIA IS BELIEVED TO BE BASED ON ORWELL'S SECOND WIFE.

Many scholars have speculated that Julia, *1984*'s female lead and romantic interest to protagonist Winston, was modeled after Orwell's second wife, Sonia Brownell. The comparison might not have been all that flattering, though: Orwell describes Julia as a "rebel from the waist downwards" and ultimately has Winston betray her to aid his own liberation.

ORWELL WROTE THE BOOK WHILE STRUGGLING WITH TUBERCULOSIS.

While most of us would use the opportunity of a mild cold to take a week off from work, Orwell did not let a 1947 bout with tuberculosis shift his focus away from his latest novel. After a stay in a hospital he kept working—supposedly collapsing after he finished his second draft.

HE NEARLY DROWNED WHILE WORKING ON THE NOVEL.

Much of the writing of *1984* was done in Jura, Scotland, where Orwell found himself to be most productive. Even in this setting, he was hardly exempt from bouts of procrastination—some of which were particularly disastrous. While taking a break from his writing one day in the summer of 1947, Orwell led his son, niece, and nephew on a boating expedition across the nearby Gulf of Corryvreckan. During the trip, the family's dinghy capsized unexpectedly, tossing them overboard without life jackets. Luckily, all four survived, but the event was hardly helpful to Orwell's already fragile health.

ORWELL DIED SEVEN MONTHS AFTER *1984* WAS PUBLISHED.

Although Orwell had seen success as a broadcaster, journalist, nonfiction writer, and as the author of *Animal Farm*, he unfortunately never got to witness the full impact that his most popular work would have on the world: *1984* was published in June of 1949, and Orwell died on January 21, 1950, due to complications from tuberculosis.

THE ORIGINS OF FIVE FAMOUS AUTHORS' PEN NAMES

Just before publishing his first novel, Eric Arthur Blair decided to write under a pen name to avoid embarrassing his family. He took the first name from patron saint of England and the reigning monarch in the first half of the 1930s, and the last name from the River Orwell, a popular sailing spot, which he loved to visit. Here are a few other pen names that might surprise you.

TONI MORRISON

Born Chloe Wofford, Morrison began going by Toni—an abbreviation of her baptismal name, Anthony—when she went to Howard University. "The people in Washington, they don't know how to pronounce C-H-L-O-E," she told NPR. Someone called her Toni, and she went with it, saying, "It's easy. You don't have to mispronounce my name." When she got married in 1958, she took her husband Harold Morrison's last name, and though they divorced in 1964, she used Morrison on her first novel, 1970's *The Bluest Eye*. She tried to get it changed back to her maiden name before publication but was told it was too late. In a 2012 *New York* magazine profile, Morrison said it was something she regretted: "Wasn't that stupid? I feel ruined!"

AYN RAND

Born Alissa Zinovievna Rosenbaum in St. Petersburg, Russia, the future *Atlas Shrugged* author changed her name when she came to the US in 1926. Though legend has it that she got her last name from a Remington Rand typewriter, Rand was probably an abbreviation of Rosenbaum. According to the author, Ayn was a variant of a Finnish name, but some believe it was actually derived from the childhood nickname Ayin; others believe the name may have had meaning to her that we'll never know.

J.K. ROWLING

"My publisher, who published Harry Potter, they said to me, we think this is a book that will appeal to boys and girls," Joanne Rowling told CNN. "And they said, so could we use your initials? Because, basically they were trying to disguise my gender . . . I was so grateful to be published, if they told me to call myself Rupert, I probably would have done [it] to be honest with you." Rowling didn't have a middle name, so she took her grandmother's—Kathleen—to get that second initial.

BELL HOOKS

Ain't I a Woman author Gloria Jean Watkins has been going by bell hooks since 1978. She took the name from her maternal great-grandmother, Bell Blair Hooks, as a way to honor her; the lower case styling puts the focus on her ideas, because the important thing is the "substance of the books, not who I am."

JOHN LE CARRÉ

The author of spy novels was *himself* a spy in England when he began publishing novels in 1961. His employers had no issues with the novel, but said he'd have to use a pseudonym. His publisher suggested that David John Moore Cornwell go by something like Chunk-Smith. But as for how he came up with John le Carré, well . . . he couldn't remember. "I was asked so many times why I chose this ridiculous name, then the writer's imagination came to my help," the author told *The Paris Review*. "I saw myself riding over Battersea Bridge, on top of a bus, looking down at a tailor's shop . . . And it *was* called something of this sort—*le Carré*. That satisfied everybody for years. But lies don't last with age. I find a frightful compulsion toward truth these days. And the truth is, I don't know."

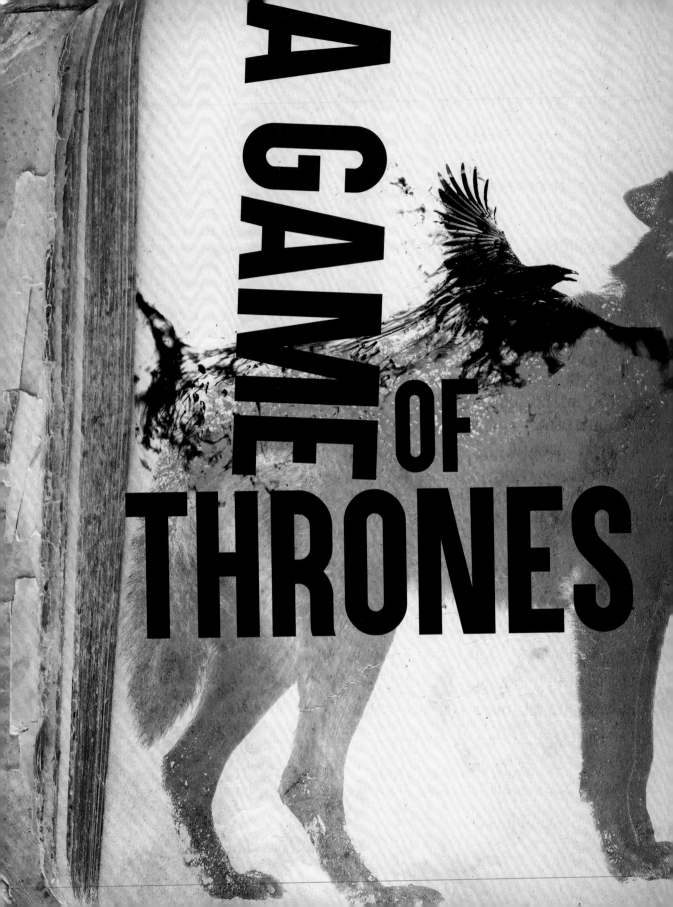

GEORGE R.R. MARTIN

September 20, 1948

BORN: Bayonne, New Jersey

OTHER NOTABLE WORKS:
The Armageddon Rag (1983)
A Clash of Kings (1998)
Fire & Blood (2018)

Growing up, George R.R. Martin was desperate to escape his hometown. "Not because Bayonne was a bad place, mind you. Bayonne was a very nice place in some ways," he once said. "But we were poor. We had no money. We never went anywhere." Unable to physically travel, Martin turned to books—and his imagination. He got his start selling his monster stories to kids in the neighborhood, first for a penny, and later a nickel. (The stories apparently gave his friends nightmares, and his mother forced him to stop selling them when she found out.)

Martin, a comic book–obsessed kid, realized he could probably write better stories than what appeared in many fanzines after he got a letter published in an issue of *Fantastic Four*—and he never looked back.

He published the novel *The Armageddon Rag* in 1983, but the reception to the novel was so terrible that Martin switched gears—and mediums—entirely, writing for *The Twilight Zone* reboot and the live-action *Beauty and the Beast* television series starring Linda Hamilton and Ron Perlman.

While working in television, he began writing the book that would become *A Game of Throne*s, the first volume in his yet-to-be-completed A Song of Ice and Fire series. The first book wasn't a best seller, but the subsequent books in the series took off: They sold more than 90 million copies and were adapted into HBO's juggernaut series *Game of Thrones*. "I had no idea when this all started where it would lead . . . or how long the road would be," Martin wrote on his blog.

TIME magazine dubbed Martin "The American Tolkien," but the author has taken a practical view of his success: "It's not something anyone could ever anticipate," he has said, and "not something I expect to ever experience again."

The first book in George R.R. Martin's A Song of Ice and Fire series, *A Game of Thrones* was published in August 1996 to a few honors (including a nomination for a Nebula) but little in the way of sales. The book—which follows characters in Westeros and across the Narrow Sea as they seek the Iron Throne and control of the seven kingdoms—wouldn't hit *The New York Times*'s best-seller list until January 2011, just a few months before the show based on it, *Game of Thrones*, debuted on HBO. The TV show has since come and gone, revealing an end to Martin's saga, but the author is still toiling away on his A Song of Ice and Fire; read up on the book that started it all while you wait for a new installment.

MARTIN THOUGHT THAT *A GAME OF THRONES* MIGHT BE JUST A SHORT STORY.

Martin recalled to *The Guardian* in 2018 that when it came to *A Game of Thrones*, inspiration struck suddenly—in fact, he said, the first chapter "came out of nowhere": "When I began, I didn't know what the hell I had," he said. "I thought it might be a short story; it was just this chapter, where they find these direwolf pups. Then I started exploring these families and the world started coming alive." Before he knew it, he had one hundred pages written, and had started drawing maps and family trees. "It was all there in my head, I couldn't not write it," he said. "So it wasn't an entirely rational decision, but writers aren't entirely rational creatures."

HE WAS INSPIRED BY AUTHOR THOMAS B. COSTAIN'S TAKE ON THE PLANTAGENETS.

"My model for this was the four-volume history of the Plantagenets that Thomas B. Costain wrote in the '50s," Martin said. "It's old-fashioned history: He's not interested in analyzing socioeconomic trends or cultural shifts so much as the wars and the assignations and the murders and the plots and the betrayals, all the juicy stuff. Costain did a wonderful job on the Plantagenets so I tried to do that for the Targaryens."

IN THE ORIGINAL OUTLINE, DAENERYS KILLS KHAL DROGO FOR A DIFFERENT REASON.

 Martin's 1993 pitch for his A Song of Ice and Fire series—then three books—shows that there was a lot of revising done between when he pitched the series and when *A Game of Thrones* was published in 1996. For one thing,

Daenerys kills Khal Drogo to avenge the death of her brother, Viserys, and rather than getting her dragon eggs as a wedding gift, she finds them beyond Vaes Dothrak.

But perhaps the most surprising axed storyline featured Jon Snow and Arya Stark falling in love. Their love affair eventually becomes a love triangle when Tyrion Lannister *also* falls in love with Arya.

One thing that *didn't* change was Martin's willingness to kill off beloved characters—in fact, he wrote that he didn't want readers to ever feel that a character was safe.

MARTIN DREW ON REAL HISTORICAL EVENTS FOR HIS SERIES.

With *A Game of Thrones*, Martin specifically wanted to write a book that didn't gloss over the brutality of Medieval Europe—and for inspiration, he turned to history. "No matter how much I make up, there's stuff in history that's just as bad, or worse," he said in 2013. Westeros itself was based on Medieval Great Britain, and the brutal Wars of the Roses was "the single biggest influence" on the story: "I've drawn from French history, and Scottish history, and other things, but at the center of it all is the Wars of the Roses. I have the Lannisters and the Starks, and in real life it was the Lancasters and the Yorks." The Wall is inspired by Hadrian's Wall in the United Kingdom, built by the Romans in the second century CE.

In *A Storm of Swords*, the Red Wedding had two events as its inspiration: The Black Dinner of 1440—a dinner-turned-trap that ended in the murder of two children—and the Massacre of Glencoe of 1692, during which soldiers claiming to need shelter due to a full fort slayed their hosts.

4 FOUR DIFFERENCES BETWEEN THE *A GAME OF THRONES* BOOK AND THE SHOW

Showrunners David Benioff and D.B. Weiss made a number of changes—big and small—in translating *A Game of Thrones* from the page to the screen. Here are just a few of them.

THE WHITE WALKERS LOOK DIFFERENT IN THE BOOKS.

The gray, frozen skin and dark armor of the White Walkers is a contrast to the books, in which they have "flesh pale as milk" and "armor [that] seemed to change color," reflecting their environment as they moved. They also largely went by a different name: The wildlings (and Old Nan) call them White Walkers, but the residents of the Seven Kingdoms call them The Others.

IN THE BOOKS, THE TARGARYEN FAMILY MEMBERS ARE NOTABLE FOR THEIR SILVER HAIR AND VIOLET EYES.

During shooting, Daenerys (Emilia Clarke) and Viserys (Harry Lloyd) Targaryen originally wore violet contact lenses, but Benioff and Weiss decided they negatively impacted the actors' ability to portray emotion.

THE STARK KIDS WERE DIFFERENT AGES IN THE SHOW THAN IN THE BOOKS.

When the book *A Game of Thrones* starts off, the Stark children are much younger than their on-screen counterparts. Bran was supposed to be seven instead of ten on the show. Arya went from nine to eleven, while Sansa went from eleven to thirteen. And the actors could have dramatic age differences as well: Daenerys is thirteen in the book and around sixteen in the TV show's first season—but Emilia Clarke was in her twenties when production began.

THE JOKE ABOUT THE HAND—A.K.A. THE KING'S CLOSEST ADVISOR—CHANGED BETWEEN THE BOOK AND THE SHOW.

In the book, people say, "The King eats, the Hand takes the shit." But in the series, it's "The King shits, and the Hand wipes."

Tools of the Trade

When it comes to writing, George R.R. Martin is delightfully old school: He writes everything in WordStar 4.0—which he has called "the Duesenberg of word processing software (very old, but unsurpassed)"—on a DOS computer that isn't connected to the internet. That's not what takes him so long to write his books, though. "When I'm actively writing, when it's really going well . . . I live in Westeros," he has said. "[I]n order to achieve this almost Zen state of obsession, I have to push away real life. There are other writers who write four pages a day, they write in hotels, they write on airplanes, they write everywhere. I've never been one of those writers. I need to have the whole day just to write, nothing else on my calendar."

A PRAYER FOR OWEN MEANY

JOHN IRVING

March 2, 1948

BORN: Exeter, New Hampshire

OTHER NOTABLE WORKS:
Setting Free the Bears (1968)
The World According to Garp (1978)
The Cider House Rules (1985)

"I never write the first sentence until I know all the important things that happen in the story, especially—and I mean exactly—what happens at the end of the novel," John Irving has said. "If I haven't already written the ending . . . I can't write the first sentence."

Born John Wallace Blunt Jr., Irving never met his father; his parents separated when his mother was pregnant, and Irving would eventually take his stepfather's last name. Irving struggled with dyslexia growing up, and credits his wrestling coach with helping to keep him in school—and his learning disability with giving him an edge in writing.

The author has published over a dozen books in more than thirty-five languages so far, winning a National Book Award (for *The World According to Garp*), a Lambda Award (for *In One Person*), and an Oscar (for his *The Cider House Rules* screenplay). Irving weaves elements of his own life into his novels—both absent parents and wrestling are recurring themes, and like the narrator of his beloved novel *A Prayer for Owen Meany*, Irving lives in Canada. He once told *The New York Times*, "You can become tyrannized by the authenticity of what you remember."

···

A Prayer for Owen Meany, Irving's novel about a boy with a "wrecked voice" who believes he's an instrument of God, is a staple on high school summer reading lists—and made *The New York Times*'s best-seller list after it was published in March 1989. Here are a few things you might not have known about the hit novel.

THE FIRST SENTENCE IS IRVING'S FAVORITE.
Irving didn't write the first sentence of *A Prayer for Owen Meany* ("I am doomed to remember a boy with a wrecked voice—not because of his voice, or because he was the smallest person I ever knew, or even because he was the instrument of my mother's death, but because he is the reason I believe in God; I am a Christian because of Owen Meany") until at least a year after he'd written the last sentence. "I may one day write a better first sentence to a novel than that of *A Prayer for Owen Meany*, but I doubt it," Irving

wrote. "What makes the first sentence of *A Prayer for Owen Meany* such a good one is that the whole novel is contained in it."

IRVING BASED OWEN MEANY ON A CHILDHOOD FRIEND.

The author was home for Christmas in the early 1980s, where he and his childhood friends were remembering other friends who had gone to Vietnam and never come back. "Suddenly one of my friends mentioned a name that drew a blank with me—a Russell somebody," Irving wrote. "Then another one of my friends reminded me that, in Sunday School, we used to lift up this little boy; he was our age, about eight or nine, but he was so tiny that we could pass him back and forth over our heads."

That jogged Irving's memory. Russell had moved away before they became teenagers, and was killed in Vietnam. "I was amazed," Irving writes. "I said one of the stupidest things I've ever said. 'But he was too *small* to go to Vietnam!' My friends looked at me with pity and concern. 'Johnny,' one of them said, 'I presume he *grew*.' That night I lay awake in bed, pondering the 'What if . . .' that is the beginning of every novel for me. What if he *didn't* grow? I was thinking." Irving would later incorporate the memory of passing Russell over the heads of kids in Sunday School into a scene in *Owen Meany*.

THE BOOK IS FULL OF HOMAGES TO OTHER NOVELS.

In the novel, Johnny's mother is killed by a baseball hit by Owen Meany—which, Irving said in an interview with *The Denver Post*, is an homage to the Robertson Davies novel *Fifth Business*, in which the protagonist's mom is hit by a snowball. "I love that novel," Irving said. "And Owen Meany has the same initials as Oskar Matzerath—the hero of Günter Grass's novel *The Tin Drum*." And, like Irving's Meany, Oskar Matzerath refuses to grow.

IRVING PLAGIARIZED HIMSELF.

"The physical description of Owen Meany who is first described as looking embryonic, not yet born, was a passage I lifted from the physical description of the orphan Fuzzy Stone who dies of respiratory failure in *The Cider House Rules*, the novel before I wrote *A Prayer for Owen Meany*," Irving said at a 2006 charity event. "If you look at the physical description of Fuzzy

and the physical description of Owen Meany, they're almost word for word the same."

OWEN'S VOICE IS PROBABLY CAUSED BY "SINGERS' POLYPS."

 The author writes Owen's weird "wrecked voice" in all caps. When asked to describe what the voice sounds like to him, Irving told *The Denver Post*, "There's gravel damage, rock dust, granite quarry residue, in Owen's throat; he probably has what they call singers' polyps. . . . It's irritating to listen to—like the effect of those capital letters, I thought. It's an insistent voice—one that demands to be heard." Another important reason it was necessary: In the novel's climactic scene, where he saves a group of Vietnamese children at an airport from the grenade-wielding half-brother of a dead soldier, "Owen has to have a voice the Vietnamese children will pay attention to, which is why he also has to be small," Irving said.

IRVING INSISTS THAT JOHNNY WHEELWRIGHT IS NOT AN AUTOBIOGRAPHICAL CHARACTER.

Despite the similarities between Irving and John Wheelwright—they share a first name and a similar childhood history, neither went to Vietnam, and both, as adults, live in Toronto—Irving emphasizes that he's not Wheelwright. "I wouldn't be playing fair if I did not admit to sharing some of his opinions emotionally, but the point about Johnny Wheelwright is that he has no distance; he has no perspective," Irving told *The New York Times* in 1989. "He is puerile. His sense of political outrage is strictly emotional." He doesn't share John Wheelwright's religious fervor, either.

IT WAS ADAPTED INTO A MOVIE—SORT OF.

Irving, who penned the screenplay for the film adaptation of his novel *The Cider House Rules* over the course of thirteen years, decided he was too busy and "had neither the desire nor the stamina to revisit the Vietnam years" to try to adapt a screenplay for a film version of *Owen Meany*—so he let Mark Steven Johnson take a whack at writing the screenplay. But he had some conditions: "I said I wanted to read the shooting script and decide at that time if I wanted them to use my title and the names of my characters. Mark agreed."

Irving liked the script, he said, which was quite different from the novel: Everything about Vietnam had been excised and the ending was changed. "I felt it would mislead the novel's many readers to see a film of that same title which was so different from the book," Irving said, and so he asked that the name be changed. The resulting movie, *Simon Birch,* hit theaters in 1998. "*Simon Birch* is really Mark Steven Johnson's story—with *Owen Meany*'s beginning," Irving said. "I think it was, therefore, a happy resolution for both Mark and me that he was able to make his film, which clearly was 'suggested by' (as credits say) *A Prayer for Owen Meany,* but which is clearly not *A Prayer for Owen Meany.*"

Afterward, rumors circulated that Irving had hated the movie. "Mark took an unfair bashing in the American press," Irving told *The Guardian.* "People wrote that I hated the film and took my title away. That is untrue." The book has since been adapted into a stage play, a college production, and a BBC radio play.

WRITING ADVICE FROM FIVE WRITERS

When setting out to write, don't let the thought of competing with famous authors leave you paralyzed—instead, harness their writing habits and tips to further your own work. Start with these five tips.

1 Use the words you're writing with // JOHN IRVING

"If you're familiar with the words you use, you'll probably spell them correctly—and you shouldn't be writing words you're unfamiliar with anyway," Irving wrote in an 1980s advertorial for International Paper. "USE a word—out loud, and more than once—before you try writing it, and make sure (with a new word) that you know what it means before you use it."

2 Don't worry about your "process" // LOUISA MAY ALCOTT

"I never copy or 'polish' so I have no old manuscripts to send you; and if I had it would be of little use, for one person's method is no rule for another," Alcott once wrote. "Each must work in his own way, and the only drill needed is to keep writing and profit by criticism."

3 Write a lot // RAY BRADBURY

"The best hygiene for beginning writers or intermediate writers is to write a hell of a lot of short stories," the sci-fi novelist said in a keynote address. "If you can write one short story a week—it doesn't matter what the quality is to start, but at least you're practicing, and at the end of the year you have fifty-two short stories, and I defy you to write fifty-two bad ones. Can't be done. At the end of thirty weeks or forty weeks or at the end of the year, all of a sudden a story will come that's just wonderful."

4 Don't wait for inspiration // JACK LONDON

"Don't loaf and invite inspiration; light out after it with a club, and if you don't get it you will nonetheless get something that looks remarkably like it," the author advised. "Set yourself a 'stint,' and see that you do that 'stint' each day."

5 Research and revise // OCTAVIA BUTLER

"Revise your writing until it's as good as you can make it," Butler advised. "Check your writing, your research (never neglect your research), and the physical appearance of your manuscript. Let nothing substandard slip through. . . . There will be plenty that's wrong that you won't catch. Don't make the mistake of ignoring flaws that are obvious to you."

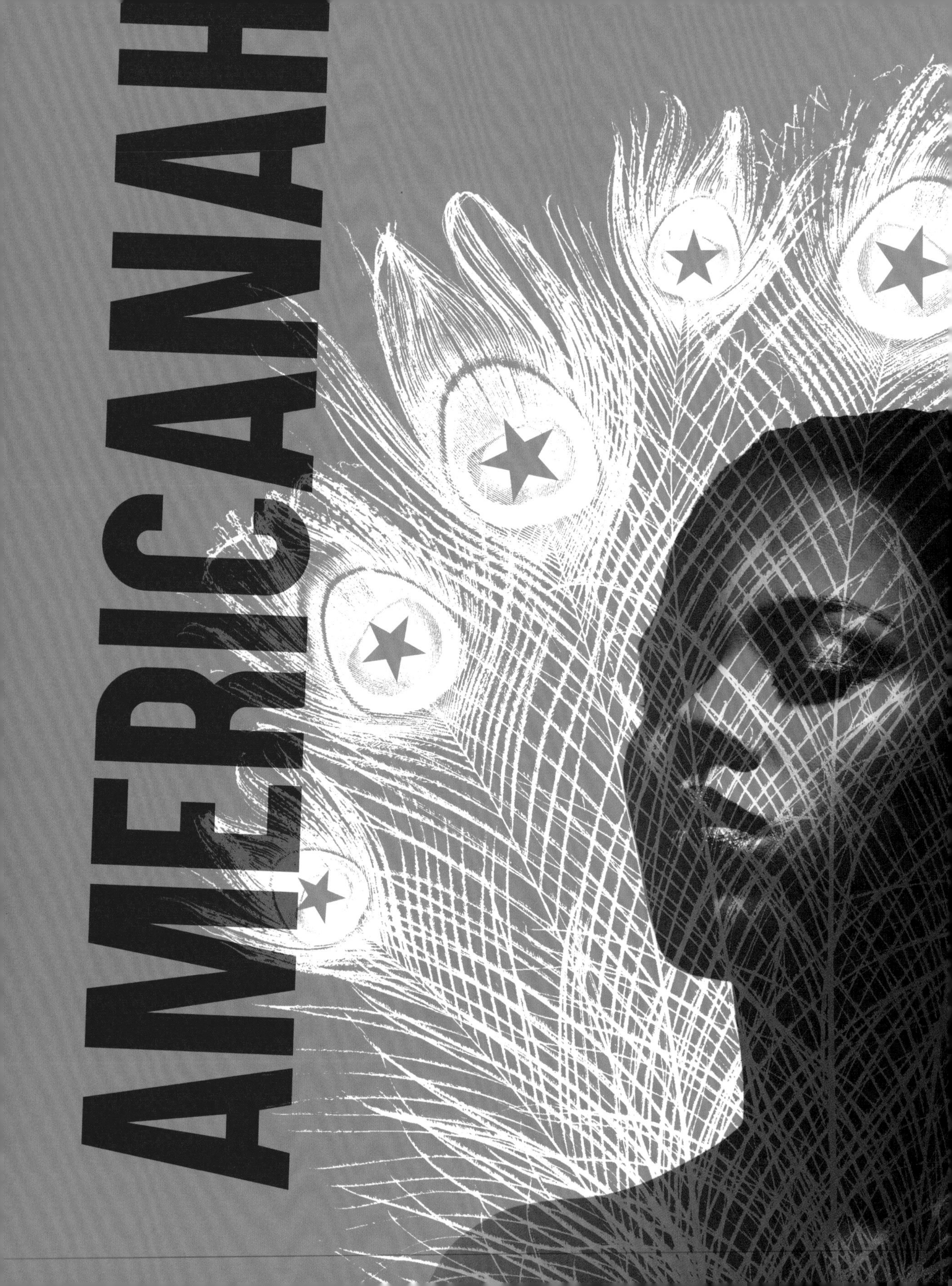
AMERICANAH

CHIMAMANDA NGOZI ADICHIE

September 15, 1977

BORN: Enugu, Nigeria

OTHER NOTABLE WORKS:
Purple Hibiscus (2003)
Half of a Yellow Sun (2006)
We Should All Be Feminists (2014)

When Chimamanda Ngozi Adichie was six years old, her family moved into a home in Nsukka, Nigeria, whose previous resident was Chinua Achebe—the author of *Things Fall Apart*. Years later, Adichie would jokingly say that she could remember "waking up at night to go to the bathroom and stopping near a staircase and hearing literary spirits whispering secrets in my ear, secrets about plot and character and sentence structure." Adichie began reading and writing early, but all of her stories featured white British people. It wasn't until she read *Things Fall Apart* at age ten that she realized "that people like me could exist in books. . . . I would not be the writer I am if it wasn't for Chinua Achebe."

Adichie began to write about the Nigerian experience in poems, essays, and her critically acclaimed debut novel, *Purple Hibiscus*, published in 2003. Three years later came *Half of the Yellow Sun*, which takes place during the Nigerian civil war—which was a shadow over Adichie's childhood—and two years after that, Adichie won a MacArthur Genius Grant. With her third novel, 2013's *Americanah*, "I wanted to write an unapologetically old-fashioned love story," she explained to *The Guardian*. "But it is also about race and how we reinvent ourselves. It is about how, when we leave home, we become another version of ourselves. And it is also about hair. . . ."

Americanah follows a young woman named Ifemelu as she leaves Nigeria for the United States to attend college, a journey that Adichie made herself. As she told *Interview* magazine, "I can write with authority only about what I know well, which means that I end up using surface details of my own life in my fiction. There are bits of me in Ifemelu, as there are in most characters I write." Ifemelu's teenage love, Obinze, is ultimately supposed to join her in America, but his visa is denied after 9/11. Ifemelu starts a successful blog that humorously discusses her observations on race in America from the perspective of an African Black woman. *Americanah* isn't just a coming-to-America story; it also follows Ifemelu as she returns to Nigeria and reunites with Obinze. The novel won the National Book Critics Circle Award for Fiction and was named one of the top ten books of the year by *The New York Times*.

THE TITLE COULD HAVE BEEN DIFFERENT.

When Ifemelu returns to Nigeria, she has a new, Americanized perspective—and the book's title reflects this: *Americanah* is a word Nigerians use to refer to people who go to the United States and put on American airs when they come back. "It's often used in the context of a kind of gentle mockery," Adichie told NPR.

Americanah was Adichie's first title for the book, because, as she told Goodreads, "I liked the playfulness and irreverence of it." But she flirted with changing it to *The Small Redemptions of Lagos*, the name of the blog Ifemelu starts writing when she comes back to Nigeria, because she thought it sounded "more poetic." But Adichie ultimately went back to *Americanah* when "a good friend told me [*The Small Redemptions of Lagos*] sounded like the title of a small book sold under the bridge in Lagos."

ADICHIE DIDN'T THINK *AMERICANAH* WOULD BE A SUCCESS.

Adichie told HuffPost that when she was writing *Americanah*, she thought the book ultimately wouldn't do well because she "didn't necessarily follow all of the literary rules. It deals with race in a way that's very overt. It's a love story that is ridiculously romanticized in a way, while also being kind of practical. I also wanted it to be a book that just felt true and raw. . . . But I also realized that these are not necessarily the things that lead to success in fiction. . . . In some ways, this book has taught me to trust readers, because . . . I think readers respond to things that feel true."

ADICHIE WROTE A REAL BLOG IN IFEMELU'S VOICE AFTER *AMERICANAH* CAME OUT.

After the release of *Americanah*, Adichie started a real blog called *The Small Redemptions of Lagos*, written in Ifemelu's voice, discussing important and timely issues like the Nigerian response to the Ebola outbreak. Like the blog in the book, this blog was supposed to be funny—but after events like the shooting of Michael Brown by a white police officer in Ferguson, Missouri, in 2014, the author stopped writing it. "I think what's going on now just doesn't give me room for humor," Adichie said at the Washington Ideas Forum in 2016. "I don't think I could find any space to wrap humor around what's been happening in the past one year, two years. I have often thought about continuing the blog, but it probably wouldn't do much with race, because I'm just exhausted."

AMERICANAH WAS THE FIRST PICK FOR NEW YORK CITY'S FIRST BOOK CLUB.

In 2017, the New York City Mayor's Office of Media and Entertainment announced a city-wide book club called One Book, One New York, which encouraged everyone in New York City to read the same book at the same time. Fifty thousand votes were cast and determined that Adichie's *Americanah* would be the first read. When asked about New York's choice in an interview with HuffPost, Adichie said she was honored, and likened the idea of the whole city reading the same book to "the idea of a village gathering under a tree in the moonlight and telling their stories."

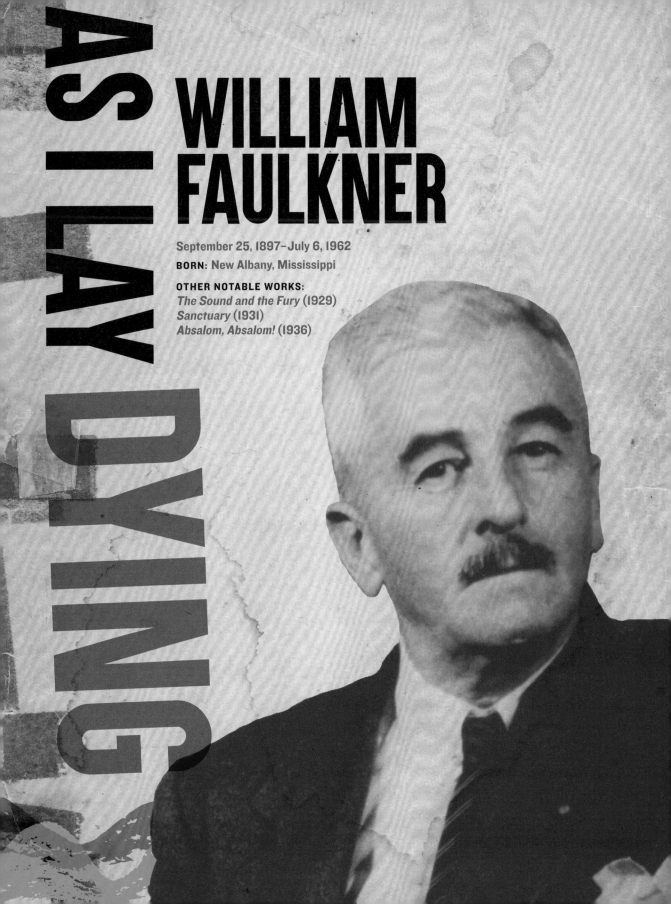

AS I LAY DYING

WILLIAM FAULKNER

September 25, 1897–July 6, 1962

BORN: New Albany, Mississippi

OTHER NOTABLE WORKS:
The Sound and the Fury (1929)
Sanctuary (1931)
Absalom, Absalom! (1936)

Few writers are as closely linked to the American South as William Faulkner. The Mississippi native wrote nineteen novels and dozens of short stories during his career, with many taking place in the fictional Yoknapatawpha County—a stand-in for Lafayette County, where Faulkner grew up. Though his first three novels failed to make much of an impact, it was his next two—1929's *The Sound and the Fury* and 1930's *As I Lay Dying*—that began establishing his genius. He would continue to explore themes like sex, race, and class through a Southern point of view in books like *Sanctuary* and *Absalom, Absalom!*

Throughout the '30s and '40s, Faulkner split much of his time between his home in Oxford, Mississippi, and Hollywood, where he contributed to movies like 1939's *Gunga Din*, 1944's *To Have and Have Not*, and 1946's *The Big Sleep*. He was awarded the 1949 Nobel Prize in Literature, and would continue to write until his death in July 1962 at the age of sixty-four.

Released in 1930, William Faulkner's *As I Lay Dying* appeared to be an impossibly ambitious undertaking. The sprawling tale of the Bundren clan and their struggles to give their matriarch, Addie, a proper burial is an astonishing literary achievement, often cited as one of the great novels of the twentieth century. As they trek through the state to deliver Addie's body to her desired burial site in Jefferson, the family struggles with obstacles, arguments, and even insanity in order to fulfill her wishes. The novel is now regarded as an American classic—and a bit of an endurance test for some readers. Here, some facts about the book and Faulkner's very deliberate undertaking of writing a "classic."

IT HAS MUCH IN COMMON WITH *THE SOUND AND THE FURY*.

For six months, William Faulkner put everything he had into writing *The Sound and the Fury*, a story that uses multiple narrators and a stream-of-consciousness style to chronicle the decline of the formerly aristocratic Compson family. It wasn't an immediate success when it was released in 1929, but it has since been recognized as one of the author's essential works.

The next year, Faulkner released *As I Lay Dying*, a similarly stylized book that utilizes fifteen different narrators over fifty-nine chapters. Though critics continue to see the two works as inextricably linked, Faulkner himself was once quoted as saying he never thought of the novels "in the same breath."

FAULKNER CLAIMED HE WROTE IT IN SIX WEEKS.

It can sometimes be difficult to sort Faulkner's own personal mythology from facts. The novelist, who was a high school and college dropout, claimed he wrote *As I Lay Dying* while working at a Mississippi power plant. (His earlier novels, while well regarded, did not provide much in the way of royalties.) For around six weeks, he wrote from midnight until four in the morning while at the plant. The book was composed on a wheelbarrow that he turned into a table.

HE DELIBERATELY SET OUT TO WRITE A CLASSIC.

Faulkner was one of the more blunt novelists of his era, having little time or regard for self-promotion or any examination of his process. In discussing *As I Lay Dying*, he was fond of saying that he was very conscious of the novel's potential to be embraced as a sprawling American classic. "I set out deliberately to write a tour de force," he said. "Before I ever put pen to paper and set down the first word I knew what the last word would be and almost where the last period would fall."

FAULKNER USED THE SAME FICTIONAL SETTING IN SEVERAL OF HIS BOOKS.

Faulkner set many of his novels, including *As I Lay Dying*, in the fictional Yoknapatawpha County, a spell-check-threatening word that Faulkner claimed came from a Chickasaw term for water running through flat lands (though modern Faulkner scholars think it's more likely "split land"). While visiting the University of Virginia, he instructed students on its proper pronunciation: *YOK-na-pa-TAW-fa*.

ONE CHAPTER IS COMPRISED OF A SINGLE SENTENCE.

Chapter Nineteen reads:

"My mother is a fish."

The perspective is that of Vardaman Bundren, the youngest son of the recently deceased Addie Bundren, whom he compares to a sea creature due to her coffin floating on a river.

TWENTY-TWO BANNED BOOKS

- ■ **RACISM**
- ■ **EXTREMISM**
- ■ **CRIMINALITY**
- ■ **SEXUALITY**
- ■ **POLITICS**
- ■ **SEXISM**
- ■ **RELIGION**
- ■ **CULTURAL DIFFERENCES**

■ **1856–1857**
Madame Bovary
FRANCE / Its depictions of adultery were seen as morally offensive.

■ **1928–1959**
The Well of Loneliness
UK / This novel was banned for its portrayal of lesbian relationships.

■ **1931**
Alice's Adventures in Wonderland
HUNAN PROVINCE, CHINA / Anthropomorphic animals were considered inappropriate.

■ **1932**
Brave New World
IRELAND / The future world's sexual promiscuity was offensive.

■ **1934–1964**
Tropic of Cancer
US / The dirty details of author Henry Miller's expat life shocked Americans.

■ **1939**
The Grapes of Wrath
KERN COUNTY, CALIFORNIA, US / Set in California, the book offended Kern County's leaders.

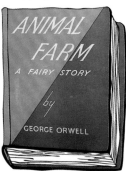

■ **1945–1990**
Animal Farm
USSR / This novel was viewed, accurately enough, as a critique of communism.

■ **1957**
The Song of the Red Ruby
NORWAY / This book was briefly banned due to the protagonist's sexual exploits.

■ **1962–present**
Nine Hours to Rama
INDIA / This title controversially dealt with Mahatma Gandhi's assassination.

■ **1978–present**
The Turner Diaries
GERMANY / The author, William Luther Pierce, was part of a pro-Nazi political group.

1979
Burger's Daughter
SOUTH AFRICA / This historical novel's treatment of apartheid got it banned for three months.

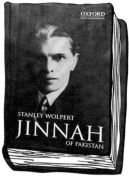

1984–present
Jinnah of Pakistan
PAKISTAN / This biography claims Pakistan's founder enjoyed wine and pork.

1985–1988
Spycatcher
UK / In this title, a former intelligence officer reveals state secrets.

1988
The Story of Little Black Sambo
JAPAN / This children's book was banned for racist depictions.

1989-present
The Satanic Verses
THROUGHOUT THE MIDDLE EAST / Salman Rushdie's novel was banned for blasphemy against Islam.

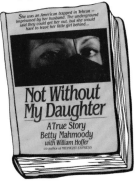

1990
Not Without My Daughter
IRAN / This memoir is considered critical of Islamic customs.

1991–present
Our Friend the King
MOROCCO / This biography of King Hassan II of Morocco divulged human rights violations.

1995–2000
American Psycho
GERMANY / The novel was widely criticized for violence and misogyny.

1996-present
Zhuan Falun
CHINA / This book details the beliefs of the banned Falun Gong sect.

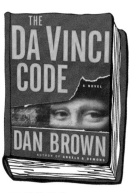

2004–present
The Da Vinci Code
LEBANON / The Catholic community in Lebanon deemed Dan Brown's novel offensive.

2007–present
The Peaceful Pill Handbook
AUSTRALIA / This guide instructs readers how to perform euthanasia.

2010-present
Dianetics
RUSSIA / All of L. Ron Hubbard's books are deemed "extremist material."

BEL♥VED

er pallet intricate Bab

ati condemnation chain gang aul D. enunc

teous muster thwart resurrection ing reminisc defer r

esolate maim offal cleave Sweet H undulate De er pallet i

oolteacher rendezvous Sethe whip noi e Cincinnati demnat

on profound malevolent bereft clabbe ghteous mu te thwa res

niscent defer repulsion me n oly ma ote esol te maim offal cleave S

ate Denver pallet intricate Baby Suggs sch endezvous Sethe whip

e Cincinnati condemnation chain gang Paul D. en n profound malevolent bereft

clabbe righteous muster thwart resurrection roiling ref n defer repulsion melanc

malice dote desolate maim offal cleave Sweet Home undu er pallet intricat

Suggs schoolteacher rendezvous Sethe whip noisome Cinc ondemnation chain

profound malevolent bereft clabber righteo s r t resur

er re sion anch

Baby

n gan

TONI MORRISON

February 18, 1931–August 5, 2019

BORN: Lorain, Ohio

OTHER NOTABLE WORKS:
The Bluest Eye (1970)
Sula (1973)
Song of Solomon (1977)

SPOILERS! Toni Morrison's first novel was written in the limited free time available to her between her day job in the publishing industry and the responsibilities of raising two children. Perhaps the dueling pressures of these two worlds lent her unique insight into "the role women play in the survival of . . . communities," as *The New York Times* described an enduring theme of hers upon her death in 2019. Morrison's first job after receiving her graduate degree was in academia, teaching at Texas Southern University and then at Howard. And while she returned to teaching intermittently even after her own success as a writer, Morrison's work avoids didacticism. Instead, perhaps influenced by the superstitions of her own young life and a grandmother who often looked to a book of dream interpretations, Morrison's work often feels more like an American-born magical realism, a less-than-literal reality that brings truth powerfully to light.

By the time *Beloved* hit bookshelves in 1987, Toni Morrison had firmly established herself as a force in the world of literature. Not only had she already published four acclaimed novels of her own—*The Bluest Eye, Sula, Song of Solomon*, and *Tar Baby*—but she had also overseen the publication of works by Angela Davis, Gayl Jones, Henry Dumas, and many other seminal authors as an editor at Random House.

When it came to *Beloved*, however, Morrison said it "was like I'd never written a book before." The story, which follows a formerly enslaved woman haunted by the daughter she killed to save her from slavery, so moved Morrison that she often doubted her ability to finish it. But she persevered, creating what many now consider one of the most important novels of all time.

MORRISON CAME UP WITH THE IDEA FOR THE STORY YEARS BEFORE SHE WROTE IT.

As an editor, Morrison spearheaded the formation of 1974's *The Black Book*, a scrapbook of sorts containing photos, advertisements, newspaper clippings, and other visual artifacts of the Black experience in America. One of them was an article about Margaret Garner, an enslaved woman who fled with her family from Kentucky to Ohio in 1856. When their enslaver's search party caught them, Garner "cut the throat of her little daughter, whom she probably loved the best."

(She also attempted to kill her other children, but was overpowered.)

Garner's desperate act—and the implication that death was better than being enslaved—lodged in Morrison's mind, but she didn't decide to adapt the story until more than a decade later. And though the author did substantial research for *Beloved*, she refrained from unearthing every detail about Garner's life. "I wanted to invent her life, which is a way of saying I wanted to be accessible to anything the characters had to say about it," she said in 1988.

MORRISON RELIED ON READERS' INNATE BELIEF IN GHOSTS TO MAKE BELOVED'S APPEARANCE MORE CONVINCING.

Though Sethe believes *Beloved* to be the spectral incarnation of her daughter, nowhere in the novel does Morrison confirm that she is, in fact, a ghost. Morrison wasn't sure if readers would be receptive to this gray area but noted that we all occupy that gray area in real life: Even skeptics make sure their hands don't dangle over the edge of the bed. In other words, Morrison didn't need readers to believe that Beloved was a ghost— she just needed them to entertain the possibility that she *could* be one.

BELOVED IS THE FIRST BOOK IN A TRILOGY.

When Morrison submitted the manuscript to her editor, Robert Gottlieb, it was a year late and far from finished. She had intended *Beloved* to be the first segment of a three-part novel. The second part would center on the Harlem Renaissance, and the final story would take place in the 1980s. Since Gottlieb insisted that *Beloved* worked as its own novel, Morrison decided the other planned volumes would complete a trilogy. Those novels, loosely connected by theme, are *Jazz* (1992) and *Paradise* (1997).

MORRISON DIDN'T HAVE HIGH HOPES FOR BELOVED'S SUCCESS.

In 1989, Morrison told *TIME* that she "had this terrible reluctance" to write about slavery. Not only did the sheer length of the era overwhelm her, but she hesitated to delve into the physical and psychological torture that white enslavers—and society at large—committed against enslaved people. After it was written, she believed

that *Beloved* wouldn't be widely read, "because it is about something that the characters don't want to remember, I don't want to remember, Black people don't want to remember, white people don't want to remember. I mean, it's national amnesia." *Beloved* ended up winning the Pulitzer Prize in Fiction.

BELOVED WAS MEANT TO MAKE UP FOR THE LACK OF PHYSICAL MEMORIALS TO ENSLAVED PEOPLE.

After finishing *Beloved*, Morrison found herself wondering why it had felt like such an essential endeavor. She noticed that the nation had virtually no monuments or public spaces commemorating enslaved people; for her, the novel helped fill the void. "There is no place you or I can go, to think about or not think about, to summon the presences of, or recollect the absences of slaves," she said in her acceptance speech for the Frederic G. Melcher Book Award. "There is no suitable memorial or plaque or wreath or wall or park or skyscraper lobby. There's no 300-foot tower. There's no small bench by the road."

The Toni Morrison Society celebrated the author's seventy-fifth birthday in 2006 by unveiling "The Bench by the Road Project," which has placed nearly two dozen black steel benches at notable sites around the country. The inaugural bench was installed on Sullivan's Island, South Carolina, where it's believed that as many as two-fifths of all enslaved Africans first entered the US.

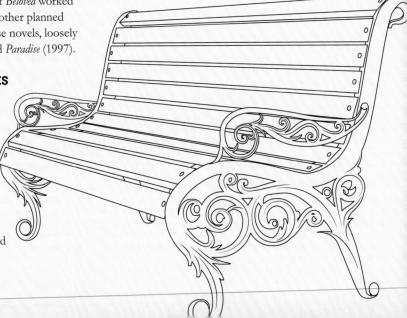

THIRTEEN AMAZING BOOKS BY BLACK AUTHORS YOU NEED TO READ

Toni Morrison was praised for adding Black stories to the overwhelmingly white world of literature. "Being a Black woman writer is not a shallow place but a rich place to write from," she told *The New Yorker* in 2003. "It doesn't limit my imagination; it expands it. It's richer than being a white male writer because I know more and I've experienced more." From literary icons to fresh, buzzworthy talent, these are some memoirs and novels by Black authors you should add to your reading list today.

1 *Hunger: A Memoir of (My) Body //* **ROXANE GAY**
While many weight-related stories are prescriptive—telling you what to do and how to live your life—Gay's is simply descriptive: a searingly vulnerable look at what it means to live obese.

2 *Between the World and Me //* **TA-NEHISI COATES**
Imagined as a letter to his teenage son, Coates shifts seamlessly between his own memories and US history to illustrate Black Americans' endless struggle against racism in all its forms.

3 *Homegoing //* **YAA GYASI**
Gyasi's sweeping epic begins with eighteenth-century Ghanaian half-sisters—Effia, who marries a British governor; and Esi, who is enslaved and sent to America—and tracks their descendants' stories through the 2000s.

4 *Their Eyes Were Watching God //* **ZORA NEALE HURSTON**
In Hurston's 1937 novel, Janie Crawford reminisces about her experiences of love, natural disaster, domestic abuse, and the legacy of slavery in rural, early twentieth-century Florida.

5 *Brown Girl Dreaming //* **JACQUELINE WOODSON**
Woodson tells the story of her childhood, from segregated South Carolina to New York at the height of the civil rights movement, through a collection of evocative, narrativized poems.

6 *I Know Why the Caged Bird Sings //* **MAYA ANGELOU**
Angelou's first autobiography chronicles her life from ages three to seventeen; a coming-of-age story that depicts rape, racism, temporary homelessness, and teen pregnancy with candor and grace.

7 *Babel-17 //* **SAMUEL R. DELANY**
As war ravages the galaxies, space captain-slash-poet Rydra Wong races to unlock the secrets of a weaponized language that can shape thoughts and turn speakers into unwitting traitors in Delany's 1966 sci-fi novel.

8 *The Hate U Give //* **ANGIE THOMAS**
In Thomas's debut novel, teenager Starr Carter witnesses a police officer shoot and kill her friend, then finds herself at the center of city-wide protests and a national demand for justice that mirrors the Black Lives Matter movement.

9 *Not Without Laughter //* **LANGSTON HUGHES**
In this seminal novel from the Harlem Renaissance, Hughes paints a portrait of the early twentieth-century Midwest through the eyes of Sandy Rogers, a young Black boy living in Kansas.

10 *The Underground Railroad //* **COLSON WHITEHEAD**
Whitehead imagines the Underground Railroad as an actual system of trains hidden beneath safehouses in this moving, multiple award–winning tale of cruelty, resilience, and hope.

11 *Devil in a Blue Dress //* **WALTER MOSLEY**
Mosley's detective thriller—his first book, and the basis for the 1995 film of the same name—follows Ezekiel "Easy" Rawlins through 1940s Los Angeles as he searches for a missing woman with a mysterious past.

12 *White Teeth //* **ZADIE SMITH**
Smith weaves a vivid, conflicted tapestry of multicultural London during the 1970s with this story about Bengali immigrant Samad Iqbal, his British friend Archie Jones, and their families.

13 *Zami: A New Spelling of My Name //* **AUDRE LORDE**
In this so-called "biomythography," an amalgam of biography, history, and myth, Lorde invites readers on an intimate journey through her early life, sharing memories of the Jim Crow era, McCarthyism, and her own personal relationships, all with the same poignant lyricism characteristic of her poetry.

BRAVE NEW WORLD

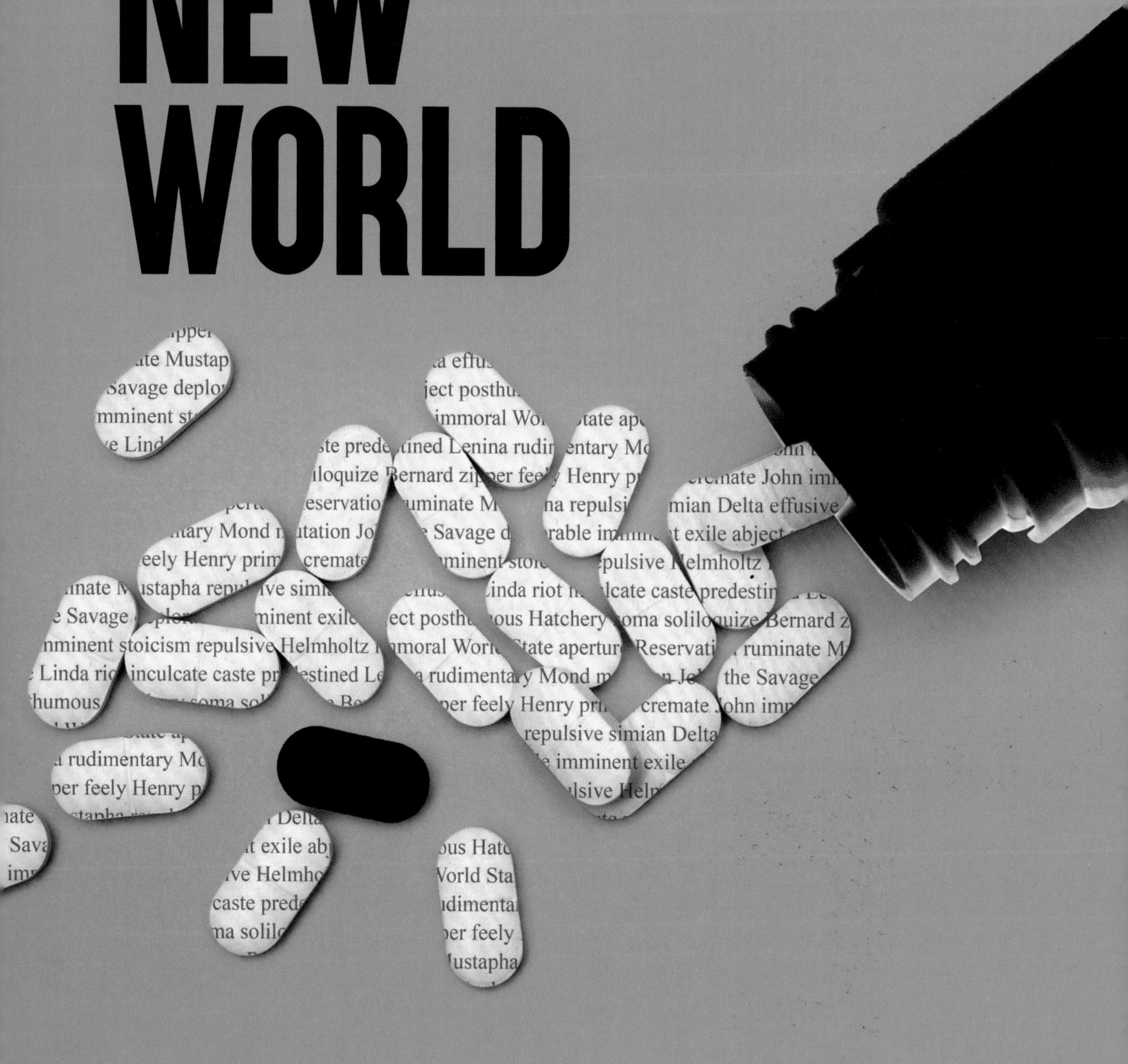

ALDOUS HUXLEY

July 26, 1894–November 22, 1963

BORN: Godalming, Surrey, England

OTHER NOTABLE WORKS:
The Doors of Perception (1954)
Island (1962)

Aldous Huxley seemed destined for a career in science at a young age. His grandfather Thomas Henry Huxley was a world-renowned biologist in the nineteenth century and a vocal defender of Charles Darwin's *On the Origin of Species*. But a condition known as keratitis would leave young Aldous partially blind as a teen and unable to pursue a career in the field, forcing him to turn his attention to his other passion: writing. Early in his career, Huxley wrote for the likes of British *Vogue* and *Vanity Fair*, before embarking upon his most celebrated novel, *Brave New World*, about a supposed utopian society where emotions and individuality are a thing of the past and the population is kept calm and happy thanks to a drug called soma.

Aldous Huxley's 1932 classic *Brave New World* is arguably one of the most inventive novels published in the twentieth century. It takes place in a futuristic setting called the World State, where every part of the dystopian society is dedicated to efficiency, and the class of each citizen is predetermined from birth. When Bernard Marx, a member of the highest class, sees how the "savages" born outside the system live, the true nature of the utopia he comes from is called into question. Here are a few interesting facts about the novel's inspiration and the legacy it spawned.

IT STARTED OUT AS A PARODY.

Before creating his most famous work, Huxley was mostly known as a satirist. His early novels *Crome Yellow*, *Antic Hay*, and *Those Barren Leaves* had served as send-ups of the avant-garde communities of the 1920s. When he began work on the project that would ultimately become *Brave New World*, Huxley was envisioning a loose and affectionate parody of the Wellsian utopia in the science fiction works of H.G. Wells like *A Modern Utopia*, *The Sleeper Awakes*, and especially *Men Like Gods*.

A BOAT TRIP SHOWED HUXLEY A KEY CREATIVE INFLUENCE.

Sheer luck led Huxley to a major inspiration for *Brave New World*. On a boat traveling between Singapore and the Philippines, Huxley happened upon a copy of Henry Ford's 1922 book *My Life and Work*. Ford would go on to be a major character—something of a deity—in the society Huxley created in *Brave New World*.

SAN FRANCISCO PROVIDED FURTHER INSPIRATION.

Though he was born and raised in a small market town in Surrey, England, Huxley was affected by a visit to the United States in the 1920s. San Francisco's youth culture made an especially large impact on the author. His indignation over what he saw as epidemics of consumerism and promiscuity in the city would inform *Brave New World*'s key themes. Disapproval of the California lifestyle notwithstanding, Huxley ended up moving to California in the 1930s.

AN ENGLISH CHEMICAL PLANT MADE ITS MARK ON THE NOVEL.

Along with the philosophies of Ford and the freewheeling lifestyle of San Francisco, Huxley found an unlikely muse in the Billingham Manufacturing Plant in Stockton-on-Tees, England. The author visited this industrial giant and was struck by how it was an "anomalous [oasis] of pure logic in the midst of the larger world of planless incoherence." The factory was set up by a businessman and politician named Sir Alfred Mond, 1st Baron Melchett, who might have lent his name to the story's Resident World Controller of Western Europe, Mustapha Mond.

A SCIENTIST HAS BEEN CREDITED WITH INFLUENCING *BRAVE NEW WORLD*'S SETTING.

While Huxley considered his principal literary influences to be H.G. Wells and D.H. Lawrence, many scholars agree that the writer's scientific leanings can be traced to physicist, geneticist, and biologist J.B.S. Haldane. One can find specific forerunners to the science fiction concepts of *Brave New World* in Haldane's 1924 text *Daedalus; or, Science and the Future*, which engages topics like transhumanism (that is, the synthetic control of human genetics and evolution) and in vitro fertilization.

HUXLEY WROTE THE BOOK QUICKLY.

Huxley set to work writing his story in 1931, and completed the novel in just four months.

GEORGE ORWELL ACCUSED HUXLEY OF PLAGIARISM . . .

Orwell, known best for *Animal Farm* and *1984*, opened this discussion in his *Tribune* magazine review of the 1924 novel *We* by Russian novelist Yevgeny Zamyatin. Orwell penned the review in 1946, stating that, "Aldous Huxley's *Brave New World* must be partly derived from [*We*]. Both books deal with the rebellion of the primitive human spirit against a rationalised, mechanised, painless world, and both stories are supposed to take place about six hundred years hence." Huxley claimed to have had never even heard of *We* until long after he had finished writing *Brave New World*.

. . . AS DID KURT VONNEGUT, THOUGH IN A MUCH FRIENDLIER WAY.

Commenting on his 1952 debut novel *Player Piano*, Vonnegut admitted to casually swiping the general premise from *Brave New World*. He softened the blow of his self-directed castigations, however, by asserting that Huxley had done the very same with Zamyatin's *We*. As Vonnegut told *Playboy* in 1973, "I cheerfully ripped off the plot of *Brave New World*, whose plot had been cheerfully ripped off from Yevgeny Zamyatin's *We*."

AS TIME WENT ON, HUXLEY BECAME MORE AND MORE AFRAID OF HIS PROPHECIES COMING TRUE.

Huxley's *Brave New World Revisited*, published in 1958 following an upswing in American counterculture and the author's own attraction to Hindu Vedanta, was a work of nonfiction detailing Huxley's apprehensions over a rapidly approaching overhaul of society by the values and practices illustrated in his 1932 original. Huxley even attempted to propose a de facto "call to arms" to reduce the likelihood of a dystopian reality.

Fascinating Facts about Aldous Huxley

There's a lot more to Aldous Huxley's life than dystopian novels. Here are a handful things you might not know about the author.

1 HE WAS ALMOST COMPLETELY BLIND AS A TEENAGER.

Born in 1894 in England, Huxley had a challenging early life. During his teenage years, his mother died of cancer, his brother died by suicide, and he began having problems with his vision. Following an infection, his corneas became inflamed (a condition called keratitis), and he couldn't see well. In an interview with *The Paris Review*, Huxley explained, "I started writing when I was seventeen, during a period when I was almost totally blind and could hardly do anything else. I typed out a novel by the touch system; I couldn't even read it."

2 HE STRUGGLED WITH EYESIGHT FOR MOST OF HIS LIFE.

Historians debate the extent and duration of Huxley's vision problems. In 1942, Huxley wrote *The Art of Seeing*, a book in which he described how he regained his sight. He used the Bates Method, a series of suggestions—get natural sunlight, do eye exercises, and don't wear glasses—for improving eyesight. *The Art of Seeing* was immediately attacked after its release by medical professionals for supporting pseudoscience, and questions remain about how much Huxley's vision actually improved.

3 HE TAUGHT GEORGE ORWELL.

In 1917, Huxley briefly worked as a teacher at Eton, the esteemed boarding school in England. One of his students was Eric Blair, who later wrote *1984* and *Animal Farm* under the pen name George Orwell. Huxley sent a letter to Orwell in October 1949, praising his work in *1984* but also getting in a slight dig at his former pupil. Huxley wrote that his own bleak view of the future was a more accurate prediction than Orwell's: "I feel that the nightmare of *1984* is destined to modulate into the nightmare of a world having more resemblance to that which I imagined in *Brave New World*."

4 HE WORKED AS A SCREENWRITER IN HOLLYWOOD.

In the 1930s, Huxley moved to California, and in the 1940s and early '50s, he worked as a screenwriter, collaborating on films such as *Pride and Prejudice*, *Jane Eyre*, and *Madame Curie*. In 1945, Disney paid Huxley $7,500 to write a treatment based on Lewis Carroll's *Alice's Adventures in Wonderland* that also incorporated Carroll's biography. That December, Huxley had a meeting with Walt Disney and his staff about the project. Disney eventually decided not to proceed with Huxley's script partly because it was, according to Disney, too literary.

5 HIS COMMITMENT TO PACIFISM PRECLUDED HIM FROM BECOMING AN AMERICAN CITIZEN.

Huxley frequently wrote about Hindu and Buddhist spiritual ideas, pacifism, and mysticism. He renounced all war, and his pacifist views ultimately prevented him from becoming a US citizen. After living in California for fourteen years, Huxley and his wife applied for citizenship. However, he refused to say that he would, if necessary, defend the US in wartime. Because his refusal to fight was based on philosophical rather than religious reasons, he realized the government would most likely deny his application, so he withdrew it before they had a chance to turn him down.

6 THE DOORS NAMED THEIR BAND AFTER HIS BOOK ABOUT MESCALINE.

Jim Morrison's band The Doors is named after Huxley's 1954 book *The Doors of Perception*, though Huxley himself took the phrase from English poet William Blake. Although Huxley depicted the pernicious effects of the fictional drug soma in *Brave New World*, he volunteered for mescaline experiments and praised the drug as physically harmless, potentially therapeutic, and spiritually enlightening in *The Doors of Perception*.

JOSEPH HELLER

May 1, 1923–December 12, 1999

BORN: Brooklyn, New York

OTHER NOTABLE WORKS:
Something Happened (1974)
Good As Gold (1979)
God Knows (1984)

Joseph Heller grew up in Brooklyn's Coney Island during the 1930s, a time he referred to as "my era" with obvious affection for the lower-middle-class treasures of his youth, from grilled hotdogs to rides on the famous Cyclone roller coaster. His otherwise idyllic childhood was marred by the sudden death of his father, perhaps embedding in Heller a penchant for gallows humor that would later serve his literary works. Described as "a sweet man" by John Updike and "a sorry soul" by his ex-wife, Heller's friends painted a picture of a man who could be riotously funny yet "suspicious of happiness," in the words of fellow writer Mario Puzo. Perhaps it was Heller's mother who best identified the gift and curse of her son's unique perspective on the world, telling Heller, years before his literary fame or the wartime experiences that preceded it, "You have a twisted brain."

Heller published *Catch-22* in 1961, and in the years after its release, he would work on a handful of plays and movie scripts before publishing his second novel, *Something Happened*, in 1974. His final novel, *Portrait of an Artist, As an Old Man,* was released in 2000, the year after his death at the age of seventy-six. In it, an aging author named Eugene Pota struggles to top the success of his first book from decades earlier.

There were countless other books focusing on World War II by the time Joseph Heller's *Catch-22* hit shelves in 1961—but none had portrayed a soldier's life through the lens of a comic farce quite like this one. Heller, a former bombardier himself, brought an absurdist twist to the battlefield in his debut novel, telling the story of Captain John Yossarian, who struggles to be relieved of his combat duties in the face of an irrational, incompetent bureaucracy. By making a mockery of war while never shying away from its brutality, Heller crafted one of the most important—and beloved—novels of the twentieth century, not to mention one of the funniest. Here's how Heller's story came to be, and the legacy it left behind.

HELLER SKETCHED OUT THE BOOK'S CONCEPT AND CHARACTERS IN ABOUT NINETY MINUTES.

Heller recalled the birth of his most famous novel as if it were a classic movie scene. While lying in bed in his apartment on the West Side of Manhattan in the early 1950s, Heller was struck with what would become the iconic opening line of the story: "It was love at first sight. The first time he saw the chaplain, 'Someone' fell madly in love with him," with "he" and "someone" holding the place for Heller's protagonist's eventual name, Yossarian. Over the course of an hour and a half, he developed the basic plot and collection of characters that he'd ultimately pour into his novel.

HE WROTE THE FIRST CHAPTER THE NEXT DAY— AT WORK.

At the time, Heller was working as an advertising copywriter, and he spent the day after his creative epiphany writing out by hand the entire first chapter of what would become *Catch-22*. He submitted the chapter to *New World Writing* magazine by way of a literary agent. A full year passed before he completed a second chapter.

HELLER WENT THROUGH FOUR NUMBERS BEFORE LANDING ON TWENTY-TWO.

The original title of the story, as published in *New World Writing*, was "Catch-18." But his publisher had qualms about the title, fearing there would be confusion with the WWII novel *Mila 18*. So Heller dragged his title through a sequence of changes: *Catch-11* (which was deemed too similar to the contemporary film *Ocean's 11*), possibly followed by *Catch-17* (which posed the same problem with Billy Wilder's war movie *Stalag 17*), and then *Catch-14* (which Heller's editor thought just didn't sound funny enough). Finally, they landed on *Catch-22*.

MANY CHARACTERS WERE BASED ON HELLER'S FRIENDS.

Yossarian was based on fellow World War II veteran Francis Yohannan. Additionally, the sociopathic Milo Minderbinder was designed with Heller's childhood friend, Marvin "Beansy" Winkler of Coney Island, in mind.

HELLER WAS FREQUENTLY ASKED ABOUT YOSSARIAN'S ETHNICITY AND RELIGION.

In *Catch-22*, Heller introduces Yossarian as Assyrian, despite the fact that his surname suggests otherwise. In response to readers' curiosity, Heller amended Yossarian's heritage in *Catch-22*'s 1994 sequel *Closing Time*, declaring the character Armenian. But the most common question Heller received regarding Yossarian's background concerned his religion, as many readers sought confirmation that the character shared Heller's Jewish faith. In 1972, Heller responded to these quandaries in a letter to Northeastern University professor James Nagel, stating, "Yossarian isn't Jewish and was not intended to be. On the other hand, no effort was expended to make him anything else."

HELLER WAS ACCUSED OF PLAGIARISM THIRTY-SEVEN YEARS AFTER THE PUBLICATION OF *CATCH-22*.

The book came under fire for similarities to the 1950 war novel *Face of a Hero*. Londoner Lewis Pollock made the connection in 1998 and contacted *The Sunday Times* to condemn *Catch-22* as a rip-off of the obscure Louis Falstein story. From there, the accusation gained international traction and eventually reached Heller himself. The author rejected Pollock's claims, insisting that he had never read *Face of a Hero* prior to the controversy. Furthermore, his editor combated the theory by asking his interrogators why Falstein, who had only passed away in 1995, would never have broadcast any such concerns if they had borne any weight. Mel Gussow wrote in *The New York Times* that "an examination of the two books leads this reader to conclude that the similarities between the two can easily be attributed to the shared wartime experiences of the authors."

NOVELS MOST OFTEN ABANDONED BY READERS

Just because you buy or borrow a book doesn't necessarily mean that you'll actually finish—or even start—reading it. Though tracking which books don't get finished is not an exact science, people have tried to figure it out; Goodreads, for example, has created a virtual shelf for members to leave their abandoned books. Since there are millions of people who *don't* report their reading habits on Goodreads, you shouldn't take any of these statistics too seriously. However, here's a list of twenty-five books they gave up on:

1. *The Casual Vacancy* by J.K. Rowling
2. *Catch-22* by Joseph Heller
3. *American Gods* by Neil Gaiman
4. *A Game of Thrones* by George R.R. Martin
5. *The Goldfinch* by Donna Tartt
6. *The Book Thief* by Markus Zusak
7. *Outlander* by Diana Gabaldon
8. *One Hundred Years of Solitude* by Gabriel García Márquez
9. *Infinite Jest* by David Foster Wallace
10. *Fifty Shades of Grey* by E.L. James
11. *Wolf Hall* by Hilary Mantel
12. *Jonathan Strange & Mr. Norrel* by Susanna Clarke
13. *The Night Circus* by Erin Morgenstern
14. *All the Light We Cannot See* by Anthony Doerr
15. *Eat, Pray, Love* by Elizabeth Gilbert
16. *Wicked: The Life and Times of the Wicked Witch of the West* by Gregory Maguire
17. *Lincoln in the Bardo* by George Saunders
18. *The Girl with the Dragon Tattoo* by Stieg Larsson
19. *Anna Karenina* by Leo Tolstoy
20. *Lolita* by Vladimir Nabokov
21. *A Discovery of Witches* by Deborah Harkness
22. *The Magicians* by Lev Grossman
23. *Life of Pi* by Yann Martel
24. *Pride and Prejudice* by Jane Austen
25. *The Handmaid's Tale* by Margaret Atwood

CRIME AND PUNISHMENT

FYODOR DOSTOEVSKY

November 11, 1821–February 9, 1881 (Gregorian calendar)

BORN: Moscow, Russian Empire

OTHER NOTABLE WORKS:
The Idiot (1869)
Demons (1872)
The Brothers Karamazov (1880)

Though Fyodor Dostoevsky (sometimes spelled Dostoyevsky) never labeled himself as an existentialist, his most famous works—including *Crime and Punishment*, *The Idiot*, and *The Brothers Karamazov*—tell a different story. Born in Moscow in 1821, Dostoevsky began his career as a military engineer. But the lure of a literary life proved too tempting to the aspiring writer. In 1845, he completed his first novel, *Poor Folk*, which made its way into the hands of some of Russia's greatest thinkers, who encouraged Dostoevsky to keep at it. Dostoevsky's tendency toward the polyphonic—a literary style in which there are multiple narratives—only strengthened his reputation as one of the great psychological novelists of all time, as his narratives could often be left open to interpretation. Friedrich Nietzsche described Dostoevsky as "the only psychologist . . . from whom I had something to learn."

Though *Crime and Punishment* was not Fyodor Dostoevsky's first book, it's arguably his most acclaimed. The 1866 novel, which is regularly cited as one of literature's greatest achievements, marked a turning point in the author's career—one that fans and critics have often referred to as the first work in his "mature" period as a writer. It tells the story of a young man named Raskolnikov who believes that he is some sort of superman—a theory he intends to test out by brutally murdering someone. What Raskolnikov does *not* plan for is the extreme guilt and alienation he'll feel in the wake of the crime, or the emotional turmoil that will haunt him.

Penned in the years following Dostoevsky's own arrest (he was targeted as a supposed revolutionary) and subsequent imprisonment and exile, *Crime and Punishment* remains true to its title in the themes it addresses. The criminal psyche, isolation from society, and nihilism are just a few of the ideas the book tackles—each of which became recurring ideas in Dostoevsky's work.

CRIME AND PUNISHMENT STARTED OUT WITH A FIRST-PERSON NARRATOR.

Having employed first-person perspectives in some of his earlier works, Dostoevsky originally planned for *Crime and Punishment* to be written as a first-person confessional.

Ultimately, he decided to switch to a third-person setup, but some authorities feel the narration style makes such use of Raskolnikov's inner thoughts that it becomes a kind of "masked first-person narrative."

RASKOLNIKOV'S CHOICE OF MURDER WEAPON SAYS A LOT ABOUT HIS THINKING.

SPOILERS! In the book, Raskolnikov kills Alyona Ivanovna—an old woman who happens to be a pawnbroker—and her younger sister, Lizaveta Ivanovna, with an ax. That weapon of choice is no mere coincidence. In James Billington's *The Icon and the Axe: An Interpretive History of Russian Culture*, the author explains that the ax represents one of the earliest tools of Russian civilization, which is why Raskolnikov's choice of weapon is later mocked by the criminals with whom he serves time in Siberia—they view him as an educated gentleman who should not have used a murder weapon linked with labor.

RASKOLNIKOV IS CONSTANTLY WRESTLING WITH THE IDEA OF GOOD VERSUS EVIL.

Raskolnikov justifies his homicidal act by rationalizing that, in the end, it will all be done for the greater good—thus validating his choice. But during his trial, we also see that Raskolnikov has a true generosity of spirit and has stepped up several times in the past to prove that. This makes it even more difficult to come to a definitive consensus on his true nature.

NOT ALL THE BOOK'S EARLY REVIEWS WERE GLOWING.

The year before *Crime and Punishment* was released as a book, it appeared in twelve monthly segments in a literary magazine. While it gained immediate attention among readers and literary critics alike, it wasn't always for positive reasons. Politically radical students argued that the book made them out to seem like homicidal maniacs, for one. One critic even asked (rhetorically): "Has there ever been a case of a student committing murder for the sake of robbery?"

CRIME AND PUNISHMENT HAS BEEN ADAPTED MORE THAN TWENTY-FIVE TIMES.

Since its original publication, *Crime and Punishment* has been adapted into dozens of languages (including English) and read by book lovers around the world. So it's hardly surprising that there are more than two dozen adaptations of it, including productions from the US, Finland, and India, among others. The most famous version might be *Raskolnikow*, a 1923 silent film directed by Robert Wiene (who also directed the classic *The Cabinet of Dr. Caligari*).

Fascinating Facts about Fyodor Dostoevsky

Thought of as one of the greatest novelists of all time, Fyodor Dostoevsky lived an extraordinary life. Here are a few things you might not know about the Russian writer.

1 DOSTOEVSKY WAS INTRODUCED TO LITERATURE AT A VERY YOUNG AGE.

Literature was an extremely important part of Fyodor Dostoevsky's childhood. Alena Frolovna, Dostoevsky's nanny, began instilling a love of books and storytelling in the future author when he was just three years old. His parents, too, were bibliophiles and exposed him to an expansive range of authors and genres, from Ann Radcliffe's pioneering works of Gothic fiction to the epic poems of Homer. They read to him nightly and his mother used the Bible to help teach him to read and write.

2 HE ABANDONED A CAREER AS A MILITARY ENGINEER.

Dr. Mikhail Dostoevsky, Fyodor's father, was a surgeon who was known to be very strict with his children. When Fyodor was just fifteen years old, his father arranged for him to begin training for a career as a military engineer at the Academy of Military Engineering in St. Petersburg. Though he graduated in 1843 and spent time working as an engineer, Dostoevsky's desire to attempt to make a living as a writer was too strong to ignore. So he followed his passion and left his engineering gig in order to devote all of his time to honing his voice as a writer.

3 HE PUBLISHED HIS FIRST BOOK AT THE AGE OF TWENTY-FOUR.

Dostoevsky was just twenty-four years old when his first book, a novella titled *Poor Folk*, was published. Through a series of letters, it tells the story of a penniless clerk and the woman he loves—who has promised herself to another man because he is a wealthy. In the hands of another writer, *Poor Folk* would have been yet another tale of the power that comes with wealth. But Dostoevsky, who had grown up on the grounds of the Mariinsky Hospital for the Poor (where his father worked as a doctor), saw poverty as a deeply complicated psychological state, which he conveyed in the highly personal emotionality of his writing. A friend ended up giving a copy of *Poor Folk* to famed poet and journalist Nikolay Nekrasov, whose own writing centered around peasant Russia. Nekrasov was amazed by the piece's depth and immediately got a copy into the hands of Russia's top literary critic, Vissarion Belinsky. Belinsky deemed Dostoevsky the next great Russian talent.

4 DOSTOEVSKY WAS ARRESTED FOR HIS RADICAL THINKING, THEN SPENT A DECADE IN PRISON AND EXILE.

With *Poor Folk*, Dostoevsky managed to capture the attention of the literature world's most elite figures and began running in the kind of intellectual circles that believed they could change Russia. Socialism and serfdom, a feudal system that ensured Russia's rural laborers would continue to exist in a state of indentured servitude, were among the group's most frequently discussed topics. In 1849, fearing that their radical ideas could lead to a societal upheaval, Dostoevsky and several of his fellow writers were arrested for suspected revolutionary activity. Dostoevsky was sentenced to death, but saw his punishment commuted at the last minute. Still, he spent the next ten years of his life alienated from society; after serving four years in a Siberian prison camp, he spent six years in exile. Unsurprisingly, the experience had a deeply profound effect on the author and led him to think about morality in a whole new way—with many of the questions he would go on to address in *Crime and Punishment*.

5 HE HAD EPILEPSY.

As a student, Dostoevsky had a number of seizures, and even suffered from a serious grand mal seizure in 1844. Later, he would record less intense seizures in his journal, writing that they were triggered by things like working too much or not getting enough sleep. He was diagnosed with epilepsy in 1849, around the time he went to prison. In 1928, forty-seven years after Dostoevsky's death, none other than Sigmund Freud weighed in on his diagnosis, saying that his seizures were caused by neurosis, and "must be accordingly classified as hystero-epilepsy—that is severe hysteria." Modern-day neurologists, however, believe Dostoevsky's epilepsy was the real thing.

FOUR FAMOUS NOVELS PENNED IN UNDER A MONTH

Fyodor Dostoevsky was heavily in debt when he wrote *The Gambler*, his semi-autobiographical novella, in just twenty-six days—he thought it might help get him out of the red. As incredible as this quick turnaround was, *The Gambler* wasn't the only book knocked out in under a month. Here are a few others.

The Boy in the Striped Pajamas:
Irish novelist John Boyne has said it took him two and a half days to write his tale of a boy living through the Holocaust. "The idea came to me on a Tuesday evening, I began writing on Wednesday morning and continued for 60 hours with only short breaks, not sleeping on Wednesday or Thursday nights and finishing the first draft by Friday lunchtime," he recalled in *The Irish Times*.

A Study in Scarlet:
Sir Arthur Conan Doyle wrote his debut novel—which also introduced detective Sherlock Holmes to the world—in a mere three weeks.

The Tortoise and the Hare:
Of this 1954 book, which she wrote in three weeks, Elizabeth Jenkins has said, "I have never looked at it since; it marked an era to which I had no desire to return." The love triangle in *Hare*, her sixth novel, reflected her real life: Jenkins wrote it in the "white heat of betrayal," after the married man she was seeing refused to leave his wife.

The Prime of Miss Jean Brodie:
"The first things I wrote about were my brothers and my mother and my father. I wrote about them, made up poems, made up stories," Muriel Spark recalled. "Then I wrote about the school, and my first writings were about the teacher who later became Miss Brodie. I wrote about her. We were given to write about how we spent our summer holidays, but I wrote about how she spent her summer holidays instead. It seems more fascinating." As an adult, Spark would funnel that fascination into writing *Jean Brodie*, a fictionalized version of her teacher, Christiana Kay. She wrote the book in four weeks.

DON QUIXOTE

MIGUEL DE CERVANTES

September 29 (assumed), 1547–April 22, 1616

BORN: Alcalá de Henares, Crown of Castile

OTHER NOTABLE WORKS:
Novelas ejemplares (1613)
Entremeses (1615)

Miguel de Cervantes left his native Spain for Italy at twenty-one years old, supposedly to escape the legal fallout from a duel. The incident, freighted as it is with notions of honor and ignominy, seems a fitting chapter in the life of the man who would give the world the idealistic (if deluded) Alonso Quixano. Cervantes's life was filled with such indignities, minor and major, from his years spent imprisoned at the hands of pirates to the financial problems that dogged him throughout his adulthood. He was nearly sixty years old when the first installment of *Don Quixote* was published. It would take a decade for the second and final part to be released, perhaps hurting the author's aspirations for greater acclaim in his own lifetime—but guaranteeing his influence on the Spanish language and the novelistic form.

Even if you've never picked up a copy of Miguel de Cervantes's novel *Don Quixote*, you're doubtlessly familiar with the story—one of delusional noblemen, portly squires, and windmill monsters. Nevertheless, there could be a few little-known facts you haven't heard about the two-volume, seventeenth-century masterpiece.

DON QUIXOTE IS CONSIDERED THE FIRST MODERN NOVEL.

Such esteemed thinkers as award-winning literary critic Harold Bloom and decorated novelist and essayist Carlos Fuentes have declared that *Don Quixote* is the very first true example of the modern novel. Bloom identifies the arcs of change bracing the story's titular character and his companion Sancho Panza as one of the markers that distinguishes it as the first of its breed, and Fuentes suggested that the nuance in the dialogue and characterization is chief in separating *Don Quixote* from all preceding texts.

CERVANTES CAME UP WITH THE STORY WHILE HE WAS IN JAIL.

Though he'd eventually go on to pen one of the most famous novels in world history, a young Miguel de Cervantes suffered from a plight familiar to any aspiring writer: working a day job to pay the bills. Among the varied gigs Cervantes kept in the years before his literary breakout was a job as a tax collector for the Spanish government. However, frequent "irregularities" landed Cervantes in the Crown Jail of Seville in 1597 and possibly again in 1602. It was in the slammer that Cervantes is believed to have first thought up the story that would become *Don Quixote*.

HE DREW FROM HIS EXPERIENCES AS A SLAVE TO WRITE THE NOVEL.

A particularly empathetic sequence in the novel sees the hero and Sancho Panza freeing a group of galley slaves from captivity. Cervantes's special sensitivity to these recipients of Don Quixote's chivalry likely stems from his own experiences in servitude in the 1570s. Cervantes spent five years enslaved in Algiers, attempting escape on more than one occasion.

CERVANTES NAMED THE MAIN CHARACTER AFTER HIS WIFE'S UNCLE.

Near the conclusion of the second volume of *Don Quixote*, Cervantes reveals the real name of his hero to be Alonso Quixano (alternatively spelled Quijano). He possibly borrowed this name from Alonso de Quesada y Salazar, the great uncle of Catalina de Salazar y Palacios, whom Cervantes married in 1584. Alonso is believed to have inspired not only the name but also the general characterization of the novel's hero. And the name Quixote came from the word for "thigh armor."

HE PLUGGED *DON QUIXOTE: PART II* IN THE FOREWORD OF ANOTHER STORY.

Cervantes released the twelve-part novella collection *Novelas ejemplares* in 1613 after having penned the series incrementally over several years. A foreword to the collection not only introduced the new work, but also promised readers that Cervantes was planning a continuation of the incomplete Gentleman of La Mancha fable. (His advertisement for an upcoming book ahead of an entirely independent work could be seen as an ancestor of the modern-day movie trailer.) This second volume was published two years later, in 1615.

A PHONY *PART II* WAS PUBLISHED AS A HOAX.

Just one year after Cervantes's *Novelas ejemplares* foreword plug, however, a volume of mysterious origin wormed its way into the *Don Quixote* canon. Written by an author who used the pseudonym Alonso Fernández de Avellaneda, the unofficial sequel was infamous for the feeble quality of writing and the numerous potshots it took at Cervantes and the source material.

THIS FAKE SEQUEL IS THOUGHT TO HAVE CONVINCED CERVANTES TO FINISH HIS OWN.

Although Cervantes had already gone on record about intending to wrap up the story of *Don Quixote* in a second text, it's generally believed that the Avellaneda debacle motivated the author to transfer his intentions to the page. Cervantes was so enraged by the hoax that he wrote the existence of Avellaneda's novel into his own *Part II*, maligning it for poor quality and misunderstanding of his original characters and story.

DON QUIXOTE HELPED ESTABLISH THE MODERN SPANISH LANGUAGE.

The variant of the Spanish language in which Cervantes penned his novel was actually a rather new development at the turn of the seventeenth century and would be much more familiar to contemporary Spanish speakers than the colloquial tongue of the era (though a 2015 survey found that over half of readers thought it was "difficult"). The popularity of *Don Quixote* cemented the modern Spanish that is now the second most commonly spoken first language in the world, behind Mandarin.

THE NOVEL IS CREDITED FOR THE SPREAD OF A POPULAR IDIOM.

Today, "the proof is in the pudding" is a regular fixture in the vernacular. The phrase is in fact a corruption of the somewhat more readily coherent—albeit admittedly less euphonic—variant, "the proof of the pudding is in the eating." While the latter traces roots to a fourteenth-century-born Middle English predecessor ("*Jt is ywrite that euery thing Hymself sheweth in the tastyng*") and would appear in various similar forms for the next few hundred years, the modern phrasing is believed to have debuted in an eighteenth-century English-language translation of *Don Quixote*. The phrase was introduced by translator Pierre Antoine Motteux in lieu of Cervantes's original maxim: "*al freír de los huevos lo verá*," or "you will see when the eggs are fried."

CERVANTES DID NOT PROFIT OFF OF THE SUCCESS OF *DON QUIXOTE*.

Despite the near-immediate popularity of the original 1605 novel, Cervantes barely made a dime off its publication, since it was common in the seventeenth century for a writer to be denied royalties on his or her published works.

DON QUIXOTE MIGHT BE THE BEST-SELLING NOVEL OF ALL TIME.

While the age of the novel makes it hard to fully estimate the scope of its distribution, many estimate that it has reached a readership of 500 million. If true, this figure would make it the best-selling novel in world history by far, topping J.R.R. Tolkien's *The Lord of the Rings* trilogy and matching the estimated sales for all seven *Harry Potter* books.

8

OF THE BEST-SELLING BOOKS IN HISTORY (MINUS RELIGIOUS TEXTS)

Which books have sold the most throughout history? The answer isn't as straightforward as it might seem. With the understanding that the definition of a book is difficult, data is often impossible to confirm, that religious books like the Bible and Qur'an will be excluded, and that this list is not exhaustive, complete, or even a top ten, these are candidates for some of the best-selling books in history.

1 *Quotations from Chairman Mao Zedong* // **Somewhere between 740 million and 5 billion copies sold**

The scale of *Quotations*, which includes 267 aphorisms on various aspects of life and politics, is difficult to fathom. Between 1966 and 1970, printing *Quotations* used 650,000 tons of paper, around the same amount as all publications produced in China between 1949 and 1965. Officially, 740 million copies were published between 1966 and 1968, and reportedly almost every citizen owned a copy.

2 *Xinhua Dictionary* // **567 million copies sold**

Considered by Guinness World Records both "Most Popular Dictionary" and "Best-selling book (regularly updated)," the Xinhua Dictionary has been one of China's best-selling books since 1953. Published by China's Commercial Press, it's the first dictionary (with pictures!) written in Mandarin Chinese, and is a widely used reference work in China in primary school and beyond.

3 *Harry Potter Series* // **500 million copies sold across the entire series**

In 2018, it was announced that 500 million copies of the entire Harry Potter series had been sold. That's a long way from 1997, when the series started with a reported 500-copy first print run for *Philosopher's Stone* (the British title).

4 *The Lord of the Rings* // **Upward of 100 million copies sold**

Before *The Lord of the* Rings movies came out, Houghton Mifflin was afraid that the trilogy might bomb and dampen sales for a generation—so much so that the publisher released new editions of the books to try to take advantage of the pre-release excitement before the first movie came out. After the movies, though, sales skyrocketed.

5 *Le Petit Prince* // **Unclear, but a common estimate is 150 million copies sold**

As with many of these numbers, actual data is difficult to come by—hence the likely undeservedly low place. But whether it's near the top of the list or near the bottom, Antoine de Saint-Exupéry's classic novella deserves its place because it's thought to be the most translated non-religious work in the world. Guinness World Records reports it has been translated into 382 languages.

6 *And Then There Were None* // **Commonly estimated at 100 million copies sold**

This Agatha Christie novel is generally considered the best-selling mystery novel of all time.

7 *The Da Vinci Code* // **Around 60 million copies sold**

After Dan Brown's *The Da Vinci Code* was released, it spent a staggering 136 consecutive weeks on *The New York Times*'s best-seller list.

8 *Betty Crocker's Cookbook* // **Probably about 60 million copies sold**

"Betty" came into existence in 1921, after flour makers the Washburn-Crosby Company began receiving an overwhelming number of baking questions in response to a contest they ran. The company decided they needed someone to sign off on the responses. They picked *Betty* as a nice, familiar name and *Crocker* in honor of retired director William G. Crocker. In 1924, "Betty" began a radio show, and even briefly appeared on television. Such was her fame that the first printing of her cookbook was 950,000 copies.

HONORABLE MENTION:
Uncle Tom's Cabin // **Probably 3 million copies sold**

Uncle Tom's Cabin deserves its place on this list for its incredible success in its own day. An 1855 *Edinburgh Review* article estimated it sold more than a million copies in England, "probably ten times as many as have been sold of any other work, except the Bible and Prayer-book." It's widely considered the most successful book of the nineteenth century.

DISHONORABLE MENTION:
A Tale of Two Cities // **Nowhere near 200 million copies sold. Probably.**

Writer and Oxford lecturer Peter Thonemann says the claim that Dickens's *A Tale of Two Cities* has sold 200 million copies appeared on Wikipedia from 2008 to early 2016. Then other writers and publishers lifted the claim and republished it, to the point that it is now a well-attested piece of literary trivia. Thonemann is unsure where the original number came from but suspects "a hyperbolic 2005 press release for a Broadway musical adaptation of Dickens's novel" that Thonemann dismisses as "pure fiction."

DUNE

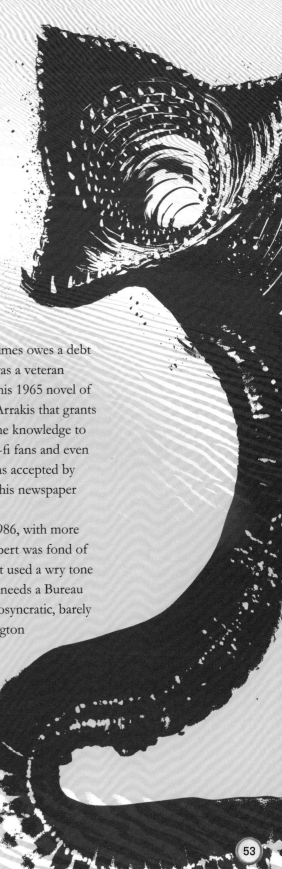

FRANK HERBERT

October 8, 1920–February 11, 1986

BORN: Tacoma, Washington

OTHER NOTABLE WORKS:
Whipping Star (1970)
The Dosadi Experiment (1977)

One of the greatest science fiction writers of modern times owes a debt to a publisher of car repair manuals. Frank Herbert was a veteran newspaper reporter when he began circulating *Dune*, his 1965 novel of galactic intrigue over spice, a compound found on the planet Arrakis that grants its users extended lives, the ability to see into the future, and the knowledge to plot ambitious space travel. Though it was well received by sci-fi fans and even serialized in *Analog* magazine, Herbert had no takers until it was accepted by automotive publisher Chilton. By 1972, Herbert had given up his newspaper career to write novels.

Though *Dune* and its myriad sequels—six by his death in 1986, with more co-authored by son Brian—remain his best-known work, Herbert was fond of exploring other worlds, authoring novels like *Whipping Star* that used a wry tone to describe a galactic government so sprawling and efficient it needs a Bureau of Sabotage to keep it from being too orderly. He was also idiosyncratic, barely paying attention during his classes at the University of Washington beyond creative writing and later prone to administering lie detector tests to his children. In *Dune*, Herbert captured a timeless obsession with royalty and resources. Under interrogation, many sci-fi fans would declare it one of the most relevant and deeply realized novels in the genre.

Before Frank Herbert unleashed the first entry in his magnificent *Dune* series—a saga many now call sci-fi's answer to *The Lord of the Rings*—almost nobody thought it had a prayer as a book. Publishers rejected the novel twenty-three times and even his own agents had their doubts. But *Dune*'s humble beginnings bolster its appeal. The first book alone has sold upward of twenty million copies and been printed in over a dozen languages. Here's some amazing stuff you might not know about this truly epic franchise.

HERBERT WAS INSPIRED BY THE "MOVING SANDS" OF OREGON.

It all started with a scrapped magazine article. By the 1950s, coastal Oregon had gotten fed up with a serious ecological menace: sand dunes. As Herbert noted in a 1957 letter, "These waves can be every bit as devastating as a tidal wave in property damage . . . and they've even caused deaths. They drown out forests, kill game cover, destroy lakes, [and] fill harbors." The US Department of Agriculture had begun experimenting with planting long-rooted beach grasses near the seaside city of Florence, Oregon, in an attempt to stop the sands from excessively shifting. Fascinated, Herbert flew in and started gathering notes for a piece entitled "They Stopped the Moving Sands." But his agent refused to send it to publishers unless it was rewritten, which Herbert never did. Still, Herbert remained intrigued and—after boning up on deserts and religious figures—outlined the story that eventually became *Dune*.

DUNE WAS ALSO INFLUENCED BY PSYCHEDELIC MUSHROOMS.

In Herbert's *Dune* universe, the single most valuable commodity is—by far—an edible substance called "melange." Also known as "spice," this highly addictive material is found only on the desert planet of Arrakis, where much of the action unfolds. Among its many properties are increased longevity and, in some cases, the ability to see the future itself.

Sound trippy? There's a reason. While conversing with fungi expert Paul Stamets, Herbert revealed that the world of *Dune* was influenced by the lifecycle of mushrooms, with his imagination being helped along by a more "magic" variety.

10 BOOKS THAT WON BOTH THE HUGO AND NEBULA AWARDS

HERBERT HAD PREVIOUSLY EXPERIMENTED WITH *DUNE*-ESQUE PLOT ELEMENTS IN AN UNCOMPLETED STORY CALLED "SPICE PLANET."

The tale's protagonist is Jesse Linkam, who must endure a hostile, otherworldly desert with his eight-year-old son, Barri. "Spice Planet" touches on several topics that *Dune* would later explore, like drug addiction. Eventually, however, Herbert went back to the drawing board, shelving this primordial narrative en route (until his son released a new story based on Frank's original outline).

IT WAS ORIGINALLY RELEASED AS A SERIAL.

Before getting published by Chilton as a novel, *Dune* started out in segments. Two main parts—*Dune World* and *Prophet of Dune*—were divided into a total of eight sections which appeared in *Analog* magazine from 1963 to 1965.

DUNE WON THE VERY FIRST NEBULA AWARD IN 1966.

These days, it's an award every sci-fi novelist craves. By the way, it also shared the 1966 Hugo Award for Best Novel with Roger Zelazny's . . . *And Call Me Conrad* (a.k.a. *This Immortal*).

A *DUNE* SEQUEL WAS THE FIRST SCI-FI NOVEL TO BECOME A *NEW YORK TIMES* BEST SELLER IN BOTH HARDCOVER AND PAPERBACK.

Sales for the original *Dune* stagnated at first, but by the time Herbert finished the third installment, 1976's *Children of Dune*, a rabid fan base had been built that couldn't wait to devour it in breathtaking numbers.

A NEVER-MADE FILM ADAPTATION WAS SUPPOSED TO BE SCORED BY PINK FLOYD AND STAR SALVADOR DALÍ.

"I wanted to do a movie that would give people who took LSD at that time the hallucinations that you get with that drug, but without hallucinating," said would-be director Alejandro Jodorowsky. It sounds like he would have been well on his way, having approached Pink Floyd to do the soundtrack and surrealist painter Salvador Dalí to portray Emperor Shaddam Corrino IV. Also, it would have been a butt-numbing twelve hours (or more!) long.

ALL THE LOW PLAINS ON ONE OF SATURN'S MOONS ARE NAMED AFTER PLANETS IN THE *DUNE* CANON.

Saturn's largest moon, Titan, contains some shady-looking terrain called planitia (low plains) that are all named after *Dune* planets. The first one named is now known as "Chusuk Planitia" in honor of the fictitious (and musically oriented) planet Chusuk.

In science fiction writing, there is no higher honor than earning a Hugo Award or Nebula Award. Unless, of course, you win both. The Hugo, named after sci-fi editor Hugo Gernsback and first presented in 1953, is voted on by members of the World Science Fiction Society. The Nebula has been handed out by the Science Fiction and Fantasy Writers of America to honor the work of their peers since 1965. Only a handful of titles have earned both in a single year. Here are ten books that join Frank Herbert's *Dune* in accomplishing this rare feat.

1. *Ringworld* by Larry Niven
2. *Rendezvous with Rama* by Arthur C. Clarke
3. *The Forever War* by Joe Haldeman
4. *Dreamsnake* by Vonda N. McIntyre
5. *Startide Rising* by David Brin
6. *Neuromancer* by William Gibson
7. *American Gods* by Neil Gaiman
8. *The Yiddish Policemen's Union* by Michael Chabon
9. *Among Others* by Jo Walton
10. *The Calculating Stars: A Lady Astronaut Novel* by Mary Robinette Kowal

RAY BRADBURY

August 22, 1920–June 5, 2012

BORN: Waukegan, Illinois

OTHER NOTABLE WORKS:
Martian Chronicles (1950)
Dandelion Wine (1957)
I Sing the Body Electric! (1969)

Ray Bradbury got in on the ground floor of the Golden Age of Science Fiction, joining sci-fi organizations and rubbing elbows with other upcoming luminaries of the genre, like Robert A. Heinlein and Leigh Brackett. All that camaraderie didn't distract him from actually writing though; Bradbury penned numerous horror, fantasy, and science fiction stories throughout the 1930s, and his byline was common in high-profile magazines—everything from *The New Yorker* to *Planet Stories*—by the following decade. Though he's best known for *Fahrenheit 451*, the novel just scratches the surface of Bradbury's legacy as one of the most imaginative sci-fi authors of all time.

For more than sixty years, Ray Bradbury's science fiction classic *Fahrenheit 451* has sparked imagination, debate, and rebellion. The dystopian story of a man who burns books to prevent the dissemination of ideas—and then comes to realize the error of his choices—criticized censorship at the height of the Cold War. The novel remains full of surprises, contradictions, and misconceptions.

ADOLF HITLER WAS THE BOOK'S DARK INSPIRATION.

Fahrenheit 451 centers on Guy Montag, a fireman tormented by his job: Instead of putting out fires, he is expected to burn books. In an interview with the National Endowment for the Arts, Bradbury explained how he came up with this concept:

"Well, Hitler, of course. When I was 15, he burned the books in the streets of Berlin. Then along the way I learned about the libraries in Alexandria burning 5,000 years ago . . . That grieved my soul. Since I'm self-educated, that means my educators—the libraries— are in danger. And if it could happen in Alexandria, if it could happen in Berlin, maybe it could happen somewhere up ahead, and my heroes would be killed."

THE NOVEL'S TITLE IS MISLEADING.

A popular tagline for the book is "the temperature at which book-paper catches fire, and burns." But 451°F actually refers the auto-ignition point of paper, meaning the temperature at which paper will burn if not exposed to an external flame, like that from Montag's flamethrower. Books can, however, ignite at temperatures between the 440s and 480s, depending on the density and type of paper.

THE NOVEL WAS ADAPTED FROM BRADBURY'S SHORT STORY "THE FIREMAN."

In 1950, Bradbury released *The Martian Chronicles*, and the following year, "The Fireman" was published in *Galaxy* magazine. From there, Bradbury would expand the tale to create *Fahrenheit 451*.

BRADBURY DID *NOT* WRITE *FAHRENHEIT 451* IN NINE DAYS.

A popular apocryphal story is that Bradbury hammered out *Fahrenheit 451* in just over a week. That story is wrong: It was the twenty-five-thousand-word "The Fireman" that he wrote in that short span of time. The author would later refer to the short story as "the first version" of the eventual novel. But over the years, he would often speak about "The Fireman" and *Fahrenheit 451* interchangeably, which has caused some confusion.

HE WROTE "THE FIREMAN" ON A RENTED TYPEWRITER IN A LIBRARY BASEMENT.

Bradbury and wife Marguerite McClure had two young children, and he was in need of a quiet place to write but had no money for renting an office. In a 2005 interview, Bradbury said:

"I was wandering around the UCLA library and discovered there was a typing room where you could rent a typewriter for 10 cents a half-hour. So I went and got a bag of dimes. The novel began that day, and nine days later it was finished. But my God, what a place to write that book! I ran up and down stairs and grabbed books off the shelf to find any kind of quote and ran back down and put it in the novel. The book wrote itself in nine days, because the library told me to do it."

Bradbury's nine days in the library cost him, by his own estimate, just under $10. That means he spent about forty-nine hours writing "The Fireman."

THE BOOK IS VIEWED AS A CRITICISM OF McCARTHYISM.

Fahrenheit 451 was published on October 19, 1953, in the midst of the Second Red Scare, an era from the late 1940s to the end of the 1950s characterized by political and cultural paranoia. Many Americans feared Communist infiltration of their values and communities. Because of the context of its publication, Montag's story has been interpreted by some critics as a challenge to the censorship and conformity that US Senator Joseph McCarthy's witch hunt sparked.

BRADBURY CONSIDERED *FAHRENHEIT 451* HIS ONLY WORK OF SCIENCE FICTION.

Though he is regarded as a master of the science fiction genre, Bradbury viewed the rest of his work as fantasy. He once explained, "I don't write science fiction. I've only done one science fiction book and that's *Fahrenheit 451*, based on reality. Science fiction is a depiction of the real. Fantasy is a depiction of the unreal. So *Martian Chronicles* is not science fiction, it's fantasy. It couldn't happen, you see?"

FAHRENHEIT 451 IMAGINED EARBUDS.

When the novel came out, headphones were large and cumbersome things. But Bradbury imagined "the little Seashells, the thimble radios," which rested in the ear canal, and played "an electronic ocean of sound" to Montag's sleeping wife. Though early in-ear headphones had been patented decades before, "seashells" went from science fiction to science fact in 2001, when Apple designer Jony Ive debuted earbuds.

Still, "predicting" wasn't something Bradbury was interested in. "I've tried not to predict, but to protect and to prevent," he said of *Fahrenheit 451*. "If I can convince people to stop doing what they're doing and go to the library and be sensible, without pontificating and without being self-conscious, that's fine. I can teach people to really know they're alive."

FOR YEARS, BRADBURY REFUSED TO LET *FAHRENHEIT 451* BE PUBLISHED AS AN E-BOOK.

As the novel makes clear, Bradbury treasured the printed word. When asked in 2009 if he'd allow one of his books to be put online, the author responded to the would-be publishers, "to hell with you and to hell with the internet. It's distracting. It's meaningless; it's not real. It's in the air somewhere." He also proclaimed that e-books "smell like burned fuel."

But in 2011, ninety-one-year-old Bradbury gave in when Simon & Schuster offered him a reported seven-figure publishing deal, in which the rights to publish an e-book version were integral.

BRADBURY KNEW WHAT HE WOULD DO IF HE LIVED IN *FAHRENHEIT 451*'S DYSTOPIA.

In the book, there is an underground band of rebels who attempt to preserve the written word by memorizing great works of literature. Asked which book he'd commit to memory in such a circumstance, Bradbury answered, "It would be *A Christmas Carol*. I think that book has influenced my life more than almost any other book, because it's a book about life, it's a book about death. It's a book about triumph."

FAHRENHEIT 451 IS BRADBURY'S MOST POPULAR NOVEL.

It's sold more than ten million copies, earned critical acclaim, and is considered one of the major novels of the twentieth century. *Fahrenheit 451* has won several awards, including a Prometheus "Hall of Fame" Award and a Hugo Award. And Bradbury earned a Grammy nomination in the spoken word category for the 1976 audiobook, which he performed himself.

Fascinating Facts about Ray Bradbury

For such a visionary futurist whose predictions for the future often came true, Ray Bradbury was rather old-fashioned in many ways.

1 HE SCORED HIS FIRST WRITING GIG WHEN HE WAS STILL A TEEN.

Most teenagers get a first job bagging groceries or slinging burgers. At the age of 14, Ray Bradbury landed himself a gig writing for George Burns and Gracie Allen's radio show—though he later said he never got any money.

2 IT TOOK HIM TWENTY-FIVE YEARS TO ASK A GIRL OUT.

At the age of twenty-five, Bradbury finally summoned up the courage to ask a girl out for the first time ever. She was a bookstore clerk named Maggie, who thought he was stealing from the bookstore because he had a long trench coat on. They went out for coffee, which turned into cocktails, which turned into dinner, which turned into marriage, which turned into fifty-six anniversaries and four children.

3 AN UNLIKELY AUTHOR LAUNCHED HIS CAREER

George Burns isn't the only famous eye Bradbury caught. In 1947, a writer at *Mademoiselle* read Bradbury's short story "Homecoming," about the only human boy in a family of supernatural beings. The magazine decided to run the piece, and Bradbury won a place in the O. Henry Prize Stories as one of the best short stories of 1947. That young writer who helped Bradbury out by grabbing his story out of the unsolicited materials pile? Truman Capote.

4 BRADBURY DIDN'T ATTEND COLLEGE.

Though he wrote *Fahrenheit 451* at UCLA, he wasn't a student there. In fact, he didn't believe in college. "I believe in libraries because most students don't have any money," Bradbury told *The New York Times* in 2009. "When I graduated from high school, it was during the Depression and we had no money. I couldn't go to college, so I went to the library three days a week for ten years."

5 HE WAS PALS WITH WALT DISNEY.

Not only was Bradbury good friends with Walt Disney (and even urged him to run for mayor of Los Angeles), he helped contribute to the Spaceship Earth ride at Epcot, submitting a story treatment that they built the ride around.

6 NASA PAID TRIBUTE TO HIM.

NASA paid the futuristic writer a tribute when they landed a rover on Mars a few months after Bradbury's death in 2012: They named the site where Mars rover Curiosity touched down "Bradbury Landing."

FAMOUS AUTHORS' FAVORITE BOOKS

One key to being a good writer is to always keep reading—and that doesn't stop after you've been published. For Ray Bradbury, the most influential books were Edgar Rice Burroughs's John Carter: Warlord of Mars series. "[They] entered my life when I was ten and caused me to go out on the lawns of summer, put up my hands, and ask for Mars to take me home," Bradbury said. "Within a short time I began to write and have continued that process ever since, all because of Mr. Burroughs."

Here are eight authors' favorite reads. Who knows, one of these books might become your new favorite.

JOAN DIDION

In an interview with *The Paris Review* in 2006, novelist and creative nonfiction scribe Joan Didion called Joseph Conrad's *Victory* "maybe my favorite book in the world . . . I have never started a novel . . . without rereading *Victory*. It opens up the possibilities of a novel. It makes it seem worth doing."

GEORGE R.R. MARTIN

It's probably not surprising that *A Game of Thrones* author George R.R. Martin has said that J.R.R. Tolkien's *The Lord of the Rings*, which he first read in junior high, is "still a book I admire vastly." But he recently found inspiration in a newer book, which he recommended in a LiveJournal entry: "I won't soon forget *Station Eleven*," he wrote. Emily St. John Mandel's book about a group of actors in a recently post-apocalyptic society, he said, is "a deeply melancholy novel, but beautifully written, and wonderfully elegiac . . . a book that I will long remember, and return to."

AYN RAND

"The very best I've ever read, my favorite thing in all world literature (and that includes all the heavy classics) is a novelette called *Calumet K* by Merwin-Webster," Rand wrote in 1945. The book was famous then, but if you haven't heard of it, allow *Chicago* magazine to outline the plot: "*Calumet K* is [a] quaint, endearingly Midwestern novel about the building of a grain elevator . . . It's a procedural about large-scale agricultural production."

GILLIAN FLYNN

When *Gone Girl* author Gillian Flynn was asked about her favorite books in a 2014 Reddit AMA, she called out her "comfort food" books—the kind "you grab when you're feeling cranky and nothing sounds good to read"— which included Agatha Christie's *And Then There Were None* and Norman Mailer's *The Executioner's Song*.

MEG WOLITZER

The Interestings author loves the novel *Old Filth* by Jane Gardam. "It's a thrilling, bold and witty book by a British writer whom I discovered rather late," Wolitzer told *Elle* in 2014. "I can't say I've read anything else like *Old Filth*, which stands out for me as a singular, opalescent novel, a thing of beauty that gives immense gratification to its lucky readers."

ERIK LARSON

The acclaimed author of *The Devil in the White City* calls *The Maltese Falcon* his "all-time personal favorite": "I love this book, all of it: the plot, the characters, the dialogue . . . The single best monologue in fiction appears toward the end, when Sam Spade tells Brigid O'Shaughnessy why he's giving her to the police."

F. SCOTT FITZGERALD

In 1936—four years before his death—Fitzgerald was living at the Grove Park Inn in North Carolina. After he fired a gun in what was said to be a suicide threat, the inn insisted that he be supervised by a nurse. While under Dorothy Richardson's care, he provided her with a list of twenty-two books that he deemed "essential reading." It included *Sister Carrie* by Theodore Dreiser, *The Life of Jesus* by Ernest Renan, Henrik Ibsen's *A Doll's House*, and *Winesburg, Ohio* by Sherwood Anderson.

EDWIDGE DANTICAT

This MacArthur Fellow and award-winning author of *Claire of the Sea Light*, *The Dew Breaker*, and *Brother, I'm Dying* told Time.com that her favorite summer read is *Love, Anger, Madness* by the Haitian writer Marie Vieux-Chauvet. "I have read and reread that book, both in French and in its English translation, for many years now," she said. "And each time I stumble into something new and eye-opening that makes me want to keep reading it over and over again."

FRANKENSTEIN

MARY SHELLEY

August 30, 1797–February 1, 1851

BORN: London, England

OTHER NOTABLE WORKS:
Valperga (1823)
The Last Man (1826)

Mary Shelley was born in London in 1797, the daughter of political philosopher William Godwin and feminist writer Mary Wollstonecraft, who passed away just days after giving birth. By the time she was a teenager, she had started a relationship with romantic poet Percy Bysshe Shelley, and by the age of twenty, she had already written and published her genre-defining sci-fi novel, *Frankenstein*. Though she'll forever be remembered as the trailblazing mind behind the horror icon, Shelley also authored a number of European travelogues, political essays, and numerous other novels, including 1826's *The Last Man*, a post-apocalyptic tale about a plague-ravaged Earth in the twenty-first century.

Frankenstein—the story of a mad scientist who brings the dead back to life, only to discover that he has created a monster—continues to be one of our lasting horror stories. Here are the nuts and bolts of the two-hundred-year-old tale that forever touched on our fears about what can go wrong when people play God.

FRANKENSTEIN WAS WRITTEN BY A TEENAGER.

Mary Shelley's teenage years were eventful, to say the least. At age sixteen, she ran away with the poet Percy Bysshe Shelley. Over the next two years, she gave birth to two children. In 1816, the couple traveled to Switzerland and visited Lord Byron at Villa Diodati. While there, eighteen-year-old Mary started *Frankenstein*. It was published in 1818, when she was twenty years old.

THE NOVEL CAME OUT OF A GHOST STORY COMPETITION.

The Shelleys visited Switzerland during the "year without a summer." The eruption of Mount Tambora in modern Indonesia had caused severe climate abnormalities and a lot of rain. Stuck inside, the group read ghost stories from the book *Fantasmagoriana*. It was then that Lord Byron proposed that they have a competition to see who could come up with the best ghost story: Byron, Mary, Percy, or the physician John Polidori.

In the end, neither Byron nor Percy finished a ghost story, although Polidori later wrote *The Vampyre*—which influences vampire stories to this day—based on Byron's offering.

SHELLEY SAID SHE GOT THE IDEA FROM A DREAM.

At first, Shelley had writer's block. Then she had a waking dream—"I did not sleep, nor could I be said to think," she said. In the introduction to the 1831 edition of *Frankenstein*, she described the vision as follows:

"I saw the pale student of unhallowed arts kneeling beside the thing he had put together. I saw the hideous phantasm of a man stretched out, and then, on the working of some powerful engine, show signs of life. . . . He sleeps; but he is awakened; he opens his eyes; behold the horrid thing stands at his bedside, opening his curtains, and looking on him with yellow, watery, but speculative eyes."

Mary opened her eyes and realized she'd found her story. "What terrified me will terrify others," she thought. She began working on it the next day.

SHELLEY WROTE *FRANKENSTEIN* IN THE SHADOW OF TRAGEDY.

Before she started *Frankenstein*, Mary gave birth to a daughter, who died just days later. (In fact, only one of the Shelleys' four children lived to adulthood.) Soon after the baby died, she wrote in her journal, "Dream that my little baby came to life again—that it had only been cold & that we rubbed it by the fire & it lived—I awake & find no baby—I think about the little thing all day." This circumstance, as well as the suicide of her half-sister, likely contributed to the novel.

FRANKENSTEIN WAS THE NAME OF THE SCIENTIST, NOT THE MONSTER.

In the novel, Victor Frankenstein is the scientist. The monster remains unnamed and is referred to as "monster," "creature," "dæmon," and "it." But if you've made the mistake of calling the monster Frankenstein, you're not alone. Everyone from *The Reef* novelist Edith Wharton to the writers of the movie *Abbott and Costello Meet Frankenstein* has done it.

THE NOVEL SHARES ITS NAME WITH A CASTLE.

Shelley made up the name "Frankenstein." However, Frankenstein is a German name that means Stone of the Franks. What's more, historian Radu Florescu claimed that the Shelleys visited Castle Frankenstein on a journey up the Rhine River. While there, they must have learned about an unbalanced alchemist named Konrad Dippel, who used to live in the castle. He was trying to create an elixir, called Dippel's Oil, which would make people live for over a hundred years. Like Victor Frankenstein, Dippel was rumored to dig up graves and experiment on the bodies. Not all historians are convinced there's a link, however, pointing out that there's no indication Frankenstein had a castle in the novel, and that Shelley never mentioned visiting the castle herself in any of her writing about her trip up the Rhine.

MANY THOUGHT PERCY SHELLEY WROTE THE WORK.

Frankenstein was first published anonymously. It was dedicated to William Godwin, Mary's father, and Percy Shelley wrote the preface. Because of these connections, many assumed that Percy was the author. This myth continued even after *Frankenstein* was reprinted in Mary's name. In fact, some people are still arguing that Percy authored the book. While he edited the book and encouraged Mary to expand the story into a novel, actual authorship is a stretch.

THE BOOK WAS ORIGINALLY SLAMMED BY CRITICS.

When *Frankenstein* came out in 1818, many critics bashed it. "What a tissue of horrible and disgusting absurdity this work presents," John Croker of the *Quarterly Review* wrote. But Gothic novels were all the rage, and *Frankenstein* soon gained readers. In 1823, a play titled *Presumption; or The Fate of Frankenstein* cemented the story's popularity. In 1831, a new version of the book was published, this time under Mary's name.

FRANKENSTEIN IS WIDELY CONSIDERED THE FIRST SCIENCE FICTION NOVEL.

In penning *Frankenstein*, Shelley was writing the first major science fiction novel, as well as inventing the concept of the "mad scientist" and helping establish what would become horror fiction. The influence of the book in popular culture is so huge that the term *Frankenstein* has entered common speech to mean something unnatural and horrendous.

THOMAS EDISON ADAPTED THE STORY FOR FILM.

In 1910, Thomas Edison's studio made a one-reel, fifteen-minute film of *Frankenstein*, one of the first horror movies ever made. It was thought lost until it was rediscovered in the 1980s.

MARY SHELLEY'S FAVORITE KEEPSAKE: *Her Dead Husband's Heart*

People grieve in different ways. Back in the 1600s, people began to make jewelry out of the hair of deceased loved ones. In some parts of Madagascar, people dig up their dead relatives every few years to dance with them. And even now, we consider it fairly normal to incinerate people, then save them in decorative urns on our mantels. Taking all that into account, maybe what Mary Shelley did when her husband died wasn't *that* weird.

Percy Bysshe Shelley was just twenty-nine when he drowned after his boat, *Don Juan*, was caught in a storm on July 8, 1822. Shelley's body and those of his two sailing companions were found days later, identifiable only by their clothing.

The poet was cremated, but for some reason, his heart (though some argue it was actually his liver) refused to burn. Modern-day physicians believe it may have calcified due to an earlier bout with tuberculosis. Though Percy's friend, Leigh Hunt, originally claimed the heart—he was there for the funeral pyre-style cremation and felt he had a right to keep the unscathed organ— it was eventually turned over to Mary.

Instead of burying it with the rest of his remains in the Protestant Cemetery in Rome, Mary kept the heart in a silken shroud and is said to have carried it with her nearly everywhere for years. In 1852, a year after she died, Percy's heart was found in her desk. It was wrapped in the pages of one of his last poems, *Adonais*. It's said the heart was eventually buried in the family vault with their son, Percy Florence Shelley, when he died in 1889.

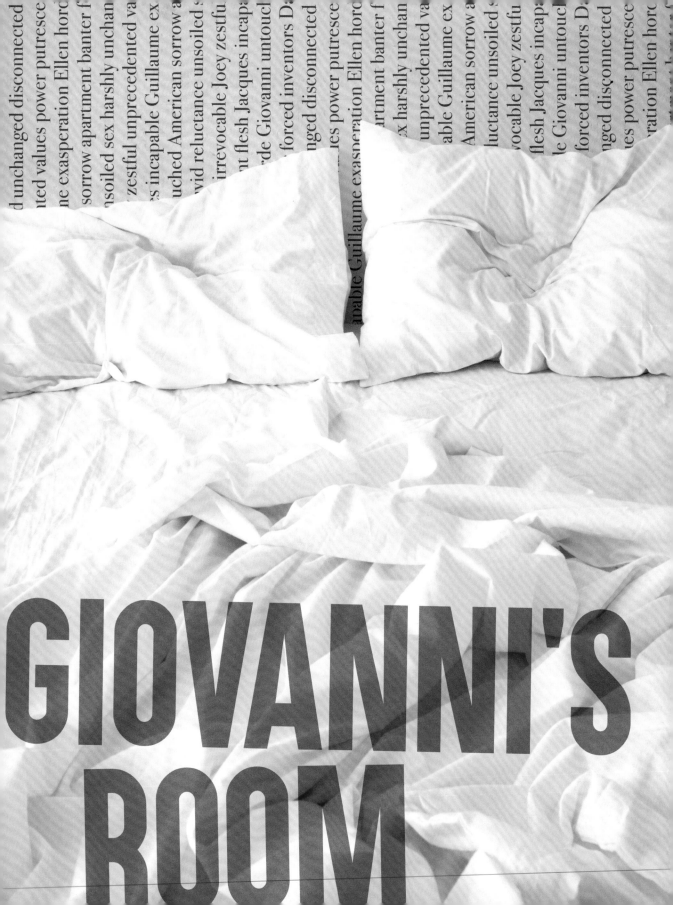

GIOVANNI'S ROOM

JAMES BALDWIN

August 2, 1924–December 1, 1987

BORN: New York, New York

OTHER NOTABLE WORKS:
Go Tell It on the Mountain (1953)
Notes of a Native Son (1955)
The Fire Next Time (1963)
If Beale Street Could Talk (1974)

James Baldwin defied categorization. His first novel, *Go Tell It on the Mountain,* was partly based on his adolescence in Harlem in the 1930s and branded him as a promising writer of Black fiction—a label he quickly eschewed. For his next novel, *Giovanni's Room,* he drew from his experience as a gay man to explore homosexuality and masculinity through the perspective of white characters. In addition to writing influential novels, he penned plays, poetry, essays, and engaged in political activism.

Baldwin moved to Paris early in his career. Despite the new environment, he continued to focus on American issues in his work, saying, "Once you find yourself in another civilization, you're forced to examine your own." He returned to the United States during the Civil Rights Movement and toured the country giving lectures on racial inequality.

Race and sexuality in America—and the relationship between the two—were topics Baldwin revisited throughout his career as a writer and activist. Today, James Baldwin is considered one of the most influential writers in LGBTQ and African American history.

In James Baldwin's 1956 novel *Giovanni's Room*, David, an American man, heads to Paris to sort himself out prior to his marriage to his fiancée, Hella. There, he meets and develops a sexual relationship with Giovanni, a waiter at a gay bar. When Hella comes to Paris, and Giovanni is accused of murdering the bar's owner, David must negotiate his feelings for Hella and Giovanni, as well as his bisexual identity. Here's what you need to know about the book *The Atlantic* said "belongs in the top rank of fiction."

BALDWIN WAS INSPIRED BY HIS TIME IN PARIS.

Readers familiar with Baldwin's biography will recognize details from the writer's life in *Giovanni's Room.* After growing up in New York City, Baldwin moved to the French capital at age twenty-four. France is where he spent most of his life and wrote some of his most influential works.

Baldwin's life in Paris was a major source of inspiration for *Giovanni's Room.* As a gay man in the 1950s, he was also able to pull from his own experiences when crafting the book's gay relationships. But while he borrowed elements from real life, Baldwin emphasized that the book wasn't autobiographical. He later explained, "it is more of a study of how it might have been or how I feel it might have been. I mean, for example, some of the people I have met. We all met in a bar, there was a blond French guy sitting at a table, he bought us drinks. And, two or three days later, I saw his face in the headlines of a Paris paper. He had been arrested and was later guillotined. That stuck in my mind."

Baldwin's novel ends with Giovanni being guillotined for murdering the owner of the bar where he worked.

THE SUBJECT MATTER WAS A DEPARTURE FOR BALDWIN.

Baldwin's first novel, *Go Tell It on the Mountain*, dealt heavily with racial injustice. For his second novel, the author decided to write strictly about white characters. He believed that racism and homophobia are connected, but when writing *Giovanni's Room*, he wasn't ready to tackle both issues at once. "I certainly could not possibly have—not at that point in my life—handled the other great weight, the 'Negro problem,'" he said in a 1980 interview. "The sexual-moral light was a hard thing to deal with. I could not handle both propositions in the same book. There was no room for it."

HIS PUBLISHER TOLD HIM TO BURN *GIOVANNI'S ROOM*.

The book's subject matter was such a shock to Baldwin's publishers at Knopf that they wanted him to burn the manuscript. The fact that it dealt with topics that were taboo at the time wasn't the only problem; because *Giovanni's Room* was so different from *Go Tell It on the Mountain*, his publisher feared Baldwin would alienate his reader base.

Knopf refused to move forward with the book, so Dial Press published it in the US instead in 1956. The new publisher had similar fears, however, and they pulled Baldwin's author photo, supposedly to hide the fact that a novel about queer white characters was written by a Black man. Despite the hand-wringing surrounding its release, *Giovanni's Room* received generally positive reviews from critics.

THE QUOTABLE BALDWIN

"If you fall in love with a boy, you fall in love with a boy. The fact that many Americans consider it a disease says more about them than it does about homosexuality."

—From an interview with Eve Auchincloss and Nancy Lynch, 1969

HOUSE MADE OF DAWN

N. SCOTT MOMADAY

February 27, 1934

BORN: Lawton, Oklahoma

OTHER NOTABLE WORKS:
The Way to Rainy Mountain (1969)
The Ancient Child (1989)

It's safe to say that stories shaped N. Scott Momaday. "I had a Pan-Indian experience as a child, even before I knew what that term meant," he told an interviewer. Though he has Kiowa and Cherokee ancestry, he grew up on Navajo, Apache, and Pueblo reservations as his family moved around trying to find work. Momaday was raised by two teacher parents with their own strong creative streaks; his mother a writer, his father a painter. As a boy, he listened raptly as his father told him stories from the Kiowa oral tradition. As he grew older, he began to write down these familiar tales. Momaday went on to study poetry and earn a PhD in English literature at Stanford University, blending aspects of his literary education with the more traditional storytelling he was immersed in as a child.

Momaday's work—a mix of novels, memoirs, folklore, and poetry—is deeply rooted in the geography of the American Southwest. The mountains, canyons, and prairies became the canvas for his work. His stories, at their core, are a celebration of language and landscape.

With his vivid prose and rich meditations on people and place, Momaday became one of the twentieth century's most prominent Native American writers. His first novel, *House Made of Dawn* (1968), ushered in a breakthrough moment for Native American literature. Critics dubbed the era the Native American Renaissance, as a flush of indigenous writers gained prominence among mainstream audiences. In 1969, *House Made of Dawn* won the Pulitzer Prize for Fiction, making Momaday the first Native American to claim that honor.

That same year, he published *The Way to Rainy Mountain*, a book that weaves together folklore, history, and memoir to tell the story of his Kiowa ancestors and his own exploration of his family roots. Momaday's latest work, 2020's *The Death of a Sitting Bear*, is a collection of poems he wrote over the last fifty years.

N. Scott Momaday's *House Made of Dawn* follows Abel, who, after serving in World War II, returns to his reservation and struggles to reacclimatize to his traditional way of life. Realizing he is no longer at home on the reservation, a world grounded in spirituality and a sense of connection with the land, Abel sets off for Los Angeles. Only after spending years away—and experiencing a series of mishaps and mistakes—is Abel finally able to realize where he truly belongs. Here's what you should know about Momaday's award-winning work.

MOMADAY'S REAL-LIFE EXPERIENCES INFLUENCED *HOUSE MADE OF DAWN.*

Kiowa oral traditions run deep throughout Momaday's work. But folklore wasn't the only aspect of his identity that influenced his critically acclaimed novel: The writer slipped in details from his own life while building the narrative. The book is set in Jemez Pueblo, New Mexico, the very same community where Momaday spent his teen years while his parents taught on the reservation.

Momaday's protagonist, Abel, may be a fictional character, but aspects of his identity and experiences were borne from reality. Momaday created him as a composite of people he knew during his time in Jemez Pueblo, and his actions represent the problems of real-life people who, like Abel, grappled with issues of identity and how to reintegrate into their communities after being uprooted to fight overseas. The protagonist also reflects aspects of Momaday's own history—he, too, grew up straddling two worlds.

THE NOVEL WAS ORIGINALLY A SERIES OF POEMS.

Momaday considers himself a poet, not a novelist. As he told an interviewer, he thinks of *House Made of Dawn* as an aberration, a deviation from his poetic norm—he didn't intend for the story to become his debut novel. When he began working on *House Made of Dawn*, he first conceived of it as a cycle of poems while pursuing his doctorate at Stanford, where he focused his dissertation on poetry. After spending several years immersed in verse, he sought a new challenge and turned his attention toward fiction. The inkling of an idea for *House Made of Dawn* then morphed into a series of short stories before finally evolving into the novel that exists today.

Though the tale changed shape, it still maintains pieces of its poetic foundation. The prose is more lyrical than linear, and each sentence is crafted with a cadence that reflects the writer's literary roots.

MOMADAY WAS SURPRISED BY *HOUSE MADE OF DAWN'S* SUCCESS.

Non-indigenous critics may have had a tough time fully understanding the elements of Native American culture braided throughout the novel, but that didn't stop *House Made of Dawn* from garnering a fair amount of praise once it arrived on the literary scene. Still, Momaday was surprised by the book's reception. When his editor called to tell him his novel had just been awarded a Pulitzer Prize, he thought she was kidding—after all, even his own publisher struggled to recall the book.

House Made of Dawn did more than startle its author with one of the writing world's top honors. Around the same time *House Made of Dawn* made its debut, other Native American writers were finding success among mainstream readers, too. Native Americans had published a wide variety of work in the English language, including novels, since the eighteenth century. But it wasn't until after *House Made of Dawn*'s historic Pulitzer win that a robust market for indigenous authors really opened up. Decades later, Momaday is still an inspiration for numerous Native American writers.

Far below, the breeze ran upon the shining blades of corn, and they heard the footsteps running. It was faint at first and far away, but it rose and drew near, steadily, a hundred men running, two hundred, three, not fast, but running easily and forever, the one sound of a hundred men running. "Listen," he said. "It is the race of the dead, and it happens here."

OTHER NATIVE AMERICAN NOVELS YOU SHOULDN'T MISS

1 *Ceremony* (1977) //
LESLIE MARMON SILKO

Like *House Made of Dawn*, *Ceremony* follows a World War II veteran's troubles reentering society. Memories of battle and his time trapped as a Japanese prisoner of war haunt Tayo, the protagonist. He struggles not only with the twentieth-century conflict, but also with the ongoing colonialism that has long threatened his home. While searching for his own inner peace, Tayo must also face the problems plaguing his society. The lyrical narrative Silko constructed covers much more than one man's attempts to use ceremony to heal from the trauma of war. As Tayo's story unfolds, readers discover that the Laguna Pueblo, his reservation, is enduring a drought of mythical proportions. By interlacing the modern plot with traditional Laguna folklore, Silko creates a tender, yet heart-wrenching, tale of pain, community, and growth.

2 *Fools Crow* (1986) //
JAMES WELCH

Welch's American Book Award–winning novel takes place in nineteenth-century America in the years following the Civil War. It's a poignant snapshot of a time marked by increasingly escalating tensions between the Blackfeet and the encroaching white settlers. The book follows Fools Crow, formerly known as White Man's Dog, as he grows from a weak warrior into a respected fighter and healer. Welch takes a big-picture approach when telling Fools Crow's story. Woven through-out the larger narrative are the broader issues the Blackfeet must face. As Fools Crow grows discontented with war, the threats of the *Napikwans* (white people) and "white-scabs disease" (smallpox) grow stronger. He attempts to find a way to save his people, along the way encountering visions of devastating disease outbreaks, forced assimilation, massacres, and long migrations plagued by illness and violence. Though the story itself is fiction, the plot includes events like the very real 1870 Marias Massacre, in which the US Army killed a camp of sleeping Blackfeet—creating a sad ode to the power of storytelling as a tool to preserve a culture's past.

3 *Mean Spirit* (1990) //
LINDA HOGAN

A wealth of oil beneath her allotment of land makes Grace Blanket one of the richest women in her area. She lived on land purchased by the Osage Nation, who settled there after being driven from their ancestral homeland. Tragically, the river of black gold lurking just beneath the surface proved to be more of a curse than a blessing. Set within Oklahoma's 1920s oil boom, *Mean Spirit* is a story of greed, grief, and disconnect from the earth. When Grace is brutally murdered, the Graycloud family takes in her daughter, who witnessed the killing. Soon, other members of the community begin dying under mysterious circumstances as well. Local law enforcement fails to investigate the violent acts until Stace Red Hawk, a Lakota Sioux officer for the US Bureau of Investigation, arrives from Washington, DC. While facing corruption and deceit, Stace, like other indigenous characters in the book, grapples with the divide between the western world's wealth and their cultures' traditional ways of life.

IN SEARCH OF LOST TIME

MARCEL PROUST

July 10, 1871–November 18, 1922

BORN: Auteuil, France

OTHER NOTABLE WORKS:
Pleasures and Days (1896)
Jean Santeuil (1952)

Readers of *In Search of Lost Time* may know Marcel Proust better than people who can only parrot the facts of his life, for it was in his seven-volume magnum opus that Proust poured his innermost ruminations on his own experiences as a lover and writer. And though he fictionalized events and characters, he only called it a novel "because it lacks that quality of the casual which is the mark of a volume of Memoirs."

The absence of any nonchalance in Proust's work may have been influenced by his feeling that he was racing to finish before his health failed him. Born into wealth, Proust could afford to focus on writing (and partake in the salon-based intellectual society of the era) but asthma-related illnesses often interrupted him. By the time he was looking for a publisher for *In Search of Lost Time*, he sensed he was nearing his end. "I have put the best of myself into it," he wrote in one letter, "and what it needs now is that a monumental tomb should be completed for its reception before my own is filled." Proust wasn't wrong—he died from pneumonia before the last three volumes were released.

It may never be possible to declare any single novel the definitive work of its era, but Marcel Proust's *In Search of Lost Time* stands as the most often-cited candidate. Published over seven volumes and running more than four thousand pages, the French language book and its unnamed aristocratic narrator in late nineteenth- and early twentieth-century France weaves a mediation on love, loss, and the nature of memory that frequently doubles back on itself. Sight, sounds, and smells trigger recollections that inform the protagonist's past and present. By the end, both the narrator and the reader have come to understand that memory—its reassurances, its faults, its emotions—is what shapes us all. Read on for a few fun facts about *Lost Time*.

PROUST'S EVOCATIVE MADELEINE COULD HAVE BEEN TOAST.

When we first meet Proust's narrator in *Swann's Way*, he's deadened by habit and inexplicably blocked from accessing most of his memories. That suddenly changes as soon as he tastes one tea-soaked morsel of a madeleine, which evokes a similar experience from his childhood and unleashes a torrent of other memories. The scene both drives the story forward and alludes to one of Proust's central themes—finding meaning through memory—and it even originated the French expression *madeleine de Proust*, used whenever a sensation or event provokes nostalgia.

Though Proust did base that pivotal moment on a real-life incident, his own *madeleine de Proust* wasn't actually a madeleine. It was a rusk—a crisp, dry, twice-baked biscuit. And in 2015, a set of newly published handwritten manuscripts revealed that Proust had initially intended the scene to mirror its source material more accurately. In his first version, the narrator eats a slice of toast with honey; and in the second, he bites into a *biscotte*, or rusk. To think, readers may never have had the pleasure of hearing Proust describe a sweet, spongey madeleine as "the little scallop-shell of pastry, so richly sensual under its severe, religious folds."

PROUST HAD TO SELF-PUBLISH THE FIRST VOLUME.

Proust had published essays and short stories in magazines and newspapers before—and some of those short stories were even released in a book called *Pleasures and Days* in 1896—but getting someone to back several hundred meandering pages of the first volume of *Lost Time* proved difficult. Proust first sent them to a well-known publisher named Fasquelle, who suggested so many edits that Proust decided to look elsewhere. The literary journal *La Nouvelle Revue Française* passed in part because they considered Proust's writing too aristocratic; and Marc Humblot, another prospective publisher, found it prohibitively verbose. "Perhaps I am as thick as two short planks," he wrote, "but I just can't understand why anyone should take thirty pages to describe how he tosses about in bed because he can't get to sleep."

In the end, Proust resigned himself to footing the bill, and enlisted the help of an as-yet-unestablished publisher named Bernard Grasset to print the books. *In Search of Lost Time* drew acclaim, and writer André Gide, who had encouraged *La Nouvelle Revue Française*'s original rejection, told Proust it was "the worst blunder they ever made." Fortunately, the journal redeemed itself by publishing the following volumes.

EVELYN WAUGH, D.H. LAWRENCE, AND JAMES JOYCE WEREN'T FANS.

It's difficult to overstate the impact that *In Search of Lost Time* had on twentieth-century writers. Graham Greene considered Proust the "greatest novelist" of the entire century, for example, and Virginia Woolf idolized him to the point of frustration. "Proust so titillates my own desire for expression that I can hardly set out the sentence," she wrote. "Oh if I could write like that! I cry."

That said, there were a few venerated authors who didn't exactly campaign to be president of the Marcel Proust fan club. In a 1948 letter, Evelyn Waugh told Nancy Mitford that he found Proust to have "absolutely no sense of time." He couldn't get past Proust's ill-plotted timelines (and boring jokes, too). D.H. Lawrence lambasted Proust—along with James Joyce and Dorothy Richardson—for trying to delay the demise of the "serious novel" by penning "a very-long-drawn-out fourteen-volume death-agony." Joyce also failed to "see any special talent" in Proust, though he did admit that he himself wasn't the best critic.

THE DISHES FIVE WRITERS WOULD BRING TO A LITERARY POTLUCK

Proust, we can assume, would be on dessert duty with his madeleines, but here are the other dishes that famous authors would probably bring to a dinner party.

PEARL S. BUCK: Sweet and Sour Fish

Buck grew up in China and considered Asian cookery the world's best. As a child, she had meals with Chinese servants instead of eating American fare with her family, an experience that inspired her to write the *Oriental Cookbook* in 1972.

HARPER LEE: Crackling Bread

If you had asked the Pulitzer-winning author why the South lost the Civil War, she might have blamed the soldiers' hankering for crackling bread, a mix of cornmeal and cracklings. "Some historians say this recipe alone fell the Confederacy," Lee wrote. Understandable, considering her recipe begins: "First, catch your pig."

F. SCOTT FITZGERALD: Turkey Leftovers

In his private papers, Fitzgerald listed thirteen uses for leftover Thanksgiving turkey. These included a vermouth bird cocktail, a side of monkey meat, and dishes stuffed with mothballs, stewed in washing machines, and blown up with bicycle pumps.

JOHN STEINBECK: Posole

Steinbeck liked to eat local. In England, he'd hunt for dandelion greens. In California, he made butter and cheese with the milk from his own personal cow. In New York, he fished for dinner. But traveling on the road, Steinbeck ate like a college freshman. His posole recipe is simply a "can of chile and a can of hominy."

SYLVIA PLATH: Tomato Soup Cake

Plath often wrote as she baked, penning "Death & Co." while she made her specialty, tomato soup cake.

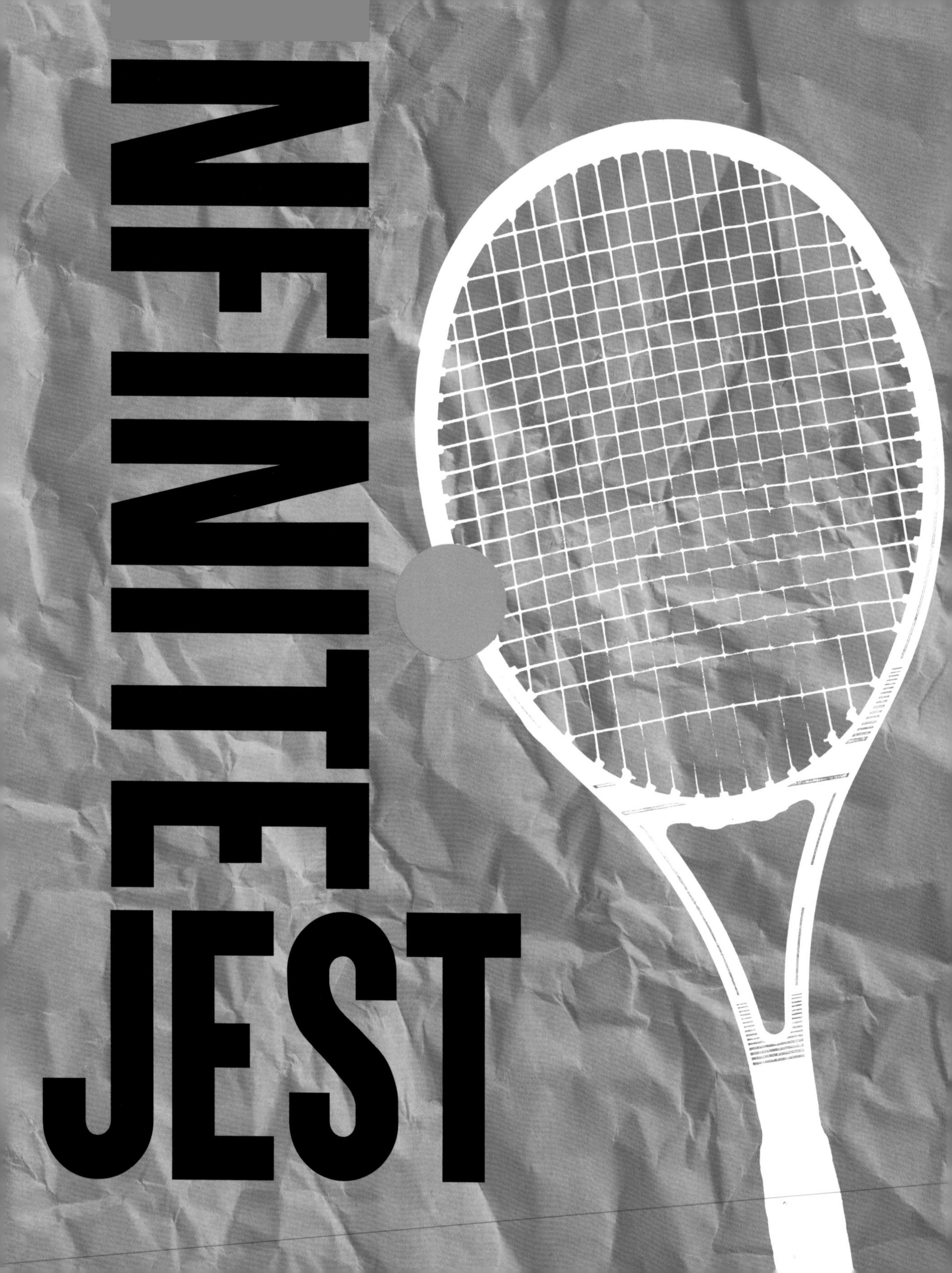
NFINITE
JEST

DAVID FOSTER WALLACE

February 21, 1962–September 12, 2008

BORN: Ithaca, New York

OTHER NOTABLE WORKS:
A Supposedly Fun Thing I'll Never Do Again:
Essays and Arguments (1997)

D avid Foster Wallace was the son of college professors and called himself a "near-great junior tennis player," but academic pursuits soon eclipsed athletics. Wallace studied modal logic and English at Amherst College and briefly pursued graduate studies in philosophy at Harvard.

He wrote with a knowing, sardonic tone, and yet cautioned readers about the withering effects of irony. His use of abundant endnotes provided a structure for his discursive, self-analyzing authorial presence in works like *Infinite Jest*. His nonfiction ranged in topics from tennis to television, rap music to lexicography. His influence can be seen in the inline annotations of modern media and the matter-of-fact existential anxiety of George Saunders and Ben Lerner.

Wallace's commencement speech at Kenyon College implored his audience to seek empathy and, above all, awareness. And yet the limits of Wallace's own empathy were revealed in his abusive behavior toward former partner (and fellow writer) Mary Karr, documented in a biography by D.T. Max. It's difficult to say that these personal failings are "irrelevant," as Wallace once contended regarding another writer's life in relation to their work. Still, his impact on postmodern literature and culture remains undeniable. Wallace died by suicide in 2008.

It's not a stretch (or very original) to call *Infinite Jest* the defining work of the 1990s. David Foster Wallace's second novel is set in an absurd (but agonizingly believable) near-future, and it explores addiction, entertainment, pleasure, commerce, technology, and tennis—lots and lots of tennis. Here are a few brief facts about Wallace's sprawling work.

WALLACE BEGAN WRITING *INFINITE JEST* IN EARNEST IN 1991.

"I wanted to do something sad," Wallace said in an interview with Salon shortly after the book's publication in 1996. "I'd done some funny stuff and some heavy, intellectual stuff, but I'd never done anything sad. And I wanted it not to have a single main character. The other banality would be: I wanted to do something real American, about what it's like to live in America around the millennium."

AUTHOR AND CRITIC STEVEN MOORE GAVE WALLACE NOTES ON EARLY DRAFTS.

Moore knew Wallace when Wallace was teaching at Illinois State, and he was one of three people to see the early manuscript. He described it as "[a] mess—a patchwork of different fonts and point sizes, with numerous handwritten corrections/additions on most pages, and paginated in a nesting pattern (e.g., p. 22 is followed by 22A-J before resuming with p. 23, which is followed by 23A-D, etc.). Much of it is single-spaced, and what footnotes existed at this stage appear at the bottom of pages . . . Throughout there are notes in the margins, reminders to fix something or other, adjustments to chronology (which seems to have given Wallace quite a bit of trouble), even a few drawings and doodles. Merely flipping through the 4-inch-high manuscript would give even a seasoned editor the howling fantods."

IT WAS A HIGHPOINT OF HIS EDITOR'S CAREER.

After reading two hundred pages of *Infinite Jest*, Michael Pietsch, Wallace's editor at Little, Brown, told Wallace's agent, "I want to do this book more than I want to breathe." Pietsch responded to the original 1,600-page manuscript of *Infinite Jest* with a letter to Wallace saying, "It's exactly the challenge and adventure I came to book publishing to find."

It was hyped like crazy before it was published. Little, Brown sent out cryptic postcards to publications teasing the book with phrases like "Infinite Pleasure" and "Infinite Writer." It worked. *Infinite Jest* was published in February 1996, and by March it was already in its sixth printing.

WALLACE MADE PREDICTIONS ABOUT THE INTERNET BUT WASN'T A FAN.

While *Infinite Jest* can be seen as prophetic regarding the Internet (especially video conferencing) and the consequences that come with such an informational firehose, Wallace had never used it as of the novel's publication. "I've never been on the Internet," he told a *Chicago Tribune* reporter in 1996. "This is sort of what it's like to be alive. You don't have to be on the Internet for life to feel this way." (A few months after that *Tribune* story, Wallace would participate in an online chatroom interview.)

INFINITE JEST BY THE NUMBERS

According to Ryan Compton's *"Infinite Jest* by the Numbers," Wallace used a vocabulary of

20,584

unique words to write the

577,608

-word *Infinite Jest*.

INVISIBLE MAN

RALPH ELLISON

March 1, 1913–April 16, 1994

BORN: Oklahoma City, Oklahoma

OTHER NOTABLE WORKS:
Shadow and Act (1964)
Juneteenth (1999)

If not for the Great Depression—and Richard Wright—Ralph Ellison might have been a musician instead of a writer. Born in 1913 (though he would later say it was 1914), Ellison was raised by his mother after his father's death and picked up the cornet when he was eight. Later, he began playing the trumpet, and at nineteen, he started studying music at Tuskegee Institute in Alabama.

In 1936, he headed to New York in order to raise funds for his final year of school and decided to stay. There, he was taken under the wings of celebrated writers like Richard Wright and Langston Hughes. Wright was editing a magazine at the time and had Ellison write a review, and, after that, a short story. (It was accepted but got bumped for space just before the magazine went out of business.) The Depression raged, and Ellison headed to Ohio, where he hunted game and sold it to get by; at night, he told *The Paris Review*, "I practiced writing and studied Joyce, Dostoevsky, Stein, and Hemingway."

Ellison never went back to school, but he did go back to New York, and more short stories and essays followed. So did *Invisible Man*, published in 1952—and then a forty-year dry spell in which Ellison wrote essays and prose but was unable to finish *Juneteenth*. (It was published posthumously in 1999.) Ellison rounded out his days as a teacher and professor at a series of colleges and universities, but his landmark work was an education unto itself.

For a generation marked by civil rights battles, the arrival of Ralph Ellison's novel *Invisible Man* signaled a new chapter in how people of color were depicted in literature. Since its publication, *Invisible Man* has been heralded as one of the most important novels of the twentieth century. Ellison won the National Book Award for Fiction in 1953, *and Invisible Man* has been heavily circulated in classrooms ever since. Take a look at some things you might not know about Ellison and his landmark work.

INVISIBLE MAN TOOK SEVEN YEARS TO WRITE.

Following the end of his service as a cook in the United States Merchant Marine during World War II, Ellison acted on Wright's encouragement and began to write what would become *Invisible Man*. He started the book in 1945 and it was published in 1952, a seven-year stretch that would foreshadow Ellison's difficulties in finishing future projects.

IT STARTED WITH JUST ONE LINE.

Although they shared similar experiences, Ellison warned that the protagonist of *Invisible Man* was not a stand-in for the author. The novel's history began when Ellison was home from the war and visiting a friend in Vermont. Ellison recalled that he typed "I am an invisible man" almost spontaneously, without having any additional idea of where he was going or what the sentence meant.

THE FIRST CHAPTER WAS PUBLISHED YEARS BEFORE THE REST OF THE BOOK.

While still toiling on the novel, Ellison published the first chapter in *Horizon* magazine in 1947. The emotionally charged nature of the scene—Ellison wrote of Black students forced to box blindfolded for the amusement of white spectators—led the literary community to brace for a potent novel by Ellison.

ELLISON WAS HIGHLY CRITICAL OF HIS OWN BOOK.

Invisible Man was an instant success: It spent sixteen weeks on best seller lists and was hailed by critics as one of the most impressive novels of the century. But in accepting his National Book Award in 1953, Ellison referred to the book as an "attempt" at a great novel.

THE FBI READ *INVISIBLE MAN* BEFORE IT CAME OUT.

Ellison's considerable success in articulating the civil rights climate of the mid-twentieth century, and his tangential relationship to the Communist Party, prompted J. Edgar Hoover's infamously paranoia-fueled FBI to keep a close watch on the author. The bureau amassed more than 1,400 pages of information about his political and professional activities. Agents were even able to preview *Invisible Man* prior to publication thanks to informers in the publishing industry.

THE BOOK WASN'T INTENDED TO BE EXCLUSIVELY ABOUT DISCRIMINATION IN AMERICA.

Although *Invisible Man* has been heralded as a definitive exploration of how people of color are minimized in America, Ellison said that that is only one interpretation of the book—another is that it's a parable about integration. "When I was a kid, I read the English novels. I read Russian translations and so on," he said in 1983. "And always, I was the hero. I identified with the hero. Literature is integrated. And I'm not just talking about color, race. I'm talking about the power of literature to make us recognize again and again the wholeness of the human experience."

Writing in Fort Greene Park

Richard Wright, Ellison's mentor, wrote most of his influential 1940 novel *Native Son* on a yellow legal pad sitting on a bench in Brooklyn's Fort Greene Park. There is now a park bench dedicated to the writer, inscribed with his line about the novel: "In the writing of scene after scene I was guided by but one criterion: to tell the truth as I saw it."

FOUR AUTHORS ON OVER-COMING WRITER'S BLOCK

Writer's block can happen to anyone—even successful novelists. Everyone from Stephen King to Leo Tolstoy has fallen victim to the phenomenon. So did Ralph Ellison: The author wrote thousands of pages of notes for a follow-up to 1952's *Invisible Man*, but thanks to what he called "a natural writer's block as big as the Ritz and as stubborn as a grease spot on a gabardine suit," a second novel never appeared. Ellison died in 1994 without publishing another book. (His friend John Callahan would eventually take Ellison's notes and turn them into *Juneteenth*.)

Ellison might not have gotten over his block, but plenty of authors have—and have offered their advice for how they did it, including these four:

RAY BRADBURY

When Bradbury became blocked in his writing, he took it as a sign of being on the wrong track. "In the middle of writing something you go blank and your mind says: 'No, that's it,'" he said in a 2001 speech. "You're being warned, aren't you? Your subconscious is saying 'I don't like you anymore. You're writing about things I don't give a damn for.'" The cure for writer's block is to "[stop] whatever you're writing and [do] something else. You picked the wrong subject." This has been echoed by Orson Scott Card. "I have never found 'writer's block' to be wrong," he said. "Whenever I'm stopped on a project, it's because I was doing something false or weak, and when I get it right, it becomes more powerful and true."

JHUMPA LAHIRI

According to Lahiri, writer's block is simply part of the process of writing, "the period during which ideas gestate in the mind, when a story grows but isn't necessarily being written in sentences on the page," she told *The Times*. Her foolproof way of getting over it? Taking a break from what she's writing and picking up a book. She's not alone in this strategy: Many other authors swear by walking away from their work and revisiting it later, including Jane Smiley, Hilary Mantel, and Neil Gaiman, who noted that by reading what you're writing from the beginning with fresh eyes, "when you get to the end you'll be both enthusiastic about it and know what the next few words are. And you do it all one word at a time."

JOHN STEINBECK

When it came to writer's block, *The Grapes of Wrath* author advised fellow writers that the easiest way to get started was to forget the audience they were supposed to be writing for and, instead, making it more personal by writing to a single person. Not only did this strategy help remove the fear of writing to an unknown audience, but "it also, you will find, will give a sense of freedom and a lack of self-consciousness," he wrote.

MAYA ANGELOU

Author and poet Maya Angelou was not fond of the term writer's block, which she felt gave the phenomenon a power that she wasn't comfortable with. But she did sometimes suffer from it and had a strategy for overcoming it: Just writing, even if what came out wasn't her finest work. "I may write for two weeks 'the cat sat on the mat, that is that, not a rat,'" she said in *Writers Dreaming*. "And it might be just the most boring and awful stuff. But I try. . . . And then it's as if the muse is convinced that I'm serious and says, 'OK. OK. I'll come.'" Other writers agree with this method of just getting it out, including one anonymous Penguin Random House author, who told the publishing house's blog, "write anything—deliberately write rubbish. Write something you'd never allow anyone to read, then burn it—or eat it." (You should maybe skip that last part.)

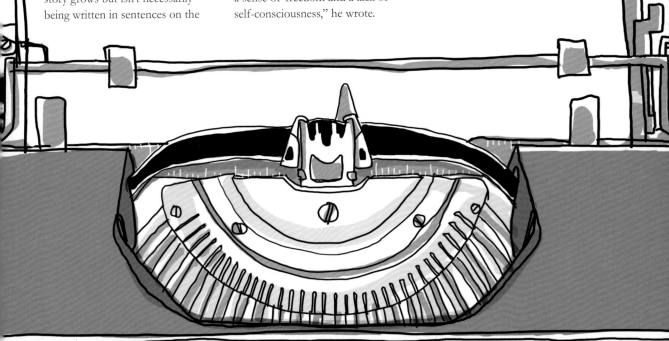

JANE EYRE

o doubt, p

of almos

untenance

ppearin

ne not

with pride; a

nciple, in a positi

e had, likewise, a

e of Mrs. Reed she

er voice was deep, its i

tical—very intolerable,

nd a shawl turban

d her (I suppose

ity.

e and Mary were of eq

oplars. Mary was too sli

was moulded like a Dian

, with special interest. First, I

ppearance accorded with Mrs. Fa

ndly, whether it at all resembled the fa

nted of her; and thirdly—it will out!

ch as I should fancy likely to suit Mr. Ro

As far as person went, she answered poin

to my picture and Mrs. Fairfax's descripti

st, the sloping shoulders, the graceful nec

black ringlets were all there—but her

CHARLOTTE BRONTË

April 21, 1816–March 31, 1855

BORN: Thornton, England

OTHER NOTABLE WORKS:
Villette (1853)

Charlotte Brontë was something of a literary visionary from an early age, penning fanciful stories and dreaming up games to play with her (equally creative) siblings on the grounds of the family's Haworth estate in Yorkshire. As an adult, she turned down several suitors, preferring to earn a living by working intermittently as a governess and a teacher—experiences that would later inform her novels. In 1847, when Brontë was thirty-one years old, she published *Jane Eyre* to wide acclaim and followed it up with *Shirley: A Tale* and *Villette*. Though she did eventually marry a colleague of her father's in 1854, her happy ending was short-lived: She died the very next year.

When Charlotte Brontë sat down to write *Jane Eyre*, she didn't know she was writing a major work of literature. The Gothic novel about a governess's romance with the brooding Mr. Rochester was an instant classic in its time and is still much loved today. After all, who can resist a tale featuring a madwoman locked in an attic? Brontë's life mirrored many of the book's plot points.

LIKE JANE, BRONTË WORKED AS A GOVERNESS.

Jane Eyre was a provincial girl hired to work as a governess among strangers—and so was Charlotte Brontë. In 1839, the wealthy Sidgwick family employed Brontë to live in their country estate and educate their children. She hated the job, writing, "I had charge given me of a set of pampered, spoilt, turbulent children, whom I was expected constantly to amuse, as well as to instruct." She became depressed and withdrawn, causing Mrs. Sidgwick to scold her.

THE MADWOMAN IN THE ATTIC WAS INSPIRED BY REAL LIFE.

That same year, Brontë visited Norton Conyers House in North Yorkshire. There she learned that sixty years before, a mentally ill woman had been confined in "Mad Mary's Room" in the attic. The story possibly inspired Bertha Mason, Rochester's insane wife. In 2004, the owners of the house discovered a blocked staircase connecting the attic and the first floor, just like the staircase described in the novel.

THE HARSH SCHOOL JANE ATTENDS WAS ALSO BASED ON EXPERIENCE.

When Brontë was five, her mother died, leaving her poor clergyman father to care for six children. He sent Charlotte, Emily (author of *Wuthering Heights*), and their two older sisters to the Clergy Daughters' School at Cowan Bridge, Lancashire. It was a harsh, disciplinary environment with bad food, cold buildings, and physical abuse. Brontë later drew on these memories when creating Lowood, the school Jane attends. The cruel headmaster, Mr. Brocklehurst, was drawn from a real person, Reverend William Carus-Wilson.

HELEN BURNS IS BASED ON BRONTË'S SISTER MARIA.

Like Helen Burns, Jane's friend who dies at Lowood, Maria Brontë was neglected and abused when she got sick at school. Brontë's biographer Elizabeth Gaskell wrote that when the child wanted to rest in bed, a teacher "took her by the arm . . . and by one vigorous movement whirled her out into the middle of the floor, abusing her all the time for dirty and untidy habits." Both Maria and the second-eldest Brontë daughter, Elizabeth, contracted tuberculosis at the school and were sent home, where they later died.

BRONTË WROTE THE NOVEL WHILE NURSING HER BLIND FATHER.

While Brontë was writing *Jane Eyre,* her father, Patrick, had a pre-anesthetic operation to have cataracts removed from his eyes. He was left blind and helpless while his eyes healed. It's no coincidence that Rochester is blind at the end of the novel, and that, like Brontë's father, he eventually regains his sight.

LOVE TRIANGLES WERE ALL AROUND HER.

When Jane discovers that Rochester is married to Bertha Mason, she leaves him rather than commit bigamy. In real life, not only was Brontë's younger brother, Branwell, having an affair with a married

woman, Charlotte herself had fallen in love with a married professor named Constantin Heger. The crush was unrequited—Heger is said to have torn up the love letter Brontë wrote him—but the situation may have inspired aspects of Jane and Rochester's relationship, as well as the novel *Villette.*

JANE EYRE WAS PUBLISHED UNDER A MALE PSEUDONYM.

In 1846, Anne, Emily, and Charlotte published a poetry book under the pseudonyms Acton, Ellis, and Currer Bell; they knew they would be taken more seriously if the public believed that they were men. Charlotte also published *Jane Eyre* under the name Currer Bell. When it became a best seller, the literary world became consumed with learning more about the mysterious Bell brothers.

Having corresponded by letter, Brontë's publishers, Smith, Elder, and Company, had no idea that Currer Bell was a woman. In 1848, circumstances forced Charlotte and Anne to go to London and meet their editors in person. Charlotte wrote later:

"Neither Mr. Smith nor Mr. Williams knew we were coming—they had never seen us—they did not know whether we were men or women, but had always written to us as men . . . 'Is it Mr. Smith?' I said, looking up through my spectacles at a tall young man. 'It is.' I then put his own letter into his hand directed to Currer Bell. He looked at it and then at me again. 'Where did you get this?' he said. I laughed at his perplexity—a recognition took place. I gave him my real name: Miss Brontë."

A year after Anne and Emily died, Charlotte Brontë outed all three of them as women writers in the preface of the combined edition of *Wuthering Heights* and *Agnes Grey.*

JANE EYRE WAS AN INSTANT SUCCESS.

From the start, the book was a success—one critic called it "the best novel of the season"—and people began to speculate about who Currer Bell was. But some reviewers were less impressed, criticizing it for being coarse in content, including one who called it "anti-Christian." Brontë was writing in the Victorian period, after all.

CAT-LOVING WRITERS

Some of history's most successful writers were devoted to their furry friends, including these nine.

THE BRONTË SISTERS

Many of the Brontë sisters' published works featured felines, and cats make appearances in Anne and Charlotte's diaries as well. In 1842, while living in Brussels, Emily wrote an essay in French called "Le Chat" ("The Cat") that defended cats against people who say they're cruel—and made points about human nature while she was at it. The sisters didn't just write about cats, either; at their home in Haworth, they had a black cat named Tom and a tabby named Tiger.

LOUISA MAY ALCOTT

Louisa May Alcott once jokingly listed a "love of cats" among her vices, and her fondness of felines shone through her writing. In *Little Women*, the March sisters have a pet cat, and at one point in the story Beth is seen playing with the cat and her kittens.

The book even includes a poem called "A Lament (For S.B. Pat Paw)" eulogizing a beloved pet cat.

MARK TWAIN

When his beloved black cat Bambino went missing, Mark Twain took out an advertisement in the *New York American* offering a $5 reward to return the missing cat to his house at 21 Fifth Avenue in New York City. It described Bambino as "Large and intensely black; thick, velvety fur; has a faint fringe of white hair across his chest; not easy to find in ordinary light." (For the record, Bambino made it back just fine.)

T.S. ELIOT

Aside from peppering his high Modernist poetry with allusions to feline friends, T.S. Eliot wrote a book of light verse called *Old Possum's Book of Practical Cats*, a collection of fifteen poems regarding the different personalities and eccentricities of kitties. Later publications of *Old Possum's* included illustrations by noted artist Edward Gorey—yet another avid cat lover.

WILLIAM S. BURROUGHS

William S. Burroughs is known for his wild, drug-induced writings, but he had a softer side as well—especially when it came to his cats. He penned an autobiographical novella, *The Cat Inside,* about the felines he owned throughout his life, and the final journal entry Burroughs wrote before he died referred to the pure love he had for his four pets: "Only thing can resolve conflict is love, like I felt for Fletch and Ruski, Spooner, and Calico. Pure love. What I feel for my cats present and past."

RAYMOND CHANDLER

British novelist Raymond Chandler's cat Taki gave him endless enjoyment,

but also occasionally got on his nerves. "Our cat is growing positively tyrannical," he once wrote to a friend. "If she finds herself alone anywhere she emits blood curdling yells until somebody comes running. She sleeps on a table in the service porch and now demands to be lifted up and down from it. She gets warm milk about eight o'clock at night and starts yelling for it about 7.30."

PATRICIA HIGHSMITH

Patricia Highsmith once said, "My imagination functions better when I don't have to speak with people," but she did virtually everything with her cats: She wrote next to them, she ate next to them, and she even slept next to them. She kept them by her side throughout her life until her death at her home in Locarno, Switzerland, in 1995.

SAMUEL JOHNSON

In *The Life of Samuel Johnson*, James Boswell writes of Johnson's cat, Hodge, saying, "I never shall forget the indulgence with which he treated Hodge, his cat: for whom he himself used to go out and buy oysters, lest the servants having that trouble should take a dislike to the poor creature." Although Boswell wasn't a fan, Johnson called Hodge "a very fine cat indeed."

CHARLES DICKENS

Charles Dickens had a soft spot for a few felines in his life. In 1862, he was so upset after the death of his favorite cat, Bob, that he had the kitty's paw stuffed and mounted to an ivory letter opener. He had the opener engraved saying, "C.D., In memory of Bob, 1862" so he could have a constant reminder of his old friend.

OCTAVIA BUTLER

June 22, 1947–February 24, 2006

BORN: Pasadena, California

OTHER NOTABLE WORKS:
Parable series (1993–1998)
Fledgling (2005)

Octavia Butler faced many obstacles on her path to becoming one the best science fiction authors of the twentieth century. Raised primarily by her grandmother and widowed mother, she grew up in Pasadena, California, poor, dyslexic, and painfully shy. Published Black women writers were rare in 1950s America—and Black women science fiction writers even more so—but that didn't keep Butler from recognizing her own potential.

While watching television at age twelve, the B-movie *Devil Girls from Mars* (1954) became an unlikely source of inspiration for her. "As I was watching this film, I had a series of revelations," she recounted at a lecture at MIT in 1998. "The first was that 'Geez, I can write a better story than that.' And then I thought, 'Gee, anybody can write a better story than that.' And my third thought was the clincher: 'Somebody got paid for writing that awful story.'"

Butler enrolled in Pasadena City College and earned an Associate of Arts degree in 1968. Though her mother encouraged her to find steady work as a secretary, Butler preferred jobs that left her with enough mental energy to wake up early every morning and write. These odd jobs included dishwasher, telemarketer, and potato chip inspector. She also continued her education past under-graduate school, attending the Clarion Science Fiction Writers' Workshop at the recommendation of her mentor and fellow science fiction writer Harlan Ellison.

In 1976, she published *Patternmaster*, the first book in the Patternist series. Her 1979 novel *Kindred*, about a Black woman in modern-day California who's sent back in time to a pre–Civil War Maryland plantation, cemented her legendary reputation in the speculative fiction world.

Throughout her career, Butler was the recipient of numerous honors and awards. The second book in her Parable series, *The Parable of the Talents*, won a Nebula award, and her short story and essay collection *Bloodchild* received both a Hugo and a Nebula Award. In 1995, she became the first-ever science fiction author to receive a MacArthur Genius Grant. Octavia Butler died in 2006 at age fifty-eight, and her body of work—which dealt with race, gender, and authoritarianism—is just as relevant.

While working as a writer, Octavia Butler famously wrote herself the motivational note: "I am a Bestselling Writer. I write Bestselling Books . . . So Be It! See to It." Her best-selling work, *Kindred*, is still widely read today. The book follows Dana, a twenty-six-year-old Black woman from California who travels back in time to an antebellum plantation in Maryland. There, she meets the white enslaver destined to become her great-great-great-grandfather. In order to ensure her existence, Dana continues to jump between the present and the past, saving her ancestor's life numerous times while enduring abuse. *Kindred* has become a staple of many school reading curriculums and a popular choice for book clubs and community reading initiatives. Since its release in 1979, it's sold over half a million copies and been adapted into an acclaimed graphic novel. Here's what you should know.

IT'S NOT SCIENCE FICTION.

Butler is one of the most esteemed science fiction authors of the twentieth century, known for her high-concept series set in the future. But while it does include time travel, *Kindred* doesn't fall under the science fiction genre, according to Butler. When discussing the book, the author clarified: "You'll note there's no science in it." She instead categorized her most famous work as a "grim fantasy." Critics have also placed it under the labels of neo-slave narrative and psychological horror.

BUTLER WANTED TO DEFEND THE INTEGRITY OF ENSLAVED PEOPLE.

Butler wrote *Kindred* in response to statements she heard from Black college students in the 1960s and '70s. In the Black Power era, it had become common for some young people to look down on their enslaved ancestors and insist they would have never put up with the same mistreatment. *Kindred* shows how Butler felt about this narrative. In the book, the violence Dana faces in the antebellum South is brutal and often inescapable. In order to ensure the existence of her future self, she must endure abuse from her white enslaver ancestor and help him survive. The story shows that surviving slavery—and all the sacrifices that required—was an act of bravery on its own. Butler said in an interview with *Publishers Weekly*, "I wanted to write a novel that would make others feel the history: the pain and fear that Black people have had to live through in order to endure."

THE ADVANCE WAS JUST ENOUGH TO LIVE ON.

Speculative fiction was a white-, male-dominated field in the 1970s, and Butler struggled to find a publisher for a time travel book that dealt with slavery. When she finally sold *Kindred*, she received an advance of $5,000. Her writing was her only source of income at the time, and she got by on meals of beans and potatoes.

KINDRED ALMOST HAD A MALE PROTAGONIST.

In the early stages of her work on *Kindred*, Butler imagined the main character who is sent back in time as a man. It didn't take her long, however, to run into logistical problems. "So many things that he did would have been likely to get him killed," she told Charles Rowell in an interview. "He wouldn't even have time to learn the rule—the rules of submission, I guess you could call them—before he was killed for not knowing them because he would be perceived as dangerous." Rather than writing a male character whose modern attitude would be a liability in the past, she made the character seem less threatening by switching the gender.

BUTLER TONED DOWN THE VIOLENCE.

The horrors of slavery are on full display in *Kindred*, and they're central to the book's themes. It may then come as a surprise to some readers that Butler held back when depicting the harsh realities of the pre–Civil War South. By writing a more realistic portrayal of slavery (and therefore a more violent one), Butler feared the book would lack mainstream appeal. She instead found a way to tone down the more brutal passages without losing the book's message.

THREE NOVELISTS WHO WON THE MacARTHUR "GENIUS GRANT"

The MacArthur Foundation Fellowship, colloquially known as "genius grants," is today "a $625,000, no-strings-attached award to extraordinarily talented and creative individuals as an investment in their potential." In 1995, Octavia Butler was the first science fiction writer to receive a fellowship. Other novelists who have received one include:

COLSON WHITEHEAD

Colson Whitehead was twenty-nine years old when he published his first novel, *The Intuitionist*, in 1999. It received critical acclaim, and his experimental approach to telling stories about Black American experiences would continue to earn him recognition in the years that followed. He received his MacArthur genius grant in 2002 at age thirty-two. Fourteen years later, he published his most well-known work, *The Underground Railroad*, which presents an alternate history of slavery in the South. The novel won him the 2016 National Book Award for Fiction and the 2017 Pulitzer Prize for Fiction.

THOMAS PYNCHON

Thomas Pynchon's first three novels—*V., The Crying of Lot 49*, and *Gravity's Rainbow*—branded him as an exciting new voice in the postmodernist literary scene. *Gravity's Rainbow* made an especially big splash, winning him the National Book Award in 1974, which he shared with Isaac Bashevis Singer for *A Crown of Feathers and Other Stories* that year. Seventeen years passed between the publication of *Gravity's Rainbow* and the release of his next novel, *Vineland*, in 1990. During that period, he was inducted into the MacArthur Fellows class of 1988 when he was fifty-one years old.

VIET THANH NGUYEN

Literary scholar Viet Thanh Nguyen was born in Vietnam and raised in America. His remarkable debut novel, *The Sympathizer*, told from a conflicted double agent's perspective, won multiple awards, including the Pulitzer Prize for Fiction in 2016. His 2017 short story collection, *The Refugees*, explores the aftermath of the Vietnam War, including a story that mirrored his own experience.

LITTLE
WOMEN

LOUISA MAY ALCOTT

November 29, 1832–March 6, 1888

BORN: Germantown, Pennsylvania

OTHER NOTABLE WORKS:
Little Men (1871)
Jo's Boys (1886)

Much like Jo March, the independent-minded writer of the family in her *Little Women*, Louisa May Alcott was a natural born writer. Louisa May was the second of four daughters born to Amos and Abigail Alcott. Though Orchard House, the Alcott family home in Concord, Massachusetts, is a quasi-celebrity in its own right, it wasn't until 1834 that the family relocated to New England. It was there, when Louisa was just nineteen years old, that she had her first work published. Though she originally wrote under the pen name Flora Fairfield, Alcott eventually grew comfortable enough with her craft to often use her given name when putting pen to paper.

Louisa May Alcott's *Little Women* is one of the world's most beloved novels, and more than 150 years after its original publication, it's still enjoyed by generations of readers. Whether it's been days or years since you've last read it, here are some things you might not know about Alcott's classic tale of family and friendship.

LOUISA MAY ALCOTT DIDN'T WANT TO WRITE *LITTLE WOMEN*.

Alcott was writing both literature and pulp fiction when Thomas Niles, the editor at Roberts Brothers Publishing, approached her in 1867 about writing a book for girls. Alcott said she would try, but she wasn't all that interested, later calling such books "moral pap for the young." Although she tried to get excited about the project, she thought she wouldn't have much to write about girls because she was a tomboy.

The next year, Alcott's father was trying to convince Niles to publish his manuscript about philosophy. He told Niles that his daughter could write a book of fairy stories, but Niles still wanted a novel about girls. Niles told Alcott's father that if he could get his daughter to write a (non-fairy) novel for girls, he would publish his philosophy manuscript. So to make her father happy and help his writing career, Alcott wrote about her adolescence growing up with her three sisters.

LITTLE WOMEN TOOK JUST TEN WEEKS TO WRITE.

Alcott began writing the book in May 1868. She worked on it day and night, becoming so consumed with it that she sometimes forgot to eat or sleep. On July 15, she sent all 402 pages to her editor. In September, a mere four months after starting the book, *Little Women* was published. It became an instant best seller and turned Alcott into a rich and famous woman.

MEG, BETH, AND AMY WERE BASED ON ALCOTT'S SISTERS.

Meg was based on Louisa's sister Anna, who fell in love with her husband, John Bridge Pratt, while performing opposite him in a play. The description of Meg's wedding in the novel is supposedly based on Anna's actual wedding.

Beth was based on Elizabeth (or Lizzie), who contracted scarlet fever in 1856. Though she recovered, the disease permanently weakened her; Lizzie passed away in her sleep from a "wasting condition" on March 14, 1858—just shy of her twenty-third birthday. Like Beth, Lizzie caught the illness from a poor family her mother was helping.

Amy was based on May (Amy is an anagram of May), an artist who lived in Europe and whose paintings were displayed in the Paris Salon.

Jo, of course, is based on Alcott herself.

THE BOOK WAS ORIGINALLY PUBLISHED IN TWO PARTS.

The first half was published in 1868 as *Little Women: Meg, Jo, Beth, and Amy. The Story of Their Lives. A Girl's Book*. It ended with John Brooke proposing marriage to Meg. In 1869, Alcott published the second half of the book. It, too, only took a few months to write.

ALCOTT REFUSED TO END THE BOOK AS THE FANS WANTED.

SPOILERS! Alcott, who never married herself, wanted Jo to remain unmarried, too. But while she was working on the second half of *Little Women*, fans were clamoring for Jo to marry the boy next door, Laurie. "Girls write to ask who the little women marry, as if that was the only aim and end of a woman's life," Alcott wrote in her journal. "I *won't* marry Jo to Laurie to please anyone." As a compromise—or to spite her fans—Alcott married Jo to the decidedly unromantic Professor Bhaer. Laurie ends up with Amy.

THERE ARE LOTS OF THEORIES ABOUT WHO LAURIE WAS BASED ON.

People have theorized Laurie was inspired by everyone from Henry David Thoreau to Nathaniel Hawthorne's son Julian, but this doesn't seem to be the case. In 1865, while in Europe, Alcott met a Polish musician named Ladislas Wisniewski, whom Alcott nicknamed Laddie. The flirtation between Laddie and Alcott culminated in them spending two weeks together in Paris, alone. According to biographer Harriet Reisen, Alcott later modeled Laurie after Laddie. How far did the Alcott/Laddie affair go? It's hard to say, as Alcott later crossed out the section of her diary referring to the romance. In the margin, she wrote, "couldn't be."

LITTLE WOMEN HAS BEEN ADAPTED A NUMBER OF TIMES.

In addition to a 1958 TV series, multiple Broadway plays, a musical, a ballet, and an opera, *Little Women* has been made into more than a half-dozen movies. The most famous are the 1933 version starring Katharine Hepburn, the 1994 version starring Winona Ryder, and the 2019 version directed by Greta Gerwig and starring Saoirse Ronan as Jo and Timothée Chalamet as Laurie. In 1987, Japan made an anime version of *Little Women* that ran for forty-eight half-hour episodes.

Fascinating Facts about Louisa May Alcott

Besides enchanting millions of readers with her novel *Little Women*, Louisa May Alcott worked as a Civil War nurse, fought against slavery, and registered women to vote. Here are a few facts about the celebrated author.

1 ALCOTT HAD MANY FAMOUS FRIENDS.

Louisa's parents, Amos Bronson and Abigail Alcott, raised their four daughters in a politically active household in Massachusetts. As a child, Alcott briefly lived with her family in a failed Transcendentalist commune, helped her parents hide enslaved people who had escaped via the Underground Railroad, and had discussions about women's rights with Margaret Fuller.

Throughout her life, she socialized with her father's friends, including Henry David Thoreau, Ralph Waldo Emerson, and Nathaniel Hawthorne. Although her family was always poor, Alcott had access to valuable learning experiences. She read books in Emerson's library and learned about botany at Walden Pond with Thoreau, later writing a poem called "Thoreau's Flute" for her friend. She also socialized with abolitionist Frederick Douglass and women's suffrage activist Julia Ward Howe.

2 SHE SECRETLY WROTE PULP FICTION.

Before writing *Little Women*, Alcott wrote Gothic pulp fiction under the nom de plume A.M. Barnard, and wrote stories with titles like "Behind a Mask" and "The Abbot's Ghost" to make easy money. The sensational, melodramatic works are strikingly different than the more wholesome, righteous vibe she captured in *Little Women*, and she didn't advertise that writing as her own after *Little Women* became popular.

3 SHE WROTE ABOUT HER EXPERIENCE AS A CIVIL WAR NURSE.

In 1861, at the beginning of the US Civil War, Alcott sewed Union uniforms in Concord and, the next year, enlisted as an army nurse. In a Washington, DC hotel-turned-hospital, she comforted dying soldiers and helped doctors perform amputations. During this time, she wrote about her experiences in her journal and in letters to her family. In 1863, she published *Hospital Sketches*, a fictionalized account, based on her letters, of her stressful yet meaningful experiences as a wartime nurse. The book became massively popular and was reprinted in 1869 with more material.

4 SHE SUFFERED FROM MERCURY POISONING.

After a month and a half of nursing in Washington, DC, Alcott caught typhoid fever and pneumonia. She received the standard treatment at the time—a toxic mercury compound called calomel, which was used in medicines through the nineteenth century. Because of this exposure to mercury, Alcott suffered from symptoms of mercury poisoning for the rest of her life. She had a weakened immune system, vertigo, and had episodes of hallucinations. To combat the pain caused by the mercury poisoning (as well as a possible autoimmune disorder, such as lupus, that could have been triggered by it), she took opium. Alcott died of a stroke in 1888, at fifty-five years old.

EIGHT RUTHLESS REJECTION LETTERS

When Louisa May Alcott wrote about her experience as a governess in the essay "How I Went Out to Service," publisher James T. Fields's stinging rejection included the line, "Stick to your teaching; you can't write." Luckily, she didn't listen to his advice—and neither did the authors who are said to have received these similarly savage rejections:

··

HERMAN MELVILLE // *Moby-Dick*

"First, we must ask, does it have to be a whale?

While this is a rather delightful, if somewhat esoteric, plot device, we recommend an antagonist with a more popular visage among the younger readers. For instance, could not the Captain be struggling with a depravity towards young, perhaps voluptuous, maidens?"

—an editor at Bentley & Son Publishing House

URSULA K. LE GUIN //
The Left Hand of Darkness

"The book is so endlessly complicated by details of reference and information . . . that the very action of the story seems to be to become hopelessly bogged down, and the book, eventually, unreadable. . . . The whole is so dry and airless, so lacking in pace, that whatever drama and excitement the novel might have had is entirely dissipated by what does seem . . . to be extraneous material."

—a rejection sent to Le Guin's agent

GEORGE ORWELL // *Animal Farm*

". . . we have no conviction (and I am sure none of the other directors would have) that this is the right point of view from which to criticise the political situation at the present time . . . Your pigs are far more intelligent than the other animals, and therefore the best qualified to run the farm—in fact, there couldn't have been an animal farm at all without them: so that what was needed, (someone might argue), was not more communism but more public-spirited pigs."

—T.S. Eliot of Faber & Faber, one of four publishers to reject *Animal Farm*

VLADIMIR NABOKOV // *Lolita*

". . . overwhelmingly nauseating, even to an enlightened Freudian . . . the whole thing is an unsure cross between hideous reality and improbable fantasy. It often becomes a wild neurotic daydream . . .

I recommend that it be buried under a stone for a thousand years."

—one editor's rejection of *Lolita*

JACK KEROUAC // *On the Road*

"Kerouac does have enormous talent of a very special kind. But this is not a well made novel, nor a saleable one nor even, I think, a good one.

His frenetic and scrambling prose perfectly expresses the feverish travels, geographically and mentally, of the Beat Generation.

But is that enough? I don't think so."

—a rejection sent to Kerouac's agent, Sterling Lord

F. SCOTT FITZGERALD // *The Great Gatsby*

"You'd have a decent book if you'd get rid of that Gatsby character."

—a revision suggested to F. Scott Fitzgerald

ROBERT GALBRAITH // *The Cuckoo's Calling*

"Owing to pressure of submissions, I regret we cannot reply individually or provide constructive criticism. **(A writers' group/ writing course may help with the latter.)**"

—a rejection from Constable & Robinson to Galbraith, a.k.a. J.K. Rowling

GERTRUDE STEIN // *The Making of Americans: Being a History of a Family's Progress*

"Being only one, having only one pair of eyes, having only one time, having only one life, I cannot read your M.S. three or four times. Not even one time. Only one look, only one look is enough. Hardly one copy would sell here. Hardly one. Hardly one."

—Arthur C. Fifield

VLADIMIR NABOKOV

April 22, 1899–July 2, 1977

BORN: St. Petersburg, Russia

OTHER NOTABLE WORKS:
Speak, Memory (1951)
Pnin (1957)

It says a lot about Vladimir Nabokov and his natural inclination toward storytelling—in any language—that the St. Petersburg native could knock out several books in his native Russian while he was living in Berlin, but find true success when he crossed the Atlantic to America and began writing in English. It was while in the US that Nabokov wrote *Lolita*—his most important, albeit controversial, book—and where he became a professor of Russian and European literature at Cornell, literally helping to shape the minds of future great thinkers like Thomas Pynchon and the late Supreme Court Justice Ruth Bader Ginsburg. She credited Nabokov with changing "the way I read and the way I write. Words could paint pictures, I learned from him. Choosing the right word, and the right word order, he illustrated, could make an enormous difference in conveying an image or an idea."

Lolita was released in 1955 to largely adulatory reviews. It was also called "highbrow pornography" in *The New York Times*, presaging its ambivalent place in the literary canon—a place guaranteed, perhaps, by the morally depraved (if unerringly eloquent) narrator of Nabokov's invention, Humbert Humbert.

Nabokov accused critics of "underestimat[ing] the power of [his] imagination," and was suspicious of readers who looked for prurient autobiographical clues in his fiction. But while few readers would doubt the author's literary imagination, there may actually be several real-life inspirations for *Lolita*.

THE AUTHOR FOUND INSPIRATION IN A NEWSPAPER ARTICLE.

Nabokov himself suggested the novel was inspired by a (still unidentified) newspaper story discussing an ape in captivity who sketched the bars of his own cage. In Nabokov's rendering, Humbert Humbert is his "baboon . . . drawing and . . . redrawing the bars of his cage, the bars between him and what he terms 'the human herd.'"

LEWIS CARROLL MAY HAVE INSPIRED *LOLITA*'S NARRATOR.

The novelist also found inspiration in another writer. Nabokov once referred to the author of *Alice's Adventures in Wonderland* as "Lewis Carroll Carroll, because he was the first Humbert Humbert." Nabokov's suspicions centered around Carroll's photographs, including portraits of nude and partially nude children.

AN INCIDENT INVOLVING CHARLIE CHAPLIN HAS BEEN LINKED TO *LOLITA*.

The true nature of Carroll's relationships with children remains a matter of contention among historians, but there is less dispute regarding the details of another real-life story that has become attached to *Lolita*. Lillita MacMurray, a.k.a. Lita Grey, was only sixteen when she became pregnant by a thirty-five-year-old Charlie Chaplin in a case of untried statutory rape. (At the urging of her family, they got married so he wouldn't be arrested.) Between the young actress's name and Nabokov's familiarity with Chaplin's work, some have suggested a connection to *Lolita*—a connection, it should be noted, that Nabokov's son Dmitri denied.

THE NOVEL IS A LOVE LETTER TO THE ENGLISH LANGUAGE.

Fittingly for a book as aware of the clarifying and obfuscating power of language as *Lolita*, Nabokov suggested that an entirely different relationship may have given rise to his defining novel. When a critic said that the book could be read as a record of the author's love affair with the romantic novel, Nabokov countered, perhaps indicating the real love motivating his text, "The substitution 'English language' for 'romantic novel' would make this elegant formula more correct."

When Vladimir Nabokov Met Dr. Seuss

In 1949, Vladimir Nabokov had the beginnings of *Lolita* knocking around in his head when he drove to Salt Lake City for the 2nd Writers' Conference at the University of Utah. In attendance were Oscar Williams, Wallace Stegner, Martha Foley, and John Crowe Ransom—all formidable figures in the literary world. But none of them caught the attention of Nabokov quite like former political cartoonist and author Ted Geisel (better known today as Dr. Seuss). The pair hit it off: Geisel penned a butterfly poem for the Russian-born novelist during their time at the conference, and Nabokov described Seuss as "a charming man, one of the most gifted people" in attendance. Later, Geisel named a character after Nabokov: *Horton Hears a Who!*'s eagle Vlad Vlad-i-koff—a blend of Nabokov's birth name, Vladimir Vladimirovich, and how he had once spelled his last name (Nabokoff).

Fascinating Facts about Vladimir Nabokov

Vladimir Nabokov described himself by saying, "I am an American author, born in Russia, educated in England, where I studied French texts." Here are a few more interesting facts.

1 HE CAME FROM MONEY.

Nabokov was born in 1899 in Saint Petersburg, Russia, to the aristocratic family of a liberal lawyer and politician, and his upbringing reflected the culture and wealth of his family. The author was raised trilingual, speaking Russian, English, and French.

Nabokov's father, who was also named Vladimir, had a fairly successful political career during his son's childhood. In the aftermath of the Russian Revolution, the family had to flee the country in 1919. The Nabokovs first went to England, where the sale of his mother's pearls financed two whole years of Vladimir's study at Cambridge. They eventually settled in Berlin, where Nabokov's father remained active in the politics of the Russian exile community. This involvement soon proved fatal for the elder Nabokov: He died while trying to protect former Russian Foreign Minister Pavel Milyukov from an assassination attempt in Berlin.

2 NABOKOV KNEW HIS BUTTERFLIES.

Nabokov was a world-renowned expert on butterflies, so much so that in the 1940s he became curator of the Harvard Museum of Comparative Zoology's butterfly collection. He discovered and named several species and families of butterflies, assembled a new taxonomy system that's still in use, and investigated butterflies' "sculpturesque" genitalia under a microscope. His collection of dissected blue butterfly genitalia is still in Harvard's holdings.

3 HE GAVE PAVAROTTI A BOOST.

Nabokov and his wife, Vera, had only one child, but their son, Dmitri, led quite a life in his own right, including stints as a mountaineer and race car driver. After graduating from Harvard, Dmitri turned down an offer to stay there for law school and instead launched a career as an opera singer. In 1961 he finally made it to the stage in a production of *La Bohème* in Reggio Emilia, Italy.

His father arranged for the performance to be recorded. While Dmitri was good as Colline, he couldn't hold a candle to the unknown tenor who was also making his operatic debut in the role of Rodolfo. The tenor, Luciano Pavarotti, quickly grew to worldwide fame, and thanks to Nabokov's doting fatherhood, the world still has documentation of the revered singer's very first performance.

4 HE WROTE ON NOTECARDS.

Years before the advent of word processing, Nabokov developed his own form of nonlinear writing and editing using a simple technology: the index card. As he told *The Paris Review,* "I fill in the gaps of the crossword at any spot I happen to choose. These bits I write on index cards until the novel is done." In the case of *Lolita,* Nabokov's preparatory cards included notes on firearms, quotes from teen-targeted magazines like *Miss America,* and even snippets of teenagers' conversations that the novelist overheard on streetcars.

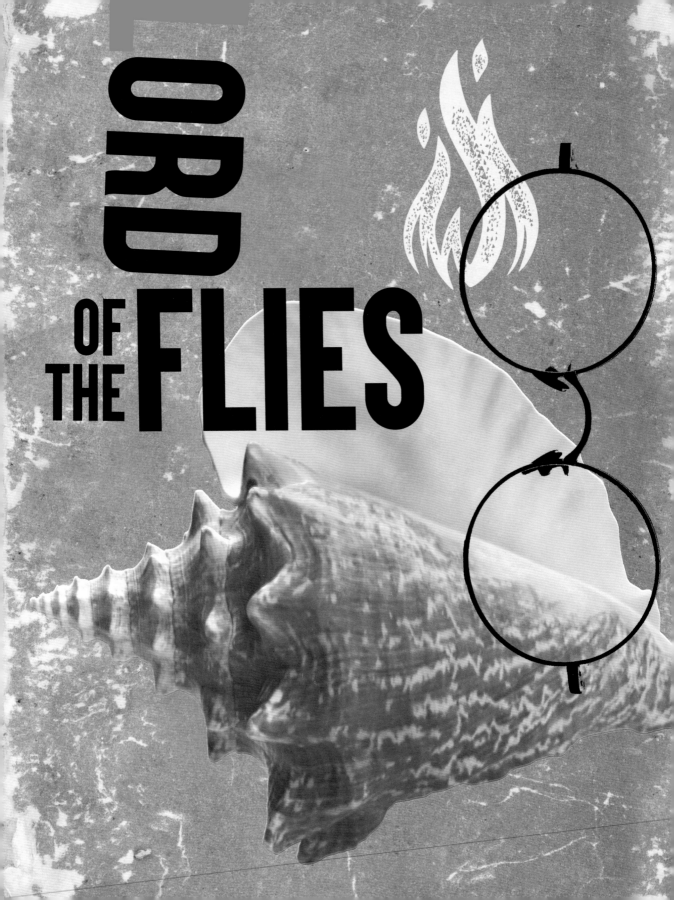

WILLIAM GOLDING

September 19, 1911–June 19, 1993

BORN: Newquay, Cornwall, England

OTHER NOTABLE WORKS:
The Inheritors (1955)
The Pyramid (1967)
Rites of Passage (1980)

William Golding's parents wanted him to be a scientist, but Golding himself embraced the literary life. His first published work, a book of poems, was released in 1934, when he was just twenty-three, though it didn't make waves. Next, Golding spent time teaching and sailed with the Royal Navy during World War II, where he saw the sinking of the *Bismarck* and took part in D-Day. "World War II was the turning point for me," he reportedly said. "I began to see what people were capable of doing. Anyone who moved through those years without understanding that man produces evil as a bee produces honey must have been blind or wrong in the head."

Golding published *Lord of the Flies*, his unforgettable debut novel, in 1954, and many more after that. He was awarded the Nobel Prize in Literature in 1983, and knighted by Queen Elizabeth II in 1988. At his Nobel lecture, Golding said that "words may, through the devotion, the skill, the passion, and the luck of writers prove to be the most powerful thing in the world."

A fixture of English class syllabi, William Golding's 1954 novel *Lord of the Flies* keeps winning over new generations of readers. In the book, a group of British schoolboys crash-land on an uninhabited island and quickly split into two factions. The plot is an allegory representing the conflict between humans' urge for social order and for individual power. Here's what you should know.

AN EARLY DRAFT OF THE STORY OPENED AND CLOSED DIFFERENTLY.

Golding's original version of *Lord of the Flies* began not on the island, but by describing a nuclear war with no main characters. Next, the action moved onto a plane that participates in an air battle and eventually releases a "passenger tube" full of students that floats down to the tropical island. The first draft closed its story with an ominous cataloguing of the story's time and date: "16.00, 2nd October 1952."

NOBODY WANTED TO PUBLISH THE NOVEL.

Since it was Golding's first novel, *Lord of the Flies* was met with little interest from the multitudes of publishing companies to whom he sent his manuscript. Golding's daughter Judy Carver remembered her cash-strapped father struggling with many rejection letters. "My earliest memory is not of the book itself but of a lot of parcels coming back and being sent off again very quickly," she told *The Guardian*. "He must have been grief-stricken every time it returned. Even paying for the postage was a commitment."

THE EVENTUAL PUBLISHER TRIED TO HIDE THE BOOK FROM T.S. ELIOT.

Even Faber and Faber, the London-based house that ultimately released the book, was resistant at first, yielding only because new editor Charles Monteith was so passionate about the story. The company even went so far as to not discuss the title within earshot of its literary advisor, acclaimed poet T.S. Eliot.

Eliot allegedly first heard about *Lord of the Flies* via an offhand remark made by a friend at his social club. In his biography *William Golding: The Man Who Wrote Lord of the Flies*, John Carey recounts that Eliot's friend warned him, "Faber had published an unpleasant novel about small boys behaving unspeakably on a desert island." In the end, Faber's fears were unfounded: The poet loved Golding's novel.

SIMON WAS INITIALLY MORE OF A CHRIST FIGURE.

Golding originally designed Simon as a sanctified, ethereal character, which Monteith thought was too heavy-handed. The Simon that appears in the final draft of *Lord of the Flies* is indeed a good deal more peaceful and conscientious than his peers, but lacks the ostentatious godliness that Monteith found problematic.

REALLY HARSH EARLY REVIEWS OF NINE CLASSIC TWENTIETH-CENTURY NOVELS

To some, *Lord of the Flies* is a brutally honest portrayal of the depth of the human spirit— but to *The New Yorker* it was just "completely unpleasant." Here are some other vicious early reviews of beloved books.

1 *Ulysses* // **JAMES JOYCE**
Joyce's magnum opus redefined literature and was a major event upon its release in 1922. Some bought into its radical structure, but others didn't—including fellow modernist Virginia Woolf. In her diary she called *Ulysses* "an illiterate, underbred book it seems to me: the book of a self-taught working man, and we all know how distressing they are, how egotistic, insistent, raw, striking, and ultimately nauseating."

2 *To the Lighthouse* // **VIRGINIA WOOLF**
The New York Evening Post's cleverly snide review of Woolf's highly abstract Modernist masterpiece, published in 1927, managed to praise her and shoot her down all in the same sentence: "Her work is poetry; it must be judged as poetry, and all the weaknesses of poetry are inherent in it."

3 *An American Tragedy* // **THEODORE DREISER**
This sprawling tale of love and deceit's influence has been made into an opera, a musical, a radio program, and more. When the novel was first published in 1925, the *Boston Evening Transcript* called its main character, Clyde Griffiths, "one of the most despicable creations of humanity that ever emerged from a novelist's brain," and called Dreiser "a fearsome manipulator of the English language" with a style that "is offensively colloquial, commonplace and vulgar."

4 *Native Son* // **RICHARD WRIGHT**
Richard Wright's *Native Son*, published in 1940, is another classic American novel about the African American experience, but *The New Statesman and Nation* found the book to be "unimpressive and silly, not even as much fun as a thriller."

5 *Henderson the Rain King* // **SAUL BELLOW**
Bellow's 1959 novel about an American millionaire who unwittingly becomes the king of an African tribe was the author's personal favorite. But it wasn't a favorite for critic Reed Whittemore. In his review for *The New Republic*, Whittemore posed this

INITIALLY, THE BOOK WASN'T A SUCCESS.

Upon its release in September 1954, *Lord of the Flies* underwhelmed at bookstores, selling only 4,662 copies through the following year and falling out of print shortly thereafter. Critical acclaim and the respect of the academic community steadily grew over the rest of the decade, and the novel eventually found enough of an audience that by 1962 it had moved 65,000 copies.

GOLDING WAS UNIMPRESSED WITH HOW HIS STORY TURNED OUT.

Although he was initially enthusiastic about the text, Golding's appraisal of his breakthrough work dimmed over time. After revisiting *Lord of the Flies* in 1972 for the first time in a decade, Golding gave it a less-than-stellar review. According to Carey's biography, the author said he found his own book "boring and crude. The language is O-level stuff." (O-level is the lower level of standardized testing in parts of the UK, which assesses basic knowledge—so Golding was saying his novel was the rough equivalent of middle school English writing.)

LORD OF THE FLIES IS A PERSONAL FAVORITE OF ANOTHER FAMOUS AUTHOR.

Stephen King has cited *Lord of the Flies* as one of his favorite books. In a foreword to the 2011 edition of the novel, King wrote, "It was, so far as I can remember, the first book with hands—strong ones that reached out of the pages and seized me by the throat. It said to me, 'This is not just entertainment; it's life-or-death.'"

King's books even include a nod to the text. King named the fictional town of Castle Rock, Maine—the setting for a number of his novels—after the geological structure featured prominently in *Lord of the Flies*.

---

question to himself: "The reviewer looks at the evidence and wonders if he should damn the author and praise the book, or praise the author and damn the book. And is it possible, somehow or other to praise, or damn, both?—he isn't sure."

6 *Winesburg, Ohio* // SHERWOOD ANDERSON

The interlaced short stories that take place in the fictional Ohio town that gives this 1919 book its name were based off of author Sherwood Anderson's recollections from his childhood hometown of Clyde, Ohio. The veracity of those memories and the town were called into question in *The Nation*'s review of the book: "We sympathize with Mr. Anderson and with what he is trying to do. . . . [he] tries to find honest mid-American gods. Yet either he never does quite find them or he can never precisely set forth what he has found. . . . It seems probable that Mr. Anderson has given a distorted view of life, that he caricatures even Winesburg, Ohio."

7 *The Sun Also Rises* // ERNEST HEMINGWAY

Hemingway's debut novel about masculinity and the Lost Generation typifies the sparse and powerful writing style that his subsequent work would become known for. Some critics still believe it is his most important work. His mother, Grace, on the other hand, did not. In a letter she wrote that Hemingway kept all his life, his mother said, "What is the matter? Have you ceased to be interested in loyalty, nobility, honor and fineness in life . . . surely you have other words in your vocabulary besides 'damn' and 'bitch'—Every page fills me with a sick loathing—if I should pick up a book by any other writer with such words in it, I should read no more—but pitch it in the fire."

8 *The Naked and the Dead* // NORMAN MAILER

Norman Mailer's debut novel, *The Naked and the Dead*, was based on his experiences with the 112th Cavalry Regiment in the Philippines during World War II. It made many readers feel like they were actually there, but other readers, like the *New Republic*'s critic, didn't agree: "For the most part, the novel is a transcription of soldiers' talk, lusterless griping and ironed-out obscenities, too detailed and monotonous to have been imaginatively conceived for any larger purpose but too exact and literal to have been merely guessed at. . . . This doesn't mean to deny Mailer his achievement. If he has a taste for transcribing banalities, he also has a talent for it."

9 *Portnoy's Complaint* // PHILIP ROTH

Ask someone for a list of the greatest American writers of the past few decades and chances are Philip Roth will make the cut. His 1969 novel *Portnoy's Complaint*—a continuous sex-filled inner monologue told to a psychoanalyst by the book's protagonist, Alexander Portnoy—put him on the map. *America* magazine's critic, however, wasn't on board, saying of the book, "it is finally a definitive something or other. I regret that it is not a definitive something."

SALMAN RUSHDIE

June 19, 1947

BORN: Bombay, British India (present-day Mumbai, India)

OTHER NOTABLE WORKS:
Shame (1983)
The Satanic Verses (1988)
Fury (2001)

Salman Rushdie was born and raised in what was then Bombay before attending boarding school and college in England. He published his first novel, *Grimus*, in 1975; it was mostly ignored. The same cannot be said for his second novel, *Midnight's Children*. The book tells the story of Saleem Sinai—whose birth at the exact moment of India's official independence confers upon him supernatural abilities—intertwined with the post-colonial history of India. *Midnight's Children* won the Booker Prize.

If *Midnight's Children* put Rushdie on the map, his fourth novel, *The Satanic Verses*, made him infamous. In Rushdie's words, *Verses* is about "migration, metamorphosis [and] divided selves." But while the novel's satirical lens points at subjects from America to India, it was the book's purported reimagining of the prophet Muhammad that led to its legacy outside of literature (Rushdie has vehemently denied all such charges and says that this view is a misrepresentation of the book).

Ayatollah Ruhollah Khomeini of Iran issued a fatwa against Rushdie for his alleged blasphemy against Islam, calling for the author's death. Several attacks launched in subsequent years seem to have targeted those involved in the novel's distribution, including the book's Japanese translator, Hitoshi Igarashi, who was fatally stabbed in 1991. Since moving to the English countryside in the immediate aftermath of the fatwa, Rushdie has remained safe and published over a dozen books. He now lives in New York.

When *Midnight's Children* was released in 1981, *The New York Times* pronounced that "the literary map of India is about to be redrawn." And while the book has much to say, directly and obliquely, about the state of India, the book may be most notable for introducing the authorial voice of Salman Rushdie, alternately ironic, reverential, scatological, and fluently conversant in the language of pop culture.

THE AUTHOR WAS NEARLY A CHILD OF MIDNIGHT.

In the novel, a critical role is played by the 1,001 "children of midnight" born in the first hour of India's postcolonial independence. Rushdie himself was born in Bombay fewer than two months before August 15, 1947, the date India's independence and partition became official. It's not hard to imagine the impact the pivotal timing of his own birth had on the book's intermingling of the personal and historical. As Rushdie once described it, "India is my kid sister."

Can't Stop Buying Books?

In English, stockpiling books without ever reading them might be called being a literary pack rat. People in Japan have a much nicer term for the habit: *tsundoku*.

According to the BBC, the term *tsundoku* derives from the words *tsumu* ("to pile up") and *doku* ("reading"), and it has been around for more than a century. One of its earliest known print appearances dates back to 1879, when a Japanese satirical text playfully referred to a professor with a large collection of unread books as *tsundoku sensei*.

THE NOVEL MIGHT NOT EXIST WITHOUT GRIMUS.

While the artistic influence of Rushdie's first book, *Grimus*, on his later work is difficult to quantify, its economic impact is much easier to trace. The author returned to his birth country in 1975 for a "journey of fifteen-hour bus rides and humble hostelries," courtesy of a £700 advance from that debut novel. The trip helped revive Rushdie's plans for a "novel of childhood" and inspired him to repurpose a character from an abandoned book (*The Antagonist*) for the sprawling story that would become *Midnight's Children*. That character, Saleem Sinai, soon became an icon in the English language oeuvre of the Indian subcontinent. As Rushdie described it, he was a character for whom the entire modern history of India "was somehow *all his fault*."

IT SEEMED, FOR A TIME, TO BE CURSED.

The publication date of *Midnight's Children* was delayed several times, according to Rushdie. In a series of coincidences befitting a novel about the unlikely confluence of the personal and the political, the initial printing of the book was delayed by a printers' strike in the United States; a transport strike led to a delay in copies of the book arriving in England; finally, a dock-workers' strike set back the unloading of the printed and transported books.

While the image of thousands of copies of a seminal work of twentieth-century literature rotting away in shipping containers would fit neatly into Rushdie's ironic worldview, in the long run, labor disputes and the sardonic wit of fate proved helpless in the face of a great book. *Midnight's Children* received plaudits around the world. As Rushdie put it in a 2006 reflection, with his characteristic blend of self-effacement and hubris, "If it can pass the test of another generation or two, it may endure."

5 FAMOUS AUTHOR FEUDS

No matter which popular author you disdain, you're bound to find yourself in good company: There was no love lost between these writers.

SALMAN RUSHDIE VS. JOHN UPDIKE

Things got a little heated between Rushdie and Updike in 2005 when Updike reviewed Rushdie's *Shalimar the Clown*, saying, "Why, oh why, did Salman Rushdie . . . call one of his major characters Maximilian Ophuls?"

"A name is just a name," Rushdie later said. "'Why, oh why . . . ?' Well, why not? Somewhere in Las Vegas there's probably a male prostitute called 'John Updike.'" He went on to say that Updike's then-latest novel, *Terrorist*, was "beyond awful. He should stay in his parochial neighborhood and write about wife-swapping, because it's what he can do."

ERNEST HEMINGWAY VS. GERTRUDE STEIN

Though they were at one point good friends, Hemingway and Stein eventually became embroiled in a feud that began when Hemingway was critical of the work of novelist Sherwood Anderson and intensified when Stein painted a not-so-flattering portrait of Hemingway in *The Autobiography of Alice B. Toklas*. Hemingway, never one to take an insult lying down, criticized Stein and her writing in *A Moveable Feast*, saying that her book *The Making of Americans* "began magnificently, went on very well for a long way with great stretches of great brilliance and then went on endlessly in repetitions that a more conscientious and less lazy writer would have put in the waste basket."

GORE VIDAL VS. NORMAN MAILER

The infamous feud started when Vidal compared Mailer to Charles Manson. When Mailer later punched Vidal at a party, Vidal still had the wherewithal to zing his enemy, saying, "Once again, words fail Norman Mailer."

HENRY JAMES VS. H.G. WELLS

Wells understandably got a little upset when his supposed pal listed him among authors he considered to be producing "affluents turbid and unrestrained." Wells responded by referring to James as a "painful hippopotamus," and after that, the duo sent nasty (but beautifully written) letters back and forth.

JOSEPH CONRAD VS. D.H. LAWRENCE

"Filth. Nothing but obscenities," Conrad once said of Lawrence—and that was *before* Lawrence wrote *Lady Chatterley's Lover*. Lawrence wasn't a fan of Conrad's, either; he felt that pessimism "pervades all Conrad and such folks—the Writers among the Ruins. I can't forgive Conrad for being so sad and giving in."

HERMAN MELVILLE

August 1, 1819–September 28, 1891

BORN: New York, NY

OTHER NOTABLE WORKS:
Typee (1846)
Mardi (1849)
Billy Budd (1924)

Like the characters in his stories, Herman Melville took to the seas aboard whaling ships and other vessels, sailing around the world to distant lands. After abandoning one voyage, he and a friend spent time among the Pacific Islanders, an experience he drew on when writing his first two novels. As he wrote *Moby-Dick* he could look out the window of his study at the summit of Mount Greylock, Massachusetts's tallest mountain. The apex, he wrote, looked "like a sperm whale rising in the distance." Melville was so inspired by the landmass, he dedicated his seventh novel, *Pierre; or, The Ambiguities* to it.

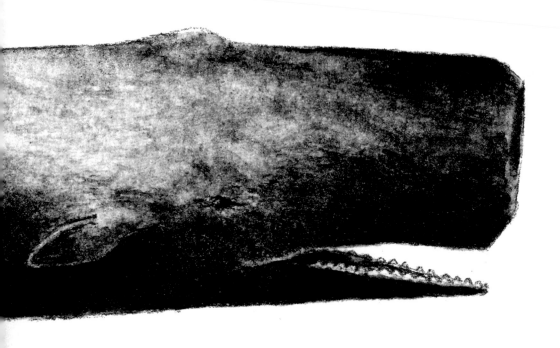

In Melville's 1851 epic, *Moby-Dick*, narrator Ishmael recounts his time aboard the whaling ship *Pequod* and Captain Ahab's quest to best Moby Dick, the monstrous sperm whale that chomped off part of his leg during a previous voyage. Fueled by Ahab's obsessive drive for vengeance, the crew leave the waters of New England behind to sail the Pacific Ocean in search of the white whale. Read on for what you need to know about *Moby-Dick*—a book that is today considered a classic but, along with Melville's genius, was not fully recognized in its time.

A REAL INCIDENT HELPED INSPIRE THE STORY.

On November 20, 1820, a Nantucket whaling ship called the *Essex* was rammed and sunk by an angry sperm whale. The twenty-man crew survived the assault by climbing onto three open boats, but their troubles were just beginning. With minimal supplies, the men drifted for three months and over three thousand miles. Most of them died en route, and those who didn't cannibalized the deceased before being rescued near Chile. Melville used the disaster to form the climax of *Moby-Dick*, in which the *Pequod* of Nantucket is destroyed by the white whale.

MELVILLE'S WORK ON WHALERS INFORMED *MOBY-DICK*.

Thanks to a national financial crisis in 1837, Melville had difficulty finding a permanent job. He served as a bank clerk, teacher, land surveyor, and crew member on a packet ship before going out to sea in 1841 on the whaler *Acushnet*. He served aboard a few different whalers and supposedly rose to the role of harpooner. His adventures at sea planted the seeds for Melville's interrogation of man, morality, and nature in *Moby-Dick*.

THE BOOK IS DEDICATED TO NATHANIEL HAWTHORNE.

The two literary titans, who lived just six miles apart in Massachusetts, met in 1850. Despite having almost finished *Moby-Dick* by late 1850, Melville felt compelled to essentially rewrite it from scratch after meeting the man behind *The Scarlet Letter*. It's likely that Hawthorne's influence completely changed the direction and tone of *Moby-Dick*. The two writers greatly admired each other: They wrote glowing reviews of each other's novels, and on more than one occasion, Melville even compared his fellow author to Shakespeare himself.

ANOTHER SPERM WHALE ATTACK OCCURRED THE SAME YEAR *MOBY-DICK* WAS PUBLISHED.

On August 20, 1851, a New Bedford, Massachusetts, whaling vessel called the *Ann Alexander* was rammed by a whale and sank. Just three months later, on November 14, *Moby-Dick* was officially released in the US. "It is really & truly a surprising coincidence—to say the least," Melville wrote in a reply to an acquaintance's letter about the *Ann Alexander* not long before the book made its stateside debut. "I make no doubt it *is* Moby Dick himself, for there is no account of his capture after the sad fate of the Pequod . . . Ye Gods! What a commentator is this *Ann Alexander* whale. What he has to say is short & pithy & very much to the point. I wonder if my evil art has raised this monster."

MOBY-DICK WAS A FLOP.

Readers who were expecting another rip-roarin' adventure like novels *Typee* or *Redburn* were sorely disappointed when Melville's masterpiece was released in November 1851. American reviewers were shocked at its obscure literary symbolism and complexity. "There is no method in his madness; and we must needs pronounce the chief feature of the volume [the character of Captain Ahab] a perfect failure, and the work itself inartistic," wrote the *New York Albion*. The reviewer added that the novel's style was like "having oil, mustard, vinegar, and pepper served up as a dish, in place of being scientifically administered sauce-wise."

Only 3,715 copies of *Moby-Dick* were purchased in Melville's lifetime (by comparison, *Typee* sold three times as many), and in the states, Melville's total earnings from *Moby-Dick* amounted to a paltry $556.37. His literary career more or less over, the writer returned to New York, where he became a customs inspector in 1866.

A POSTHUMOUS REPRINTING SAVED *MOBY-DICK* FROM OBSCURITY.

When Melville passed away on September 28, 1891, his *New York Times* obituary cited him as the author of "Mobie Dick." Readers had to work hard to track down his novels, all of which had gone out of print by 1876.

Then, in late 1891, *Moby-Dick* was reprinted and, this time around, critics started to take it more seriously. Leading the charge was acclaimed author Carl Van Doren, who had found a copy at a used book store in 1916 and soon after proclaimed "the immense originality of *Moby Dick* must warrant the claim of its admirers that it belongs with the greatest sea romances in the whole literature of the world." Within the next few decades, *Moby-Dick* became universally recognized as an American classic.

STARBUCKS COFFEE IS NAMED AFTER A MAIN CHARACTER.

The world's largest coffeehouse company was almost named Pequod in honor of Captain Ahab's vessel. Co-founder Gordon Bowker liked the idea, but his creative partner Terry Heckler was much less enthusiastic. "No one's going to drink a cup of Pee-quod," he said. They began looking at historic mining camps in the area when they found the name Starbo, and a quick connection brought them back to Mr. Starbuck, Ahab's first mate.

MELVILLE'S LAST MAJOR WORK WAS DISCOVERED BY ACCIDENT.

The centennial of Melville's birth renewed interest in his novels and poems, most of which were long out of print by then. Raymond Weaver, an English professor at Columbia University working on the first major biography of Melville, collaborated with Eleanor Melville Metcalf, Melville's granddaughter and literary executor, who gave him access to the author's papers. In 1919, while poking through letters and notes, Weaver discovered the unfinished manuscript of *Billy Budd* in a tin breadbox. Melville had started to write the short story about a tragic sailor in 1888 but, by his death in 1891, had not completed it. Weaver edited and published the story in 1924, but initially considered the tale "not distinguished." Other scholars asserted that *Billy Budd* was Melville's final masterpiece.

MELVILLE'S CHIMNEY OBSESSION

Melville moved to Arrowhead, his home in Pittsfield, Massachusetts, with his wife and son in 1850. (He wrote *Moby-Dick* in an upstairs study.) He grew very attached to the house, especially to the massive central chimney, which he immortalized in his 1856 short story "I and My Chimney." Yet his financial struggles after *Moby-Dick* failed to find an audience led Melville to sell Arrowhead to his brother Allan in 1863. As an homage, Allan painted a few lines from "I and My Chimney" on the chimney's stonework, which are still visible today.

THE INSPIRATIONS FOR FOUR FAMOUS LITERARY ANIMALS

From terrifying encounters to history to Dame Judi Dench, here's what inspired four iconic animal characters.

MOBY-DICK

Melville's white whale was partially based on a real-life albino sperm whale called Mocha Dick. Named after the Chilean island of Mocha (near which the beast was first encountered), the seventy-foot-long whale was famous for swimming gently next to the whaling boats—but at the first sign of aggression, Mocha Dick tried to destroy any boat that attacked him. When the notorious animal was finally brought down around 1838, at least twenty harpoons were found lodged in his sides. For his novel, Melville replaced "Mocha" with "Moby," though no one is sure why.

CUJO

Though Stephen King has said he doesn't remember anything about writing *Cujo*—he was apparently drinking too much at the time— he does remember the inspiration for the rabid St. Bernard in the novel. One summer, he took his motorcycle to be fixed at a shop, where he encountered what he called "the biggest Saint Bernard I ever saw in my life." The dog growled menacingly at him and went for the writer's hand. "I remember how scared I was because there was no place to hide," King said. "I was on my bike but it was dead, and I couldn't outrun him." The encounter stuck with King, and would eventually become the kernel of an idea that led to *Cujo*.

FIVER

We have a long car ride and Dame Judi Dench to thank for the rabbit story that led to *Watership Down*. "One day we were going to Stratford-upon-Avon to see Judi Dench in *Twelfth Night*," Richard Adams once explained. His daughter, then eight, demanded that he tell a story they hadn't heard before. "I just began off the top of my head: 'Once upon a time there were two rabbits, called eh, let me see, Hazel and Fiver, and I'm going to tell you about some of their adventures.' What followed was really the essence of *Watership Down*." To nail rabbit behavior, Adams consulted Ronald Lockley's *The Private Life of the Rabbit: An Account of the Life History and Social Behavior of the Wild Rabbit*.

NAPOLEON

Though he may be named for the French emperor, George Orwell based the personality of the pig that takes over Manor Farm in *Animal Farm* on Joseph Stalin, the dictator of Soviet Russia. Like Stalin, Napoleon took part in a revolution (in this case, to overthrow the humans running the farm); executed his enemies and threats to his power; exiled his former partner, Snowball (a stand-in for Stalin's one-time collaborator, Leon Trotsky); and subverted a revolution into a brutal dictatorship.

MURDER ON THE ORIENT EXPRESS

AGATHA CHRISTIE

September 15, 1890–January 12, 1976

BORN: Torquay, Devon, England

OTHER NOTABLE WORKS:
The Mysterious Affair at Styles (1920)
The Murder of Roger Ackroyd (1926)
And Then There Were None (1939)

COMPAGNIE INTERNATIONALE DES W

VOITURE-LITS

Britain mystery author Agatha Christie holds the Guinness World Record as the best-selling fiction writer of all time. Beginning with first novel *The Mysterious Affair at Styles* (1920), Christie has sold more two billion copies of her mysteries, short story collections, and plays, many starring her detectives Hercule Poirot and Miss Marple. Christie drew inspiration for her mysteries from her work in a pharmacy during World War I (that's where she learned the ins and outs of poisons) and from her second marriage to archaeologist Max Mallowan. While accompanying her husband to his dig sites in the Middle East, Christie came up with some of her best-known stories, *Murder on the Orient Express* (1934) and *Death on the Nile* (1937). She continued to write best sellers until her death in 1976 at age eighty-five.

. . . .

Who could equal the fierce intellect of Hercule Poirot, the gloriously mustached detective who takes passengers to task following the onboard murder of a wealthy American in a snowbound Orient Express? It would have to be Agatha Christie, the celebrated mystery writer who created puzzles for Poirot and then devised the brilliant man's solutions.

Murder on the Orient Express (1934) is both Christie and Poirot's finest hour, with Christie perfecting the template of a dogged inspector tackling an assembly of eccentric suspects—virtually the entire middle portion of the book is devoted to interrogations—until the culprit is identified in one sweeping declaration of guilt. Is it the Russian princess? The Italian car agent? Or the German maid? The book is renowned for providing a resolution that's somehow plausible while remaining unpredictable. *Express* hums along with the precision of a handcrafted timepiece, ticking away until Poirot uncovers the means and motive in a clever twist on the whodunit genre. "The impossible cannot have happened," Christie writes of the seemingly perfect murder. And yet the impossible did happen: She wrote a seemingly perfect mystery. Here's what you should know.

THE PLOT WAS INSPIRED BY A REAL-LIFE KIDNAPPING.

In the novel, Poirot must determine who murdered a man named Ratchett on the Orient Express. He discovers that Ratchett is actually a man named Cassetti who had kidnapped a toddler named Daisy Armstrong and extorted $200,000 in ransom money from her parents, who died shortly after their daughter's body was found. Christie based some of the details of this plot on the kidnapping and death of the twenty-month-old son of aviator Charles Lindbergh in 1932. Charles Lindbergh, Jr. was taken from his crib, and the Lindberghs paid the $50,000 ransom that had been demanded in a note left in his room. Sadly, their son's body was found a few miles away from their home two months later.

CHRISTIE ALSO TOOK INSPIRATION FROM HER OWN TRIPS ON THE ORIENT EXPRESS.

Christie took her first trip on the Orient Express in 1928, and it was love at first sight; later, she and her second husband, an archaeologist, frequently rode the train to the locales of his digs. In *Murder on the Orient Express*, Christie translated the train's details onto the page and even incorporated one of her own experiences. On one 1931 trip, there was a flood that necessitated stopping the train in its tracks. "Started out from Istanbul in a violent thunder storm," she wrote to her husband. "We went very slowly during the night and about 3 a.m. stopped altogether."

It wasn't the first time the Orient Express had ground to a halt: In 1929, a snowstorm stranded it in the mountains for days. Christie wasn't on board at the time, but she used it in her book nonetheless.

IT INITIALLY HAD A DIFFERENT NAME.

Murder on the Orient Express was originally published in a serialized format in *The Saturday Evening Post* under the title *Murder in the Calais Coach*. When it was published in book format in 1934, its title had been changed to *Orient Express*—at least in the UK. In the US, however, it was still *Calais Coach*. The book's publishers didn't want it to be confused with Graham Greene's 1932 book *Stamboul Train*, which had been published in the states as *Orient Express*.

CHRISTIE HAD AN ISSUE WITH THE FILM ADAPTATION.

Murder on the Orient Express was adapted as a film for the first time in 1974, with Sidney Lumet directing and Albert Finney playing Poirot. (Supposedly, Lord Louis Mountbatten, a member of Britain's royal family and father-in-law of one of the producers, was a key player in convincing Christie to allow the movie to be made.) Though the film was a huge success—Finney nabbed an Oscar nomination for playing Poirot, and Ingrid Bergman won an Oscar for Actress in a Supporting Role—Christie did have a tiny issue with it. "It was well made except for one mistake," she's quoted as saying. "It was Albert Finney, as my detective Hercule Poirot. I wrote that he had the finest mustache in England—and he didn't in the film. I thought that a pity—why shouldn't he have the best mustache?"

THE AGATHA CHRISTIE BOOK LINKED TO REAL MURDERS

Arsenic, cyanide, even nicotine: No toxic substance escaped the attention of Agatha Christie. Slipped into nightcaps, eye drops, even seeping from wallpaper, a variety of fatal chemicals provided her characters with mysterious ailments and puzzling clues that made for ideal murder mystery material. The author's assured handling of poisons came from her time volunteering as an apothecary's assistant at a hospital during both World Wars, and her descriptions of dosages, reactions, and mortality rates were often rivaled only in specialist texts.

While this attention to detail was normally celebrated, there was one instance when a hysterical news media—and even Christie herself—became alarmed that her work may have inspired a real-life killer.

The book was *The Pale Horse*, a novel about a group of contract killers using thallium, a heavy metal discovered in 1861 but largely obscure until Christie wrote about it. The real-life murderer was Graham Young, who was sentenced to life in prison for using thallium to poison an untold number of people, killing at least two, and possibly three. His experiments began in 1961, while he was just fourteen years old. *The Pale Horse*, the first and only time Christie used thallium as a plot device, was published the same year.

Odorless and tasteless, thallium is treated by the body as potassium and creates significant damage to the nervous system. Numbness of the hands, slurred speech, and lethargy are common symptoms. In ingestion cases, small doses can build to lethal levels within two to three weeks. Victims who succumbed to it were often thought to have suffered from encephalitis or epilepsy.

During the trial, much was made of Christie's use of thallium in *The Pale Horse* and its relative rarity as a murder weapon. Pathologist Hugh Molesworth-Johnson said Christie's descriptions of the drug were so accurate that they rivaled the reference books of his profession—and that Christie's book was the only source outside of reference books where such specific and accurate information about thallium could be found.

The news media began to speculate about whether the boy had been influenced by the work. Had Christie's fiction turned into Young's horrific fact?

A month after his sentencing, Christie, then eighty-one, expressed concern she could have given Young ideas. Her husband, Sir Max Mallowan, told reporters he wondered if "this fellow read her book and learned anything from it." According to the book *A is for Arsenic*, *The Daily Mail* published a list of similarities between *The Pale Horse* and the criminal case. They could hardly resist the implication that the author had created a literal monster. But it's unclear if Young ever read The Pale Horse; it's possible his knowledge came from studying medical texts during his library days as an adolescent.

What is clear is that *The Pale Horse* actually saved one life—that of a 19-month-old girl from Qatar who, according to a 1977 report, was flown to London after she became ill with a mysterious condition doctors couldn't figure out. Her nurse was reading *The Pale Horse* at the time, and thought she recognized the symptoms of thallium poisoning. Tests confirmed that the nurse was right. The baby was treated and made "remarkable improvement."

Fascinating Facts about Agatha Christie

Agatha Christie has kept countless readers up into the early-morning hours with her books—and occasionally, the mystery surrounding her personal life has rivaled the best of her fiction. Let's take a look at some of the verifiable details of the famed crime writer's life and times.

1 HER MOTHER DIDN'T WANT HER TO LEARN HOW TO READ UNTIL SHE WAS OLDER.

Christie's mother was said to be against her daughter learning how to read until she was eight years old. As the author recalled in her autobiography, her mother thought waiting was "better for the eyes and also for the brain." So instead, Christie taught herself to read before she turned five, which she said left her mother "much distressed." Her mother insisted on homeschooling, meaning that Agatha had little formal education until the age of fifteen, when her family dispatched her to a Paris finishing school.

2 CHRISTIE'S FIRST NOVEL WAS WRITTEN ON A DARE.

After an adolescence spent reading books and writing stories, Christie's sister, Madge, dared her sibling to attack a novel-length project. Christie accepted the challenge and wrote *The Mysterious Affair at Styles*, a mystery featuring a soldier on sick leave who finds himself embroiled in a poisoning at a friend's estate. The novel, which featured Hercule Poirot, was rejected by six publishers before being printed in 1920.

3 SHE ONCE DISAPPEARED FOR TEN DAYS.

In 1926, Christie—who was already garnering a large and loyal fan base—left her home without a trace. It could have been the beginning of one of her stories, particularly since first husband Archie had recently disclosed he had fallen in love with another woman and wanted a divorce. A police manhunt ensued, although it was unnecessary: Christie had simply driven out of town to a spa, possibly to get her mind off her tumultuous home life. The author made no mention of it in her later autobiography; some speculated it was a publicity stunt, while others believed the family's claim that she had experienced some kind of amnesic event.

4 CHRISTIE LOVED TO SURF.

With her husband Archie, Christie went on a traveling spree in 1922, starting in South Africa and winding up in Honolulu. At each step, the couple got progressively more capable riding surfboards; some historians believe they may have even been among the first British surfers to learn how to ride standing up.

5 CHRISTIE HAD AN ALIAS.

Not all of Christie's work had a mortality rate. Beginning in 1930 and continuing through 1956, she wrote six romance novels under the pen name Mary Westmacott. The pseudonym was a construct of her middle name, Mary, with Westmacott being the surname of her relatives.

6 SHE LOVED ARCHAEOLOGY.

After divorcing alleged cad Archie, Christie married archaeologist Max Mallowan in 1930 and joined him for regular expeditions to Syria and Iraq. In 2015, Harper-Collins republished *Come, Tell Me How You Live*, the author's long-forgotten 1946 memoir of her experiences traveling. Although she assisted her husband on digs, she never stopped working on her writing: Their preferred method of transport was frequently the Orient Express.

ELENA FERRANTE

BIRTHDATE: Unknown

BORN: Naples, Italy

OTHER NOTABLE WORKS:
L'amore molesto (1992); English translation *Troubling Love* (2006)
La frantumaglia (2003); English translation *Frantumaglia* (2016)

MY BRILLIANT FRIEND

Elena Ferrante's books have sold millions of copies and been translated into forty-five languages. Reading the richly rendered account of a decades-long friendship between the two main characters of the books that make up her Neapolitan quartet, many readers felt they knew Ferrante themselves. That literary intimacy was complicated by the fact that Ferrante's true identity remains unconfirmed; "Elena Ferrante" is a pen name.

Frantumaglia (a "jumble of fragments") is a collection of Ferrante's ostensibly non-fiction writing. Despite her self-professed goal "to orchestrate lies that always tell . . . the truth" in interviews, those fragments offer an opportunity to draw conclusions about the "real" Ferrante. Naples apparently holds a central place in her life, though she "ran away as soon as [she] could." She loves to write, but is beset by fear and self-doubt. The book offers numerous explanations for Ferrante's anonymity, including "a somewhat neurotic desire for intangibility" and a lack of "physical courage." These self-deprecating remarks surely represent a facet of Ferrante's reluctance, but she suggests a deeper current guiding her decision: "Writing with the knowledge that I don't have to appear produces a space of absolute creative freedom. It's a corner of my own that I intend to defend."

Readers around the world were transported to post-war Naples by *My Brilliant Friend*, the first entry of Ferrante's sprawling but intensely personal Neapolitan quartet. Though the novel's famously anonymous author can be taciturn and even contradictory in interviews, we can glean some insights about the book from her limited public words and those of her collaborators.

THE FIRST DRAFT LET BOTH FRIENDS NARRATE.

One of the driving tensions of *My Brilliant Friend* revolves around identifying the eponymous brilliant friend. Readers might easily imagine the title being spoken by the novel's narrator, Elena "Lenù" Greco. She describes her friend Lila as "the best among us" while calling herself "second in everything." And though the book revolves, in many ways, around the ever-changing perceptions the girls have of themselves and one another, it still can feel revelatory to read, for the first time, the moment when Lila tells Elena (emphasis added), "you're *my brilliant friend*, you have to be the best of all, boys and girls."

This sudden yet seemingly inevitable upending of our expectations may not have landed with the same weight if the narrative wasn't told completely from Elena's perspective. Interestingly, the choice to tell the story in this way wasn't always clear to Ferrante.

She told an interviewer that "there were long episodes" written by Lila in the first draft of the novel. Ferrante eventually decided that the book required a single narrator, leaving readers to wonder what Lila might have written about the moment her formal education ends, or imagining the prose she may have crafted in writing her story of *The Blue Fairy*.

THE AUTHOR CAN'T PIN DOWN THE INSPIRATION FOR THE NOVEL.

The Italian director Saverio Costanzo was entrusted with bringing *My Brilliant Friend* to the screen for a television series coproduced by HBO and Italy's RAI. Costanzo tells a story of facing budgetary and schedule restrictions, and nearly removing the novel's culminating wedding scene from his adaptation. Ferrante, whom he collaborated with through email, apparently pressed upon him: "Listen, the first moment I thought about *My Brilliant Friend*, the first image I had was a banquet, a very vulgar banquet of Neapolitan life. Please put the banquet back in."

Costanzo acquiesced, but he would perhaps not be entirely surprised to learn that his enigmatic colleague has told different versions of the novel's inception. In an interview, Ferrante declared that she's unable to give a "precise answer" identifying the original idea for the book, mentioning a friend's death, a wedding, and even her own novel, *The Lost Daughter*, as possible kernels that would eventually develop into the four-part story.

MY BRILLIANT FRIEND IS A LITERARY FUNHOUSE MIRROR.

Events and identities seem to echo throughout Ferrante's work, not just within individual novels but through wide swaths of literature. Ferrante has said that she "read[s] a lot, but in a disorderly way," and one can imagine her writing, among other things, serving a kind of organizing and complicating function as she traces and retraces memories, real and literary.

Elena is the name of the narrator in *My Brilliant Friend*, and of the main character's child in Ferrante's earlier book, *The Lost Daughter*. It's also the first name in her nom de plume, of course, an identity with its own echoes of the Italian author Elsa Morante, whose work Ferrante has expressed admiration for on numerous occasions. From Virgil to Louisa May Alcott to Lenù and Ferrante themselves, writers seem to float in and out of the book's margins, influencing the author and characters all at once.

BOOK SERIES TO BINGE-READ

Blown through Ferrante's Neapolitan novels? Here are a handful of other great book series to read:

My Struggle // KARL OVE KNAUSGÅRD
The quotidian details of this Norwegian writer add up to so much more than the sum of their parts in this autobiographical series. You'll find yourself unable to put the books down, wondering how a seemingly inconsequential high school party from thirty years ago turned out and why you care so much.

The Millennium Series // STIEG LARSSON
Stieg Larsson's expertly crafted psychological thrillers spawned a franchise that now includes films and additional novels written after the author passed away, but his original Millennium trilogy—*The Girl with the Dragon Tattoo*, *The Girl Who Played with Fire*, and *The Girl Who Kicked the Hornet's Nest*—is truly binge-worthy content at its finest. If you end up pulling an all-nighter (or more) to find out what wild thing Lisbeth Salander, the haunted genius at the center of the stories, does next, you won't have been the first one. To get an idea of what themes you'll encounter, Larsson's original Swedish title for *The Girl with the Dragon Tattoo* was *Men Who Hate Women*.

The Mars Trilogy // KIM STANLEY ROBINSON
Kim Stanley Robinson's Mars trilogy imagines what humanity's inevitable presence on the Red Planet would look like, warts and all. The series begins with *Red Mars*, which details the growing pains and cultural difficulties of adjusting to life on a new planet. The next two books in the series continue to look at how humans terraform the once-dead Martian landscape into something more habitable for the long term, while escalating the drama with conflicts between rival factions vying for control.

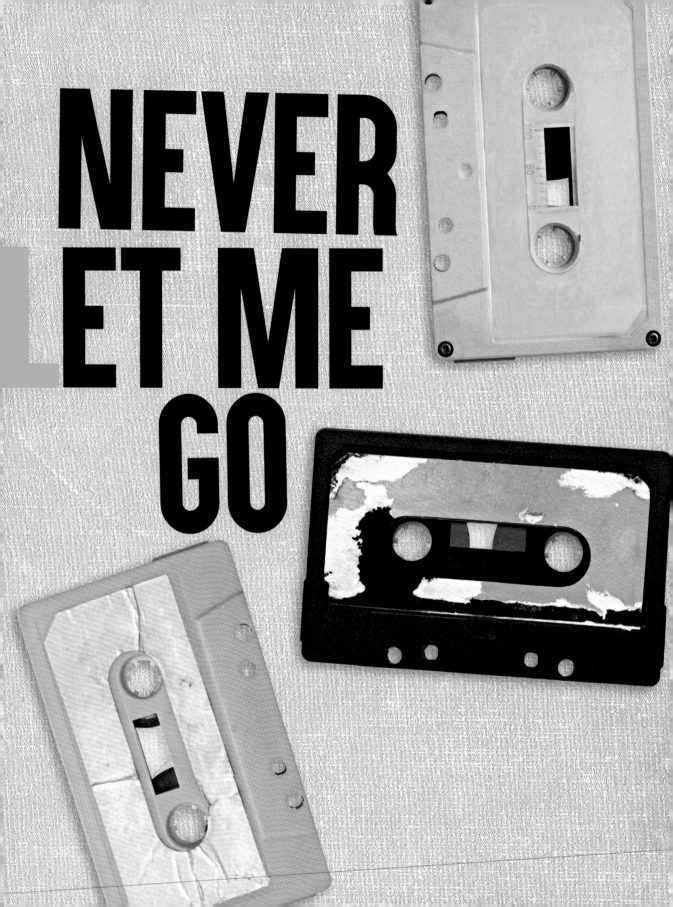

KAZUO ISHIGURO

November 8, 1954

BORN: Nagasaki, Japan

OTHER NOTABLE WORKS:
A Pale View of the Hills (1982)
An Artist of the Floating World (1986)
The Remains of the Day (1989)
When We Were Orphans (2000)

Kazuo Ishiguro, who played piano from the age of five and picked up the guitar when he was fifteen, initially thought he'd be a musician, not a writer—but it wasn't meant to be. He had many meetings with A&R representatives, but as he recalled to *The Paris Review*, "After two seconds, they'd say, 'It's not going to happen, man.'" It worked out for Ishiguro and for the rest of us. He instead became a celebrated author, publishing eight novels and a short story collection as well as numerous short works of fiction and four screenplays. And he's still working on music, albeit in a different way than he might have imagined: He sometimes writes lyrics for musicians. In 2017, he won the Nobel Prize for Literature for being an author "who, in novels of great emotional force, has uncovered the abyss beneath our illusory sense of connection with the world."

The Guardian named Ishiguro's sixth novel, *Never Let Me Go*—a subtle, heartbreaking sci-fi tale set at an English boarding school—one of its one hundred best books of the twenty-first century. "Unless you have a real sense of precious things under threat there would be nothing sad about time being limited," the author has said about the book. "The people in the novel believe, irrationally, like we all believe, that love can do all kinds of things that make you exempt from your fate."

ISHIGURO CAME UP WITH NARRATOR KATHY H. FIFTEEN YEARS BEFORE HE PUBLISHED *NEVER LET ME GO*.

Initially, the character who would become the narrator of *Never Let Me Go* popped up in a vague idea for a book about young people hanging out and arguing about books in a time like the 1970s. "I knew there was this strange fate hanging over them, but I couldn't work out exactly what it was," Ishiguro told *The Guardian*.

THE AUTHOR NIXED A FEW IDEAS FOR WHAT THAT STRANGE FATE WOULD BE.

SPOILERS! Ishiguro at first thought his characters would be young people who lived went through the regular human lifespan more quickly than normal people—in thirty years rather than eighty.

"I thought that they were going to come across nuclear weapons that were being moved around at night in huge lorries and be doomed in some way," he told *The Paris Review*.

But when he heard a radio show about biotechnology, he decided to make his students clones who eventually "complete"—die after donating all of their organs to the people they're clones of. Having his characters be clones didn't just give him a reason for why their lifespans would be cut short; it also made his readers immediately ask themselves what, exactly, it means to be a human being—what he said was "a secular route to the Dostoevskian question, 'What is a soul?'"

ACCORDING TO THE AUTHOR, THE BOARDING SCHOOL IN THE NOVEL IS "A PHYSICAL MANIFESTATION FOR WHAT WE HAVE TO DO TO ALL CHILDREN."

Ishiguro's clones are raised in a boarding school called Hailsham, where the truth about their purpose is hidden from them. For the author, Hailsham was a physical representation of what adults have to do to protect children from the harsh realities of life that they might not be ready for. "When you become a parent, or a teacher, you turn into a manager of this whole system," he told *The Guardian*. "You become the person controlling the bubble of innocence around a child, regulating it. All children have to be deceived if they are to grow up without trauma."

ISHIGURO THINKS OF IT AS HIS "CHEERFUL NOVEL."

Prior to *Never Let Me Go*, Ishiguro wrote what he called "how-not-to-lead-your-life books" about his characters' failings, as a sort of warning to himself. But *Never Let Me Go* was his "cheerful novel," one where he focused on his character's positive traits in addition to their flaws. His goal, he said, was to make his three main characters "essentially decent." When they finally become aware of their purpose—and the fact that they don't have the luxury of time—"I wanted them to care most about each other and setting things right," he told *The Paris Review*. "So for me, it was saying positive things about human beings against the rather bleak fact of our mortality."

WHAT'S THE DIFFERENCE BETWEEN A NOVELLA AND A SHORT STORY?

We typically put fiction into one of two categories—it's either a short story, or it's a novel. But there is another variation that lands somewhere in between the two: the novella. What exactly separates a short story from a novella from a novel, you ask?

Fascinating Facts about Kazuo Ishiguro

Kazuo Ishiguro had many jobs—he worked at a homeless shelter, as a grouse beater for the Queen Mother at Balmoral, and even tried to make it as a musician—but it was in fiction where he found success: He published his first novel, the Nagasaki-set *A Pale View of Hills*, when he was twenty-seven, to critical acclaim. Here's what you need to know about the Nobel Prize-winning author.

1 ISHIGURO GREW UP WRITING.

When Ishiguro was five, he and his family moved from Japan to the UK so his father, an oceanographer, could work on an invention with the British National Institute of Oceanography. They settled in Guildford, and there, Ishiguro was enrolled in a primary school that, instead of defined lessons, allowed its students to choose activities, like using a manual calculating machine; making a cow using clay; or writing stories that the students would then bind and decorate like books and read aloud.

Ishiguro chose stories, creating a spy he called Mr. Senior. The experience, beyond being "good fun," taught him to "think of stories as effortless things"—something that stuck with him as he got older.

"I've never been intimidated by the idea of having to make up a story," he said. "It's always been a relatively easy thing that people did in a relaxed environment."

2 HE WAS OBSESSED WITH SHERLOCK HOLMES.

As a kid, Ishiguro's Sherlock Holmes obsession ran deep. "I'd go to school and say things like: 'Pray, be seated' or 'That is most singular,'" the author told *The New York Times*. "People at the time just put this down to my being Japanese." *The Hound of the Baskervilles* remains his favorite Sherlock Holmes story: "It was scary and gave me sleepless nights, but I suspect I was drawn to Conan Doyle's world because, paradoxically, it was so very cozy."

As an adult, Ishiguro counts Charlotte Brontë and Fyodor Dostoevsky as his favorite novelists. "I owe my career, and a lot else besides, to *Jane Eyre* and *Villette*," he told the *Times*.

3 HIS PORTRAIT ONCE HUNG AT 10 DOWNING STREET.

Over the course of his career, Ishiguro has received a number of awards and honors, including the Booker Prize, the *Chevalier de l'Ordre des Arts et des Lettres*, and the Nobel Prize in Literature. Ishiguro was knighted in 2018 for his services to literature, and declared himself "deeply touched to receive this honor from the nation that welcomed me as a small foreign boy." For a bit, his portrait—painted by Welsh artist Peter Edwards for the British National Portrait Gallery—even hung in 10 Downing Street when Tony Blair was Prime Minister.

As with most art forms, the label is somewhat malleable. When it comes down to it, though, it's all about word count. Short stories are usually only a few thousand words long and written for publication in a magazine or as part of a collection, and most are under 7,500 words or so. Novellas, on the other hand, can run from twenty thousand to fifty thousand words. Anything more than that is probably a full novel. (There's another in-between category for those stories between seven thousand and twenty thousand words: the "novelette.")

Novellas have been around since the Middle Ages, and some standard English class assignments are on the list. Even if you don't know it, you've surely read one: Joseph Conrad's *Heart of Darkness*, Charles Dickens's *A Christmas Carol*, Franz Kafka's *The Metamorphosis*, Edith Wharton's *Ethan Frome*, and H.G. Wells's *The Time Machine* can all be classified as novellas.

9 NOBEL PRIZE–WINNING NOVELISTS

The Swedish Academy has been awarding Nobel Prizes in Literature since 1901. Here are a few laureates beyond Ishiguro whose work you might have on your shelf.

JEAN-PAUL SARTRE

Sartre, Existentialist philosopher and author of *Roads to Freedom*, won the Nobel Prize for Literature in 1964 "for his work which, rich in ideas and filled with the spirit of freedom and the quest for truth, has exerted a far-reaching influence on our age." But the author refused to accept the prize—and was the first person to willingly do so. "My refusal is not an impulsive gesture, I have always declined official honors," he wrote later. "A writer who adopts political, social, or literary positions must act only with the means that are his own—that is, the written word."

GÜNTER GRASS

The Tin Drum author won the Nobel Prize in 1999, the year he published *My Century.* Grass's "frolicsome black fables," the committee wrote, "portray the forgotten face of history."

ISAAC BASHEVIS SINGER

Singer, author of books such as *The Family Moskat*, was a journalist who emigrated to the United States four years before the rise of the Nazis. He wrote almost exclusively in Yiddish and won in 1978 "for his impassioned narrative art which, with roots in a Polish-Jewish cultural tradition, brings universal human conditions to life."

PEARL S. BUCK

The 1938 Nobel Prize for Literature went to *The Good Earth* author, "for her rich and truly epic descriptions of peasant life in China and for her biographical masterpieces."

HERMANN HESSE

Hesse, author of *Siddhartha* and *Narcissus* and *Goldmund*, was awarded the Nobel Prize in Literature in 1946 "for his inspired writings which, while growing in boldness and penetration, exemplify the classical humanitarian ideals and high qualities of style."

NADINE GORDIMER

The South African author of ten novels, including *The Conservationist* and *My Son's Story,* was part of the anti-apartheid movement and made it a background of her work. She won in 1991 for being an author "who through her magnificent epic writing has—in the words of Alfred Nobel—been of very great benefit to humanity."

ALBERT CAMUS

Three years before his death in 1960, the Nobel Prize committee awarded Camus, author of The Stranger, "for his important literary production, which with clear-sighted earnestness illuminates the problems of the human conscience in our times."

DORIS LESSING

Lessing sold her first short stories when she was fifteen and would go on to write dozens of works over the course of her life, including *The Grass Is Singing* and *Children of Violence.* When she was awarded the Nobel Prize in Literature in 2007, the committee called her "that epicist of the female experience, who with scepticism, fire and visionary power has subjected a divided civilisation to scrutiny."

NAGUIB MAHFOUZ

The *Adrift on the Nile* author wrote more than thirty novels and 350 short stories and frequently used Cairo—his birthplace—as the setting for his works. He won the Nobel Prize in Literature in 1988, for being an author "who, through works rich in nuance—now clear-sightedly realistic, now evocatively ambiguous—has formed an Arabian narrative art that applies to all mankind."

ON THE ROAD

JACK KEROUAC

March 12, 1922–October 21, 1969

BORN: Lowell, Massachusetts

OTHER NOTABLE WORKS:
The Dharma Bums (1958)
Big Sur (1962)

orn Jean-Louis Kerouac, Jack was a football star at his Massachusetts high school, which led him to be awarded a scholarship to Columbia University in New York City. He ended up dropping out of school and enlisted in both the Merchant Marine and the Navy at the same time he began to write. After he returned to New York in 1943, he befriended members of what would become known at the Beat Generation, including the poet Allen Ginsberg and the novelist William S. Burroughs. In 1947, while working on his first published novel, *The Town and the City*, Kerouac decided his next topic would be the American road. In the following years, he would traverse America several times with friend Neal Cassady, the basis for the novel's character Dean Moriarty, in search of the breadth of humanity in the world and the ever-elusive "It," the magic "moment when you know all and everything is decided forever."

On the Road, Jack Kerouac's stream-of-consciousness travelogue charts the adventures of two friends—narrator Sal Paradise and his wild co-pilot Dean Moriarty—as they road trip their way across the United States to find a deeper meaning within their country, as well as themselves. The novel is a largely autobiographical tale with Paradise standing in for Kerouac. Here's what you should know.

THE SCROLL STORY IS A LITTLE MISLEADING.

Literary legend has it that Kerouac wrote *On the Road* spontaneously over three weeks in April 1951. It's a tale that Kerouac played up himself, but in fact, he prepared extensively, keeping journals and buying roadmaps to study. "I have another novel in mind—'On the Road'— which I keep thinking about: two guys hitchhiking to California in search of something they don't really find, and losing themselves on the road, and coming all the way back hopeful of something else," he wrote in an August 1948 journal entry. He produced a draft of the novel—one of several—not long after.

THE FIRST DRAFTS OF THE NOVEL WERE DIFFERENT FROM THE FINISHED PRODUCT.

Kerouac often used his own life, and his friends, as inspiration for his fictional works, and *On the Road* was no exception. The novel was based on several road trips Kerouac had taken, and protagonist Sal Paradise was based on Kerouac himself; Dean Moriarty is a stand-in for Kerouac's friend Neal Cassady.

In the first drafts of the novel, however, the protagonist was named Ray Smith, then Smitty. Early drafts also had a more conventional structure than the final result. Kerouac toyed around with other titles, too, including *Beat Generation* and *Shades of the Prison House*.

HE WAS INSPIRED BY A LETTER FROM NEAL CASSADY.

Kerouac had a breakthrough in December 1950, courtesy of a letter he received from Cassady, who had penned the thirteen-thousand-word, forty-page missive on a three-day Benzedrine high. It was, Kerouac would later say, "All first person, fast, mad, confessional, completely serious, all detailed." He dubbed the style "spontaneous prose."

In April 1951, Kerouac sat down at his typewriter and, in twenty days, wrote more than 120,000 words on a scroll of tracing paper he'd taped together.

THE SCROLL VERSION WAS EDITED EXTENSIVELY.

The scroll wasn't the final version of *On the Road*; it would take a few more revisions and many, many rejections before the novel was finally published. As author Joyce Johnson, who dated Kerouac off-and-on for two years, would later recall, "each paragraph had to be a 'poem.'" One tale Kerouac told about the scroll—that a friend's dog had chewed off some paragraphs at the end—may have actually been a cover for the fact that he wanted to tweak the ending.

A SINGLE REVIEW MADE *ON THE ROAD* A SUCCESS.

When *On the Road* was finally published in September 1957, it was quickly a best seller, thanks to a review from critic Gilbert Millstein, who wrote in *The New York Times* that the novel was "the most beautifully executed, the clearest and the most important utterance yet made by the generation Kerouac himself named years ago as 'Beat', and whose principal avatar he is."

CASSADY'S LETTER WAS LOST FOR DECADES.

Neal Cassady's "Joan Anderson letter," the inspiration for *On the Road*'s "spontaneous prose," got lost after Kerouac gave the letter to Allen Ginsberg. (Ginsberg said poet Gerd Stern had thrown it into San Francisco Bay, which Stern denied.) Then, in 2012, the letter was rediscovered: It had been in the "to read" pile of mail that had belonged to Richard Emerson, owner of Golden Goose Press. When the business folded, he sent his archives to his colleague Jack Spinosa, where his daughter found it after Spinosa's death. The letter was sold at auction for $200,000.

THE SCROLL VERSION WAS REISSUED IN 2007.

In 1962, Kerouac wrote that his books, including *On the Road*, *The Dharma Bums*, and *Visions of Cody*, were "one vast book like Proust's [*Remembrance of Things Past*] . . . chapters in the whole work which I call *The Duluoz Legend*." The author noted that "Because of the objections of my early publishers I was not allowed to use the same personae names in each work," so instead he created new names for the people in his stories. To mark the fiftieth anniversary of *On the Road* in 2007, Penguin Classics re-released Kerouac's scroll version of the novel, featuring scenes that had been cut prior to publication and swapping out the character names for the names of the people who had actually inspired them.

Young Jack Kerouac's Reading List

It's not every day that you get a chance to peek at a reading syllabus of sorts from one of the great American authors of the twentieth century. In 1940, a young Jack Kerouac (then eighteen) scrawled a reading list on a piece of notebook paper. The titles included span eras and cultures and offer a rare glimpse at the works of literature that were molding his teenage mind.

In two years' time, Kerouac would join the United States Merchant Marine and then the Navy, where he'd write his first attempt at a novel, *The Sea Is My Brother*—a work he later described as a "crock [of shit] as literature" that wouldn't be published until after his death. We all have to start somewhere.

Required Reading for J.K.

1. Indian Scripture
2. Chinese [Scriptures]
3. Old and New Testament
4. Gibbon and Plutarch
5. Homer (again)
6. Shakespeare (again)
7. Wolfe (always)
ETC. ETC.
"Finnegans Wake"
"Outline of History" (again)
Thoreau and Emerson ([again])
Joseph Conrad
Proust's "Remembrance"

Dante (again)

ONE HUNDRED YEARS OF SOLITUDE

GABRIEL GARCÍA MÁRQUEZ

March 6, 1927–April 17, 2014

BORN: Aracataca, Colombia

OTHER NOTABLE WORKS:
Love in the Time of Cholera (1985)
News of a Kidnapping (1996)

As a boy, Gabriel García Márquez preferred drawing over writing—but eventually, he would win the Nobel Prize in Literature for his stories, "in which the fantastic and the realistic are combined in a richly composed world of imagination, reflecting a continent's life and conflicts." Raised and educated by his grandparents until the age of ten, he attended a Jesuit secondary school and enrolled in law school before dropping out and becoming a journalist amidst the savage, ten-year-long Colombian civil war known as La Violencia. And he read, and read, and read, everyone from Hemingway to Woolf.

García Márquez frequently drew inspiration from his own life for his books; most notably, his hometown of Aracataca became the Macondo of his first novella, 1955's *Leaf Storm*, as well as 1967's *One Hundred Years of Solitude*, a book that came to him while he was driving his family from Mexico City, their residence at the time, to a vacation in Acapulco. "It was so ripe in me," he said later, "that I could have dictated the first chapter, word by word, to a typist." *One Hundred Years of Solitude* made García Márquez a literary giant and one of Latin America's most esteemed writers. When he died at eighty-seven in 2014, García Márquez's native Colombia mandated three days of mourning for the author popularly known as "Gabo."

Gabriel García Márquez's body of work is filled with influential novels, but none have impacted culture quite like *One Hundred Years of Solitude*. The book tells the story of seven generations of one family living in the same village, and it tackles ambitious themes like the nature of reality. Half a century after its publication, *One Hundred Years of Solitude* is regarded as one of the best works of literature ever written. Here are some facts about the Spanish language masterpiece.

ONE HUNDRED YEARS OF SOLITUDE ENDED THE AUTHOR'S WRITING SLUMP.

García Márquez came close to never committing his magnum opus to paper. Following the publication of his first four books, the author felt demoralized, and stopped writing everything but movie scripts for five years. "It was a very bad time for me, a suffocating time," he told *The Atlantic* in 1973. "Nothing I did in films was mine. It was a collaboration, incorporating everybody's ideas, the director's, the actors'. I was very limited in what I could do and I appreciated then that in the novel the writer has complete control." But everything changed that day in January 1965, when the first chapter of the story came to him en route to his planned vacation. He immediately turned around so he could start writing. At his desk—which he called "The Cave of the Mafia"—he spent up to ten hours every day for the next eighteen months in front of his typewriter until he had a finished manuscript.

HE ACCIDENTALLY MAILED THE WRONG PART OF THE BOOK TO HIS PUBLISHER.

While García Márquez wrote on his novel, money was tight. His wife, Mercedes, worked and handled the bills and, when they didn't have enough funds, convinced their landlord to let them skip the rent. Then, when García Márquez had a complete manuscript to send to his publisher, he couldn't afford the postage required to send all 590 pages at once. As the author later recalled, "We divided [the manuscript] into two equal parts and sent one part to Buenos Aires . . . Only later did we realize that we had not sent the first part, but the last. But before we got the money to send it, Paco Porrúa, our man in the South American publisher, eager to read the first half of the book, sent us the money we needed to send the first part. That was how we came to be born in our lives today."

(Some modern scholars feel that there is some mythologizing is going on here, however: Historian Álvaro Santana-Acuña, author of *Ascent to Glory: How One Hundred Years of Solitude Was Written and Became a Global Classic*, has noted that the story of the book's development changed over the years, with the divided manuscript appearing four years after publication, and the second-half mistake not appearing until ten years after publication.)

THE BOOK GOT SUPPORT FROM OTHER LATIN AMERICAN NOVELISTS.

Two early readers of *One Hundred Years of Solitude* were *Hopscotch* author Julio Cortázar and Carlos Fuentes, author of *The Death of Artemio Cruz*. Both were enthusiastic in their praise. Fuentes described the first three chapters of the book as "absolutely magisterial," adding, "All 'fictional' history coexists with 'real' history, what is dreamed with what is documented, and thanks to the legends, the lies, the exaggerations, the myths . . . Macondo is made into a universal territory, in a story almost biblical in its foundations, its generations and degenerations, in a story of the origin and destiny of human time and of the dreams and desires by which men are saved or destroyed."

GARCÍA MÁRQUEZ'S MAGICAL WORLD IS BASED IN LIVED EXPERIENCE.

One Hundred Years of Solitude helped popularize magical realism, a style of fiction that blends a grounded world with fantastical elements. The genre is heavily associated with Latin American literature, and it's been praised as a more accurate representation of certain cultures than the more literal writing that's typical to the Western canon. For García Márquez, this style wasn't difficult to achieve. He said the story came directly from experiences he had and stories he heard as a child, noting, "There's not a single line in my novels which is not based on reality."

IT WASN'T THE KIND OF BOOK ITS AUTHOR LIKED TO READ.

García Márquez's book was successful from the get-go—which, under other circumstances, meant it wouldn't have been his type of book. As he told *The Atlantic*, "If I hadn't written [*One Hundred Years of Solitude*], I wouldn't have read it. I don't read best sellers."

MAGICAL REALISM BOOKS YOU NEED TO READ

Somewhere between the fantasy realms of Mordor and Narnia and the real world lies magical realism, a literary genre in which fantastical elements are incorporated into grounded and often mundane settings. Gabriel García Márquez didn't invent it, but he helped popularize magical realism when his epic novel *One Hundred Years of Solitude* was published in 1967. Here are a few other books in the genre you should add to your reading list.

1 *The House of Spirits //* **ISABEL ALLENDE**
Chilean author Isabel Allende's 1982 debut novel *The House of Spirits* tells the story of one family, a member of which possesses clairvoyant abilities. *The Wall Street Journal* called the book "an alluring, sometimes magical tale . . . In its tumultuous story of rebellion and love among three generations, it is an allegory in which any family should be able to recognize a bit of itself."

2 *Like Water for Chocolate //* **LAURA ESQUIVEL**
Published in Mexico in 1989, *Like Water for Chocolate* features a main character who is able to impart her emotions onto others through her cooking. This detail is more than just a plot device, as it may have been employed in a more conventional fantasy book—author Laura Esquivel uses it to develop her protagonist and build relationships between the characters.

3 *Red Sorghum //* **MO YAN**
Magical realism is also viewed as way to more accurately depict certain cultures where the literal style typical to Western literature falls short. In the Chinese novel *Red Sorghum*, published in 1986, author Mo Yan weaves folklore into a story about real-life events like the Second Sino-Japanese War. When he won the Nobel Prize for Literature in 2012, the committee said, "Through a mixture of fantasy and reality, historical and social perspectives, Mo Yan has created a world reminiscent in its complexity of those in the writings of William Faulkner and Gabriel García Márquez, at the same time finding a departure point in old Chinese literature and in oral tradition."

4 *The Ocean at the End of the Lane //* **NEIL GAIMAN**
In 2013, British author Neil Gaiman wrote *The Ocean at the End of the Lane*, a book that uses magical elements to explore the divide between childhood and adulthood. Upon returning home, the protagonist—an ordinary man from the real world—uncovers extraordinary memories from his youth that he had forgotten.

5 *The Life of Pi //* **YANN MARTEL**
Perhaps the best-known example of magical realism in literature from the twenty-first century is *Life of Pi*. Yann Martel's novel follows a boy stranded at sea for hundreds of days while sharing a lifeboat with a Bengal tiger. The surreal premise is part of the book's theme, which calls on readers to reflect on the subjectivity of reality.

DIANA GABALDON

January 11, 1952

BORN: Williams, Arizona

OTHER NOTABLE WORKS:
The Lord John series (1998–2017)

n Claire nurse hero soul Jacobite high
'ort hope stone blood Jamie fire Fr
acKenzie surgery chest kiss hea
'nder Frank hearth sigh British
'vant bones safe honor bed Jac
rse hero soul Jacobite highla
ne blood Jamie fire Fran'
'urgery chest kiss h'
' hearth sigh '
safe ho
oul Jacol
Jamie f
y chest ki.
...k hearth sigh Bı..
.it bones safe honor bed Ja
ırse hero soul Jacobite highlan
tone blood Jamie fire Frank R'

T hough Diana Gabaldon's books have brought her international acclaim as an author, her background is actually in science. She earned a bachelor's degree in zoology, a master's degree in marine biology, and a PhD in quantitative behavioral ecology. As a master's student, she studied hermit crabs; as part of her PhD research, she examined the nest selection habits of pinyon jays, which included squirting syringes of water down nestlings' throats to see what they ate.

So how did she jump from studying animal behavior to penning steamy Scottish fantasies? After becoming an expert in scientific computation while working as a professor at Arizona State University, Gabaldon set her sights on a new endeavor: writing a novel. The result, *Outlander*, would become the first installment of a now-best-selling series.

Readers have swooned over Jamie Fraser's love for his time-traveling wife Claire since 1991. The two are the stars of Diana Gabaldon's *Outlander* series, a genre-bending whirlwind of romance, historical, and science fiction. But when Gabaldon started writing *Outlander*, she never intended for anyone to read it, let alone publish it—it was originally just a practice book. Here are a few other facts you should know about the novel.

OUTLANDER WAS PARTIALLY INSPIRED BY DOCTOR WHO.

You'd be forgiven for thinking a foray into Scotland's dreamy landscape inspired *Outlander*. But Gabaldon didn't set foot in the country until after she'd received some of the book's advance money. It was a popular science fiction franchise, not real-world experience, that sparked the series. While noodling on potential ideas for her practice novel, Gabaldon watched "War Games," an old *Doctor Who* rerun on PBS. It was then that she spotted the character Jamie McCrimmon. The Scotsman, played by Frazer Hines, gave her an idea. Soon, Gabaldon was penning her own fantastical tale set in eighteenth-century Scotland. But apart from the ruggedly beautiful setting and a handsome man in a kilt—plus, of course, a fair amount of time travel—the two series share little in common. Instead of hurtling through time and space in a boxy contraption, the time-traveling Outlander characters step through mysterious portals, aided by genetic luck and some gemstones. Gabaldon did pay homage to her inspiration, though; Jamie Fraser's first name is a nod to the *Doctor Who* character.

IT WAS ORIGINALLY MEANT TO BE A HISTORICAL NOVEL.

People have yet to reach a consensus on which bucket of literature the *Outlander* series belongs in. The books are a blend of historical fiction, science fiction, mystery, and fantasy—and the regular risqué bedroom scenes add some strong romance elements, too. But Gabaldon didn't intend to burst onto the literary scene with a masterpiece mishmash of genres. Originally, she planned for *Outlander* to be a historical novel.

The arrival of Claire, a twentieth-century World War II nurse, changed that. "The time-travel was all her fault," the author writes on her website. She concocted the character on her third day of writing, and before long, she was telling the story from her point of view, braiding together two worlds two centuries apart. Time travel was Gabaldon's way of plugging the modern protagonist into the eighteenth-century tale she'd started crafting. Elements of the story are based on fact, though. The Jacobite Rebellion and 1746 Battle of Culloden, which feature heavily in the series' earlier books, are real historical events. In fact, you can even visit a memorial to the real Clan Fraser and other Highland fighters at the Culloden Battlefield—just make sure you treat the area with respect.

WRITING THE OUTLANDER BOOKS REQUIRES A LOT OF RESEARCH.

Gabaldon researches as she writes, piecing together bits of plot laced with historical details. She used a whopping 2,200 books for her core research. Claire's botany skills and knowledge of healing plants comes from the author's century-spanning collection of more than one hundred tomes on herbs and folk medicine; her more modern medical skills were pulled from surgeons' memoirs and history of medicine books. Nonfiction works on weaponry and battle history inform the many skirmishes Jamie and his fellow men often find themselves pulled into, and a hearty mix of dictionaries and Britain-based novels dictate the characters' speech. (Gabaldon originally cobbled together the books' Gaelic phrases from a dictionary, then later received aid from a native speaker.)

Not every detail the author uses comes from a book, though. Gabaldon drew on her science background while writing one particularly grisly scene for *Dragonfly in Amber*, book two in the series. Her postdoctoral work at the University of Pennsylvania involved butchering seabirds, using a hammer and chisel to remove their brains. According to Gabaldon's website, that gory skill helped her create the description of drawing and quartering featured in the book.

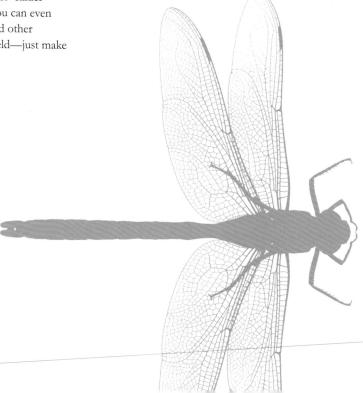

FIVE OTHER GREAT LOVE STORIES IN NOVELS

Jamie and Claire's romance in *Outlander* is just one of many incredible love stories to have graced the pages of classic novels. Once you've read *Pride and Prejudice* and *Jane Eyre*, consider picking up these novels whose love stories will make your heart skip a beat.

1 *Love in the Time of Cholera* (1985) // **GABRIEL GARCÍA MÁRQUEZ**
Like many young loves, Florentino Ariza and Fermina Daza's secret romance is destined for heartbreak. Fermina later marries and grows old with Dr. Juvenal Urbino, a physician fighting to eradicate cholera. When her husband dies, Florentino—who continued to nurture his feelings for her, despite spending the decades engaging in many romantic affairs— attends the funeral, ready for a second chance with his first love.

2 *Their Eyes Were Watching God* (1937) // **ZORA NEALE HURSTON**
Set in early twentieth-century Florida, this Harlem Renaissance staple cemented Zora Neale Hurston's place in history as a literary great. The story, a celebration of Black love, blossoms into a complex narrative about gender roles and women's independence. Janie's love for Tea Cake is intense and imperfect, ending in tragedy, but her quest for romance and partnership rather than ownership and control celebrates a type of love that is joyful and enduring.

3 *The Thorn Birds* (1977) // **COLLEEN MCCULLOUGH**
This tale about the forbidden romance between protagonist Meggie Cleary and an older priest topped *The New York Times*'s best-seller list for more than a year. When the novel begins, Meggie is just a four-year-old child living in the harsh Australian Outback. As the decades pass, deception and death continue to dog the Cleary family. Family secrets unravel, testing both love and loyalty.

4 *Norwegian Wood* (1987) // **HARUKI MURAKAMI**
This is no lighthearted coming-of-age story. In the novel, Toru Watanabe reminisces on his years as a student in 1960s Tokyo; a time defined by love, longing, and loss. His attempts to navigate his relationships with two starkly different women, set against the backdrop of the era's civil unrest and student protests, is poignant and powerful.

5 *The Notebook* (1996) // **NICHOLAS SPARKS**
It's safe to say Sparks's entry into the literary world was a smashing one. Elderly Noah Calhoun reads a story to Allie, who is suffering from dementia. It's soon revealed that the tale he's telling is their own love story—a husband's gentle-yet-raw attempt to reignite his wife's memory of their decades-long romance.

JANE AUSTEN

December 16, 1775–July 18, 1817

BORN: Steventon, Hampshire, England

OTHER NOTABLE WORKS:
Sense and Sensibility (1811)
Mansfield Park (1814)
Emma (1815)

In the late eighteenth century, a woman's main role was to be a good wife and mother. Jane Austen was neither of those things (she never married so had no children). She wasn't afraid to write about empowered women with minds and views of their own—even if they did (eventually) often find their happily-ever-afters with men of substantial means. Yet Austen only published four novels during her lifetime—*Sense and Sensibility*, *Pride and Prejudice*, *Mansfield Park*, and *Emma*—and even then, they were published anonymously. In fact, it wasn't until after Austen's death in 1817, at the age of forty-one, that her identity was eventually revealed, and that her three remaining books—*Northanger Abbey*, *Persuasion*, and, eventually, the unfinished manuscript for *Sanditon*—were published.

Jane Austen's *Pride and Prejudice* appears on best-loved literature lists across the globe, is a fixture in high school classrooms, and has spawned a rabid fan base and countless film and television adaptations. The story of how Miss Elizabeth Bennet's disdain for the wealthy, prideful Mr. Fitzwilliam Darcy turned to love has sold more than twenty million copies since its first appearance more than two hundred years ago.

Austen's family, however, probably didn't see much of that success: She sold the novel's copyright to her publisher and died just a few years later, in 1817. Though the novel was reviewed positively and was well-received by the upper classes at the time, it was no widespread

sensation. It wasn't until the twentieth century that the book and its author were rediscovered and lifted to the rarefied place in the English literature pantheon they hold today.

LIKE HER CHARACTERS, AUSTEN EXPERIENCED REJECTION.

Pride and Prejudice is about young women trying to find good marriage matches. This issue must have been fresh on the young author's mind when she wrote the book. At age twenty, she flirted scandalously with a young man named Tom Lefroy at a ball. "Imagine to yourself everything most profligate and shocking in the way of dancing and sitting down together," she wrote to her sister Cassandra. "He is a very gentlemanlike, good-looking, pleasant young man, I assure you." But for some reason the romance never extended beyond a few ballroom dances—Austen would write her sister: "At length the day is come on which I am to flirt my last with Tom Lefroy . . . My tears flow as I write this, at this melancholy idea."

MR. DARCY WOULD BE THE EQUIVALENT OF A ROCKEFELLER OR A VANDERBILT.

The characters in *Pride and Prejudice* constantly exclaim over Mr. Darcy's £10,000 a year, but how rich is that exactly? In 2014, *The Telegraph* calculated that adjusting for financial changes, a decent estimate might be £12 million, or US$18.7 million a year. And that's just income on top of a much larger fortune. It's no wonder Mrs. Bennet gushed about Elizabeth's engagement—"How rich and how great you will be! What pin-money, what jewels, what carriages you will have!" Marrying Darcy would be like marrying a Rockefeller or a Vanderbilt.

LYDIA SAYS SHE'S ELOPING TO THE LAS VEGAS OF HER DAY.

SPOILERS! In the book, the Bennet family is almost ruined when Lydia takes off with the nefarious soldier George Wickham. "I am going to Gretna Green," Lydia writes her friend, "and if you cannot guess with who, I shall think you a simpleton."

Unlike England, Scotland allowed people under twenty-one to get married without parental consent, and without the same legal and religious bureaucracy. Gretna Green was the first town over the Scottish border. There, a young couple could be joined with "marriage by declaration," which often occurred in a blacksmith shop.

Lydia and Wickham don't actually go to Scotland, however—they don't marry until later, after Darcy pays Wickham's gambling debts.

Fascinating Facts about Jane Austen

More than two hundred years after her death, Jane Austen continues to be celebrated for her sharp, biting prose on love's various entanglements. The strong female characters in her books are as resonant today as when Austen first pressed her pen to paper. Though her bibliography totals just six novels (alongside some unfinished books and other works) in all, Austen's books and her insightful quotes have been subject to hundreds of years of analysis and—for the Austen die-hards—numerous re-readings. For more on the writer's life, influences, and curious editing habits, take a look at our compendium of all things Austen below.

1 JANE AUSTEN'S FATHER DID EVERYTHING HE COULD TO HELP HER SUCCEED.

Austen, the second-youngest in a brood of eight kids, was born to George Austen, a rector, and Cassandra Austen. She developed a love for the written word partially as a result of George's vast home library. When she wasn't reading, Austen was supplied with writing tools by George to nurture her interests along, and later, he would send his daughters to a boarding school, furthering their education.

2 AUSTEN BACKED OUT OF A MARRIAGE OF CONVENIENCE.

Many of Austen's characters carry great agency in their lives, and Austen scholars enjoy pointing to the fact that Austen herself bucked convention when it came to affairs of the heart. The year after her family's move to the city of Bath in 1801, Austen received a proposal of marriage from Harris Bigg-Wither, a financially prosperous childhood friend. Austen accepted but quickly had second thoughts. Though his money would have provided for her and her family (and, at the time, she was twenty-seven and unpublished, meaning she had no outside income and was fast approaching Georgian-era spinster status), Austen decided that a union motivated on her part by economics wasn't worthwhile. She turned the proposal down the following day and later cautioned her niece about marrying for any reason other than love. "Anything is to be preferred or endured rather than marrying without affection," she wrote.

LIKE ELIZABETH AND JANE BENNET, AUSTEN WAS CLOSE TO HER SISTER.

In *Pride and Prejudice*, the relationship between the two sisters is central to the novel. In real life, Austen was very close to her sister Cassandra. They wrote constantly when they were apart and family tradition says they would voluntarily share a bedroom, even when they could sleep separately. When Jane died, Cassandra wrote her niece: "She was the sun of my life, the gilder of every pleasure, the soother of every sorrow."

A PUBLISHER REJECTED *PRIDE AND PREJUDICE* WITHOUT EVEN READING IT.

Austen finished the book, then titled *First Impressions*, when she was twenty-one years old. In 1797, her father George wrote to the publisher Thomas Cadell, writing that he had "a Manuscript Novel comprised in three Vols., about the length of Miss [Fanny] Burney's *Evelina*." He asked how much it would cost him to publish the book and what Cadell would pay for copyright. In response, Cadell scrawled "Declined by Return of Post" on the letter and sent it back with insulting speed. It's not clear if Austen was even aware that her father had approached Cadell on her behalf. Much later, in 1810, her brother Henry would act as her literary agent, selling *Sense and Sensibility* to London publisher Thomas Egerton. *Pride and Prejudice* would be published in 1813 when she was thirty-seven years old.

PRIDE AND PREJUDICE WAS PUBLISHED ANONYMOUSLY.

From *Sense and Sensibility* through *Emma*, Austen's published works never bore her name. *Sense and Sensibility* carried

3 SHE TOOK A FEW YEARS OFF WRITING.

Because so little of Austen's writing outside of her novels survives—her sister, Cassandra, purportedly destroyed much of her correspondence in an effort to keep some of Austen's scathing opinions away from polite society— it can be hard to assign motivations or emotions to some of her major milestones in life. But one thing appears clear: Following her father's death in 1805, Austen's writing habits were severely disrupted. Once prolific—early versions of three of her novels were completed by 1801—a lack of a routine kept her from producing work for roughly four years. It wasn't until she felt her home life was stable after moving into property owned by her brother, Edward, that Austen resumed her career.

4 AUSTEN USED STRAIGHT PINS TO EDIT HER MANUSCRIPTS.

Austen had none of the advancements that would go on to make a writer's life easier, like typewriters or computers. In at least one case, her manuscript edits were accomplished using the time-consuming and prickly method of straight pins. For an unfinished novel titled *The Watsons*, Austen took the pins and used them to fasten revisions to the pages of areas that were in need of correction or rewrites. The practice dates back to the seventeenth century.

5 SOME BELIEVE AUSTEN'S DEATH WAS A RESULT OF BEING POISONED.

Austen lived to see only four of her six novels published. She died on July 18, 1817 at the age of forty-one following complaints of symptoms that medical historians have long felt pointed to Addison's disease or Hodgkin's lymphoma. In 2017, the British Library floated a different theory—that Austen was poisoned by arsenic in her drinking water due to a polluted supply or possibly accidental ingestion due to mismanaged medication. Though they stop short of endorsing the idea, it was put forth based on Austen's notoriously poor eyesight (which they say may have been the result of cataracts) as well as her written complaint of skin discoloration. Both can be indicative of arsenic exposure. Critics of the theory say the evidence is scant and that there is equal reason to believe a disease was the cause of her death.

the byline of "A Lady," while later works like *Pride and Prejudice* featured credits like, "By the Author of *Sense and Sensibility*." Its likely Austen chose anonymity because female novelists were frowned upon for having selected what was viewed at the time as a potentially lewd, male-dominated pursuit (though it should be noted that around half of all novels of this time were published anonymously). Her nephew claimed that if she was interrupted while writing, she would quickly conceal her papers to avoid being asked about her work. Austen was first identified in print following her death in 1817, thanks to a eulogy accompanying the posthumous publications of *Persuasion* and *Northanger Abbey*.

The Real Mr. Darcy

Though Jane Austen never herself said who Mr. Darcy was based on (if anyone), some have speculated that it was Lefroy, the man Austen had flirted with at several holiday balls, who was the inspiration for the character. Austen certainly seemed smitten with him; in 1796, she wrote to her sister Cassandra that Lefroy "has but one fault, which time will, I trust, entirely remove—it is that his morning coat is a great deal too light."

If Austen and Lefroy were so well suited to each other, why didn't they end up together? The world may never know. In 1799, Lefroy—who would go on to become a politician and judge—married Mary Paul, whom some Austen scholars argue he had met and planned to marry long before meeting Austen (which is perhaps the reason why Austen and Lefroy had relatively few meetings).

A year after Lefroy's death in 1869, one of his nephews wrote to Austen's nephew to say: "My late venerable uncle . . . said in so many words that he was in love with [Jane], although he qualified his confession by saying it was a boyish love."

SHE SOLD HER COPYRIGHT FOR £110— BUT WANTED £150.

Austen sold the copyright for *Pride and Prejudice* to her publishers for £110, even though she said in a letter that she wanted £150. She chose this one-time payment, forfeiting any risk or reward connected to the future of the book. It was a bad gamble—the book was a best seller, and was on its third edition by 1817.

PRIDE AND PREJUDICE HAS BEEN ADAPTED HUNDREDS OF TIMES.

The adaptations of *Pride and Prejudice* seem endless (and sometimes bizarre). There have been at least eleven film and TV versions of the book, including the 1995 BBC miniseries starring Colin Firth as a memorable Darcy. Other (looser) adaptations include *Bridget Jones's Diary* (2001), *Pride and Prejudice and Zombies* (2016), the Bollywood-style movie *Bride and Prejudice* (2004), and the 2012-2013 web series *The Lizzie Bennet Diaries*.

Prejudice featured credits like, "By the Author of *Sense and Sensibility*." It's likely Austen chose anonymity because female novelists were frowned upon for having selected what was viewed at the time as a potentially lewd, male-dominated pursuit (though it should be noted that around half of all novels of this time were published anonymously). Her nephew claimed that if she was interrupted while writing, she would quickly conceal her papers to avoid being asked about her work. Austen was first identified in print following her death in 1817, thanks to a eulogy accompanying the posthumous publications of *Persuasion* and *Northanger Abbey*.

AUSTEN WORRIED THE NOVEL WAS TOO FRIVOLOUS.

Because *Pride and Prejudice* humorously deals with women getting married, it's often described as "chick lit," a label some fans find reductionist. But Austen herself worried the book wasn't serious enough. "The work is rather too light, and bright, and sparkling," she wrote. "It wants shade; it wants to be stretched out here and there with a long chapter of sense, if it could be had." Overall, though, Austen was "well satisfied enough" with the novel, especially with the character of Elizabeth. In another letter, she said, "I must confess that I think her as delightful a creature as ever appeared in print, and how I shall be able to tolerate those who do not like *her* at least I do not know."

PRIDE AND PREJUDICE'S GREATEST CRITICS

Pride and Prejudice is beloved by many, but not by all—including the following three literary titans, who had some very harsh things to say about Austen's book.

CHARLOTTE BRONTË

"**Why do you like Miss Austen so very much? I am puzzled on that point.**

What induced you to say you would rather have written *Pride and Prejudice* or *Tom Jones* than any of the Waverly Novels? I had not seen *Pride and Prejudice* till I read that sentence of yours, and then I got the book and studied it. And what did I find? An accurate daguerrotyped portrait of a common-place face; a carefully fenced, highly cultivated garden with near borders and delicate flowers—but no glance of a bright vivid physiognomy—no open country—no fresh air—no blue hill—no bonny beck. I should hardly like to live with her ladies and gentlemen in their elegant but confined houses."

—From an 1848 letter to friend and literary critic George Henry Lewes

MARK TWAIN

"**I haven't any right to criticize books, and I don't do it except when I hate them. I often want to criticize Jane Austen, but her books madden me so that I can't conceal my frenzy from the reader; and therefore I have to stop every time I begin.**

Every time I read *Pride and Prejudice* I want to dig her up and beat her over the skull with her own shin bone."

—From an 1898 letter

RALPH WALDO EMERSON

"**I am at a loss to understand why people hold Miss Austen's novels at so high a rate, which seems to me vulgar in tone, sterile in artistic invention, imprisoned in the wretched conventions of English society, without genius, wit, or knowledge of the world. Never was life so pinched and so narrow. The one problem in the mind of the writer in both of the stories I have read, *Persuasion* and *Pride and Prejudice*, is marriageableness ... Suicide is more respectable.**"

—From an 1861 journal entry

JESMYN WARD

April 1, 1977

BORN: Berkeley, California

OTHER NOTABLE WORKS:
Where the Line Bleeds (2008)
Men We Reaped (2013)
Sing, Unburied, Sing (2017)

When Jesmyn Ward was three years old, she and her parents moved from California's Bay Area to DeLisle, Mississippi, an unincorporated coastal town where both sides of her family had lived for generations. Many of DeLisle's residents were poor and Black, and Ward's experiences growing up in this rural, marginalized community would later inspire much of her work.

The eldest of four siblings, Ward loved reading from an early age, and her mother worked as a maid for a few families who paid for her to attend a private middle and high school. As one of the only Black students there, she often felt like an outsider—an impression that persisted through her years at Stanford University, where she rarely spoke in class.

After completing a bachelor's degree in English and a master's degree in communication, Ward returned to DeLisle to plot her next move; something practical, like law school. But when her younger brother was killed by a drunk driver, Ward surrendered to the underlying ache to share her community's stories with the world. She enrolled in an M.F.A. program at the University of Michigan, and she's been writing ever since. Ward has won two National Book Awards to date, for *Salvage the Bones* and *Sing, Unburied, Sing*.

In Ward's second novel, *Salvage the Bones*, a young Black teenager named Esch is living with her father and brothers in a low-income, rural patch of Mississippi when Hurricane Katrina arrives on the coast. As the family fights for survival, Esch carries the weight of another life-changing event: She's pregnant. Here's what you need to know about the book *The New York Times* called "a taut, wily novel, smartly plotted and voluptuously written."

WARD'S OWN EXPERIENCE IN HURRICANE KATRINA INSPIRED *SALVAGE THE BONES*.

Anyone who reads both *Salvage the Bones* and Ward's memoir, *Men We Reaped*, will pick up on a certain number of parallels between the fictional story of Esch and the author's real life. Ward also grew up with pit bulls, for example, and lived in a house on her grandmother's land in rural Mississippi. But the most notable similarity by far is that Ward herself was in Mississippi during Hurricane Katrina.

She had finished her MFA program and was spending some time back in DeLisle before returning to Ann Arbor, Michigan, to start teaching in the fall. Having no idea how severe the storm would be, Ward decided to stay put until after it passed. Once the hurricane hit, she and her family fled her grandmother's rapidly flooding house and ended up parking their trucks in a field (the white land owners claimed their house was too full to shelter any more people). Ward's family survived, but the trauma of the storm—and its aftermath—didn't easily fade.

"It took me a few years to commit to writing about the hurricane," Ward said in a 2011 radio interview for The World. "I think that the hurricane was so awful and so devastating that it actually silenced me for a while."

WARD'S CHARACTERS SOMETIMES SURPRISED HER.

The characters in *Salvage the Bones* took shape in ways that even their creator didn't always expect. Ward was surprised when Esch's mother, who dies in childbirth before the novel even begins, was still so present in the story; and she told *BOMB* Magazine that Esch's father just "walked on the page" as a weak character. When he began exhibiting small shows of strength later on, that surprised her, too.

And while Ward intentionally included Greek mythology in Esch's story to subvert the idea that those so-called "universal" classics are reserved for white authors, she didn't anticipate that her young protagonist would feel such a powerful connection to the myths, and relate to the sorceress Medea on such a personal level.

That said, Ward always knew that Esch would have an affinity for literature—just like Ward herself did.

BOIS SAUVAGE TRANSLATES TO *WILD WOOD*, A NOD TO DELISLE'S HISTORY.

Trying to separate Ward's work from her hometown of DeLisle would be about as easy as detaching a Charles Dickens novel from nineteenth-century industrial London. (In other words, not easy.) In *Salvage the Bones*—and in her other novels, too—Ward captures the varied struggles of life in the low-income area, where many locals are just scraping by and the pillowy humidity is both oppressive and comforting.

What she doesn't do is simply label the town "DeLisle." Instead, she presents a lightly fictionalized place called Bois Sauvage, French for *wild wood*. Not only does the name emulate the rural nature of the region, but it's also a subtle reference to the real-life history of DeLisle. When French explorers first settled there, they called it *La Riviere des Loups*, or *Wolf River*, which eventually became Wolf Town. Ward chose *sauvage* as a linguistic link to DeLisle's once-savage wildlife. The *salvage* in the novel's title is also a play on *savage*, a word that now often has a positive connotation.

"At home, among the young, there is honor in that term," Ward told *The Paris Review*. "It says that come hell or high water, Katrina or oil spill, hunger or heat, you are strong, you are fierce, and you possess hope."

7 NATIONAL BOOK AWARD WINNERS YOU SHOULD READ

Since its inception in 1950, The National Book Award in Fiction has recognized the best the world of literature has to offer. Dozens of influential authors—including Ward—have been honored for their achievements over the decades. Here are some of the standouts.

1 SUSAN CHOI //
Trust Exercise (2019)
Though *Trust Exercise* has all the trappings of a typical high-school drama, writer Susan Choi uses competing—and unreliable—narrators to explore how the different characters in the book perceive the truth. By building a narrative in the first half only to dismantle it later on, Choi leaves readers guessing until the end.

2 LOUISE ERDRICH //
The Round House (2012)
In *The Round House*, author Louise Erdrich journeys to the Ojibwe Native American reservation in North Dakota to tell a story about the ripple effects that one violent act has on the community. Confronting subjects like bigotry, injustice, and misogyny, this book is a microcosm of the larger issues facing society.

3 JONATHAN FRANZEN //
The Corrections (2001)
The Lambert family is beginning to fray: Alfred, the patriarch, is rapidly declining due to Parkinson's disease, while his three children are all on the East Coast and dealing with failing careers, troubled marriages, and worsening mental health. Despite everyone's private turmoil, Enid, Alfred's wife, attempts to convince her children to come home for one last Christmas.

4 JOYCE CAROL OATES //
Them (1970)
Them—you can almost hear the disgust in the title as author Joyce Carol Oates paints a version of America that is full of violence and desperation for the disenfranchised. Chronicling the ongoing tragedy of a dysfunctional working-class family in the middle of the twentieth century, this is a book that will break your heart one moment and repulse you the next.

5 THOMAS PYNCHON //
Gravity's Rainbow (1974)
Clocking in at over seven hundred pages and featuring a plot that can only be described as dense, *Gravity's Rainbow* isn't so much a book as it is an experience. It's full of biting satire, intense paranoia, and plenty of conversations about death—and depending on who you ask, it's either an unapproachable mess or the stuff of brilliance.

6 PHILIP ROTH //
Goodbye, Columbus (1960), *Sabbath's Theater* (1995)
The recipient of two National Book Awards, author Philip Roth won his first in 1960 for *Goodbye, Columbus*, a novella about the issues that two young Jewish Americans from different classes face after embarking on a summer romance. Then, in 1995, he won for *Sabbath's Theater*, a darkly comic novel about a depraved puppeteer searching for meaning in his autumn years.

7 SAUL BELLOW //
The Adventures of Augie March (1954), *Herzog* (1965), *Mr. Sammler's Planet* (1971)
Saul Bellow's first National Book Award came in 1954 for *The Adventures of Augie March*, a picturesque novel in the Dickensian mold that follows the spirited exploits of the titular Augie March. In 1965, he won for *Herzog*, in which he gets into the corroding mind of an academic in crisis by partially telling the story through the unsent letters he writes to friends, family, and enemies alike. And in 1971, he won his final National Book Award for a story about a world-weary Holocaust survivor in *Mr. Sammler's Planet*.

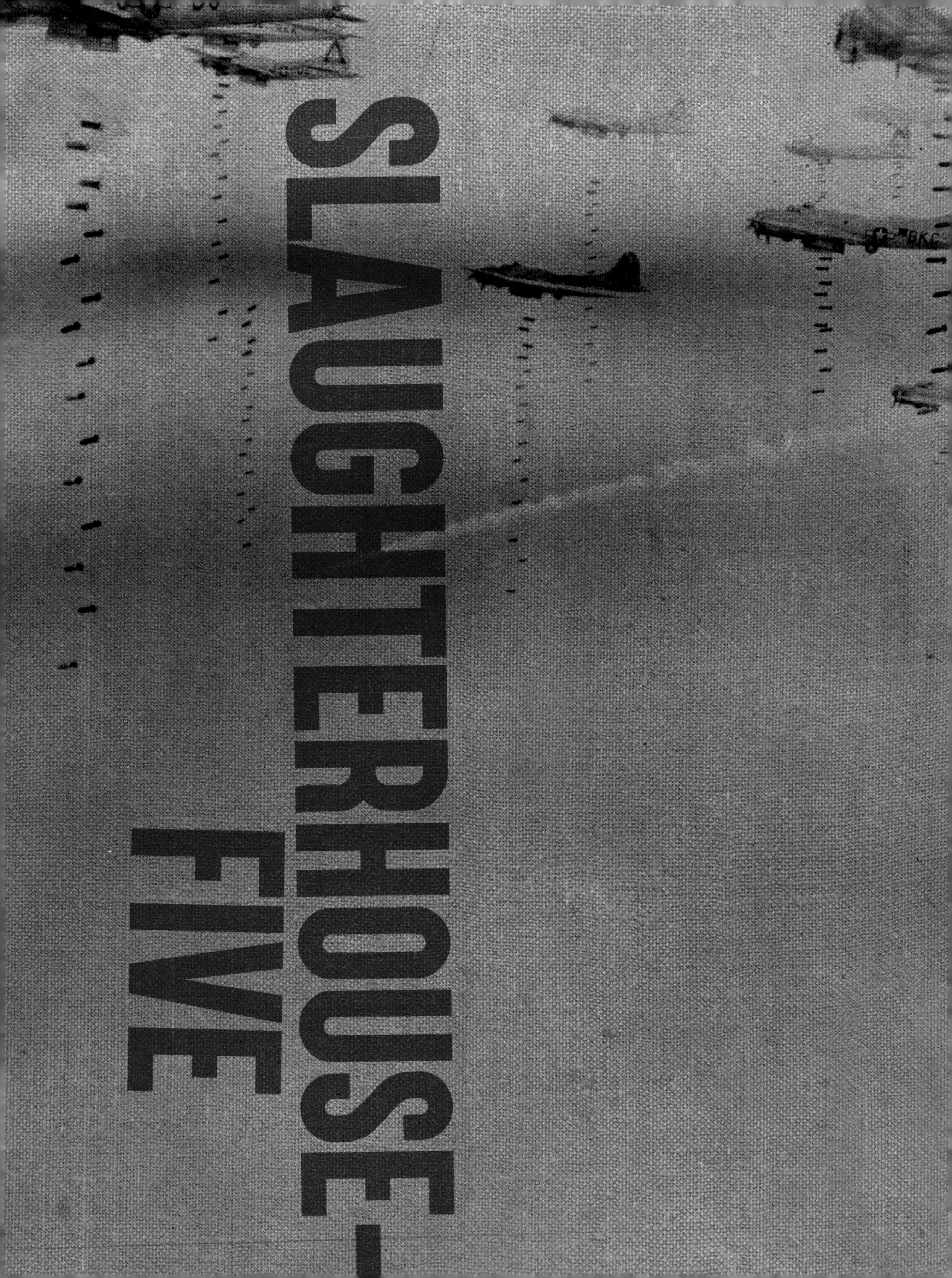
SLAUGHTERHOUSE-
FIVE

KURT VONNEGUT

November 11, 1922–April 11, 2007

BORN: Indianapolis, Indiana

OTHER NOTABLE WORKS:
The Sirens of Titan (1959)
Cat's Cradle (1963)

Kurt Vonnegut's career took off in the 1950s with the release of early sci-fi novels like *Player Piano* and *The Sirens of Titan*. As his work progressed, he started tackling loftier subject matter, such as religion and the arms race in 1963's *Cat's Cradle* and touching on his own experience as a POW in Dresden during World War II in 1969's *Slaughterhouse-Five*. Vonnegut continued his genre-bending work over the next few decades before eventually moving into non-fiction essays in 2005's *A Man Without a Country*. Despite his reputation as a curmudgeonly nihilist, Vonnegut was a champion for human decency, as summed up in one of his most famous quotes from 1965's *God Bless You, Mr. Rosewater*: "There's only one rule that I know of, babies—God damn it, you've got to be kind."

Based on his experiences as a prisoner of war during the Allied bombing of Dresden in 1945, Kurt Vonnegut's **Slaughterhouse-Five** is (rightfully) considered a modern literary masterpiece. It propelled Vonnegut to fame and literary acclaim.

The novel follows Billy Pilgrim, a man who has become "unstuck in time," and weaves together different periods of his life—his stint as a hapless soldier, his post-war optometry career, and a foray in an alien zoo where he served as an exhibit—with humor and profundity. "The inhumanity of many of man's inventions to man," Vonnegut wrote in 1994, "is the dominant theme of what I have written during the past forty-five years or so." Here are some things you might not know.

VONNEGUT'S POW EXPERIENCE LED TO THE BOOK.

When Vonnegut was flunking his classes at Cornell, he decided to drop out and join the army to fight in World War II. During the Battle of the Bulge in 1944, German forces captured him, along with other American prisoners of war, in Dresden. Forced to work long hours in a malt-syrup factory, he slept in a subterranean slaughterhouse. In a letter he later wrote to his family, Vonnegut described the unsanitary conditions, sadistic guards, and measly food rations. After surviving the February 1945 Allied bombing of Dresden, in which tens of thousands of people were killed, Vonnegut was forced by his captors to remove jewelry from the corpses before cremating them. "One hundred thirty thousand corpses were hidden underground. It was a terribly elaborate Easter-egg hunt," he said in an interview with *The Paris Review*.

In a "Special Message" penned for the Franklin Library's limited edition of *Slaughterhouse-Five*, Vonnegut writes, "The Dresden atrocity, tremendously expensive and meticulously planned, was so meaningless, finally, that only one person on the entire planet got any benefit from it. I am that person. I wrote this book, which earned a lot of money for me and made my reputation, such as it is . . . One way or another, I got two or three dollars for every person killed. Some business I'm in."

THE BOOK WAS JUMPSTARTED IN IOWA.

After repeated and failed attempts to start his "Dresden book," Vonnegut finally began what would become *Slaughterhouse-Five* during a two-year teaching stint at the University of Iowa Writers' Workshop. He had stopped writing fiction and was in a considerable funk when he accepted the invitation, offered by his former editor George Starbuck, who was a full-time professor of English at the university.

Vonnegut credited the program for rekindling his love of literature: "Suddenly writing seemed very important again. This was better than a transplant of monkey glands for a man my age," he said. Vonnegut became friends with Nelson Algren, Jose Donoso, Vance Bourjaily, Donald Justice, and Richard Yates while there, and some of his students included Gail Godwin, John Irving, Jonathan Penner, Bruce Dobler, John Casey, and Jane Casey.

THE BOOK MIXES FACT AND FICTION.

The character "Wild Bob" is based on William Joseph Cody Garlow, grandson of Buffalo Bill Cody and commander of the 423rd regiment in World War II. A private in that regiment, Vonnegut was captured along with Garlow on December 19, 1944 at the Battle of the Bulge.

While Vonnegut fills the novel with non-fiction asides and excerpts from real accounts, the pornographic postcard carried around by Roland Weary depicting a woman with a pony flanked by doric columns is non-existent; the story of the photographer André Le Fèvre is completely fictionalized. However, the name "André Le Fèvre" may come from André Lefèvre, a famous French scoutmaster—the equivalent of a Boy Scout leader.

SLAUGHTERHOUSE-FIVE WAS AN IMMEDIATE BEST SELLER.

Published on March 31, 1969, *Slaughterhouse-Five* became an instant and surprise hit. It spent sixteen weeks on *The New York Times*'s best-seller list and went through five printings by July.

The novel owes much of its immediate success to two rave reviews; one in *The New York Times Book Review*, which was featured on the section's front page, and another in the *Saturday Review*. Robert Scholes, who wrote the *Times* review, was a colleague of Vonnegut's at Iowa. As Jerome Kinkowitz writes in *Vonnegut in Fact*, "A correlation exists between the first two major reviews of *Slaughterhouse-Five*: Each was written by a critic who had heard Vonnegut speak to audiences, and who had been, moreover, deeply impressed by the personal voice in the author's fictive statement."

THE BOOK IS FREQUENTLY BANNED.

Slaughterhouse-Five was banned from Oakland County, Michigan, public schools in 1972. The circuit judge there accused the novel of being "depraved, immoral, psychotic, vulgar, and anti-Christian." In 1973, a school board in North Dakota immolated thirty-two copies of the book in the high school's coal burner.

"My books are being thrown out of school libraries all over the country—because they're supposedly obscene," Vonnegut told the *Paris Review*. "I've seen letters to small-town newspapers that put *Slaughterhouse-Five* in the same class with *Deep Throat* and *Hustler* magazine. How could anybody masturbate to *Slaughterhouse-Five*?"

The American Library Association listed the book as the forty-sixth most banned or challenged book of the first decade of the twenty-first century, and *Slaughterhouse-Five* is still being banned in schools. In 2011, Wesley Scroggins, a professor at Missouri State University, called on the Republic, Missouri, school board to ban Vonnegut's novel. He wrote in the local paper, "This is a book that contains so much profane language, it would make a sailor blush with shame. The 'f word' is plastered on almost every other page. The content ranges from naked men and women in cages together so that others can watch them having sex to God telling people that they better not mess with his loser, bum of a son, named Jesus Christ." The board eventually voted to remove the novel from the high school curriculum and its library.

In response to this ban, the Kurt Vonnegut Memorial Library in Indianapolis gave away 150 free copies of *Slaughterhouse-Five* to Republic, Missouri, students who wanted to read it.

"So it goes."

The book's melancholic refrain appears in the text 106 times

Fascinating Facts about Kurt Vonnegut

Kurt Vonnegut filled his novels, plays, and short stories with irreverence, satire, and wry wit. He wrote about dystopian societies, disillusionment with war, and skepticism, particularly connecting with millions of readers in the 1960s counterculture. Here are a few facts you may not know about him.

1 HE MET HIS FIRST WIFE IN KINDERGARTEN.

Vonnegut was born in Indianapolis, Indiana, in 1922, and he met his future wife, Jane, in kindergarten. Although they dated as teenagers in high school, their relationship paused when Vonnegut went to Cornell University, dropped out to serve in World War II, and became a prisoner of war in Germany. After returning to the US, he married Jane in 1945. The couple had six children—three biological and three adopted—but divorced in 1979.

2 HIS MOTHER DIED BY SUICIDE ON MOTHER'S DAY.

When Vonnegut was born, his parents were well-off. Kurt Sr., his father, was an architect and Edith, his mother, was independently wealthy from the brewery that her family owned. But due to Prohibition and the Great Depression, the family struggled to make ends meet, sold their home, and switched their son to a public school. Edith, who suffered from mental illness, became addicted to alcohol and prescription pills. In 1944, when Vonnegut came home from military training to celebrate Mother's Day, he found Edith had died by suicide. The twenty-one-year-old Vonnegut soon

went to Germany to fight in World War II. In an interview with *The Paris Review*, Vonnegut remembered his mother as being highly intelligent, cultivated, and a good writer. "I only wish she'd lived to see [my writing career]. I only wish she'd lived to see all her grandchildren," he said.

3 VONNEGUT ADOPTED HIS SISTER'S THREE KIDS.

In the late 1950s, Vonnegut's sister, Alice, died of cancer and Alice's husband died in a train accident within the span of a few days. Although Vonnegut already had three children with his wife, he adopted his sister's three sons. Since he now had six children to support, Vonnegut spent even more time writing to earn money.

4 HE ATTEMPTED SUICIDE.

Vonnegut struggled with depression in the midst of his literary success. After separating from his wife in 1971, he lived alone in New York City and had trouble writing, and his son was diagnosed with schizophrenia (though his son later said his symptoms are more consistent with bipolar disorder). Vonnegut married his second wife in 1979 and they adopted a daughter together, but his depression got worse, and in 1984, he tried to kill himself,

an experience he wrote about in 1991's essay collection *Fates Worse Than Death*.

5 HE GRADED ALL HIS BOOKS.

In an interview with Charlie Rose, Vonnegut discussed his grading system for his books (he also wrote about this system in *Palm Sunday*, a collection of his works published in 1981). He gave himself an A+ for his writing in *Cat's Cradle* and *Slaughterhouse-Five*, but in *Palm Sunday* he gave *Happy Birthday, Wanda June* and *Slapstick* Ds.

6 EVEN DEAD, HE HAS OVER 214,000 TWITTER FOLLOWERS.

Wake up, you idiots! Whatever made you think that money was so valuable?
— *Kurt Vonnegut (@Kurt_Vonnegut) November 11, 2017*
Although Vonnegut died in 2007 at eighty-four years old, his ideas live on in 280 characters or less. A Twitter account dedicated to the writer tweets his quotes several times a day to more than 214,000 followers. Examples of his tweets? "How embarrassing to be human," and "We could have saved the Earth but we were too damned cheap." Fittingly, the account follows just one person, @TheMarkTwain, for Vonnegut greatly admired the *Tom Sawyer* and *Huckleberry Finn* author.

KURT VONNEGUT QUOTES ABOUT WRITERS AND WRITING

"I get up at 7:30 and work four hours a day. Nine to twelve in the morning, five to six in the evening. Businessmen would achieve better results if they studied human metabolism.

No one works well eight hours a day.

No one ought to work more than four hours."

—*To Robert Taylor*. Boston Globe Magazine. *July 20, 1969.*

"Nothing in real life ends.

That's the horrible part of being in the short-story business—you have to be a real expert on ends. 'Millicent at last understands.' Nobody ever understands."

—*To Mel Gussow*. The New York Times. *October 6, 1970.*

"When I used to teach creative writing, I would tell the students to make their characters want something right away—even if it's only a glass of water.

Characters paralyzed by the meaningless of modern life still have to drink water from time to time."

—*To* The Paris Review. *Spring 1977.*

"I try to keep deep love out of my stories because, once that particular subject comes up, it is almost impossible to talk about anything else. Readers don't want to hear about anything else. They go gaga about love. If a lover in a story wins his true love, that's the end of the tale, even if World War III is about to begin, and the sky is black with flying saucers."

—*To* The Paris Review. *Spring 1977.*

D.H. LAWRENCE

September 11, 1885–March 2, 1930

BORN: Eastwood, Nottinghamshire, England

OTHER NOTABLE WORKS:
The Rainbow (1915)
Women in Love (1920)
Lady Chatterley's Lover (1928)

SONS AND LOVERS

D.H. Lawrence often used his coal mining hometown as inspiration. Two years after he started writing at the encouragement his friend Jessie Chambers, he published his first piece in a newspaper in 1907. He earned his teacher's certificate from the University College, Nottingham, graduating in 1908 and moving to London, where he wrote poetry and short stories and was published in *The English Review.*

In 1911, he published his first novel, *The White Peacock.* It was the beginning of a long and controversial career that culminated with his last major novel, 1928's *Lady Chatterley's Lover*—which, due to its erotic content, was banned in America until 1959. Today, D.H. Lawrence is widely considered one of the twentieth century's most influential writers, and his third novel, *Sons and Lovers,* is regarded as a masterpiece.

In *Sons and Lovers*, Gertrude Morel—trapped in an unhappy marriage—shifts her affections for her husband to her older son William. When he dies, her younger son Paul becomes the object of her love. As he grows up, Paul is forced to reconcile his unconventional relationship with his mother and his sexual attraction to other women. Here's what you should know about the novel.

THE BOOK IS SEMI-AUTOBIOGRAPHICAL.

Sons and Lovers draws heavily from the characteristics of Lawrence's own life. His father Arthur was a coal miner in a colliery near Nottingham, England. His mother Lydia came from a middle-class family, but a machinery accident had put her father out of work and the family's financial status suffered. Still, many people in their town felt that Lydia had married beneath her.

Their marriage was not happy. While Lydia drifted away from her husband, she transferred her affection to her two younger sons, Ernest and David Herbert (or D.H.). She saw a pathway back to respectability through the achievements of her children. But in 1901, Ernest died from an infection, and D.H. came down with life-threatening pneumonia. Lydia assuaged her grief over losing her older son by nursing her younger son back to health. From then on, their bond was so tight that it stood in the way of D.H's full coming of age.

All of these themes appear in *Sons and Lovers*, published in 1913. The protagonist, Paul Morel, is a stand-in for the author. Morel's working-class background and unbalanced family dynamics drive the tension between his love for his mother and his search for marriage and sexual fulfillment. He forms a new relationship with a country girl, Miriam (who represented Lawrence's real-life friend Chambers), and has a steamy affair with a sophisticated feminist, Clara (a stand-in for his eventual wife, Frieda, a German aristocrat). But Morel cannot find peace with either, and returns to his mother's orbit just before she dies of cancer and leaves him completely alone. In real life, Lydia's death in 1910 had a similarly traumatic effect on Lawrence.

AN OEDIPUS COMPLEX IS CENTRAL TO THE PLOT OF *SONS AND LOVERS.*

Sigmund Freud coined the phrase *Oedipus complex* to describe a child's psychosexual feelings for his or her parent of the opposite sex and rivalry with the parent of the same sex. Freud suggested that these feelings are a normal part of a child's psychological development from age three to five. In Lawrence's case, they lasted much, much longer.

Lawrence learned of this concept from Frieda and, recognizing it as a theme in his own life, explored it in *Sons and Lovers.* He described how the Oedipus complex features prominently in the plot: "As [the mother's] sons grow up she selects them as lovers—first the eldest, then the second. These sons are *urged* into life by their reciprocal love of their mother—urged on and on. But when they come to manhood, they can't love, because their mother is the strongest power in their lives, and holds them."

NOT EVERYONE THOUGHT *SONS AND LOVERS* WAS A WORK OF GENIUS.

Duckworth & Co., the publisher of *Sons and Lovers*, ran newspaper ads in 1913 touting the novel with reviewers' rosy comments. "The mother of the family is a wonderful piece of portraiture," the *Westminster Gazette* opined, while the *Standard* gushed, "*Sons and Lovers* is a great book. No other English novelist of our time has so great a power. Mr. Lawrence shows that he is a master."

The Guardian was not as taken with the book's modernist structure or analysis of family life, however. "The constant juxtaposition of love and hatred looks like an obsession, and like all obsessions, soon becomes tiresome," its reviewer wrote. "It has no particular shape and no recognizable plot; themes are casually taken up, and then as casually drop[ped], and there seems no reason why they should have been taken up unless they were to be kept up."

FIVE MEMORABLE D.H. LAWRENCE QUOTES

D.H. Lawrence was much more than a novelist: He was also a prolific playwright, poet, literary critic, and painter. Here are five memorable quotes from the famously controversial author.

ON THE ROOT OF ALL THINGS
"The fairest thing in nature, a flower, still has its roots in earth and manure."
—*From the introduction to* Pansies

ON EMBRACING PASSION
"Be still when you have nothing to say; when genuine passion moves you, say what you've got to say, and say it hot."
—*From* Studies in American Literature

ON MONEY
"Money poisons you when you've got it, and starves you when you haven't."
—*From* Lady Chatterley's Lover

ON FINDING LOVE
"Those that go searching for love
Only make manifest their own lovelessness,
And the loveless never find love,
Only the loving find love,
And they never have to seek for it."
— "Search for Love" *from*
The Complete Poems of D.H. Lawrence

ON DREAMS
"I can never decide whether my dreams are the result of my thoughts, or my thoughts the result of my dreams."
—*From a 1912 letter*

THE ADVENTURES OF HUCKLEBERRY FINN

MARK TWAIN

November 30, 1835–April 21, 1910

BORN: Florida, Missouri

OTHER NOTABLE WORKS:
The Adventures of Tom Sawyer (1876)
A Connecticut Yankee in King Arthur's Court (1889)

Samuel Clemens's "school days ended when he was twelve," according to *The New York Times*. His first job, working as a printer at local newspapers, may have spoken to an interest in letters, but it was his next position, as a steamboat pilot on the Mississippi River, that led most directly to his later literary work, especially in his memoir, *Life on the Mississippi*. His time on the river could have also given Clemens his pen name, Mark Twain—a moniker that would earn great renown, first as the author of humorous short stories like "Jim Smiley and His Jumping Frog," and later for his pivotal contribution to American literature, *The Adventures of Huckleberry Finn*. Sometime between the publication of those two pieces, Twain became a celebrity, partially through public performances around the country (and, eventually, around the world). Befitting a comic voice that influenced generations of writers, many commenters have read these traveling lectures as a precursor to modern standup comedy.

On its surface, Mark Twain's *The Adventures of Huckleberry Finn* is a straightforward story about a boy and a fugitive from slavery floating down the Mississippi River. But underneath, the book—which was published in the US on February 18, 1885—is a subversive confrontation of slavery and racism. It remains one of the most loved, and most banned, books in American history.

HUCKLEBERRY FINN MAY BE BASED ON MARK TWAIN'S CHILDHOOD FRIEND.

Twain once said that Huck is based on Tom Blankenship, a childhood friend whose father, Woodson Blankenship, was a poor drunkard and the likely model for Pap Finn. "In *Huckleberry Finn* I have drawn Tom Blankenship exactly as he was," Twain wrote in his autobiography. "He was ignorant, unwashed, insufficiently fed; but he had as good a heart as ever any boy had." However, Twain may be exaggerating here. In 1885, when the *Minneapolis Tribune* asked who Huck was based on, Twain indicated it was no single person: "I could not point you out the youngster all in a lump; but still his story is what I call a true story."

IT TOOK TWAIN SEVEN YEARS TO WRITE THE BOOK.

Huckleberry Finn was written in two short bursts. The first was in 1876, when Twain wrote four hundred pages that he told his friend he liked "only tolerably well, as far as I have got, and may possibly pigeonhole or burn" the manuscript. He stopped working on it for several years to write *The Prince and the Pauper* and *Life on the Mississippi* and to recharge in Germany. In 1882, Twain took a steamboat ride on the Mississippi from New Orleans to Minnesota, with a stop in Hannibal, Missouri. It must have inspired him, because he dove into finishing *Huckleberry Finn*.

"I have written eight or nine hundred manuscript pages in such a brief space of time that I mustn't name the number of days," Twain wrote in August 1883. "I shouldn't believe it myself, and of course couldn't expect you to." The book was published in 1884 in the UK and 1885 in America.

LIKE HUCK, TWAIN'S VIEW ON SLAVERY CHANGED.

Huck, who grows up in the South before the Civil War, not only accepts slavery, but believes that helping Jim run away is a sin. The moral climax of the novel is when Huck debates whether to send Jim's enslaver a letter detailing his whereabouts. Finally, Huck says, "All right, then, I'll go to hell," and tears the letter up.

As a child, Twain didn't question the institution of slavery. Not only was Missouri a slave state, but his uncle owned twenty enslaved people. In *Autobiography of Mark Twain, Volume 1,* Twain wrote, "I vividly remember seeing a dozen black men and women chained to one another, once, and lying in a group on the pavement, awaiting shipment to the Southern slave market. Those were the saddest faces I have ever seen." At some point, Twain's attitudes changed and he married into an abolitionist family. His father-in-law, Jervis Langdon, was a "conductor" on the Underground Railroad and helped Frederick Douglass escape from slavery.

MANY CONSIDER *HUCKLEBERRY FINN* TO BE THE FIRST TRUE "AMERICAN" NOVEL.

"All modern American literature comes from one book by Mark Twain called *Huckleberry Finn*," Ernest Hemingway wrote in *Green Hills Of Africa*. "There was nothing before. There has been nothing as good since." While this statement ignores great works like *The Scarlet Letter*, *Huckleberry Finn* was notable because it's considered the first major novel to be written in the American vernacular. Huck speaks in dialect, using phrases like "it ain't no matter" or "it warn't no time to be sentimentering." Since most writers of the time were still imitating European literature, writing the way

Americans actually talked seemed revolutionary. It was language that was clear, crisp, and vivid, and it changed how Americans wrote.

MANY PEOPLE CONSIDER THE END OF THE BOOK TO BE A BIT OF A COP-OUT.

A major criticism of *Huckleberry Finn* is that the book begins to fail when Tom Sawyer enters the novel. Up until that point, Huck and Jim have developed a friendship bound by their mutual plight as runaways. We believe Huck cares about Jim and has learned to see his humanity. But when Tom Sawyer comes into the novel, Huck changes. He becomes passive and doesn't even seem to care when Jim is captured. To make matters worse, it turns out that Jim's owner has already set him free, and that Huck's abusive dad is dead. Essentially, Huck and Jim have been running away from nothing. Many critics, including American novelist Jane Smiley, believe that by slapping on a happy ending, Twain was ignoring the complex questions his book raises.

THE BOOK IS FREQUENTLY BANNED.

Huckleberry Finn was first banned in Concord, Massachusetts, in 1885 ("trash and suitable only for the slums") and continues to be one of the most-challenged books. Some say that the portrayal of African Americans is stereotypical, racially insensitive, or racist. And there are objections over the n-word, which occurs over two hundred times in the book. In 2011, Alan Gribben, a professor at Auburn University, published a version of the book that replaced that offending word with *slave*. Around the same time came *The Hipster Huckleberry Finn*, where the word was replaced with *hipster*. The book's description says, "the adventures of Huckleberry Finn are now neither offensive nor uncool."

A PENIS DRAWING ALMOST RUINED ITS PUBLICATION

Twain, who ran his own publishing firm, hired twenty-three-year-old E.W. Kemble to illustrate the first edition of *Huckleberry Finn*. Right as the book went to press, someone—it was never discovered who—added a penis to the illustration of Uncle Silas. The engraving shows Uncle Silas talking to Huck and Aunt Sally while a crude penis bulges from his pants.

According to Twain's business manager Charles Webster, 250 books were sent out before the mistake was caught. They were recalled and publication was postponed for a reprint. If the full run had been sent out, Webster said, Twain's "credit for decency and morality would have been destroyed."

Fascinating Facts about Mark Twain

Mark Twain's rollicking tales aren't the only legacy he left behind. His poignant quotes and witticisms have been told and retold (sometimes erroneously) over the last century and a half, and over the course of his legendary career, Twain wrote more than a dozen novels plus countless short stories and essays and still found time to invent new products, hang out with famous scientists, and look after a house full of cats.

1 "MARK TWAIN" IS A NAUTICAL REFERENCE.

Like many of history's literary greats, Samuel Langhorne Clemens decided to assume an alias early on in his writing career. He tried out a few different *noms de plume*—Thomas Jefferson Snodgrass, Sergeant Fathom, and, more plainly, Josh—before settling on Mark Twain, which means two fathoms (twelve feet) deep in boating jargon. Where Mark Twain picked up the name has long been debated—one popular nineteenth century story was that he'd walk into a bar and call out, "mark twain!," prompting the bartender to take a piece of chalk and make two marks on a wall for twain—two—drinks. Twain denied this, however, saying that he swiped it from a captain named Isaiah Sellers who used it at the *New Orleans Picayune*. But according to the *LA Review of Books*, there's no evidence Sellers used that name, and stories of Twain picking it up while working as a steamboat pilot are unlikely, because mark twain was a relatively uncommon term at the time. Instead, it's possible that he stole it from an 1861 maritime sketch in a magazine—or some as-yet-unknown origin.

2 A STORY HE HEARD IN A BAR LED TO HIS BIG BREAK.

In 1864, Twain headed to Calaveras County, California, in hopes of striking gold as a prospector (he didn't). However, it was during his time there that he heard the bartender of the Angels Hotel in Angels Camp share an incredulous story about a frog-jumping contest. Twain recounted the tale in his own words in "Jim Smiley and His Jumping Frog" (later retitled "The Celebrated Jumping Frog of Calaveras County"). It was published in 1865 in *The New York Saturday Press* and went on to receive national acclaim.

3 TWAIN CREATED "IMPROVED" SCRAPBOOKS AND SUSPENDERS.

Twain tinkered at inventions and patented two products. One was inspired by his love of scrapbooking, while the other came about from his hatred of suspenders. He designed a self-adhesive scrapbook that works like an envelope, which netted him about $50,000. His "improvement in adjustable and detachable straps for garments" also ended up being useful, but for an entirely different purpose than Twain originally intended. According to *The Atlantic*, "This clever invention only caught on for one snug garment: the bra. For those with little brassiere experience, not a button, nor a snap, but a clasp is all that secures that elastic band, which holds up women's breasts. So not-so-dexterous ladies and gents, you can thank Mark Twain for that."

4 THOMAS EDISON FILMED TWAIN AT HOME.

Only one video of Twain exists, and it was shot by none other than his close friend Thomas Edison. The footage was captured in 1909—one year before the author died—at Twain's estate in Redding, Connecticut. He's seen sporting a light-colored suit and his usual walrus mustache, and one scene shows him with his daughters, Clara and Jean. On a separate occasion that same year, Edison recorded Twain as he read stories into a phonograph, but those audio clips were destroyed in a fire. No other recording of Twain's voice exists.

5 TWAIN ACCURATELY PREDICTED WHEN HE WOULD DIE.

Twain was born on November 30, 1835, just weeks after Halley's Comet was at perihelion (the point at which it was closest to the sun). It appears roughly every 75 years, and Twain predicted he would die the next time it graced the sky. As he put it in 1909, "I came in with Halley's Comet in 1835. It is coming again next year, and I expect to go out with it. It will be the greatest disappointment of my life if I don't go out with Halley's Comet. The Almighty has said, no doubt: 'Now here are these two unaccountable freaks; they came in together, they must go out together.' Oh, I am looking forward to that." He ended up passing away at his Connecticut home on April 21, 1910, one day after Halley's Comet's perihelion.

THREE THINGS MARK TWAIN DIDN'T REALLY SAY

Mark Twain provided us with some of the best quips of all-time—but he's also one of the most misquoted people who ever lived. Here are three quotes the author likely never uttered, despite popular belief.

"The secret of getting ahead is getting started."

This quote has also been attributed to Agatha Christie, though neither source can be verified as the author of this line.

WHAT MARK TWAIN *DID* SAY:

"Never put off till to-morrow what you can do day after to-morrow just as well."

—*From an 1870 article in* The Galaxy

"There are three kinds of lies: lies, damned lies, and statistics."

Twain did make this observation, but denied inventing it—he claimed British politician Benjamin Disraeli was the one who created it (though that is likely incorrect, too). It is thanks to Twain, however, that the saying became popular in the US.

WHAT MARK TWAIN *DID* SAY:

"Yes, even I am dishonest. Not in many ways, but in some. Forty-one, I think it is."

—*From a 1905 Letter to Joseph Twichell*

"Twenty years from now you will be more disappointed by the things you didn't do than by the ones you did do."

WHAT MARK TWAIN *DID* SAY:

"One cannot have everything the way he would like it. A man has no business to be depressed by a disappointment, anyway; he ought to make up his mind to get even."

—*From* A Connecticut Yankee in King Arthur's Court

THE ADVENTURES OF SHERLOCK HOLMES

ARTHUR CONAN DOYLE

May 22, 1859–July 7, 1930

BORN: Edinburgh, Scotland

OTHER NOTABLE WORKS:
The White Company (1891)
The Stark Munro Letters (1895)
The Lost World (1912)

Arthur Ignatius Conan Doyle transcended an often-chaotic early life to create one of the most beloved characters in English literature: Sherlock Holmes.

Growing up, Doyle shuttled between boarding schools until enrolling at the University of Edinburgh to study medicine. He began writing and publishing short stories while he was still a student. In 1887, Doyle published *A Study in Scarlet*, the first appearance of the enigmatic sleuth Sherlock Holmes and his trusty assistant and friend Dr. Watson. Doyle followed it with three more novels and fifty-six short stories featuring Holmes. Controversially, Doyle killed his hero in the short story *The Final Problem* in 1893. The public was so upset that he brought Holmes back for the terrifying masterpiece *The Hound of the Baskervilles*. He continued to write Holmes stories for serialization in *The Strand Magazine* until 1927.

Doyle also wrote historical fiction, autobiographies, histories, plays, mysteries, and true crime accounts. He was also drawn to spiritualism, and he wrote several books on the subject toward the end of his own life. He died in 1930 at his home in what is now East Sussex.

There is perhaps no more iconic detective than Sherlock Holmes, a keenly observant sleuth with remarkable deductive reasoning skills.

The Adventures of Sherlock Holmes

is a collection of short stories, with each tale recalling how Holmes and Watson solve crimes and attempt to right social wrongs. The duo encounter everything from a Bohemian king on a quest to recover a racy photograph to a governess working a dodgy job.

SHERLOCK HOLMES WAS INSPIRED BY A REAL PERSON.

Arthur Conan Doyle based the character of Sherlock Holmes at least in part on Dr. Joseph Bell, a surgeon and professor at Edinburgh's Royal College of Surgeons. Doyle, his student, was captivated by Bell's observational acuity and ability to diagnose illnesses with just a few clues. Bell also studied handwriting analysis and dialectology (the art of identifying one's origin by their words and accent), which added to his diagnostic powers. "Poe's masterful detective, M. Dupin, had from boyhood been one of my heroes. But could I bring an addition of my own? I thought of my old teacher Joe Bell, of his eagle face, of his curious ways, of his eerie trick of spotting details. If he were a detective, he would surely reduce this fascinating but unorganized business to something nearer an exact science . . . such examples as Bell gave us every day in the wards," Doyle wrote in *Collier's Magazine* in 1923.

HOLMES WAS THE FIRST FICTIONAL SLEUTH TO USE A MAGNIFYING GLASS.

When he whips out his magnifying glass in *A Study in Scarlet*, Holmes became the first detective in a work of fiction to use one on a case. Magnifying glasses had been used for hundreds of years in microscopy and allowed scholars to observe the world more closely. With magnifying lenses, scientists could form theories using evidence that was not visible with the naked eye. Doyle, as a practicing physician, knew all about the use of microscopy in medicine. When he put the magnifying glass into Holmes's hands, he signaled to readers that the detective would make scientific observations of the crime scenes and solve cases based on the evidence.

HOLMES IS THE MOST-DEPICTED HUMAN LITERARY CHARACTER.

Sherlock Holmes holds the Guinness World Record as the "most-portrayed human literary character" in television and film, with more than 254 depictions. In 1899, American actor William Gillette collaborated with Doyle on the first official Holmes play, titled *Sherlock Holmes*, which Gillette starred in; the actor introduced several motifs that are now synonymous with Holmes, including the deerstalker cap, curved pipe, and cloak (though cloaks and deerstalkers did make appearances in some early illustrations of Doyle's stories). Actors Basil Rathbone and Nigel Bruce enjoyed a long string of movies playing Holmes and Watson, respectively, in the 1940s. More recently, Benedict Cumberbatch and Robert Downey Jr. have played the famed sleuth. But Holmes isn't the most-portrayed of *any* literary character—that record belongs to Dracula.

HOLMES NEVER ACTUALLY SAYS "ELEMENTARY, MY DEAR WATSON."

The detective has become a subject of the Mandela Effect—a phenomenon in which people collectively misremember things like famous phrases. Holmes often calls his devoted sidekick "my dear Watson," and describes his amazing powers of deduction and talent for solving cases as "elementary." But in the original four novels and fifty-six stories, Holmes never puts the two phrases together. In Doyle's "The Crooked Man" Holmes says both "my dear Watson" and then a few

sentences later "Elementary," but not the full phrase. Some historians point to a 1929 film, *The Return of Sherlock Holmes*, as the first instance in which Holmes speaks the full phrase, but others note the phrase was being used and parodied from at least twenty years prior. Swedish Sherlockian Mattias Boström, author of *From Holmes to Sherlock*, suspects William Gillette as the source of the phrase as well, though actual hard evidence is lacking.

PAULO COELHO

August 24, 1947

BORN: Rio de Janeiro, Brazil

OTHER NOTABLE WORKS:
Brida (1978)
The Pilgrimage (1990)
The Devil and Miss Prym (2000)

From a young age, Paulo Coelho knew he wanted to write—but he wouldn't actually become a writer until later in life, after a spiritual awakening. Once he made the leap, he wanted his written work to be widely shared; not only did he work with local publishers and help ensure *The Alchemist* would be affordable for a wide audience, he also advocated for pirating his own prose. Coelho went as far as to launch a site that collected pirated editions of the book and audiobook that anyone could easily download. His tips for other writers are fitting for a person who has eschewed a traditional life. "Writers . . . need to understand that before putting anything down on paper, they should be free enough to change direction as their imagination wanders," he once wrote. "When a sentence comes to an end, the writer should tell himself: 'While I was writing I traveled a long road. Now I can finish this paragraph in the full awareness that I have risked enough and given the best of myself.'"

In Brazilian author Paulo Coelho's allegorical novel, *The Alchemist*, a Spanish shepherd named Santiago sets off for the Egyptian pyramids after having a recurring dream about treasure. Guided by omens, he travels the desert, encountering luck, loss, love, and a wise old alchemist while fulfilling his destiny. The book has inspired millions of readers to set out searching for their own personal treasures. Here are a few things you may not know about the literary blockbuster.

COELHO ONLY NEEDED TWO WEEKS TO WRITE THE NOVEL.

In 2009, the author explained to *The Guardian* that he was able to write *The Alchemist* so quickly because, as he put it, "The book was already written in my soul."

IT WAS NOT AN INSTANT SUCCESS.

The Alchemist's journey to becoming a commercial juggernaut almost reads like its own Coelho story. When a small Brazilian publisher took a chance on the book in 1988, it hedged its bets by only printing nine hundred copies. After that tiny first run, the book went out of print, and Coelho got to keep the rights to the novel.

In a new foreword written in 2014, Coelho explained his situation after his publisher dropped *The Alchemist*: "I was forty-one and desperate. But I never lost faith in the book or ever wavered in my vision. Why? Because it was me in there, all of me, heart and soul. I was living my own metaphor."

A SECOND BRAZILIAN PUBLISHER GAVE COELHO ANOTHER SHOT.

As Coelho would later write, the fate of the book proved the book's recurring theme of "when you want something, the whole universe conspires to help you." Another local publishing house agreed to back the book. The second publishing run fared better than the first, and eventually thousands of copies were being sold.

THE ENGLISH TRANSLATION WAS THE BIG BREAK COELHO NEEDED.

Coelho writes that eight months after the rerelease of *The Alchemist*, an American tourist found the book and wanted to help him find an American publisher for an English translation. HarperCollins took on the project, and Coelho would later credit the 1993 release of the English version with catapulting the novel to new heights. As he told *The New York Times* in 1999, "To have a book published in more than 119 countries, you need to have a language that can be read in Thailand or Lithuania. Translation into English made it possible for other editors to read me."

THE BOOK'S SUCCESS WAS STAGGERING.

If Coelho's Personal Legend involved selling millions of books, he certainly followed it. *The Alchemist* spent over three hundred weeks on *The New York Times*'s best-seller list. The 1994 French translation was a similar smash. The book gradually spread through the rest of Europe, finding great success in each new market. By 2002 a Portuguese literary journal determined it was the best-selling book in the history of the language.

WIDE TRANSLATION HELPED COELHO SET A WORLD RECORD.

The Alchemist has now sold over sixty-five million copies and has been translated into eighty languages. This wide success helped Coelho set a quirky Guinness record in 2003: "Most translations of a single title signed by the author in one sitting." Coelho signed fifty-three different translations of *The Alchemist* at a book fair in Frankfurt, Germany.

THE FILM ADAPTATION OF *THE ALCHEMIST* IS STILL ON ITS OWN JOURNEY.

Coelho sold the film rights to *The Alchemist* to Warner Bros. for a reported $250,000 in 1994. The project never got off the ground, in part because producers insisted on adding epic battle scenes to juice the story's action. At one point Coelho even supposedly offered $2 million to buy the rights back from the studio. In a 2008 Goodreads interview, Coelho admitted that while he was open to allowing an adaptation of *The Alchemist*, he was usually hesitant about movies because "seldom do I find that film adaptations of books work well." Though *Variety* reported in 2008 that Laurence Fishburne had signed on to direct and star in the film, the project still hasn't come together. Perhaps Hollywood should start looking for omens.

NOT EVEN COELHO CAN FULLY EXPLAIN THE BOOK'S APPEAL.

Coelho has always been ready to share sage words on most any topic, but in 2011 he admitted to *The New York Times* that the runaway sales of *The Alchemist* surprised him. "It's difficult to explain why. I think you can have ten thousand explanations for failure, but no good explanation for success," Coelho said.

Fascinating Facts about Paulo Coelho

The author of one of the most successful books of all time almost didn't become a writer at all. Here's what you need to know about the long and winding path that Paulo Coelho took to his destiny.

1 HIS PARENTS COMMITTED HIM TO AN ASYLUM BECAUSE THEY DIDN'T WANT HIM TO BE A WRITER.

Coelho was raised in a devoutly Catholic household and went to Jesuit school. He knew as a kid that he wanted to be a writer, but his parents weren't thrilled—they wanted him to be an engineer instead. "My parents tried everything to dissuade me," Coelho told Oprah Winfrey. "They tried to bribe me. Then they cut off all the money they gave me to buy, I don't know, soft drinks. Then they tried a psychiatrist. Then they lost hope and said, 'This guy is crazy. We love him, but he's crazy.'" His parents put him in a mental institution three times, starting when he was seventeen—but Coelho always escaped.

2 COELHO WAS ARRESTED AND TORTURED BY THE BRAZILIAN GOVERNMENT.

After Coelho escaped from the institution for the final time, at the age of twenty, he briefly enrolled in law school but eventually dropped out and embraced the hippie lifestyle, indulging in sex and drugs and writing lyrics for Brazilian rocker Raul Seixas that were inspired by occultist Aleister Crowley (the Portuguese lyrics translate to "Do what you want/Because it's the whole of the law/Long live the Alternative Society/The number 666 is Aleister Crowley"). The songs were a hit, but the lyrics were too subversive for the Brazilian government, which repeatedly arrested the future author. Coelho was even subjected to torture.

The experience of being committed, along with being tortured, led him to "behave like a normal person," he told *The Guardian*. He got married, found a job. "I was normal for seven years," he said. "I could not stand to be normal." So he got divorced, married again, and decided to "travel and try to find the meaning of life."

3 HE HAD A SPIRITUAL AWAKENING IN SPAIN.

In 1986, Coelho walked more than five hundred miles to Santiago de Compostela, a Galician pilgrimage site. "When I arrived at Santiago de Compostela, I understood, finally, that I had to make a choice in my life," he said. "And the choice would be: I have to fulfill my dream or I have to forget my dream forever. My dream was to be a writer. I was forty years old, probably too old to change my path. But I said, 'No. I'm going to change . . . I'm going to follow my heart from now on, even if I have a price to pay.'" His experiences on the road would become the basis for his first novel, *The Pilgrimage*.

4 COELHO FOLLOWS OMENS IN HIS WRITING LIFE.

The author practices what he preaches when it comes to divining symbolism. Coelho must find a white feather before he starts a new book. Even if it takes a while, Coelho waits until he finds the sign. Once he has the feather in hand, he touches it to each page of the work when he prints out his manuscripts.

SYLVIA PLATH

October 27, 1932–February 11, 1963

BORN: Boston, Massachusetts

OTHER NOTABLE WORKS:
The Colossus (1960)
Ariel (1965)

Now considered one of the most important poets of the twentieth century, Sylvia Plath's recognition came posthumously. Plath published her first poem in the children's section of a local paper at age eight, and by the time she attended Smith College, she had published more than fifty works of prose and poetry. A Fulbright fellowship to Cambridge introduced her to leading British poets and their milieu, as well as her husband, future poet laureate Ted Hughes. Her collection *The Colossus and Other Poems*, published in 1960, established her as a confessional poet in the tradition of Anne Sexton. Plath took her own life in 1963.

Published one month before Plath died by suicide at age thirty, *The Bell Jar*—her only novel—follows a young woman, Esther Greenwood, through a mental breakdown, a suicide attempt, and electroshock therapy in a hospital. The novel and the spate of brilliant poems Plath wrote right before her death still reverberate today.

PLATH WAS INSPIRED BY *THE SNAKE PIT.*

Plath always called *The Bell Jar* a "potboiler"—a term used to refer to something created with the popular tastes of the day in mind. In 1959, Plath wrote in her journal, "Must get out *Snake Pit,*" referring to Mary Jane Ward's 1946 novel about her experiences in a mental hospital. "There is an increasing market for mental-hospital stuff. I am a fool if I don't relive, recreate it."

THE STORY IS PARTIALLY BASED ON PLATH'S "GUEST EDITORSHIP" AT *MADEMOISELLE.*

The first half of *The Bell Jar* follows Esther though a summer internship at *Ladies' Day* magazine in New York—a stand-in for *Mademoiselle*, where Plath won a "guest editorship" in 1953. The experiences in the novel are based on real events and people. The character Philomena Guinea, for example, was based on Plath's literary patron, Olive Higgins Prouty. And the scene in which Esther eats an entire bowl of caviar by herself was a real thing Plath did. There were other similarities as well: After returning from New York, Esther discovers that she didn't get into a writing course. Likewise, Plath was rejected from Frank O'Connor's writing class at Harvard.

LIKE PLATH, ESTHER TRIES TAKE HER OWN LIFE AND IS SENT TO A HOSPITAL.

In 1953, Plath attempted to die by suicide, and Esther's actions in *The Bell Jar* mirror Plath's. Esther is found—just as Plath was—and taken to a mental hospital. Plath was sent to McLean Hospital in Massachusetts, which has also treated Robert Lowell, Anne Sexton, David Foster Wallace, James Taylor, and Ray Charles, among others.

AFTER YEARS OF WRITER'S BLOCK, PLATH WROTE THE BOOK VERY QUICKLY.

Plath repeatedly tried to write about her breakdown but was hopelessly blocked on the subject. Then, in 1961, when her poetry collection *The Colossus and Other Poems* was accepted for publication, the block suddenly disappeared. After "a night of inspiration," she started working on the novel every morning at "a great pace," according to her husband Ted Hughes. She completed a draft in seventy days.

THE BELL JAR WAS REJECTED BY AMERICAN PUBLISHERS.

When Plath received a $2,080 novel-writing fellowship associated with publishers Harper & Row, she must have thought that publication was a sure thing. But Harper & Row rejected *The Bell Jar*, calling it "disappointing, juvenile and overwrought." British publisher William Heinemann eventually accepted the book, but Plath still had trouble finding an American publisher. "We didn't feel that you had managed to use your materials successfully in a novelistic way," one editor wrote.

THE BOOK WAS INITIALLY PUBLISHED UNDER THE PSEUDONYM VICTORIA LUCAS.

Plath used a pseudonym to protect the people she fictionalized in the book, both to save her mother from embarrassment and because her publisher was worried about libel suits. She also wanted to separate her serious literary reputation from her "potboiler" and protect the book from being judged as the work of a poet. (Originally, the protagonist was also named Victoria Lucas, but Plath was persuaded by her editor to find an alternative; she went with Esther Greenwood.)

THE BELL JAR DIDN'T GET THE ATTENTION PLATH WAS EXPECTING.

When *The Bell Jar* was published in January 1963, it didn't seem likely to become a literary sensation. Reviews weren't terrible—some were even positive—but they were all, for the most part, indifferent.

PLATH'S MOTHER DIDN'T WANT THE BOOK TO COME OUT IN THE UNITED STATES.

The Bell Jar was published under Plath's name in England in 1966, but it didn't come out in the United States until 1971. Plath's mother, Aurelia, didn't want people she knew to recognize themselves in the book, believing it showed "the basest ingratitude" to Plath's friends and family. Much to Aurelia's displeasure, Hughes finally published *The Bell Jar* in the US because he wanted money to buy a country house.

THE BELL JAR IS PLATH'S ONLY PUBLISHED NOVEL.

When Plath died, she was writing another novel titled, at different points, *Double Exposure* or *Doubletake*, about the breakdown of her marriage to Hughes. Plath told friends it was "better than *The Bell Jar*" and made her "laugh and laugh, and if I can laugh now it must be hellishly funny stuff." Whether she finished the novel is unclear. Originally Hughes said the book was 130 pages, but he later revised that number to sixty or seventy pages. In any case, Hughes claimed the novel disappeared in 1970.

Fascinating Facts about Sylvia Plath

Poet and novelist Sylvia Plath has been both celebrated for her candid, confessional style and mourned for her personal struggles. Her tumultuous life and work—and how they often became entwined—continue to resonate today. Here are a few things you should know about *The Bell Jar* author.

1 PLATH WROTE FOR *SEVENTEEN* MAGAZINE.

Born October 27, 1932 in Boston's Jamaica Plain neighborhood, Plath attended Smith College and, later, Cambridge University in England. Before heading over the pond, Plath got an early taste of seeing her name in print in the pages of *Seventeen* magazine, which had not yet turned into a chronicle of teen idols. Her story, "And Summer Will Not Come Again," was published in their August 1950 issue. Before that, Plath submitted an answer to an editorial question asking readers what kind of parent they might eventually become.

2 SHE ALSO WROTE A CHILDREN'S BOOK.

After Plath's death, stories she had written for children were discovered in her papers. One, *The It-Doesn't-Matter Suit*, was published in 1996. It tells the story of Max Nix, a resident of Winkelburg, who covets a new mustard-yellow suit that arrives in the mail. The label is damaged (only the letters N-I-X are legible), so no one knows who it belongs to; after various relatives try it on, Max discovers the suit is perfect— for the very reasons the other members of the family refused it.

3 SHE WAS A SKILLED VISUAL ARTIST.

Plath is best known for her prose work, but she originally had designs on becoming a visual artist. At Smith College, she studied art before her teachers convinced her to switch to English because of her talent for writing. Some of her work, including paper dolls made in her youth and a self-portrait created in high school, were put on display at the Smithsonian National Portrait Gallery in 2017, alongside letters, manuscripts, family photos, and objects from her life.

4 *ARIEL* WASN'T PUBLISHED AS PLATH ORIGINALLY INTENDED.

Thought to be her signature work, 1965's *Ariel* shows Plath at her acerbic best, with her poems arranged so it appears as though the author is spiraling down to a feeling of hopelessness. But Plath didn't intend for the collection to end that way. The order of the poems was decided by her husband, Ted Hughes, who opted to end the volume on a downbeat note. She originally wanted to end the work with her celebrated "bee poems," an optimistic look at a beekeeper's curation of life. (Her father, Otto, was an authority on honeybees.)

5 SHE LIVED IN THE SAME HOUSE WHERE POET W.B. YEATS GREW UP.

Plath moved with her family to England in 1959. After she and Hughes separated in 1962, she moved to 23 Fitzroy Road in Primrose Hill, which she selected because it bore a plaque outside that announced it as the one-time home of Irish poet William Butler Yeats. Plath was herself later memorialized by a plaque at a previous address: 3 Chalcot Square, also in Primrose Hill.

6 SHE HAS A STRANGE CONNECTION TO *THE IRON GIANT*.

The Iron Giant, a 1999 animated film directed by Brad Bird about a boy who befriends a giant robot (voiced by Vin Diesel), was based on Hughes's book *The Iron Man*. Hughes is said to have written the book following Plath's death in 1963 to help comfort their two children.

FIVE IMPORTANT NOVELS ABOUT MENTAL ILLNESS

1 The Awakening (1899) // KATE CHOPIN

Many scholars cite *The Awakening* as one of the first great feminist novels. Through the story of Edna Pontellier—a housewife living in Louisiana at the turn of the nineteenth century—author Kate Chopin was able to explore topics rarely discussed in public circles at the time. *The Awakening* focuses on Edna's resistance to conform to the gender roles expected from her as a wife and mother—a conflict that manifests as symptoms closely resembling clinical depression. When describing the character's mental state, Chopin wrote, "There were days when she was unhappy; she did not know why—when it did not seem worth while to be glad or sorry, to be alive or dead." Another quote from the book reads, "Despondency had come upon her there in the wakeful night, and had never lifted. There was no one thing in the world that she desired." Edna's struggle with mental illness culminates with her dying of suicide by drowning herself in the Gulf of Mexico.

2 Mrs. Dalloway (1925) // VIRGINIA WOOLF

Mrs. Dalloway is set after World War I, but the psychological impact of the war on its survivors is a major presence in Woolf's novel. The character Septimus Warren Smith is a former World War I soldier whose post-traumatic stress disorder has disconnected him from the world around him. He suffers from hallucinations, many of which involve a friend who died in the war. After he's involuntarily committed to a psychiatric hospital, Septimus dies of suicide by jumping from a window.

Having suffered from mental illness herself, Woolf often incorporated these issues into her work. In *Mrs. Dalloway,* the writer explores the reality of living with mental illness as well as the way medical professionals treating such patients in the early twentieth century could cause more harm than good. Her novel was also one of the first to examine military post-traumatic stress disorder, or PTSD (formerly known as "shell shock") before it was a proper diagnosis.

3 One Flew Over the Cuckoo's Nest (1962) // KEN KESEY

Set in a psychiatric hospital, themes related to mental illness are front-and-center in Ken Kesey's 1962 novel *One Flew Over the Cuckoo's Nest*. When Randle Patrick McMurphy arrives at the institution after faking insanity so he won't have to serve his sentence in prison, he challenges the authority of the tyrannical Nurse Ratched. Rather than just focusing on mental health from a personal level, *One Flew Over the Cuckoo's Nest* looks at the systemic abuses victims of mental illness faced in the mid-twentieth century. Electroshock therapy and lobotomies were a few of the controversial treatments highlighted in the book. The story was still relevant more than a decade after its release when *One Flew Over the Cuckoo's Nest* was adapted into an Oscar-winning film.

4 Ordinary People (1976) // JUDITH GUEST

Judith Guest's debut novel *Ordinary People* follows one family dealing with the fallout of a tragedy. While sailing on Lake Michigan, teenage brothers Buck and Conrad Jarrett get caught in a storm that causes Buck's death. Conrad attempts suicide months later, and with guidance from his therapist, he eventually grapples with the sources of his depression and survivor's guilt.

Conrad isn't the only character who suffers from grief in the novel. Though his parents may look more outwardly composed than he does, Guest makes it clear that they have their own mental issues to confront. One major theme of *Ordinary People* is the many forms that grief, and mental illness in general, can take in different patients.

5 A Little Life (2015) // HANYA YANAGIHARA

Hailed as a modern-day classic, *A Little Life* tells the story of a group friends living New York City through many stages of their lives, and one character's struggle with mental illness makes up the central conflict of the novel. Jude suffers from depression and self-harm, and because of the sexual trauma he experienced as a child, he has trouble forming intimate relationships with others. Rather than depicting a character's recovery from trauma, Yanagihara set out to show the destructive effects of mental illness over time. The author told Vulture in 2015, "One of the things I wanted to do with this book was create a protagonist who never gets better."

THE CALL OF THE WILD

JACK LONDON

January 12, 1876–November 22, 1916

BORN: San Francisco, California

OTHER NOTABLE WORKS:
The Sea-Wolf (1904)
White Fang (1906)
Martin Eden (1909)

One of the most popular American novelists at the turn of the twentieth century, Jack London's tales of adventure and survival mirrored his real life. As a teenager, London worked as an oyster pirate, then an oyster pirate catcher, and later he joined a ship bound for the north Pacific. Back in the US, he rode freight trains across the country and became an ardent socialist.

London joined the Klondike Gold Rush in 1897, but didn't strike it rich until he turned his Yukon experience into novels and short stories. He published his first collection of stories as *The Son of the Wolf* in 1900. For his best-known novel, *The Call of the Wild* (1903), London chose as his protagonist a sled dog named Buck, and it became an instant best seller. Later books included *White Fang* (1906), the semi-autobiographical *Martin Eden* (1909), and *The Cruise of the Snark* (1911), about his 1907 voyage to the South Pacific.

London built a ranch in Glen Ellen, California, where he intended to live and write. But his adventures often left him in poor health. He died of kidney failure at forty, and was buried at his ranch.

The Call of the Wild—which follows a dog named Buck from a cushy life in California to the decidedly less comfortable Alaska Gold Rush—made Jack London a literary star and became one of the most popular books of the twentieth century. Here's what you should know.

THE BOOK WAS INFLUENCED BY HIS TIME IN THE KLONDIKE—AND MILTON'S *PARADISE LOST*.

Though he had been writing furiously, London had basically no success as an author by the time he was twenty-one. Looking to make some money, he joined the thousands of people going to the Klondike Gold Rush, and staked eight claims. Unfortunately, they yielded little gold, and London endured the Alaskan winter reading John Milton's *Paradise Lost* and Darwin's *The Origin of Species*—both influences on *The Call of the Wild*. Finally, after nearly a year living on a diet of beans, bread, and bacon, London got scurvy and returned to California. He was as penniless as the day he left, but he had a wealth of new material.

BUCK WAS BASED ON A DOG NAMED JACK.

In the frozen north, London met brothers Marshall and Louis Whitford Bond. The brothers had a dog, a St. Bernard-Collie mix also named Jack, who must have made an impression on London. "Yes, Buck was based on your dog at Dawson," London later wrote to Marshall Bond. In that letter, London acknowledged that Jack the dog wasn't the only thing he had borrowed from the Bonds: Their father, Judge Hiram Gilbert Bond, served as inspiration for Judge Miller, and his ranch in the book is based on the family's ranch, which London had visited in 1901.

THE CALL OF THE WILD STARTED AS A SHORT STORY.

In 1902, London published a short story called "Diable—A Dog" (later, "Bâtard"), where a dog named Bâtard kills his master. He started a companion piece, this one about a "good dog," which he also intended to be a short story. But, as he would later say, "it got away from me, and instead of 4,000 words it ran 32,000 before I could call a halt."

IT WAS FIRST SERIALIZED BY *THE SATURDAY EVENING POST.*

The magazine paid London $750 for *The Call of the Wild*, which it published in four installments during the summer of 1903. Soon after, the book was published by Macmillan, whose initial run of ten thousand copies sold out in a day. *The Call of the Wild* received rave reviews, and *The Atlantic Monthly* noted that London was being called "the American Kipling."

LONDON WAS ACCUSED OF PLAGIARISM.

In 1907, *The Independent* suggested that London had plagiarized Egerton R. Young's nonfiction book *My Dogs in Northland*, placing passages of both books side by side so readers could compare. In an accompanying letter, London admitted that he had used Young's book as a source, and had informed Young of that fact. But he didn't consider it plagiarism, because Young's story was nonfiction, and London didn't use the same language. "Fiction writers have always considered actual experiences of life to be a lawful field for exploitation," he wrote. "Really, to charge plagiarism in such a case [as this] is to misuse the English language. To be correct, 'sources of materials used in *The Call of the Wild*' should be substituted for 'Plagiarism.'"

LONDON DIDN'T RECEIVE ROYALTIES FOR THE BOOK—BUT IT STILL MADE HIM RICH.

London, who had sold all book rights to Macmillan for a flat fee of $2,000, didn't profit from *The Call of the Wild*'s runaway success. But it did make him a household name, which led to the success of his future books: When he followed up with *White Fang*, it wasn't long before he was the highest-paid author in the United States. London wrote more than fifty books in his lifetime, and it all started with *The Call of the Wild*, which is still widely read today—and considered to be one of the books that shaped America.

Persistence Pays Off

When he was a young guy living in Oakland, London wrote for fifteen hours, often forgetting to eat. But his passion didn't yield results in those early days: In five years, London received 664 rejections. He impaled every rejection on a spindle in his writing room, and soon had a column of paper four feet high. Eventually he got an acceptance letter that offered a mere $5. A demoralized London resolved to go shovel coal—but then an acceptance letter from the literary magazine *The Black Cat* soon arrived offering him $40 and allowed him to keep writing.

5 FAMOUS NOVELISTS' HOMES YOU CAN VISIT

Who wouldn't want to see, with their own eyes, the places where great novelists did their work? Many homes of famous novelists have opened their doors to the public, including Jack London's Beauty Ranch in the Sonoma Mountains in California, which now sits in Jack London State Park. A few other novelists' homes that you can put on your vacation itinerary are:

Thomas Hardy's Max Gate
LOCATION: **DORCHESTER, DORSET, ENGLAND**

Hardy was both an author and an architect, and he designed Max (named after a local tollkeeper whose name was not Max but Mack) House in 1885. He wrote *Tess of the d'Urbervilles* and *Jude the Obscure* in the Victorian-style home, whose gardens are still as they were originally planned. You can also visit the cob-and-thatch cottage where Hardy was born, located just outside Dorchester.

Leo Tolstoy's Yasnaya Polyana
LOCATION: **TULA, RUSSIA**

Tolstoy was born at this Central Russian estate, which had belonged to his family since the 1760s. The writer himself inherited the estate in 1847, and wrote many of his classic works there, including *War and Peace.* Today, Yasnaya Polyana has the estate's original furniture and library and looks

just as it did in the late eighteenth and early nineteenth centuries.

Pearl S. Buck's Houses
LOCATIONS: **CHINA; WEST VIRGINIA; PENNSYLVANIA**

Those heading to China can put two Pearl S. Buck homes on their itinerary: the two-story Dengyun Hill house in Zhenjiang City, where she lived for a time, and the Pearl S. Buck Memorial House on the grounds of Nanjing University, where she wrote *The Good Earth.* Those planning a trip stateside also have two potential places to visit: Her West Virginia birthplace and the Pearl S. Buck House near Dublin, Pennsylvania, where Buck moved after returning from China. She and her second husband raised their large family of adopted children there, and visitors can see everything from their closet full of board games and the typewriter Buck used to write her most famous work to the property's cultural center and the author's grave.

Goethe House
LOCATION: **FRANKFURT, GERMANY**

Before he kicked off the Romantic movement, Johann Wolfgang von Goethe was just a kid growing up

with sister Cornelia in a four-story bourgeois-style house in Frankfurt. Today, Goethe's birthplace has been turned into a museum where visitors can see where Goethe was supposedly born as well as the room where he wrote his early works, including *The Sorrows of Young Werther.* There's also a grand staircase that takes up a third of the building, a puppet theater room, and lavishly decorated rooms for entertaining.

La Maison de Colette
LOCATION: **SAINT-SAUVEUR EN PUISAYE, FRANCE**

Sidonie-Gabrielle Colette, a.k.a. Colette, was born at this home in 1873, and lived there until the age of eighteen, when financial issues forced her family to sell. The house and its grounds frequently pop up in the author's books, including *Claudine at School, The Vagabond,* and *Gigi.* Today, the home has been renovated and restored with the late nineteenth-century décor "of Colette's happy childhood," in the words of the museum's director. There are no barriers or displays; instead, the house is meant to be less like a museum and more like a home, where Colette herself could walk in at any moment.

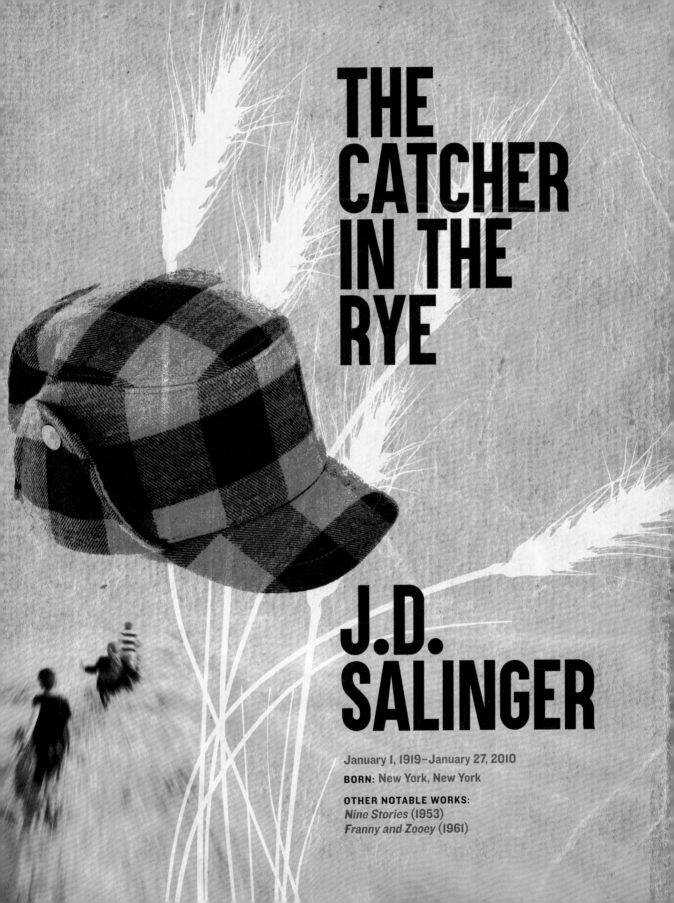

J erome David Salinger, better known as J.D. Salinger to his millions of fans, had a problem with preconceived notions. It's the reason why he refused to allow his publishers to draw representations of his characters on the dustjackets of his work (he thought that imagining what a character might look like should be up to the reader), and would seemingly explain why he preferred to keep the details of his own life as mysterious as possible, too. Along with being the literary world's least prolific titan—*The Catcher In the Rye* is the only novel he ever published—Salinger was painfully private, and went to great lengths to ensure that the enormous success of his quintessential ode to teenage rebellion did not come attached with the trappings of fame. Though it was long believed that he never stopped writing, it would be tough to confirm that fact as Salinger, who was born in New York City on January 1, 1919, spent the last fifty or so years of his life in New Hampshire, where he lived largely in seclusion until his death in 2010.

J.D. Salinger's *bildungsroman* (coming of age) story about an aimless young man named Holden Caulfield on a mission to find himself after being expelled from a private school, ***The Catcher in the Rye*** ushered in a new era of philosophical literature, becoming a staple of classrooms across the country. But there still might be a few things you didn't learn about the book in class.

SALINGER WORKED ON *THE CATCHER IN THE RYE* WHILE FIGHTING IN WORLD WAR II.

Salinger was a restless student who attended New York University, Ursinus College, and Columbia University in succession. While taking classes at the latter, he met Whit Burnett, a professor who also edited *Story* magazine. Sensing Salinger's talent for language, Burnett encouraged him to pursue his fiction. After World War II broke out, Salinger was drafted into the Army, and during his service from 1942 to 1944, he worked on chapters for what would later become *The Catcher in the Rye*, keeping pages on his person even when marching into battle.

HE HAD A NERVOUS BREAKDOWN.

Following his service, Salinger experienced what would later be labeled PTSD: He was hospitalized after suffering a nervous breakdown in Nuremberg in 1945 after seeing some very bloody battles on D-Day and in Luxembourg. Writing to Ernest Hemingway, whom he had met while the latter was a war correspondent for *Collier's*, he said his despondent state had been constant and he sought out help "before it got out of hand." Shortly thereafter, he wrote "I'm Crazy"—the first appearance of Holden Caulfield. *Collier's* published the story in December 1945.

HE REFUSED TO BE REWRITTEN.

After settling back in New York after the war, Salinger continued to write, contributing short stories to *The New Yorker* and other outlets before finishing *The Catcher in the Rye*. In literary circles, his name was already becoming known for insisting that editors not change a single word of his writing. A.E. Hotchner recalled how, when he was working as a magazine editor, he got a story from Salinger with a note attached reading "Either as-is or not at all." After ensuring the story wasn't changed, Hotchner found out that another editor had changed the title—and it was too late to change it back. When he met with Salinger to let him know, the writer was apoplectic. "He said it was a terrible deceit on my part," Hotchner said. Salinger stormed out, and they never saw each other again.

SALINGER AVOIDED PUBLICITY FROM THE START.

Early on, it became apparent that Salinger wasn't going to embrace whatever celebrity *The Catcher in the Rye* brought to his doorstep. At some point after the book's publication, he insisted that Little, Brown remove his photo from the dust jacket and turned down any opportunities to publicize it—with one exception. After moving to New Hampshire, Salinger agreed to give an interview to a local high school paper. Salinger was later dismayed to find out an editor wound up putting that interview on the front page of the local paper. Annoyed and feeling betrayed, he put up a six-foot, six-inch tall fence around his property, further walling himself off from prying eyes.

HE SUED HIS BIOGRAPHER.

When author Ian Hamilton insisted on pursuing a biography of Salinger in the 1980s, Salinger was so peeved that he sued Hamilton to prevent him from using excerpts of unpublished letters. The courts gave him a victory, barring Hamilton from using the passages.

SALINGER PROBABLY DRANK HIS OWN PEE.

Salinger's reclusive habits made him easy prey for a litany of rumors, but some of his more intriguing habits were disclosed by his daughter, Margaret, in a memoir that described her father as speaking in tongues and occasionally sipping his own urine. That practice, called urophagia, is said to have health benefits, although no reputable studies have been able to demonstrate as much.

HE ALWAYS LOATHED THE IDEA OF A *CATCHER IN THE RYE* MOVIE.

With its persistent interior monologues, *The Catcher in the Rye* might be almost unfilmable—but that hasn't stopped directors as revered as Billy Wilder and Steven Spielberg from trying. Throughout his life, Salinger famously rebuffed any attempt to purchase the rights to make a film from his book, but did leave open a small possibility that it could possibly happen after he died. "It pleasures me to no end, though," he once wrote, "to know that I won't have to see the results of the transaction."

SALINGER DID WIND UP SELLING A MOVIE IDEA.

Although his most celebrated work has been kept offscreen, Salinger did have a brief courtship with Hollywood. In 1948, producer Darryl Zanuck purchased the rights to one of his short stories, "Uncle Wiggily in Connecticut," which was released as *My Foolish Heart* in 1949. Actress Susan Hayward earned an Oscar nomination for her role, and the film was also nominated for Best Original Song. Salinger reportedly hated the swooning love story.

THERE ARE TWO UNPUBLISHED STORIES ABOUT HOLDEN CAULFIELD'S FAMILY.

"The Last and Best of the Peter Pans" and "The Ocean Full of Bowling Balls" were both donated to Princeton University's Firestone library. "Bowling Balls," a prequel of sorts to *Rye* about the death of Caulfield's brother, was supposed to run in *Harper's Bazaar* in 1949—but Salinger opted not to publish. The stories weren't supposed to be published until around 2060, fifty years after Salinger's death, but in 2013, "Bowling Balls" leaked online.

MARK DAVID CHAPMAN HAD *RYE* ON HIM WHEN HE MURDERED JOHN LENNON.

On December 8, 1980, Chapman shot the former Beatle outside his apartment building in New York City. In Chapman's pocket was a copy of *The Catcher in the Rye* in which he'd written, "This is my statement," with "this" underlined, and signed Caulfield's name. A few years later, the book was still on his mind: Chapman wrote to the police officer who arrested him, asking, "Is there any way you can help me locate my copy of *The Catcher in the Rye* that was taken from me on the night of my arrest? . . . Have you read *The Catcher in the Rye* yet? I would like you to read it and tell me what you think of it. As you remember, in the copy that was taken from me I had written 'This is my statement.' I'm wondering if you now understand this."

8

AUTHORS WHO HATED MOVIE VERSIONS OF THEIR WRITING

1 STEPHEN KING //
The Shining

Stephen King probably made movie buffs cringe when he said he hated what Stanley Kubrick did to *The Shining*. "I'd admired Kubrick for a long time and had great expectations for the project, but I was deeply disappointed in the end result," King said. The author believed that Kubrick was ultimately too rational to grasp the concept of the supernatural world—let alone "the sheer inhuman evil of the Overlook Hotel." Instead, King said, the director looked "for evil in the characters and made the film into a domestic tragedy with only vaguely supernatural overtones. That was the basic flaw: because he couldn't believe, he couldn't make the film believable to others."

He was also unhappy with Jack Nicholson's performance—King wanted it to be clear that Jack Torrance wasn't crazy until he got to the hotel and felt that Nicholson made the character crazy from the start. King recently described the movie as "a big, beautiful Cadillac with no engine inside it." King ended up working on another version of *The Shining* with director Mick Garris that aired on ABC in 1997.

2 ANNE RICE //
Queen of the Damned

After casting was completed for the movie version of Anne Rice's *Interview with the Vampire*, Rice said Tom Cruise was "no more my vampire Lestat than Edward G. Robinson is Rhett Butler." The casting was "so bizarre," she said, "it's almost impossible to imagine how it's going to work." When she saw the movie, however, she actually loved Cruise's portrayal and told him what an impressive job he had done. Indeed, on her website she lists it as the only film adaptation of her work she recommends—cold comfort for *Queen of the Damned*, which she reportedly has said mutilated her book.

3 WINSTON GROOM //
Forrest Gump

Note to filmmakers: Don't anger the author of the book before its sequel has been written. On the first page of the sequel, author Winston Groom wrote, "Don't never let nobody make a movie of your life's story," and "Whether they get it right or wrong, it don't matter." You can't blame Groom for being mad: He was promised 3 percent net profits for the film, which he hadn't received because producers claimed that by the time they took out production costs and advertising and promotional costs, the movie didn't turn a profit. To add insult to injury, Groom wasn't mentioned in any of the six Academy Award acceptance speeches given by various cast and crew members of *Forrest Gump*.

4 CLIVE CUSSLER //
Sahara

Clive Cussler's Dirk Pitt tales have a cult following. Dirk Pitt movies don't, especially 2005's *Sahara* starring Matthew McConaughey and Penélope Cruz. In fact, it was a certified flop: The $160 million production made just $68 million at the domestic box office. Cussler said it was because the producer failed to give him total script control as agreed upon and sued for millions. He lost. In fact, Cussler was ordered to pay $13.9 million for legal fees incurred by the *Sahara* production company, though that order was overturned in 2010.

5 ANTHONY BURGESS //
A Clockwork Orange

Not only did Anthony Burgess dislike the movie based on his novella *A Clockwork Orange*, he later regretted writing any of it in the first place. "The book I am best known for, or only known for, is a novel I am prepared to repudiate: written a quarter of a century ago, a *jeu d'esprit* knocked off for money in three weeks, it became known as the raw material for a film which seemed to glorify sex and violence. The film made it easy for readers of the book to misunderstand what it was about, and the misunderstanding will pursue me till I die. I should not have written the book because of this danger of misinterpretation."

6 BRET EASTON ELLIS //
American Psycho

Bret Easton Ellis doesn't think any of the film adaptations of his books are that great (save for maybe *The Rules of Attraction*), but he dislikes some more than others. The author believes *American Psycho* never should have happened: "*American Psycho* was a book I didn't think needed to be turned into a movie. I think the problem with *American Psycho* was that it was conceived as a novel, as a literary work with a very unreliable narrator at the center of it and the medium of film demands answers. It demands answers. You can be as ambiguous as you want with a movie, but it doesn't matter—we're still looking at it. It's still being answered for us visually. I don't think *American Psycho* is particularly more interesting if you knew that he did it or think that it all happens in his head. I think the answer to that question makes the book infinitely less interesting."

7 KEN KESEY // One Flew Over The Cuckoo's Nest

Despite the fact that *One Flew Over the Cuckoo's Nest* swept the Academy Awards—it won Best Picture, Best Director, Best Actor, Best Actress and Best Adapted Screenplay—author Ken Kesey was not impressed. He was originally slated to help with the production, but left not long into the process. He claimed for a long time that he didn't even watch it and was especially upset that they didn't keep the viewpoint of Chief Bromden.

8 RICHARD MATHESON //
I Am Legend

Richard Matheson has been annoyed with the adaptations of his book *I Am Legend* since 1964. The first one, *The Last Man on Earth*, starred Vincent Price. "I was disappointed in *The Last Man on Earth*, even though they more or less followed my story," the author said. "I think Vincent Price, whom I love in every one of his pictures that I wrote, was miscast. I also felt the direction was kind of poor." Another version, *The Omega Man*, starred Charlton Heston. "*The Omega Man* was so removed from my book that it didn't even bother me," Matheson said.

Before *I Am Legend* starring Will Smith was announced, the author commented, "I don't know why Hollywood is fascinated by my book when they never care to film it as I wrote it." The most recent adaptation, by the way, completely changed Matheson's ending because it didn't test well with audiences.

THE
COLOR
PURPLE

ALICE WALKER

February 9, 1944

BORN: Eatonton, Georgia

OTHER NOTABLE WORKS:
The Third Life of Grange Copeland (1970)
The Temple of My Familiar (1989)

When Alice Walker was a young woman living in the Jim Crow South, her mother gave her three things—a typewriter, a suitcase, and a sewing machine—that would be the keys to making her presence known in the world. The daughter of sharecroppers Willie Lee and Minnie Lou Grant Walker, she experienced a seismic event in her life at age eight, when an errant shot from a BB gun caused her to lose sight in her right eye, which turned white. Self-conscious about her appearance, Walker distanced herself from the world and turned to reading and writing poetry. The scar tissue was eventually removed, and Walker regained her confidence. She excelled in school, graduating valedictorian, and attended Spelman College on scholarship in 1961. She later transferred to Sarah Lawrence College in New York and studied abroad in Africa.

It was in college that Walker was first drawn to activism, moving to social work after graduation while pursuing her writing aspirations. Her first poetry collection, *Once*, was published in 1968, and a novel, *The Third Life of Grange Copeland*, followed in 1970. Moving between poetry, novels, and children's books, Walker's profile was greatly elevated by the success of 1982's *The Color Purple*, written as a series of letters penned by a Black woman named Celie. The novel earned Walker the Pulitzer Prize in 1983.

Walker's work often reflects what she describes as a "Womanist" perspective of Black women confronting gender as well as racial barriers. Her ruminations on gender roles are afforded the same careful thought as the civil rights actions that Walker has taken on, marching, protesting, and speaking in favor of equality for all.

Taking the Arrow Out of the Heart, published in 2018, is the latest entry to Walker's body of work. Her achievements can be traced back to those three gifts: the typewriter that allowed her to express herself, a suitcase to escape the prejudices of her community, and a sewing machine to teach her self-sufficiency. Her eclectic career is proof she made good use of all three.

⋯⋯⋯⋯⋯⋯⋯⋯⋯⋯⋯⋯⋯⋯⋯⋯⋯⋯⋯⋯⋯⋯⋯⋯⋯⋯⋯⋯⋯⋯

With its epistolary structure, frank depictions of same-sex love, and powerful treatments of religions themes, Alice Walker's **The Color Purple** (1982) has remained an unforgettable reading experience. The novel, which tells the story of Celie and her sister Nettie living in a prejudiced South of the early 1900s under the thumb of their abusive stepfather, remains Walker's best-known work and was further popularized by the 1985 film adaptation directed by Steven Spielberg. Here are a few more things you should know about *The Color Purple*.

WALKER WAS INSPIRED BY THE LOVE TRIANGLE INVOLVING HER GRANDMOTHER.

At the heart of *The Color Purple* is Celie's relationship with Shug Avery, a woman singer and lover of Mister, Celie's abusive husband. Their complex emotional entanglement was inspired by Walker's real grandmother, who also rejected her abusive husband in order to find a more fulfilling relationship with his lover, "a beautiful woman who was kind to her, the only grown person who ever seemed to notice how remarkable and creative she was," Walker said.

WALKER FELT SHE HAD TO MOVE IN ORDER TO WRITE THE BOOK.

When Walker began writing *The Color Purple*, she had just gotten divorced and was an editor at *Ms.* magazine in New York City. She realized that living in an urban area was making it difficult to write for characters in the 1930s South that had never heard a car engine, let alone a chorus of them. So Walker moved to Boonville, a small town in northern California that allowed for a quieter atmosphere. It was there, walking through nature, that Walker was struck by the presence of the color purple, something she believed people often overlooked—much like the challenges faced by Celie. The thought gave the book its title.

THE BOOK EARNED WALKER THE FIRST PULITZER PRIZE GIVEN TO A BLACK WOMAN FOR FICTION.

The impact of *The Color Purple* was immediate, with Walker winning a National Book Award for her efforts. (The reaction wasn't all positive, however: Then and now, the book is often banned in schools for its depictions of incest as well as consensual sex.) She also made history when the book won the 1983 Pulitzer Prize for fiction. It was the first time a book authored by a Black woman had ever won the award.

OPRAH WAS OBSESSED WITH THE COLOR PURPLE BEFORE STARRING IN THE MOVIE.

"*The Color Purple* was a seminal moment in my life," Oprah told *Collider* in 2014. She recounted how, one Sunday morning in 1983, she came across the review of the book in *The New York Times*. "I was in my pajamas, and I put my coat on, over my pajamas, and went to the book store," she said. "I got the book and read it, in one day. And then, I went back, the next day, and bought every copy they had." Winfrey gave the book to friends, coworkers, and "everybody that I knew . . . I moved to Chicago and I would literally walk around with a backpack filled with books because I didn't have a book club, and I would just start a conversation with people and say, 'Have you read *The Color Purple*?' And if they hadn't, I'd say, 'Here, have a copy, right here.' I was literally obsessed with it."

5 QUOTES FROM *THE COLOR PURPLE*

Written as a series of letters to God from a woman named Celie, Alice Walker's classic novel about a Black woman overcoming racial and emotional oppression is full of passages that have spoken to readers worldwide since its publication in 1982. Here are just a few quotes we love from *The Color Purple*.

"Everything want to be loved. Us sing and dance, make faces and give flower bouquets, trying to be loved. You ever notice that trees do everything to git attention we do, except walk?"

"Lord, I wants to go so bad. Not to dance. Not to drink. Not to play card. Not even to hear Shug Avery sing. I just be thankful to lay eyes on her."

"Why any woman give a shit what people think is a mystery to me."

"They had a lot of love to give. But I needed love plus understanding. They run a little short of that."

"I don't know who tried to teach him what to do in the bedroom, but it must have been a furniture salesman."

THE
GIRL WITH THE
DRAGON TATTOO

STIEG LARSSON

August 15, 1954–November 9, 2004

BORN: Skelleftehamn, Sweden

OTHER NOTABLE WORKS:
The Girl Who Played with Fire (2006)
The Girl Who Kicked the Hornet's Nest (2007)

Born in northern Sweden in 1954, Stieg Larsson lived with his grandparents for most of his early childhood while his parents looked for work in Stockholm. He moved back in with his parents after his grandfather died in 1962, and soon the young Larsson was honing his authorial prowess in notebook after notebook (and, finally, on a typewriter his father purchased for him). Though he did pen one adventure novel as a preteen, Larsson's interest in writing was mainly journalistic.

By his mid-twenties, he had served his compulsory fourteen months in the national army, trained Eritrean revolutionaries in Ethiopia, and committed himself to combating Sweden's lingering wave of right-wing radicalism through his own socialist, antifascist writing. Larsson took a job at a graphic design firm and spent every spare moment composing articles for leftist publications like Britain's *Searchlight*. In 1995, he helped found his own: *Expo*.

Then, in 2002, he decided to author a fictional series, hoping that its success would help fund his other endeavors. But while *The Girl with the Dragon Tattoo* and its two sequels did achieve international acclaim, Larsson himself didn't live long enough to reap the benefits—he died of a heart attack at age fifty, before any of his books were published.

In *The Girl with the Dragon Tattoo*, disgraced financial journalist Mikael Blomkvist retreats to the Swedish countryside on a peculiar assignment: to uncover the truth about the decades-old disappearance of a young girl. As sinister details emerge, he seeks help from an unlikely source—Lisbeth Salander, a countercultural, intensely private young hacker with a convenient disregard for playing by the rules. Read on for more you should know about the novel.

ITS ENGLISH TITLE IS NOTHING LIKE ITS SWEDISH ONE.

When discussing the English title of Larsson's first novel, a more apt expression than "lost in translation" might be "intentionally changed to something completely different in translation." It was released in Sweden in 2005 under its original name: *Män som hatar kvinnor*, or *Men Who Hate Women*. But British booksellers recommended an overhaul after publisher Christopher MacLehose acquired the English language rights, so he came up with *The Girl with the Dragon Tattoo*. According to Sonny Mehta, who published Larsson's work in the US, the shift was partially motivated by worry that prospective readers might mistake *Men Who Hate Women* for a self-help book. And as he explained in a 2010 *BookPage* interview, the new title also took the focus off the novel's criminally misogynistic villains and placed it instead on the indomitable heroine, Lisbeth Salander.

The second novel's Swedish title, *Flickan som lekte med elden*, matches its English one—*The Girl Who Played with Fire*—but English language publishers again diverged from their Swedish counterparts for the third and final work in the Millennium Trilogy. *Luftslottet som sprängdes* roughly translates to *The Air Castle That Blew Up*, which became *The Girl Who Kicked the Hornet's Nest*.

LISBETH SALANDER'S DRAGON TATTOO IS SUPPOSED TO BE MASSIVE.

Salander isn't exactly known for subtle gestures, so it makes sense that her fearsome dragon tattoo takes up a considerable portion of her back—in the Swedish version, that is. In *The Tattooed Girl: The Enigma of Stieg Larsson and the Secrets Behind the Most Compelling Thrillers of Our Time*, authors Dan Burstein, Arne de Keijzer, and John-Henri Holmberg explain that Larsson describes the tattoo as "stretching across her back, from her right shoulder blade down to her buttock," in the first novel, and mentions that the dragon's tail extends all the way to her thigh in the sequel. The English versions, on the other hand, place a pint-sized dragon "on her shoulder blade."

LARSSON'S PARTNER WAS INVOLVED IN HIS WRITING PROCESS.

The fact that Larsson went from never having written a novel (his one childhood project notwithstanding) to churning out three future best sellers in a two-year span drew skepticism from colleagues and strangers alike. Anders Hellberg, a journalist who had edited some of Larsson's earlier work—which he described to *The New York Times* as "impossible"—actually suggested that Larsson hadn't written the Millennium series at all, and others have theorized that his longtime partner Eva Gabrielsson was steering the ship.

Gabrielsson, also a writer, maintains that Larsson himself penned the unforgettable escapades of Lisbeth Salander and Mikael Blomkvist, but she has admitted to participating in the process. "The actual writing, the craftsmanship, was Stieg's," she told *The Guardian* in 2011. "But the content is a different matter. There are a lot of my thoughts, ideas, and work in there." While Larsson was writing the series, Gabrielsson was busy with her own book on Swedish architect Per Olof Hallman, and her research also helped Larsson choose where certain scenes would take place.

THE GOD OF SMALL THINGS

ARUNDHATI ROY

November 24, 1961

BORN: Shillong, India

OTHER NOTABLE WORKS:
The Algebra of Infinite Justice (2001)
The Ministry of Utmost Happiness (2017)
My Seditious Heart: Collected Non-Fiction (2019)

As a fierce supporter of human rights, author Arundhati Roy uses her body of fiction and nonfiction work to compel supporters and critics alike to take a deeper look at the issues our world faces today, touching on topics like war, bigotry, and misogyny. Born in Shillong, India, many of the causes Roy focuses on involve her home country. Her 1998 essay *The End of Imagination* takes aim at India's nuclear weapons program, and her 2009 collection *Listening to Grasshoppers* includes writings about Hindu nationalism and the country's justice system.

Roy, who originally went to school for architecture, has also written an award-winning screenplay for the Indian film industry and regularly takes part in speeches concerning the humanitarian issues that she champions. As a fiction writer, the highlight of her career came in 1997 with the release of her first novel, *The God of Small Things*, a story about how India's caste system impacts the lives of an estranged set of twins, Rahel and Esthappen.

The story of Estha and Rahel, fraternal siblings who struggle with the cultural influences of their native India, is at the heart of ***The God of Small Things***, Arundhati Roy's 1997 novel. As children, the two attempt to process the struggles of their mother, Ammu, and their extended family, with the book's perspective filtered through their young eyes. Roy then revisits the two as adults, who reunite and attempt to sift through their shared grief. The book's examination of Indian culture, politics, social structure, and misogyny was heralded, and it won the Booker Prize in 1997.

ROY DREW UPON HER REAL LIFE FOR MANY OF THE BOOK'S DETAILS.

Though *The God of Small Things* is a work of fiction, Roy took inspiration from her own life when crafting the story. In the book, much of the action takes place in Ayemenem, India, the village where Roy grew up and saw the archaic caste system firsthand. Roy's grandmother also ran a pickle factory like the one owned by Rahel and Estha's family. This is where readers are introduced to Velutha, one of the workers at the factory and a member of India's "untouchable" caste, who begins an ill-fated affair with Ammu, Rahel and Estha's mother. Like Ammu, Roy's mother was a divorcee who had to deal with the stigma of a failed marriage.

Even the family's trips to see *The Sound of Music* have some basis in reality—in an interview, Roy recalled her family taking two-hour car rides to the city of Cochin to see the movie around seven times when she was a kid. If you read the book, you'll know that she wasn't exactly a fan of Julie Andrews's big-screen classic.

SHE WAS CHARGED WITH OBSCENITY BECAUSE OF THE BOOK.

The God of Small Things, which Roy spent more than four years writing, pokes and prods at the political and social issues facing India, questioning everything from the caste system to the treatment of women in the country to India's views of the British. And while the book won support from critics and readers worldwide, the reception for Roy at home was far more complex, especially among politicians on both the left and right. For one lawyer in particular, the depiction of sex between a Syrian Christian woman and a member of a lower class at the end of the book was grounds to file obscenity charges against Roy.

The attorney, Sabu Thomas, brought the charges against Roy in Kerala, India, the same region where both the book takes place and Roy grew up. The ordeal dragged on for ten years, with Roy being summoned to multiple court appearances; failing to show up even once could have led to her arrest. In the end, a new judge took over the case and dismissed it.

AFTER *THE GOD OF SMALL THINGS*, ROY WOULDN'T WRITE ANOTHER WORK OF FICTION FOR TWENTY YEARS.

In addition to winning the Booker Prize in 1997, *The God of Small Things* has been translated into more than forty languages and sold more than eight million copies since it hit shelves. Still, fans hoping Roy would be quick with a follow-up had to learn to be patient—at least in terms of her fiction work. After *The God of Small Things* was published, Roy doubled down on her non-fiction writing, releasing political essays and interview collections.

Her second novel, *The Ministry of Utmost Happiness*, was published in 2017. The book explores India's culture through the lens of Anjum, a transgender woman, and Tilo, an architect on the cusp of activism. Roy spent ten years writing the book, and once it was finally published, *The Ministry of Utmost Happiness* was met with critical acclaim—it even found its way onto the longlist for the Man Booker Prize in 2017. As if history was repeating itself, the novel was followed up by her 2019 collection *My Seditious Heart: Collected Non-Fiction*.

Why do we love old book smell?

There's nothing quite like the aroma of old books, a scent caused by volatile organic compounds (VOCs) released as the materials that books are made of decay and react with their environments—and absorb the odors around them. The scents can be as individual as books themselves: For example, scientists from Oxford University found that one of Shakespeare's first folios is emitting VOCs that smell like maraschino cherries and moldy furniture, but the book had also picked up a strong scent of tobacco. As for why we can't get enough of it? Because scent and memory are closely linked, the smell of old books can trigger happy memories like an old library or a favorite story (maybe that's why it has been turned into both perfume and candles). In 2017, one paper even suggested adding old book smell to UNESCO's intangible heritage list.

THE GRAPES OF WRATH

JOHN STEINBECK

February 27, 1902–December 20, 1968

BORN: Salinas, California

OTHER NOTABLE WORKS:
Of Mice and Men (1937)
East of Eden (1952)

As a native of rural Salinas, California, John Steinbeck witnessed the hardships of the region's migrant workers up close while going from job to job in his youth. Those memories would end up being the driving force behind his writing career, with many of his stories questioning the role of government, the morality of capitalism, and the integrity of the American dream itself. From the nostalgia of 1945's *Cannery Row* to the generation-spanning drama seen in *East of Eden*, Steinbeck was as comfortable writing a slice-of-life novella as he was confronting a story that was biblical in scope. By staying true to his role as an authentic observer of twentieth-century struggles, Steinbeck was awarded the Nobel Prize in Literature in 1962.

The Grapes of Wrath is John Steinbeck's award-winning political novel about the Great Depression. It follows the Joad family as they're forced to leave their Oklahoma farm and go west to California for work. The 1939 book humanized the "Okies," captured history as it was happening, and earned its author so much personal trouble that he started carrying a gun for protection.

THE NOVEL WAS INSPIRED BY VISITS TO LABOR CAMPS.

In 1936, the *San Francisco News* hired Steinbeck to write a series of articles about migrant labor camps in California. The articles were later reprinted in a pamphlet along with Dorothea Lange's iconic photographs. In the pieces, Steinbeck described Americans living in filthy shacks without running water and suffering from malnutrition, illness, and death. He used much of what he saw in *The Grapes of Wrath*.

STEINBECK INADVERTENTLY USED RESEARCH FOR SOMEONE ELSE'S NOVEL.

The author dedicated *The Grapes of Wrath* in part to Tom Collins, who managed the Migratory Labor Camp in Kern County, California, and helped Steinbeck research the novel. "I need this stuff," Steinbeck wrote of the detailed reports Collins gave him about the camps.

"It is exact and just the thing that will be used against me if I am wrong." But Steinbeck didn't know that another writer, Sanora Babb, had written some of the notes he was using. Babb was working on her own novel, *Whose Names Are Unknown,* and had used her notes as the foundation for the book, which was going to be published by Random House. Then *The Grapes of Wrath* hit the best seller list. Steinbeck's novel upstaged Babb and her book was shelved until 2004, the year before she died.

STEINBECK FOUND WRITING THE NOVEL HARROWING.

While writing *The Grapes of Wrath*, Steinbeck kept a journal of his process that shows the emotional ups and downs of an intense writing experience. He knew he was writing something that could be potentially great, but he doubted his ability to do it. "This book has become a misery to me because of my inadequacy," the journal reads. He seemed to find writing not only mentally difficult, but hard on the nerves: "My stomach and my nerves are screaming merry hell in protest against the inroads." And again later: "And now home with a little stomach ache that doesn't come from the stomach."

THE TITLE COMES FROM "THE BATTLE HYMN OF THE REPUBLIC."

Steinbeck's first wife Carol thought of taking *The Grapes of Wrath* from "The Battle Hymn of the Republic": "Mine eyes have seen the glory of the coming of the Lord/He is trampling out the vintage where the grapes of wrath are stored." The poem/song was written by Julia Ward Howe in 1861. She got "grapes of wrath" from Rev. 14:19 in the Bible, which mentions the "winepress of the wrath of God." In choosing the title, Steinbeck was emphasizing that his novel was American, not Communist propaganda—an accusation he knew would be hurled at the book.

THE BOOK WAS BURNED AND BANNED.

The novel was critically acclaimed and a best seller— some 430,000 copies had been printed by February 1940. But it was also controversial. The Associated Farmers of California was angered by the book, which implied that they used the migrants for cheap labor. They called *The Grapes of Wrath* a "pack of lies" and launched an attack against it, publicly burning the work and calling it Communist. Other institutions banned the book because of profanity and because of the ending, when a woman breastfeeds a starving man.

STEINBECK GREW SO AFRAID THAT HE STARTED CARRYING A GUN.

Steinbeck encountered so much hostility after *The Grapes of Wrath* came out that he considered giving up writing altogether. Articles in the press, buoyed by the Associated Farmers of California, launched a "hysterical personal attack" on Steinbeck. "I'm a pervert, a drunk, a dope fiend," he wrote. For a time, the FBI monitored him. In Salinas, people he knew his entire life became unfriendly toward him. He received death threats and was advised by the Monterey County Sheriff to carry a gun. Steinbeck complied. His son, Thomas Steinbeck, said, "My father was the best-armed man I knew, and went most places armed."

THE 1940 MOVIE VERSION WAS A BOX OFFICE SMASH.

While the book did well on its own, the 1940 movie cemented *The Grapes of Wrath* as a classic. Directed by John Ford, it starred Henry Fonda as Tom Joad. Steinbeck reportedly liked Fonda's performance, and said of the film, "with descriptive matter removed, it is a harsher thing than the book, by far. It seems unbelievable, but it is true." Ford won an Oscar for Best Director and Jane Darwell won Best Supporting Actress as Ma Joad.

WOODY GUTHRIE WROTE "THE BALLAD OF TOM JOAD."

After the movie came out, Victor Records asked Woody Guthrie to write twelve songs about the Dust Bowl for an album called *Dust Bowl Ballads*. One song was supposed to be based on the movie, so Guthrie borrowed a friend's typewriter, sat down with a jug of wine, and typed out the lyrics to "Tom Joad."

THE GRAPES OF WRATH GAVE ROUTE 66 ITS NICKNAME.

In the book, Steinbeck writes about US Route 66, the 2,500-mile-road between Chicago and Los Angeles, which used to be a major artery in the United States and what Steinbeck called "the mother road, the road of flight." Since then, the "Mother Road" has been portrayed in everything from Bobby Troup's song "Route 66" to Jack Kerouac's novel *On the Road*.

THE NOVEL LED STEINBECK TO THE NOBEL PRIZE.

The Grapes of Wrath won the 1940 Pulitzer Prize in Fiction and was a major factor for Steinbeck winning the Nobel Prize in 1962. In his acceptance speech, he emphasized the artist's duty to believe in goodness of man, stating, "the writer is delegated to declare and to celebrate man's proven capacity for greatness of heart and spirit—for gallantry in defeat—for courage, compassion and love. In the endless war against weakness and despair, these are the bright rally flags of hope and of emulation."

STEINBECK'S TEMPLATE FOR DUMPING A BAD FRIEND

Extricating yourself from a toxic friendship can be tough. Unlike romantic relationships, there's not a ton of advice out there about how to tactfully "dump" a friend. Fortunately, if you're struggling to find the right words, you can take a few pointers from John Steinbeck.

In the mid-1930s, Steinbeck was close with an aspiring writer named George Albee. But by 1938, the friendship was beginning to sour, and a jealous Albee began gossiping behind his friend's back. Despite Steinbeck's literary successes, including the recent publication of *Of Mice and Men*, the author was in the midst of a profoundly trying time. He'd been accused of getting a childhood friend pregnant, and was surrounded by gossip and unkind rumors.

Steinbeck soon discovered that, rather than standing up for his friend, Albee had been fueling these rumors. In response, Steinbeck began subtly retreating from the friendship, giving Albee the cold shoulder. Finally, Albee pressed Steinbeck for a reason for his withdrawal from the relationship. Steinbeck, who famously preferred written correspondence to phone calls, responded with an artfully written breakup letter, writing:

The reason for your suspicion is well founded. This has been a difficult and unpleasant time. There has been nothing good about it. In this time my friends have rallied around, all except you. Every time there has been a possibility of putting a bad construction on anything I have done, you have put such a construction . . . I'd like to be friends with you, George, but I can't if I have to wear a mail shirt the whole time. I wish to God your unhappiness could find some other outlet. But I can't consider you a friend when out of every contact there comes some intentionally wounding thing . . . And that is the reason and I think you always knew it was the reason.

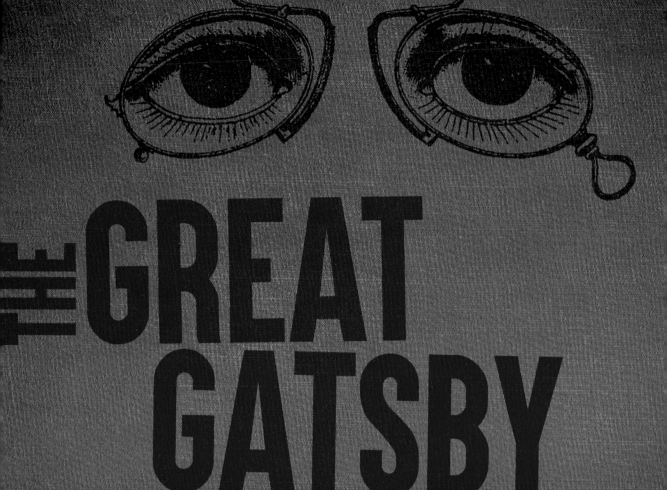

F. SCOTT FITZGERALD

September 24, 1896–December 21, 1940

BORN: St. Paul, Minnesota

OTHER NOTABLE WORKS:
This Side of Paradise (1920)
Tender is the Night (1934)

It's hardly surprising that F. Scott Fitzgerald is regularly referred to as the preeminent chronicler of the Jazz Age: The phrase—which refers to the flapper-filled decade of excess between the end of World War I and the beginning of the Great Depression—is erroneously credited to the writer himself. It's this lifestyle that Fitzgerald and his wife Zelda lived, and the one that's at the center of *The Great Gatsby*, the 1925 novel that has become a classic of English literature. While it received mixed reviews upon its release, today it would be tough to find a more serious contender for the title of "The Great American Novel." Unfortunately, much like the characters he wrote about, Fitzgerald's romantic ideals proved impossible to achieve in real life. In 1930, Zelda was diagnosed with schizophrenia and eventually institutionalized. Fitzgerald completed just one more novel, 1934's *Tender Is the Night*, but struggled with alcoholism. He passed away in 1940 at the age of forty-four, leaving an unfinished novel—*The Last Tycoon*—behind.

Fitzgerald's classic novel, ***The Great Gatsby***, chronicles the louche lives of several wealthy Long Islanders at the height of the Jazz Age. The mysterious Jay Gatsby—a hard-partying representative of the nouveau riche—pines for his former lover, Daisy Buchanan, a spirited socialite with an unfaithful husband. The drama, as narrated by Daisy's cousin, Nick Carraway, unfolds in the manner of a boozy reverie. From its real-life inspirations to its terrible early reviews, here's what you need to know about Fitzgerald's third novel.

THERE WERE SOME TERRIBLE TITLE OPTIONS.
F. Scott Fitzgerald had considered calling his tragic Jazz Age story about a self-made millionaire's pursuit of a rich young woman he'd loved in his youth *Trimalchio* and *Trimalchio in West Egg*—until someone persuaded him that the reference was too obscure. The original Trimalchio was a character in a first century work of fiction called *Satyricon*. The story had other famous fans, too: You can find mentions of Trimalchio in *Les Misérables*, *Pompeii*, and works by H.P. Lovecraft, Henry Miller, and Octavio Paz, among others.

THE STORY HAD REAL-LIFE INSPIRATIONS.

When writing *Gatsby*, Fitzgerald drew from his surroundings: He, Zelda, and their daughter Scottie had moved to Great Neck on Long Island in 1922. There, Fitzgerald witnessed the collision of "old money" and "new money." People who came from Great Neck had recently acquired money, while those who came from nearby Manhasset Neck or Cow Neck had inherited theirs.

Fitzgerald also drew from real architecture to create Jay Gatsby's lavish mansion. One of them was Oheka Castle in Huntington, New York, the second-largest private house in the United States. Some literary scholars also liken Fitzgerald's description of the mansion to the structure Beacon Towers, a mansion with around 140 rooms that was owned by William Randolph Hearst and demolished in 1945.

FITZGERALD'S FRIENDS POPULATED THE NOVEL.

Gatsby's estate wasn't all that was inspired by real-life; many of the characters were based on Fitzgerald's flesh-and-blood friends and lovers. Daisy was based on Ginevra King, a Chicago-area debutante and one of Fitzgerald's girlfriends. One Fitzgerald scholar says his romance with King was the most important relationship he experienced, even more so than the one with his wife. That may be true, considering that these words, found written in Fitzgerald's ledger, are thought to have been said by King's father: "Poor boys shouldn't think of marrying rich girls."

Similarly, Daisy Buchanan's best friend Jordan was modeled on one of Ginevra's good friends, Edith Cummings. Cummings was not only a fellow debutante—one of Chicago's "Big Four," the most eligible women in the city—she was also a famous amateur golfer. Dubbed "The Fairway Flapper," Cummings won the US Women's Amateur in 1923, two years before *Gatsby* was released.

Gatsby himself—or at least his line of work and one of his famous phrases—may have been inspired by a World War I vet named Max Gerlach, a "gentleman bootlegger" Fitzgerald knew from Great Neck. Fitzgerald scholar Matthew Bruccoli discovered a newspaper clipping in one of the Fitzgeralds' numerous scrapbooks. The clipping, apparently sent from Gerlach, was a photo of the Fitzgeralds accompanied by a handwritten note that said, "Here for a few days on business—How are you and the family old Sport? Gerlach." "Old sport," of course, is the way Gatsby constantly refers to narrator Nick Carraway.

THE COVER CHANGED THE STORY.

The iconic cover of the book was designed by Francis Cugat, who later went on to become a designer for actor/director/producer Douglas Fairbanks. Fitzgerald so loved Cugat's art that he incorporated it into the book.

THE EPIGRAPH IS FICTIONAL.

The poet Thomas Parke D'Invilliers, who "wrote" the novel's epigraph, is actually a character in Fitzgerald's previous book, *This Side of Paradise*. Fitzgerald also occasionally used it as his pen name. Here's the epigraph:

> "Then wear the gold hat, if that will move her;
> If you can bounce high, bounce for her too,
> Till she cry "Lover, gold-hatted, high-bouncing lover,
> I must have you!"

THE NOVEL WASN'T INITIALLY A SUCCESS.

Unlike Fitzgerald's previous two novels, *Gatsby* wasn't a commercial success. It sold just twenty thousand copies in the entire first year of publication.

Fitzgerald was convinced that the reason the book didn't take off was because *Gatsby* didn't have a single admirable female character—and, at the time, the majority of people reading novels were women. He also thought that the title, which was only "fair," resulted in poor sales.

Gatsby wasn't a universal critical success, either. A few of the not-so-rave reviews:

"Why [Fitzgerald] should be called an author, or why any of us should behave as if he were, has never been explained satisfactorily to me."
—*Brooklyn Daily Eagle*

"We are quite convinced after reading *The Great Gatsby* that Mr. Fitzgerald is not one of the great American writers of to-day."
—*The New York Evening World*

"Scott Fitzgerald's new novel, *The Great Gatsby*, is in form no more than a glorified anecdote, and not too probable at that."
—*The Baltimore Evening Sun*

WORLD WAR II HELPED MAKE *THE GREAT GATSBY* A SUCCESS.

So what great sum did Fitzgerald receive for writing one of the most beloved novels of all time? A $3,939 advance (plus an extra $325 later), and around $1,980 when it was published. He later received $16,666 for the movie rights.

Sadly, when Fitzgerald died of a heart attack at only forty-four years old in 1940, he had mostly disappeared into obscurity. At the time of his death, *Gatsby*'s publisher still had copies of the book in its warehouse—and that was from a second printing of just three thousand books. Fitzgerald's works saw a revival in 1945. Helping in that revival: 150,000 copies of *Gatsby* were sent to Americans serving in World War II. Today, nearly a half a million copies sell each year.

FIVE GREAT F. SCOTT FITZGERALD QUOTES ON WRITING

Though he was just forty-four when he died, F. Scott Fitzgerald left us with a wealth of wisdom and no shortage of quips. Here are five of our favorites.

ON WRITING
"You don't write because you want to say something, you write because you've got something to say."
—*From* The Crack Up

ON EXCLAMATION POINTS
"Cut out all these exclamation points. An exclamation point is like laughing at your own joke."
—*As recounted by Sheilah Graham in her memoir* Beloved Infidel

ON WHAT MAKES A GOOD STORY
"What people are ashamed of usually makes a good story." —*From* The Last Tycoon

ON LITERATURE
"That is part of the beauty of all literature. You discover that your longings are universal longings, that you're not lonely and isolated from anyone. You belong."
—*As recounted by Sheilah Graham in her memoir* Beloved Infidel

ON INTELLIGENCE
"The test of a first-rate intelligence is the ability to hold two opposed ideas in the mind at the same time, and still retain the ability to function. One should, for example, be able to see that things are hopeless and yet be determined to make them otherwise."
—*From a 1936 essay published in* Esquire

THE HANDMAID'S TALE

MARGARET ATWOOD

November 18, 1939

BORN: Ottawa, Ontario, Canada

OTHER NOTABLE WORKS:
Cat's Eye (1988)
Alias Grace (1996)
The Testaments (2019)

Margaret Atwood might be best known as the author of *The Handmaid's Tale*, her eerily prescient 1985 dystopian novel-turned-hit Hulu series. But there's much more to Atwood, and her bibliography, than bleak satire.

Since releasing *Double Persephone*, her first book of poetry (and first published work) in 1961, Atwood has published more than fifty works in a variety of genres: In addition to seventeen novels, the two-time Booker Prize winner has earned just as much acclaim for her books of poetry, nonfiction titles, short story collections, children's books, and graphic novels—and racked up a number of awards in the process. But regardless of the medium, Atwood has a way of infusing the topics that interest her most, including gender, politics, environmental factors, and female oppression.

The Handmaid's Tale is set in a discomfortingly familiar future, where a newly installed theocracy has instituted a sweeping series of misogynistic laws and practices. Because so few women in The Republic of Gilead are fertile, "handmaids" are enlisted to bear the children of the ruling class. The novel follows one such handmaid, Offred, as she struggles to acclimate to (and, perhaps, to resist) her new reality. Even if you've binge-watched the Emmy Award-winning adaptation of *The Handmaid's Tale*, there's still much to be learned from, and about, the book.

THE BOOK WAS PARTLY INSPIRED BY COLD WAR GERMANY.

Officially, *The Handmaid's Tale* is set at some point in the not-too-distant future (from whenever you're reading it). The book's oppressive themes were partly inspired by the fact that Atwood began writing it while she was living in Germany in 1984, at the height of the Cold War. "I was living in West Berlin, which was still encircled by the Berlin Wall," Atwood wrote in *The New York Times*. It was during this time, and through her visits to several other Iron Curtain countries, that the Republic of Gilead began to take shape. "I experienced the wariness, the feeling of being spied on, the silences, the changes of subject, the oblique ways in which people might convey information, and these had an influence on what I was writing," Atwood recalled.

ATWOOD WROTE *THE HANDMAID'S TALE* LONGHAND.

In 1984, the same year Atwood began writing *The Handmaid's Tale*, Apple released its first Macintosh computer. But the author took an old-school approach to penning her novel: She wrote the entire book out in longhand on yellow legal pads. It was only once she had completed the book that she transcribed it onto a (rented) typewriter.

THE BOOK IS DEDICATED TO ALLEGED WITCH MARY WEBSTER, A.K.A. "HALF-HANGED MARY."

Atwood's aunt once told her the story of Mary Webster, a resident of the Puritan town of Hadley, Massachusetts—and the author's supposed ancestor. In 1683, Webster was put on trial for suspicion of witchcraft but ultimately found not guilty. The following year, a prominent local named Philip Smith laid dying and said that he thought "himself under an evil hand," and decided Webster was to blame.

"The townspeople didn't like her, so they strung her up," Atwood said. "But it was before the age of drop hanging, and she didn't die. She dangled there all night, and in the morning, when they came to cut the body down, she was still alive." (According to eighteenth century politician and historian Thomas Hutchinson, things went down a little differently: The mob cut Mary, who was near death, down, then buried her in snow—but she survived.) The incident earned Webster the nickname of Half-Hanged Mary, and *The Handmaid's Tale* is dedicated to her memory.

ATWOOD DOESN'T CONSIDER THE BOOK SCIENCE FICTION, EVEN THOUGH IT'S OFTEN CLASSIFIED THAT WAY.

While many of Atwood's books, including *The Handmaid's Tale*, have been described as "science fiction," the author rejects that genre label: She has repeatedly said that *The Handmaid's Tale* isn't sci-fi because she ensured that the elements already exist in some form. Atwood has always contended that something like Gilead could happen under the right conditions. "I'm not a prophet," she told *The Guardian*. But when it comes to this particular novel, she is "sorry to have been so right."

THE BOOK HAS BEEN ADAPTED INTO A NUMBER OF MEDIUMS.

While Hulu's *The Handmaid's Tale* is the best-known adaptation of Atwood's book, it's hardly the only—or even the first—retelling. A stage version of the book debuted at Tufts University in Medford, Massachusetts, in 1989, just a few years after the book was published. It returned to the stage in Boston again in 2018. There has also been an opera, a ballet, a radio play, and a 1990 movie starring Natasha Richardson and Faye Dunaway, with a screenplay by Harold Pinter.

THE HULU SERIES CHANGED ONE IMPORTANT ASPECT OF THE BOOK.

In the novel, Gilead's cruelty extended to banishing all non-white "Children of Ham," which means that every character is white. But Bruce Miller, the Hulu series's executive producer and showrunner, couldn't imagine having such a homogenous cast. "That was a very big discussion with Margaret about what the difference was between reading the words, 'There are no people of color in this world' and seeing an all-white world on your television, which has a very different impact," Miller told *TIME*. "What's the difference between making a TV show about racists and making a racist TV show where you don't hire any actors of color?"

THE HANDMAID'S TALE HAS A SEQUEL.

In 2019, Atwood published *The Testaments*. The sequel to *The Handmaid's Tale* takes place approximately fifteen years after the events of the original novel and helps to fill in the ambiguity of the ending of *The Handmaid's Tale* and what became of Offred. The book also gave Atwood the chance to personally address the prescience of the first book with her readers, writing: "Everything you've ever asked me about Gilead and its inner workings is the inspiration for this book. Well, almost everything! The other inspiration is the world we've been living in."

SEVEN POWERFUL QUOTES FROM MARGARET ATWOOD

It turns out the woman behind *The Handmaid's Tale* and *Oryx and Crake* is just as wise as her tales are haunting. Here are seven of the most profound quips from author, activist, and Twitter enthusiast Margaret Atwood.

ON HER PERSONAL PHILOSOPHY

"Optimism means better than reality; pessimism means worse than reality. I'm a realist."

—From a 2004 interview with The Guardian

ON THE REALITY OF BEING FEMALE

"Men often ask me, 'Why are your female characters so paranoid?' It's not paranoia. It's recognition of their situation."

— From a 1990 interview with The Paris Review

ON THE CHALLENGES OF WRITING NON-FICTION

"When I was young I believed that 'nonfiction' meant 'true.' But you read a history written in, say, 1920 and a history of the same events written in 1995 and they're very different. There may not be one Truth—there may be several truths—but saying that is not to say that reality doesn't exist."

— From a 1997 interview with Mother Jones

ON THE DISCORD BETWEEN MEN AND WOMEN

"'Why do men feel threatened by women?' I asked a male friend of mine. . . . 'They're afraid women will laugh at them,' he said. 'Undercut their world view.' . . . Then I asked some women students in a poetry seminar I was giving, 'Why do women feel threatened by men?' 'They're afraid of being killed,' they said."

— From Atwood's Second Words: Selected Critical Prose, 1960-1982

ON HOW WE'RE ALL BORN WRITERS

"[Everyone] 'writes' in a way; that is, each person has a 'story'—a personal narrative—which is constantly being replayed, revised, taken apart and put together again. The significant points in this narrative change as a person ages—what may have been tragedy at twenty is seen as comedy or nostalgia at forty."

— From a 1990 interview with The Paris Review

ON THE OPPRESSION AT THE CENTER OF *THE HANDMAID'S TALE*

"Nothing makes me more nervous than people who say, 'It can't happen here.' Anything can happen anywhere, given the right circumstances."

— From a 2015 lecture to West Point cadets

ON WHY EVEN THE BLEAKEST POST-APOCALYPTIC NOVELS ARE, DEEP DOWN, FULL OF HOPE

"Any novel is hopeful in that it presupposes a reader. It is, actually, a hopeful act just to write anything, really, because you're assuming that someone will be around to [read] it."

— From a 2011 interview with The Atlantic

THE
HAUNTING
OF HILL HOUSE

SHIRLEY JACKSON

December 14, 1916–August 8, 1965

BORN: San Francisco, California

OTHER NOTABLE WORKS:
"The Lottery" (1948)
We Have Always Lived in the Castle (1962)

American author Shirley Jackson imbued her works, including "The Lottery" (1948) and *The Haunting of Hill House* (1959), with horror and Gothic glee. She grew up in California but spent her adult life in North Bennington, Vermont, where her husband was a university professor. Jackson staged many of her stories in familiar, mid-century settings—such as the small New England town in "The Lottery"—but then exposed their false morality and cruel social conventions through ghosts, hauntings, and psychological terror. She wrote six novels and more than two hundred short stories as well as works for children. Jackson died in 1965 at age forty-eight, but her stories continue to influence horror writers today.

Can a house be born bad? That's the question Shirley Jackson asks in her classic novel, *The Haunting of Hill House*. Released in 1959, the Gothic novel follows four strangers who converge on a purportedly haunted house to "scientifically" seek out evidence of the paranormal. Things rapidly devolve and the characters—in particular, the novel's lonely protagonist, Eleanor—realize, too late, that they're in over their heads.

Upon its release, the novel sold briskly, earning Jackson a National Book Award nomination and high praise from critics. In its review, *The New York Times* called the story "caviar for connoisseurs of the cryptic" and described Jackson as "the finest master currently practicing in the genre of the cryptic, haunted tale." Here's what you should know about the novel.

IT WAS INSPIRED BY REAL-LIFE PARANORMAL INVESTIGATORS.

Jackson was inspired to write *Hill House* after reading about a group of nineteenth century "psychic researchers" who rented a house they believed to be haunted so they could study paranormal phenomena. The researchers recorded their experiences in the house in order to present them in the form of a treatise to the Society for Psychic Research. In her essay "Experience and Fiction," Jackson explained that she was intrigued by the way the researchers revealed their own personalities and backgrounds throughout the study. "They thought they were being terribly scientific and proving all kinds of things," she explained, "and yet the story that kept coming through their dry reports was not at all the story of a haunted house, it was the story of several earnest, I believe misguided, certainly determined people, with their differing motivations and backgrounds."

JACKSON HAD A TERRIFYING SLEEPWALKING EXPERIENCE WHILE WRITING THE NOVEL.

Early on in the writing process, Jackson awoke one morning to find something terrifying atop her writing desk: A note, with the words "DEAD DEAD" scrawled upon it, written in her own handwriting. Jackson, who loved ghost stories but did not believe in ghosts, brushed the strange discovery off as sleepwalking. In "Experience and Fiction," she wrote that she used the strange note to motivate her: "I decided that I had better write the book awake, which I got to work and did."

SHE MADE AN UNSETTLING DISCOVERY WHILE RESEARCHING HAUNTED HOUSES.

Before she began writing *The Haunting of Hill House*, Jackson scoured magazines and newspapers for photos of houses that seemed haunted. During her research, she stumbled upon a photo of a house in California that had a particular air of "disease and decay." She was so struck by it that she asked her mother, who lived in California, if she could find any additional information about the house. Her mother's response shocked Jackson: Not only was she familiar with the house, but Jackson's own great-grandfather had built it. After standing empty for many years, the house had been set on fire—possibly by a group of townspeople.

THERE WAS ORIGINALLY MORE THAN ONE VERSION OF ELEANOR.

In *A Rather Haunted Life*, Shirley Jackson biographer Ruth Franklin writes that Jackson initially struggled to decide what kind of character her protagonist, Eleanor, would be. Jackson wrote three different iterations of Eleanor. One, according to Franklin, was "a spinster with a swagger"—a far cry from the introverted Eleanor of the finished novel.

IT'S A GHOST STORY WITHOUT GHOSTS.

Jackson often referred to the novel as a "good ghost story" despite the fact that it doesn't have any overt ghosts. In her notes for the novel, Jackson explained,

"The House *is* the haunting." The author was clear about the connections between Hill House and her protagonist, Eleanor. "Jackson clearly intended the external signs of haunting to be interpreted as manifestations of Eleanor's troubled psyche," Franklin explains in *A Rather Haunted Life*. At the same time, Franklin notes, "The novel makes it clear that something in the house brings out the disturbance in Eleanor."

JACKSON'S HUSBAND WAS TOO AFRAID TO READ IT.

Jackson's husband Stanley Edgar Hyman was a well-known literary critic and professor who enthusiastically read all of his wife's books—but not *The Haunting of Hill House*. According to Franklin, "For the first time he refused to read her manuscript: He found the concept of ghosts too frightening."

THE NOVEL HAS EARNED COMPARISONS TO *THE TURN OF THE SCREW*.

Since its release, critics and fans have drawn comparisons between *The Haunting of Hill House* and the writings of everyone from Edgar Allan Poe to Hilary Mantel. But the comparison that comes up the most is to Henry James's classic novella *The Turn of the Screw*. In her introduction to *The Haunting of Hill House*, Laura Miller explains that the two works share common themes, including "a lonely, imaginative young woman" and "a big isolated house." In his 1981 book *Danse Macabre*, Stephen King writes, "It seems to me that [*The Haunting of Hill House*] and James's *The Turn of the Screw* are the only two great novels of the supernatural in the last hundred years."

IT WAS JACKSON'S FIRST PROFITABLE NOVEL.

The Haunting of Hill House wasn't just Jackson's most popular novel—it was also her first profitable one. "For the first time, a novel of [Jackson's] had finally earned back its advance and was even making a profit," Franklin writes. When Jackson sold the movie rights to *Hill House* for $67,500 ("an astronomical fee for the time," notes Franklin), it propelled her family into true financial stability for the first time. They used the money from the film to buy living room drapes, a player piano, and a washing machine and dryer.

Fascinating Facts about Shirley Jackson

Jackson has long been known for her spooky short story "The Lottery," which caused widespread controversy when it came out in *The New Yorker* in 1948. But there are many more things you should know about this master of Gothic horror.

1 JACKSON WAS HER FAMILY'S CHIEF BREAD-WINNER.

Jackson's husband was a writer, too. Hyman was a literary critic who taught literature at Bennington College, and it was his job that brought the couple to the small Vermont city, where Jackson often chafed at being placed in the role of faculty wife. Yet it was Jackson's work that supported the family. (Like many wives of her day, she also did all the cooking, cleaning, taking care of their four kids, and driving the family around town— as one of Hyman's former students wrote of him, "Stanley never did anything practical if he could help it.")

In addition to the fees she earned selling short stories and novels, Jackson had a lucrative career writing lighthearted essays on motherhood and family life for women's magazines, which she eventually parlayed into two successful memoirs.

2 SHE CLAIMED TO BE A WITCH.

In keeping with the haunted themes in her writing, Jackson studied the history of witchcraft and the occult, and often told people she was a witch—though that may have been in part a publicity tactic. According to Franklin in *A Rather Haunted Life*, Jackson mentioned being a "practicing amateur witch" in the biography of an early novel and brought up her witchy abilities in interviews, "even claiming that she had used magic to break the leg of publisher Alfred A. Knopf, with whom her husband was involved in a dispute." Reviewers ate it up: "Miss Jackson writes not with a pen," one wrote, "but with a broomstick."

3 JACKSON CONSIDERED BECOMING A PROFESSIONAL CARTOONIST.

Jackson wasn't just good with words. She loved to draw, and even considered becoming a professional cartoonist at one point, according to Franklin. While her favorite subjects were cats, she regularly made minimalist, humorous sketches of herself and the people around her (particularly her husband), keeping a kind of cartoon diary of her life.

"They're Thurber-esque in style, but they're kind of edgy, too," her son, Laurence Jackson Hyman, told *The Guardian* of the drawings. "There's one in which she is trudging up a hill carrying bags of groceries, and my father is sitting in his chair, reading. 'Dear,' he says, without bothering to get up. 'You know you're not supposed to carry heavy things when you're pregnant!'"

4 JACKSON DIED BEFORE FINISHING HER FINAL NOVEL.

Jackson died unexpectedly from heart failure in 1965 at the age of forty-eight. (At the time, newspapers listed her age as forty-five—she often lied about how old she was, perhaps to minimize the age difference between her and her husband, who was two years younger than she.)

A significant chunk of her work has been published since her death, though. When she died, she was in the midst of writing a novel, *Come Along with Me*, which was published in its incomplete format by her husband in 1968. In the early '90s, a crate of unpublished stories were uncovered, and Laurence and his sister Sarah Hyman Dewitt used that as the core of a new collection called *Just an Ordinary Day*. In 2015, they edited and released *Let Me Tell You*, a collection of stories, essays and lectures from her archive that were mostly unfinished or unpublished at the time of her death.

EIGHT WOMEN HORROR WRITERS YOU NEED TO READ

While they have written some of the most blood-curdlingly scary stories of all time, they haven't always gotten the credit they deserve. Here are eight women horror writers you need to read once you've finished *The Haunting of Hill House*.

DAPHNE DU MAURIER

If you love Alfred Hitchcock movies, chances are that you already love Daphne du Maurier—Hitchcock adapted three of her novels into films, starting with *Jamaica Inn* in 1939, then *Rebecca* in 1940, and finally *The Birds* in 1963. Hitchcock wasn't the only director who wanted to bring her work to the big screen. Her short story "Don't Look Now" was adapted into an extremely creepy movie starring Julie Christie and Donald Sutherland in 1973. In all, du Maurier's works have been adapted for film more than a dozen times, and for television even more frequently. But, as with many adaptations, her original stories are even more haunting than their on-screen counterparts.

CHARLOTTE RIDDELL

For great Victorian-era ghost stories, look no further than Charlotte Riddell. Scholar E.F. Bleiler once called her "the Victorian ghost novelist par excellence," and her stories are both extraordinarily spooky and subtly snarky. Born in Ireland in 1832, she was a prolific writer of supernatural tales, haunted house stories in particular. Though she and her husband often struggled financially, Riddell—who initially wrote under the masculine pen names F.G. Trafford and R.V.M. Sparling—was a popular writer in her time, publishing classic short stories like "The Open Door" and "Nut Bush Farm" along with four supernatural novellas. Today, Riddell's stories feel old-fashioned in the best possible way—they're full of dusty, deserted mansions and ghosts with unfinished business.

JOYCE CAROL OATES

The Pulitzer Prize-nominated author Joyce Carol Oates, who has been called "America's foremost woman of letters," is famous for writing stories that will scare your pants off. Her catalogue of more than a hundred books can be overwhelming, so we'd recommend starting off with her story collection *Haunted: Tales of the Grotesque*. Or, try her famous short story "Where Are You Going, Where Have You Been?," which was inspired by the real-life serial killer Charles Schmid.

ASA NONAMI

Asa Nonami's writing has been compared to everything from *Rosemary's Baby* to *The Twilight Zone*. She's an award-winning crime and horror writer whose novels often feature complex female characters in impossible situations. In her short story collection *Body*, Nonami tells five tales of terror, each inspired by a different body part, while her novel *Now You're One of Us* tells the story of a young bride who discovers her husband and his family may not be quite what they seem. It's a ghost-free horror tale that builds its sense of suspense from its sheer unpredictability.

LISA TUTTLE

Remember those '80s horror paperbacks that tantalized with terrifying covers, then disappointed with incomprehensible plots? Lisa Tuttle is the antidote to that. She's everything you hoped mass-market horror could be, in fact. Her novels are disturbing, creative, and most importantly, well written. Tuttle got her start collaborating with George R.R. Martin on the science fiction novel *Windhaven* before emerging as an important voice in '80s horror fiction with works like *Familiar Spirit*, *Gabriel*, and the short story collection *A Nest of Nightmares*. She's also written fantasy, young adult fiction, and nonfiction—in 1986, she even published the reference book *Encyclopedia of Feminism*.

TANANARIVE DUE

Tananarive Due isn't just one of the best contemporary horror writers around, she's also one of the coolest. Back in the mid-1990s, when she was still an up-and-coming young author, Due somehow ended up onstage, in a rock band, with Stephen King. She then proceeded to get King to write a blurb for her second novel, *My Soul to Keep* (he called it an "eerie epic"). Nowadays, Due is an accomplished scholar and short story writer in addition to being a novelist. Her works include the African Immortals series, the haunted house novel *The Good House*, and *Ghost Summer*, a collection of short stories that somehow manages to be both nightmare-inducing and extremely moving. She also taught a course at UCLA inspired by Jordan Peele's 2017 horror movie *Get Out* called "The Sunken Place: Racism, Survival, and Black Horror Aesthetic."

MARIKO KOIKE

Mariko Koike is an award-winning Japanese author of suspense, romance, and, of course, horror. Her novel *The Cat in the Coffin* is a thrilling exercise in the macabre. But her greatest work of pure horror is the 1986 novel *The Graveyard Apartment*, which tells the story of a young family that moves into a brand new apartment complex overlooking an old graveyard and crematorium. The novel patiently builds dread from seemingly ordinary images: a bird's feather, a yellow hat, a smudge on the TV screen. It's a chillingly tense haunted house novel from an author who understands that the greatest horrors often hide in the mundane.

HELEN OYEYEMI

Helen Oyeyemi's writing defies classification, blending horror, fantasy, fairy tales, and folklore. Though her works don't always fit comfortably into the horror genre, they range from unsettling to truly frightening and often employ elements of the paranormal or bizarre. In *The Icarus Girl*, which Oyeyemi published when she was just twenty, an awkward young girl makes a strange new friend who may or may not be real. The novel mixes paranormal and Gothic themes with Nigerian folklore. In her 2009 novel *White is For Witching*, meanwhile, Oyeyemi tells the story of a mysterious house in Dover, England, and the secrets of the family who lives there. Reviewing that novel, *The Austin Chronicle* dubbed Oyeyemi the "direct heir to [Shirley Jackson's] Gothic throne."

DOUGLAS ADAMS

March 11, 1952–May 11, 2001

BORN: Cambridge, England

OTHER NOTABLE WORKS:
The Restaurant at the End of the Universe (1980)
Dirk Gently's Holistic Detective Agency (1987)

d computer planet one galaxy Deep Thou
ive infinite dolphin Arthur sections space Den
Beeblebrox drive towel exploration connections
ive 42 alien Marvin mostly harmless don't panic sa
Ford Prefect android Zahod computer planet one gala
Thought alpha plural emotive infinite dolphin
ons space Dent seconds The Beeblebro
oration connections Trillian em
y harmless don't panic saf
d comput   net one g
          hin Art
      ve towe
      Marvi
      t a

Though Douglas Adams will always be best-known as the author of *The Hitchhiker's Guide to the Galaxy* series, "novelist" was only one of this creative Renaissance man's many titles. As a student at the University of Cambridge, Adams began dabbling in sketchwriting as part of a comedy group (Adams-Smith-Adams) as well as for the university's performing arts society—a skill he managed to parlay into an early career writing a sketch for *Monty Python's Flying Circus* in 1974. Between 1978 and 1980, Adams worked as a writer and script editor on the BBC's original *Doctor Who*, and at the same time launched *The Hitchhiker's Guide to the Galaxy* as a BBC radio series. He would go on to satirize another genre staple with 1987's *Dirk Gently's Holistic Detective Agency*.

Much like his ahead-of-their-time tomes, Adams was a technophile with a keen interest in what the future held for humanity. He was a co-founder of a digital media and internet company, The Digital Village, where he created *Starship Titanic*, an interactive computer game in which the player is charged with repairing the eponymous interstellar cruise ship. In 1997, Monty Python's Terry Jones brought Adams's career full circle by adapting *Starship Titanic* into a book of his own.

In *Hitchhiker's Guide*, Douglas Adams combines the absurd (nuclear missiles that become sperm whales, names like *Slartibartfast*) with the utterly mundane (bath towels, economic recession) for a portrait of the universe that is both unbelievable and completely relatable. Human Arthur Dent is rescued from Earth's destruction by an undercover alien working as a guidebook researcher. Together, they embark on a series of rip-roaring interstellar adventures that bring them closer to the meaning of life (and, at the same time, leave them more confused about it than ever). Read on for more you should know about the delightful sci-fi tale.

ADAMS CAME UP WITH THE IDEA WHILE HITCHHIKING THROUGH EUROPE.

One fateful night in 1971, a young, drunk, "frantically depressed" Douglas Adams was found pondering the cosmos from a field in Innsbruck, Austria. With his copy of Ken Welsh's *Hitch-hiker's Guide to Europe* nearby, an idea struck him. "When the stars came out I thought that someone ought to write a Hitchhiker's Guide to the Galaxy because it looked a lot more attractive out there than it did around me," he later wrote to Welsh.

The concept lay dormant for several years, until Adams was working on a scripted radio show tentatively titled *The Ends of the Earth*. He originally planned for each episode to have its own storyline—which would all culminate in Earth's demise—but his long-forgotten idea came floating back, and he soon pivoted to a single-plot series that involved an alien field researcher collecting data for a galactic guidebook. *The Hitchhiker's Guide to the Galaxy* first aired on the BBC as a radio show, and Adams later adapted it as a novel.

ARTHUR DENT WAS ALMOST "ALERIC B."

For his rather aimless protagonist, Adams wanted a name that, in his words, was both "perfectly ordinary" and "distinctive." So he chose *Arthur*—classic, but not overused. *Dent*, meanwhile, seemed fitting for "somebody who reacted to things that happened to him, rather than being an instigator himself." When Adams first conceived of the character, however, he hadn't quite worked out this rationale. In an early outline for the story, Arthur Dent had a much less ordinary moniker: *Aleric B.* He made the switch in a taxi on the way to the pitch meeting at the BBC.

ADAMS WORRIED THAT THE TOWELS WOULD SEEM MEANINGLESS.

Among the many impossible technologies in Adams's novel is one laughably mundane Earthly convention: the towel. While on holiday in Greece, Adams fell into a pattern of forcing his friends to wait while he searched the premises for his towel, which he couldn't seem to keep track of. By the end of the trip, Adams viewed the towel as a symbol of the organized mind, and he gave it a similar significance in *The Hitchhiker's Guide*. Though he was nervous that readers wouldn't get such a personal joke, they responded with overwhelming enthusiasm. "I began to think, 'Well, maybe I've hit some kind of towel lodestone at the heart of people's psychology,'" he said in a 1992 interview. After Adams's death in 2001, fans launched "Towel Day," an annual celebration on May 25 when everyone takes their towel everywhere.

BUT THE NUMBER FORTY-TWO ACTUALLY *WAS* MEANINGLESS.

Considering that the number forty-two is the answer to the "Ultimate Question of Life, the Universe, and Everything," many fans assumed Adams had a good reason for picking it. Theories abounded. Some people thought it was a reference to Lewis Carroll's "Rule Forty-two" in *Alice's Adventures in Wonderland* ("All persons more than a mile high to leave the court"), while others hypothesized various mathematical origins. Adams actually just chose it as a joke. "Binary representations, base thirteen, Tibetan monks are all complete nonsense," he once confessed. "I sat at my desk, stared into the garden and thought 'Forty-two will do.' I typed it out. End of story."

ADAMS DIDN'T EXACTLY PLAN THE NOVEL'S ABRUPT ENDING.

If anybody thought Adams would shake his infamous reputation for missing due dates when he shifted from scripts to novels, they quickly shed that notion. The manuscript deadline for *The Hitchhiker's Guide* came and went, and publisher Pan Books started to get antsy. Instead of extending the deadline, they simply called and asked how many pages he had written so far. After he answered, they said, "Well, finish the page you are on, and we'll send a motorbike 'round to pick it up in half an hour."

FIVE FAMOUS LITERARY CHARACTERS BASED ON REAL PEOPLE

Douglas Adams once explained that his *Hitchhiker's Guide to the Galaxy* alien had done "minimal research" of Earth and thought he was choosing an inconspicuous name for himself, because he "had simply mistaken the dominant life form." The Ford Prefect, by the way, was a British car produced from 1938 to 1961. Here are a few more literary characters with real-life inspirations—though these are based on people, not cars.

NORA CHARLES

One of the wittiest female characters in literary history, Nora Charles from *The Thin Man*, doesn't hold a candle to her inspiration, Lillian Hellman. Lillian was author Dashiell Hammett's significant other for thirty years, but she was also a respected playwright, screenwriter, author, and outspoken political activist. Hammett apparently told Hellman that she was the inspiration for his female villains as well.

MISS HAVISHAM

It's almost hard to imagine that the furious and completely insane jilted bride of Charles Dickens's *Great Expectations* has a flesh-and-blood counterpart. But she does—in fact, there are a couple of people who might fit the bill.

One was Eliza Emily Donnithorne, an Australian woman who thought she was getting married in 1856. But after she was stood up by the groom, she refused to change anything about the house; the wedding feast even sat out until it rotted away. Legend has it that Donnithorne never left the house again.

Another was Madame Eliza Jumel, who may have gone a little crazy in her desperate attempts to break into New York high society. After finally throwing a successful dinner party for Joseph Bonaparte, she supposedly left the banquet and place settings out for decades to commemorate her social acceptance.

HESTER PRYNNE

The modest grave of Elizabeth Pain in Boston's King's Chapel Burying Ground holds a secret if you look at it closely. Some believe the *A* inscribed on the stone shows that she was "whipt with twenty stripes," though it was for the murder of her child, not for adultery (she was found not guilty, by the way). The damning mark may have served as Nathaniel Hawthorne's inspiration for Hester Prynne in *The Scarlet Letter*. There's also a record of one Hester Craford who was severely flogged for "fornication" with a man named John Wedg in the 1660s. At the very least, Hawthorne may have borrowed her name.

SEVERUS SNAPE

"Snape is the very sadistic teacher loosely based on a teacher I myself had," Harry Potter creator J.K. Rowling once said. "Children are very aware and we're kidding ourselves if we don't think that they are—that teachers do sometimes abuse their power and this particular teacher does abuse his power. He is not a particularly pleasant person at all."

That teacher, John Nettleship, wasn't thrilled with the comparison when he found out about it, saying, "I knew I was a strict teacher but I didn't think I was that bad." He later came to terms with it enough to write a booklet called *Harry Potter's Chepstow* about various locations from Rowling's school days that may have inspired people and places from her successful series. Nettleship died of cancer in 2011.

ARTEMIS FOWL

Eoin Colfer's little brother, Donal, was "a mischievous mastermind who could get out of any trouble he got into," and seeing a picture of Donal in a dapper first communion suit reminded Colfer of a tiny James Bond villain.

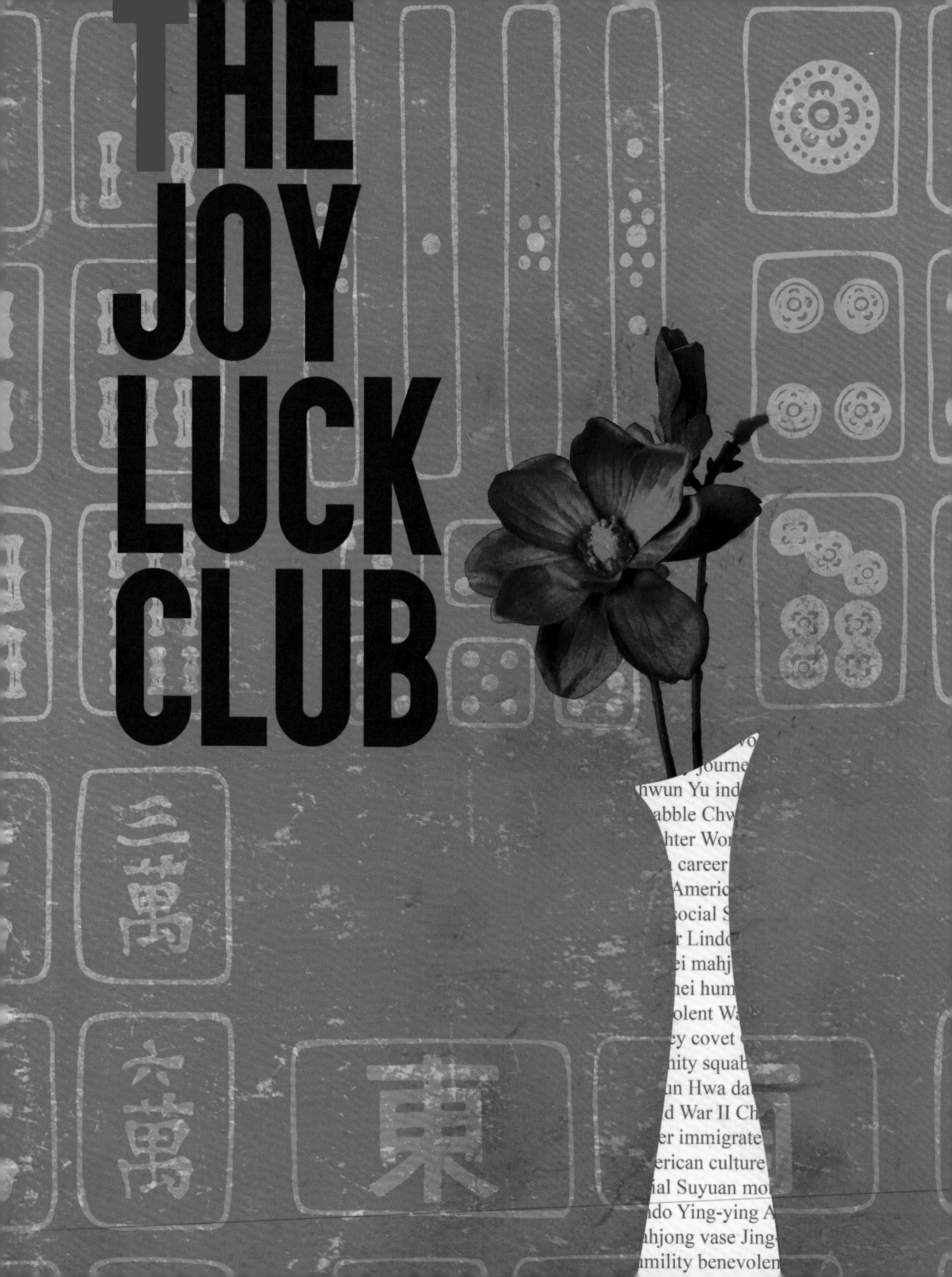
THE
JOY
LUCK
CLUB

AMY TAN

February 19, 1952

BORN: Oakland, California

OTHER NOTABLE WORKS:
The Kitchen God's Wife (1991)
The Hundred Secret Senses (1995)

If lived experiences inform a writer's best work, then Amy Tan has a deep reservoir to draw from. Before the age of eighteen, Tan had lived in twelve homes around the San Francisco area. At fifteen, her father John and brother Peter both succumbed to brain tumors, prompting her mother to take Tan and her younger brother John Jr. to travel Europe before Tan graduated from high school in Switzerland. (In 1949, her mother, Daisy, had been forced to leave three daughters behind in China to escape both communism and an abusive husband.)

After stints at five different colleges, Tan graduated with degrees in English and linguistics and worked as a language development specialist before turning to freelance business writing. Becoming a novelist was the furthest thing from her mind, but Tan did have an interest in short fiction and attended a writer's group led by Molly Giles. Tan's short stories led to what would become *The Joy Luck Club,* published in 1989.

The novel, structured as a series of sixteen vignettes, centers on the cultural rift that sometimes divides Chinese immigrants and their Chinese-American children, a topic Tan knew well. Her mother had resisted Tan leaving one college to pursue a relationship with future husband Lou DeMattei and grew even more upset when Tan abandoned her pre-med courses.

A movie adaptation of *Club* followed in 1993, and so did a celebrated writing career that earned more awards than Tan might have shelf space for. Her cultural footprint has extended to a guest appearance as herself on *The Simpsons* and even a namesake in a species of terrestrial leech, *Chtonobdella tanae*, in honor of her support of zoological field research. Her 2001 novel *The Bonesetter's Daughter* was turned into an opera, for which Tan wrote the libretto. In 2017, Tan published *Where the Past Begins*, which explores her sometimes-tumultuous relationship with her mother and her creative process.

Tan's defining work remains *Club*, in large part because its focus on Chinese immigration reveals the relationship between mothers and daughters to be common across cultures—equally rewarding, equally challenging, and equally unique.

Upon its publication in 1989, author Amy Tan's *The Joy Luck Club* was much different from other novels that were occupying the best-seller lists. In describing the emotional connection between the mothers and daughters who gather for games of mahjong at a social club, Tan was shining a light on an underrepresented culture. The book became a sensation, helping open doors for other depictions of Asian life in media. Here are some other facts about Tan's influential work.

THE BOOK WAS INSPIRED IN PART BY A TRIP TO CHINA.

The daughter of immigrants, Tan had never been to China prior to 1987, when the then-thirty-five-year-old traveled with her mother Daisy to visit the three daughters Daisy had been forced to leave behind after fleeing the communist country in 1949. The experience pushed Tan to complete a book of short stories about Chinese mothers and their Chinese-American daughters.

IT WASN'T WRITTEN AS A NOVEL.

Tan originally conceived *The Joy Luck Club* as a series of sixteen vignettes about four pairs of mothers and daughters, effectively making it a short story collection. Tan said she was inspired by *Love Medicine* by Louise Erdrich, which used a similar structure. But when one early review for the book referred to it as a novel, the publisher decided that was better from a marketing perspective and took "stories" off the title page. Tan still considers it a collection of short stories.

MORE FAMOUS AUTHORS' FAVORITE BOOKS

Amy Tan's favorite piece of classic Chinese literature is *Jing Ping Mei (The Plum in the Golden Vase)*, penned by an anonymous scribe. "I would describe it as a book of manners for the debauched," she said in a 2013 interview with *The New York Times*. "Its readers in the late Ming period likely hid it under their bedcovers, because it was banned as pornographic. It has a fairly modern, naturalistic style—'Show, don't tell'—and there are a lot of sex scenes shown. For years, I didn't know I had the expurgated edition that provided only elliptical hints of what went on between falling into bed and waking up refreshed. The unexpurgated edition is instructional."

SAMUEL BECKETT

Winner of the 1969 Nobel Prize in Literature and author of *Waiting for Godot*, Beckett was always a private individual, even after garnering acclaim for his writing. In 2011, a volume of the author's letters from 1941 to 1956 was published, giving the world a glimpse into his friendships and reading habits. Beckett wrote about many books in his correspondence: He described *Around the World in 80 Days* by Jules Verne as "lively stuff," wrote that his fourth reading of *Effi Briest* by Theodor Fontane caused "the same old tears in the same old places," and that he liked *The Catcher in the Rye* by J.D. Salinger "more than anything for a long time."

LYDIA DAVIS

Reading John Dos Passos's *Orient Express* was "a turning point for me," award-winning novelist Lydia Davis said in 1997. "That was one of the first 'grown up' books that made me excited about the language."

GEORGE SAUNDERS

In 2014, Saunders—one of the most famous short story writers of our time—detailed some of his favorite books for Oprah Winfrey's *O* magazine. On the favorites list for the author were Tobias Wolff's *In the Garden of the North American Martyrs*, Michael Herr's Vietnam memoir *Dispatches*, Stuart Dybek's short story collection *The Coast of Chicago*, Toni Morrison's *The Bluest Eye*, and several classics of Russian literature, including Isaac Babel's *Red Cavalry* and Nikolai Gogol's *Dead Souls*.

MOST OF THE BOOK WAS WRITTEN IN JUST FOUR MONTHS.

After receiving positive feedback to three of the stories that would eventually be included in *The Joy Luck Club*, Tan decided to quit her job as a freelance business writer and devote all her time to completing the book. The remaining thirteen stories were written in just four months.

THE BOOK IS—AND ISN'T—AUTOBIOGRAPHICAL.

Because Tan has been so outspoken about her mother's influence on *The Joy Luck Club*, many readers have come to assume it was autobiographical. This isn't accurate, as the scenarios in the book aren't based on Tan's life. The author has instead described it as being emotionally accurate, with the themes and conflicts based in Tan's real relationship with her mother—who wound up loving the book. "She loved that the feelings in [it] were absolutely true, and she believed that I had listened to her and that I appreciated what she was trying to teach me," Tan told *Entertainment Weekly*. "And that was the best review I could have gotten for that book. It was the best, the absolute best that I got."

THE JOY LUCK CLUB IS TAUGHT IN HIGH SCHOOLS.

Owing to its rich depiction of Chinese culture, Chinese history, and familial bonds, *The Joy Luck Club* is a popular title to read and review in classrooms. It's sometimes used in tandem with the 1993 movie adaptation of the same name. "In the past, *The Joy Luck Club* was included on required reading lists because the stories were different from the mainstream and thus would give young readers exposure to another culture," Tan has said. "Those were in the days when communities were not that diverse. The irony today is that educators select my book so that young readers can *identify* with the story. The student population is multicultural and the same books once selected to understand *others* are now chosen to understand *ourselves*."

HENRY MILLER

The *Tropic of Cancer* author wrote an entire book that, he explained in the preface, "[dealt] with books as a vital experience." *The Books in My Life* included an appendix titled "The Hundred Books Which Influenced Me Most." Classics like *Wuthering Heights, Adventures of Huckleberry Finn, Les Misérables*, and *Leaves of Grass* all made the cut.

JOYCE CAROL OATES

In a 2013 interview with *The Boston Globe*, Oates revealed Dostoevsky as one of her favorite authors. When asked for her all-time favorite book, she said: "I would say Dostoevsky's *Crime and Punishment*, which had an enormous effect on me. I think young people today might not realize how readable that novel is. The other book that I worry no one reads anymore is James Joyce's Ulysses. It's not easy, but every page is wonderful and repays the effort."

MAYA ANGELOU

The poet and author had a number of favorite books, including Dickens's *A Tale of Two Cities*, the Bible, *Look Homeward, Angel* by Thomas Wolfe, *Invisible Man* by Ralph Ellison, and Louisa May Alcott's *Little Women*. "When I read Alcott, I knew that these girls she was talking about were all white," Angelou told *The Week* in 2013. "But they were nice girls and I understood them. I felt like I was almost there with them in their living room and their kitchen."

JOHN STEINBECK

One of *The Grapes of Wrath* and *East of Eden* author's favorite books later in life was Sherwood Anderson's *Winesburg, Ohio*, but his first favorite book was *Le Morte d'Arthur*, a collection of Arthurian tales by Sir Thomas Malory, which Steinbeck received as a gift when he was nine. It was a major influence on the author's writing, and ultimately led to *The Acts of King Arthur and His Noble Knights*, which Steinbeck hoped would be "the best work of my life and the most satisfying." He had completed drafts of just seven chapters of the book when he died in 1968; it was published posthumously eight years later.

CHERYL STRAYED

When the author of the bestselling memoir *Wild* set off on her journey up the Pacific Coast Trail, she only had room to take a few books. One was a book of Adrienne Rich's poetry, *The Dream of a Common Language*, which she had already read enough times to almost memorize it in its entirety. At one point during her arduous hike, she considered burning the book to save weight in her pack, as she did with other books she read along the trail. "There was no reason not to burn this book too," she wrote. "Instead, I only hugged it to my chest."

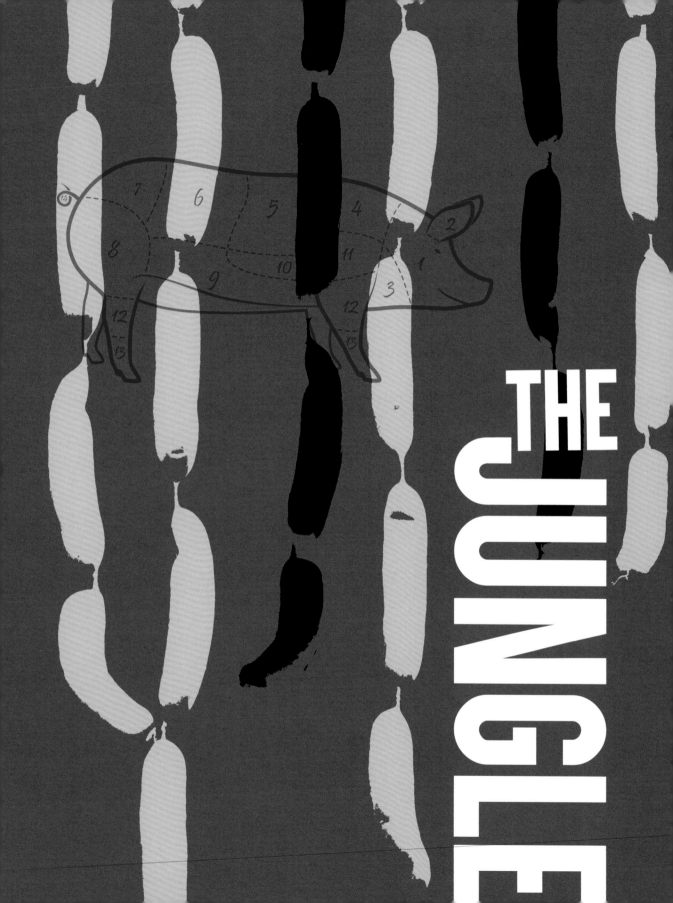

THE JUNGLE

UPTON SINCLAIR

September 20, 1878–November 25, 1968

BORN: Baltimore, Maryland

OTHER NOTABLE WORKS:
Oil! (1927)
Dragon's Teeth (1942)

U pton Sinclair gave Americans a literal look at how the sausage got made. Throughout his career, the staunch anti-capitalist penned prose advocating for social justice. His reporting on Chicago's meatpacking industry formed the basis of 1906's *The Jungle*, which dredged up dirty details on the conditions immigrant workers faced. The novel sparked public outrage and spurred Congress to pass the Food and Drug Act of 1906. *The Jungle* transformed the author from a "penniless rat" into a muckraking maven—and made him a staple in AP US History curricula decades later.

But that wasn't his only moment in the literary spotlight. Sinclair wrote nearly one hundred books; his 1942 novel about the Nazi takeover of Germany, *Dragon's Teeth*, won the Pulitzer Prize for Fiction. His politics seeped beyond his pages, too: He used earnings from *The Jungle* to fund a short-lived utopian community and dove into politics, running as a Socialist candidate in California's 1920 Congressional election and 1922 Senate race. In 1934, he was the Democratic nominee in the state's gubernatorial election. The book *I, Candidate for Governor: And How I Got Licked* detailed his campaign.

Upton Sinclair conceived *The Jungle* as a political game-changer, a book that would get people talking and instigate some major reforms. The book certainly did both of those things—but for reasons its author didn't quite expect.

THE BOOK WAS COMMISSIONED BY A SOCIALIST NEWSPAPER EDITOR.

Sinclair began his literary career as a teenager, supporting himself by writing jokes and short stories for newspapers while he was a student at the City College of New York. His first novel—a romance titled *Springtime and Harvest*—was released in 1901. By 1903, Sinclair had embraced socialism, and a year later, he became a regular contributor to *Appeal to Reason*, America's leading socialist newspaper. Its editor, Fred D. Warren, admired Sinclair's fourth novel, *Manassas*, a historical epic set in the Civil War that was written as a salute to the abolitionist movement. Warren gave Sinclair a $500 advance (the equivalent of about $14,000 today) to pen a similar novel about the problem of "wage slavery" in industrialized cities. Sinclair accepted the challenge, made tracks for the Chicago stockyards, and got to work.

SINCLAIR DID SEVEN WEEKS OF RESEARCH ON LOCATION.

From the start, Sinclair believed that *The Jungle* was destined to change history—and said as much when he met journalist Ernest Poole as he was starting his field research. "I've come here to write the *Uncle Tom's Cabin* of the labor movement," the then-twenty-six-year-old author told Poole.

Sinclair spent a total of seven weeks taking field notes in and around Chicago's meatpacking district. To access local factories, he contacted Windy City socialists and union leaders, many of whom were familiar with his work in *Appeal to Reason*. Disguised in well-worn clothes, Sinclair blended right in. On top of checking out the stockyards, he also took a few peeks into Chicago's big banks and the famous Jane Addams Hull House.

FIVE PUBLISHERS REJECTED *THE JUNGLE*.

In exchange for his $500 advance, Warren secured the right to publish *The Jungle* as a serial in *Appeal to Reason*, where it ran in (mostly) weekly installments from February to November 1905. Sinclair concurrently tried to get a shortened version published in book form, but it proved challenging. At first, Macmillan offered to put it out, but only if Sinclair made some huge changes to the text. Though the company gave him another $500 advance to implement these tweaks, the two parties never saw eye-to-eye and Macmillan eventually decided against publishing *The Jungle*. (Luckily for the cash-strapped Sinclair, they never asked him to return the money.)

Afterward, four other publishers turned down the book. Just as Sinclair was printing it himself using donations from readers, publisher Doubleday, Page & Company approached him with an offer. Sinclair asked that they allow him to self-publish his edition so he could fulfill the existing pre-orders. Doubleday acquiesced, and Sinclair released five thousand copies of the so-called "Sustainer's Edition" under The Jungle Publishing Company in February 1906, the same month that Doubleday released its almost identical version.

Calling the book a best seller feels like an understatement. Doubleday, Page sold 25,000 copies in six weeks—and in one day managed to move 5,500. In the blink of an eye, *The Jungle*'s author had become a household name. "Not since

[the British poet Lord Byron published *Childe Harold's Pilgrimage*] has there been such an example of worldwide celebrity won in a day by a book as has come to Upton Sinclair," reported the *New York Evening World*. Sinclair would later self-publish four more editions of the book.

SINCLAIR NEVER LIKED THE ENDING.

For the most part, *The Jungle* takes a "show, don't tell" narrative approach. The story centers on Jurgis Rudkus, a luckless Lithuanian immigrant who immigrates to America with his family, and follows his trials and tribulations across the stockyards, saloons, and prisons of Chicago. But during the book's final chapter, the character basically fades into the background: Jurgis ends up in the employ of a kindly Socialist who converts him to the cause; he then attends a socialist dinner party, where he passively listens to armchair intellectuals debate the movement's finer points. The novel ends with some welcome news about increased Socialist vote totals in elections around the country.

Critics panned the ending, which was seen as preachy and patronizing. Sinclair later admitted in his autobiography that "the last chapters were not up to standard." When the time came to write the novel's final third, he found himself distracted by marital difficulties and political commitments. Sinclair had also managed to waste Macmillan's $500 advance, which put him in a tight spot financially and thwarted his plans to revisit Chicago on a second fact-finding trip.

Desperate to wrap up his story on a satisfactory note, Sinclair explored every option he could think of. At one point, he approached Macmillan with a proposal to split the book into two volumes, with the first installment ending after the death of Ona—Jurgis's wife—in Chapter Nineteen. Sinclair hoped that this would buy him more time to cook up a conclusion for *The Jungle*, but Macmillan nixed the whole two-volume idea. So, with some help from Warren, Sinclair sat down and gave the novel its underwhelming finale. Five years later, an embittered Sinclair told one correspondent, "Think of my having had to ruin *The Jungle* with an ending so pitifully inadequate."

THE JUNGLE GOT SINCLAIR INVITED TO THE WHITE HOUSE.

It didn't take long for *The Jungle* to trigger a massive public outcry. Readers were sickened by the book's revolting asides about the unsanitary conditions at meatpacking factories, which had huge consequences for America's food industry—according to one packer who testified before Congress, sales of US meats went down by 50 percent after Sinclair's book was published in 1906. (For the record, though, this statement is unprovable because national statistics on meat consumption did not yet exist.)

Multiple copies of the novel were sent to President Theodore Roosevelt, who also received hundreds of letters from angry citizens demanding that his administration regulate slaughterhouses more thoroughly. In response, Roosevelt asked Sinclair to come and visit him at the White House. On April 4, 1906, the author arrived at 1600 Pennsylvania Avenue, where he met up with Roosevelt in the study. The president informed Sinclair that although a team of investigators from the Agriculture Department had already been sent to Chicago to verify *The Jungle*'s claims, he was dissatisfied with their conclusions and was forming a second team.

THE BOOK PROVOKED AN AVALANCHE OF LEGISLATION.

By the end of 1906, Congress had passed the Meat Inspection Act and the Pure Food and Drug Act. The former mandated—among other things—that packing factories comply with new sanitation standards while also allowing the USDA to inspect all livestock animals before and after they were slaughtered. Meanwhile, the Pure Food and Drug Act banned "the manufacture, sale, or transportation of adulterated or misbranded or poisonous or deleterious foods, drugs, medicines, and liquors."

Both were vigorously backed by Roosevelt, whose second team of investigators was able to confirm most of what Sinclair had written in his novel. Given this, and the degree to which it had shaped public opinion, historians credit *The Jungle* with helping to push the acts forward.

ONE OF THE BOOK'S MOST REPULSIVE INSINUATIONS IS (PROBABLY) BASELESS.

Roosevelt's men found that Sinclair's assessment of the workplace environment at American slaughterhouses was uncomfortably spot-on—in fact, according to biographer Anthony Arthur, every claim in *The Jungle*, with "one notable exception," has been backed up by "corroborating evidence or some sort of assurance that it was [at least] close to being true."

The lone outlier he noted was Sinclair's suggestion that a few workers at lard factories may have fallen into vats and been converted into lard themselves. "[When] they were fished out," Sinclair wrote, "there was never enough of them left to be worth exhibiting—sometimes they would be overlooked for days, till all but the bones of them had gone out to the world as Durham's Pure Leaf Lard!" Arresting as this image is, it's never been verified.

SINCLAIR BELIEVED THAT MOST READERS TOOK THE WRONG LESSONS FROM HIS BOOK.

The Jungle is the rare activist novel that measurably changed the world—but the effect it had on society was far removed from the author's intentions. Sinclair set out to write an exposé about the systemic exploitation of working-class people in industrialized cities. But instead, the public chose to fixate on his gruesome food-related anecdotes. In the process, most readers completely ignored Sinclair's Socialist pleas. As the author famously said in hindsight, "I aimed at the public's heart, and by accident I hit it in the stomach."

A READER-IN CHIEF

Theodore Roosevelt might have lived his own life in an exceptionally regimented fashion, but his outlook on reading was surprisingly free-spirited. Apart from being a staunch proponent of finding at least a few minutes to read every single day—and starting young—he thought that most of the details should be left up to the individual.

"The reader, the booklover, must meet his own needs without paying too much attention to what his neighbors say those needs should be,"

he wrote in his autobiography, and rejected the idea that there's a definitive "best books" list that everyone should abide by. Instead, Roosevelt recommended choosing books on subjects that interest you and letting your mood guide you to your next great read. He also wasn't one to roll his eyes at a happy ending, explaining that "there are enough horror and grimness and sordid squalor in real life with which an active man has to grapple."

BOOKS YOU DIDN'T KNOW WERE ORIGINALLY SELF-PUBLISHED

Though the wild success of a few self-published books has created a new wave of DIY authors, it's not a novel idea: Many of history's great authors went it alone. Here are a few books beyond *The Jungle* that were self-published.

1 *The Martian* // ANDY WEIR

Andy Weir's novel about an astronaut who must survive after being stranded on Mars took a roundabout route to bookshelves: He first published the story as a free serial on his website. Next, he self-published the e-book on Amazon. *The Martian* was picked up by an audiobook company before being discovered by Crown Publishing and printed at last.

2 *A Christmas Carol* // CHARLES DICKENS

Dickens was struggling financially when he wrote *A Christmas Carol*, which he finished in six weeks. Bitter about the lack of profits being made on his previous book, *Martin Chuzzlewit*, Dickens decided to forego a one-off payment from his publishers and instead paid them to print the book so he could profit directly. Unfortunately, after expenses, he made just £137 (though in following years it would begin making more money).

3 *Maggie: A Girl of the Streets* // STEPHEN CRANE

Stephen Crane is perhaps best known for traumatizing generations of elementary schoolchildren with grisly, gory depictions of the Civil War in his novel *The Red Badge of Courage*. Before that, he financed the publication of his first work, *Maggie: A Girl of the Streets*, an equally bleak examination of poverty, prostitution, and alcoholism in nineteenth-century New York. Just twenty-one years old at the time, Crane released the novella in 1893 under the pseudonym Johnston Smith and even devised a clever strategy to publicize it: He paid four men to read it on a New York elevated train. "It fell flat," he said later, according to *The New Yorker*. But *Maggie* did pique the interest of fellow writers William Dean Howells and Hamlin Garland, which helped Crane gain confidence and momentum for his next works.

4 *The Celestine Prophecy* // JAMES REDFIELD

James Redfield's novel/ spiritual guide began with a three-thousand-copy print run that set him back about $7,000. Redfield and his wife packed up their van and spent a month at a time traveling to independent bookstores across the nation to give a copy to each manager and whatever customers were present, reprinting as needed. The strategy reinforced the old publishing adage that the best way to sell books is by word of mouth: After a few months on the road, Redfield said that everybody was talking about it, and he estimates that they had sold around 160,000 copies. It was enough to ignite an informal rights auction between Warner Books and another unnamed publishing house, which Warner won. When asked at the Southern California Writers' Conference if Warner requested any revisions, Redfield said yes. "But we didn't do any of them," he added. Warner published the book anyway, which then spent an impressive three years on *The New York Times*'s best-seller list.

5 *Fifty Shades of Grey* // E.L. JAMES

The story that would become *Fifty Shades of Grey* was originally *Twilight* fan fiction published on FanFiction.net under the title *Master of the Universe*. Eventually, author E.L. James (a pen name) moved the stories onto her own website, changed the characters' names, and then self-published the novel as an e-book and print-by-demand book. From there, it went straight to *The New York Times*'s best-seller list.

THE KITE RUNNER

KHALED HOSSEINI

March 4, 1965

BORN: Kabul, Afghanistan

OTHER NOTABLE WORKS:
A Thousand Splendid Suns (2007)
And the Mountains Echoed (2013)
Sea Prayer (2018)

When fifteen-year-old Khaled Hosseini came to the United States as a refugee in 1980 after a communist coup in his home country of Afghanistan, he only knew a few words of English. He and his family settled in California, and though Hosseini wanted to be a writer, "it seemed outlandish that I would make a living writing stories in a language I didn't speak," he told *The Atlantic*. So he eventually chose a more "serious" profession, becoming a doctor. Later, he wrote what would become his first novel, *The Kite Runner*, in the mornings before going to work as an internist at a hospital in Los Angeles. That hard work paid off: *The Kite Runner* was a huge success, paving the way for more novels.

Hosseini has served as a Goodwill Ambassador for the UN Refugee Agency since 2006, and later founded The Khaled Hosseini Foundation to assist women, children, and refugees. He hasn't practiced medicine since 2004, but there are elements of his life as a doctor that still come in handy as a writer: "Qualities you need to get through medical school and residency: Discipline. Patience. Perseverance. A willingness to forgo sleep. A penchant for sadomasochism. Ability to weather crises of faith and self-confidence. Accept exhaustion as fact of life. Addiction to caffeine a definite plus. Unfailing optimism that the end is in sight," he told *The New York Times*. "Qualities you need to be a novelist: Ditto."

The Kite Runner is set in Afghanistan against a backdrop of the country's tumultuous history—from the fall of the monarchy to the rise of the Taliban. The book became a *New York Times* best-seller. It was also challenged after its release for offensive language and scenes depicting sexual abuse. Here's what you should know about Hosseini's debut novel.

IT STARTED AS A SHORT STORY INSPIRED BY NEWS REPORTS.

In 1999, Hosseini was watching the news when he saw a story about the Taliban banning kite flying in Afghanistan. The report "kind of struck a personal chord for me, because as a boy I grew up in Kabul with all my cousins and friends flying kites," he told RadioFreeEurope. He wrote a twenty-five-page short story—which "became this kind of a much darker, more involved tale than I had anticipated"—and submitted it to *The New Yorker* and *Esquire*, both of which rejected it. In 2001, he found the short story in his garage and, at the urging of a friend, decided to turn it into a novel.

THE AUTHOR WAS CRITICIZED BY SOME AFGHANS FOR HOW HE PORTRAYED AFGHANISTAN.

Hosseini told *The Atlantic* in 2013 that he had heard from "older, more conservative, religious members of my community" that his books "have somehow blemished the reputation of Afghanistan in Western eyes." But he doesn't see it that way, and doesn't think his Western readers do either.

"Most readers have come away with a sense of empathy for Afghanistan and its people; there's been awareness of the richness of its culture, its heritage, and its history," he said. "And as a result of connecting with the characters of my novels, they have achieved a more nuanced understanding of Afghanistan, and they certainly feel a sense of personal stake when they hear about an Afghan village being bombed. I've received emails and letters to this effect."

THE AUTHOR WOULD MAKE EXTENSIVE EDITS TO *THE KITE RUNNER* NOW.

It's probably true that every writer looks back on their previous work and finds at least a few things they'd change, and Hosseini is no exception. In speaking to *The Guardian* about *The Kite Runner* and *A Thousand Splendid Suns*, Hosseini said the books seemed like "the work of somebody younger than me," adding, "I think if I were to write my first novel now it would be a different book, and it may not be the book that everybody wants to read. But if I were given a red pen now and I went back . . . I'd take that thing apart."

THE LORD OF THE RINGS

J.R.R. TOLKIEN

January 3, 1892–September 2, 1973

BORN: Bloemfontein, Modern South Africa

OTHER NOTABLE WORKS:
The Hobbit (1937)
The Adventures of Tom Bombadil (1962)
The Silmarillion (1977)

Though he would become famous for his sweeping fantasy novels, John Ronald Reuel Tolkien was first a scholar specializing in Old and Middle English who reconstructed extinct languages—and invented new ones—for fun. Between 1925 and 1959, he taught at Oxford University, where he tackled between as many as 136 lectures a year even though his contract required just thirty-six. While recovering with his wife, Edith, after contracting trench warfare in World War I, he got the idea that would lead to *The Hobbit* and *The Lord of the Rings*.

When *Fellowship of the Ring* hit shelves in 1954, there wasn't much to compare *The Lord of the Rings* to. In the sprawling blend of high fantasy and real-world mythology, Tolkien transported readers to the fictional land of Middle-earth and introduced them to a dense mythology with its own languages, civilizations, and conflicts. Some sixty-five years later, *The Lord of the Rings* still stands as a cultural touchstone, inspiring new generations of authors, filmmakers, and other creative minds in the fantasy genre. But the roots of the books are far humbler than its success would suggest.

In J.R.R. Tolkien's sprawling *The Lord of the Rings* saga, the Dark Lord Sauron has returned to threaten Middle-earth as he also hunts for the One Ring. The ring, however, now rests in the hands of a lowly hobbit named Frodo Baggins, who, alongside his trusty fellowship, must travel to the fires of Mount Doom to destroy it. Here are a few things even Middle-earth superfans might not know.

TOLKIEN ORIGINALLY PITCHED THE *SILMARILLION* AS HIS FOLLOW-UP TO *THE HOBBIT*.

Tolkien's first published foray into Middle-earth, *The Hobbit*, was a huge success when it came out in 1937, earning acclaim and hitting surprising sales numbers for publisher George Allen & Unwin. Naturally, the publisher wanted Tolkien to produce a follow-up story in his fantastical world, preferably with more hobbits at the center of the action.

What they got, though, was a pitch for what would eventually become *The Silmarillion*, a dense prequel of sorts detailing the genesis of Middle-earth and its mélange of cultures. Hobbits themselves were to play virtually no role in the grandiose cosmic ballet. His publisher rejected the idea, and instead, Tolkien proceeded with the more straightforward sequel, *The Lord of the Rings*. In the end, *The Silmarillion* wouldn't see the light of day until four years after Tolkien's passing.

IT WASN'T SUPPOSED TO BE A TRILOGY.

Tolkien began writing *The Lord of the Rings* in late 1937 at the age of forty-five, and it would be twelve years before his novel was finally completed (and a few more years after that until publication). Although it was envisioned as a one-off work, the sheer size of Tolkien's book—more than one thousand pages and around 500,000 words—coupled with a post-war paper shortage in the UK, forced his publisher to split the tome into three separate volumes: *The Fellowship of the Ring*, *The Two Towers*, and *The Return of the King*—certainly not the simple sequel to a children's book that the publisher originally had in mind.

THE BOOK ALMOST CENTERED ON THE ADVENTURES OF BINGO BAGGINS.

When Tolkien actually set out to write *The Lord of the Rings*, he didn't quite know where to take the story. "I cannot think of anything more to say about hobbits," Tolkien wrote in a letter to Stanley Unwin in October 1937. But knowing that more hobbits was exactly what people wanted, he pressed on. Originally he was going to focus on young Bingo Baggins, the son of *The Hobbit* protagonist Bilbo Baggins, and some vague idea to "make return of ring a motive." Soon, Bingo became Frodo, and Tolkien added a hobbit named Trotter (who later evolved into Aragorn). Earlier drafts also left out Samwise Gamgee completely, but they did include a hobbit named Odo, who would mostly turn into Pippin. There was even a point very early on when Tolkien toyed with the idea of making Bilbo the main character yet again—or have him revealed to be Trotter in disguise.

TOLKIEN'S SON DREW THE BOOK'S MAPS OF MIDDLE-EARTH.

For Tolkien, art was key to bringing the fictional land of Middle-earth to life. He produced several paintings and illustrations for both *The Hobbit*—including the cover of the first edition—and *The Lord of the Rings*. But perhaps more important than the paintings of lush hillsides and foreboding dragon lairs were the maps drawn by Tolkien's son, Christopher. Beginning his work more than a decade before the books were ever published, these maps helped give a real sense of geography to the Shire, Mordor, and the other iconic locales, and a handful made their way into the first editions of all *The Lord of the Rings* volumes. Christopher would later go on to provide more maps for *The Silmarillion* when it was published in 1977 and would redraw his originals for inclusion in 1980's *Unfinished Tales*.

THE FIRST US PAPERBACK VERSION OF *THE LORD OF THE RINGS* WAS PIRATED.

In 1965, *The Lord of the Rings* came out in the US in paperback form, courtesy of sci-fi publisher Ace Books—and it did so without the authorization of Tolkien himself. Ace editor Donald A. Wollheim claimed that the works weren't copyrighted in the United States, leaving them unprotected and ripe for publication. Selling for seventy-five cents each, the Ace version of *The Lord of the Rings* was a success, leading Tolkien to return to his books to make enough revisions to qualify them for copyright protection in the US.

Tolkien called upon his fans to boycott the Ace versions in favor of the newly updated, and official, paperbacks from Ballantine Books—though they cost around twenty cents more. Ace later agreed to stop printing the books and pay Tolkien a royalty for every copy sold. The combined sales totals of the Ace and Ballantine versions of *The Lord of the Rings* reached $250,000 in just ten months.

FIVE REGAL FACTS ABOUT THE ELVES OF MIDDLE-EARTH

1 **ELVES WERE ROAMING MIDDLE-EARTH LONG BEFORE BILBO BAGGINS WAS EVEN A TWINKLE IN TOLKIEN'S EYE.** Tolkien is most famous as a novelist, but his first love was language, and the elves were pretty much an excuse to make up imaginary tongues. He started with Quenya (one of the Elven languages) around 1915, the year he finished his degree from Oxford and joined the military for World War I.

2 **YOU WOULDN'T KNOW IT TO LOOK AT HER, BUT GALADRIEL IS REALLY, REALLY, REALLY OLD.** Based on Tolkien's hundreds of pages of elf history and mythology, fans estimate she's over seven thousand years old. Galadriel married the elf Celeborn and gave birth to a daughter, Celebrían. Celebrían went on to marry Elrond. The couple had three children: the twin boys Elladan and Elrohir, and their younger sister Arwen.

3 **BY THE TIME *THE LORD OF THE RINGS* NOVELS ROLLED AROUND, TOLKIEN'S CATALOG OF ELF LANGUAGES HAD EXPANDED.** The writer created complete dictionaries and grammars for two primary languages, Quenya and Sindarin, and laid the foundations for many others. In early writings, Tolkien described Galadriel's husband using his Quenya name, Telporno, which means "silver tree" or "silver tall." The author later decided to go with the Sindarin version, although we can't imagine why.

4 **THERE'S AN ELVISH WORD FOR "BUTT."** Tolkien was serious about his languages, and he put so much work into them that they can be read and spoken. Fans teach Elvish language classes, organize linguistic societies, and produce scholarly works on the subject. Others make it their business to learn rude words in Quenya (and thank goodness for these people). The word, by the way, is *hakka*, which literally translates to "hams."

5 **TOLKIEN'S ELVES MAY HAVE BEEN ALLEGORICAL.** The author was a devout Roman Catholic, and he imbued Middle-earth with all kinds of religious themes. Biographer Humphrey Carpenter reported that Tolkien intended his elves to be a symbol of purity, of the human race before it fell from grace in Eden. The elves were Tolkien's ideal people: noble, insular, and monogamous.

THE LOWLAND

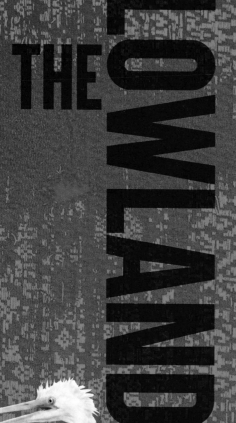

univers
dical Tollyg
gri
nd foot
avan d ce tremor golf violence
gunge H olation boycott Naxalite death
i police su te philosophy Bela bullet regre
otprints egret Calcutta university Subhas
distance tremo violence radical Tollyg
olation boycott Naxalite death grief G
philosophy Bela bullet regret po
cutta university Subhash flood Ul
radical Tollygunge Holly lett
ef Gauri police sunlight ex
footprints egret broths
nce tremor golf
n boycott Naxa
philo nyl a

JHUMPA LAHIRI

July 11, 1967

BORN: London, England

OTHER NOTABLE WORKS:
Interpreter of Maladies (1999)
The Namesake (2003)
Unaccustomed Earth (2008)

Born in London and raised in Rhode Island by Bengali parents, Jhumpa Lahiri co-wrote books with a friend during recess as a seven year old, but didn't truly begin writing until she was in graduate school, fitting it in between schoolwork and classes. It was during those years that the phrase that would become the title of her first book, *Interpreter of Maladies*, came to her: She had run into an acquaintance who was working in a doctor's office, serving as a translator between the doctor and his patients. "As I walked back home," she later recalled, "the phrase interpreter of maladies popped into my head as a way of describing what this person was doing. It lingered long enough for me to jot the phrase down on a piece of paper."

After facing years of rejection of her short stories, *Interpreter of Maladies* was published in 1999—and won the Pulitzer Prize. "I always thought of the Pulitzer as something people won when they were deep into their careers," Lahiri told *Publisher's Weekly*. Her father advised her to "accept it graciously, keep it in its place, and move on." She followed *Maladies* with her first novel, *The Namesake*, in 2003.

In her writing—which has been compared to the likes of E.M. Forster, Alice Munro, and Philip Roth—Lahiri has drawn on her own upbringing and life. "Throughout my life I have worked to reconcile the two traditions that have formed me—the world of my parents and their ways of looking at life, and the opposing views of an American culture that I've grown up with," she has said. "Through my characters I can figure things out about myself."

Jhumpa Lahiri's second novel, *The Lowland*, takes place partly in the lowland of Calcutta, India, where her grandparents lived, and in Rhode Island, where she grew up. The book, about two brothers divided by politics, has been called "Shattering and satisfying in equal measure," by *The New York Review of Books*, and was nominated for both the Man Booker Prize and the National Book Award. Here's what you should know.

THE LOWLAND WAS THE FIRST BOOK LAHIRI TRIED TO WRITE.

When she was thirty, Lahiri had a fellowship at the Fine Arts Work Center in Provincetown, Massachusetts, and it was there that she attempted to write the book that would eventually become *The Lowland* for the first time. "*The Lowland* was in fact one of my earliest projects, that I was trying to write in some repeatedly failed fashion, from a fairly early point in my life as a writer," Lahiri told *The Wall Street Journal*. "I couldn't make it work." She had already written some of the stories that would appear in *Maladies*, so it made sense for that to be her first book. She followed *Maladies* with *The Namesake*, but *The Lowland* was never far from her mind: "I was just circling around and around something I was trying to get to."

IT WAS INSPIRED BY A REAL INCIDENT.

When she was growing up, Lahiri frequently visited India. On one of these trips, she heard about an incident in the 1970s in which two brothers active in the radical Communist Naxalite movement were executed not far from her grandparents' home—while their family watched. "That was the scene that, when I first heard of it, when it was described to me, was so troubling and so haunted me," Lahiri told NPR, "and ultimately inspired me to write the book."

The author did, however, make some adjustments for her story. The real-life event was "the seed of the book," she told Goodreads, "and it incorporated both

place and character and event in different ways. I chose then to work with it to suit my own needs." Instead of having both brothers be involved in the Naxalite movement, Lahiri opted to have just one of the brothers get involved, which she thought was more interesting. "I took what I knew—which wasn't a whole lot—and went from there," she said.

WRITING THE BOOK INVOLVED A LOT OF RESEARCH.

Though Lahiri visited Calcutta in the 1970s and '80s—including in 1972 and 1973, "when the embers were quite hot"—she didn't start looking into the Naxalite movement until she began working on *The Lowland*. Before she wrote anything, she did her research, reading up not just on the origins the movement but on India after its independence as well as communism in Bengal. The drama of history, she told Goodreads, wasn't the same kind of drama that goes into creating a work of fiction. "So for the first time I had to incorporate the real, as it were—actual events, actual place, actual setting—along with the story and characters I was inventing," she said.

She also drew on her own perception of the Naxalite movement, which she, living in Rhode Island at the time, experienced from afar: "It can be all-consuming and devastating and yet you're sealed off from it and there's very little information," she said. "It's almost as if it's not happening. And I wanted the characters to be experiencing that sensation as well."

SIX OTHER PULITZER PRIZE-WINNING NOVELISTS

Established in newspaperman Joseph Pulitzer's will, the first Pulitzer Prizes were awarded in 1917, with the first Pulitzer Prize for the Novel following a year later (it went to Ernest Poole for *His Family*, and in the 1940s, the prize was renamed to award fiction in general). In 2000, Jhumpa Lahiri won; here are a few other authors whose books have nabbed the prestigious prize.

EDITH WHARTON

The jury's initial pick for the 1921 Pulitzer Prize for the Novel was Sinclair Lewis's *Main Street*, but it was rejected by the trustees for not meeting the criteria of the prize (namely, that the work be "wholesome"). The award instead went to Edith Wharton for her twelfth novel, *The Age of Innocence*, making her the first woman to win a Pulitzer. Wharton wrote in her autobiography that in *Innocence*, she had found "a momentary escape in going back to my childish memories of a long-vanished America ... it was growing more and more evident that the world I had grown up in and been formed by had been destroyed in 1914."

JEFFREY EUGENIDES

When *Middlesex*—about intersex man Cal Stephanides, who, due to a genetic mutation called 5-alpha-reductase deficiency, is assigned female at birth—was published in 2002, Eugenides told *The Guardian* that he wanted to write a medically accurate portrayal of an intersex person, "rather than a fanciful creature like Tiresias or Orlando who could shift in a paragraph." The author said he had received many letters of thanks from intersex people, but the book wasn't without controversy: Emi Koyama, director of the Intersex Initiative, wrote in 2007 that while "the book *Middlesex* is beautifully written," Eugenides "is definitely not an expert about intersex issues, and he did not

meet with any intersex person before writing the novel." The book's subject matter inevitably led to the author getting asked questions about intersex in interviews—questions which Koyama said "need to be directed toward intersex advocates who are actually familiar with the topic, and not some novelist with limited knowledge about the issue."

COLSON WHITEHEAD

Author of nine books, Whitehead was nominated for his first Pulitzer in 2002. He won his first Pulitzer in 2017 for *The Underground Railroad*, a book the jury called "a smart melding of realism and allegory that combines the violence of slavery and the drama of escape in a myth that speaks to contemporary America." He won again in 2020 for *The Nickel Boys*. He's one of only four authors to have won two Pulitzers in Fiction.

JUNOT DÍAZ

It took Junot Díaz eleven years to write his debut novel, *The Brief Wondrous Life of Oscar Wao,* about an overweight Dominican boy living in New Jersey dealing with a family curse. Writing the book may have taken awhile, but it paid off: Díaz won the Pulitzer for *Oscar Wao* in 2008.

JOHN UPDIKE

SPOILERS! Updike, the author of more than twenty-five novels, won Pulitzers for two books in his series that follows ex-athlete Harry "Rabbit" Angstrom: *Rabbit Is Rich* (1981) and *Rabbit at Rest* (1990), the latter of which ends with Rabbit's death. In 1997, Updike described ending the series as "kind of a relief . . . It wasn't as sad for me as perhaps for some of my readers. Writers are cruel. Authors are cruel. We make, and we destroy." The character of Rabbit, Updike said, "opened me up. As a writer, I could see things through him that I couldn't see by any other means."

JOHN KENNEDY TOOLE

The manuscript for *A Confederacy of Dunces* was found by John Kennedy Toole's mother after he died by suicide in 1969. Determined to get the novel published, she approached a number of publishers; finally, she went to author Walker Percy with the manuscript—and would not give up until he read it. As he later recalled, "the lady was persistent, and it somehow came to pass that she stood in my office handing me the hefty manuscript." He'd hoped to read a few pages and be able to put it aside. But that was not the case: "I read on. And on. First with the sinking feeling that it was not bad enough to quit, then with a prickle of interest, then a growing excitement, and finally an incredulity: surely it was not possible that it was so good." The novel was finally published in 1980, eleven years after Toole's death, and won the Pulitzer the next year.

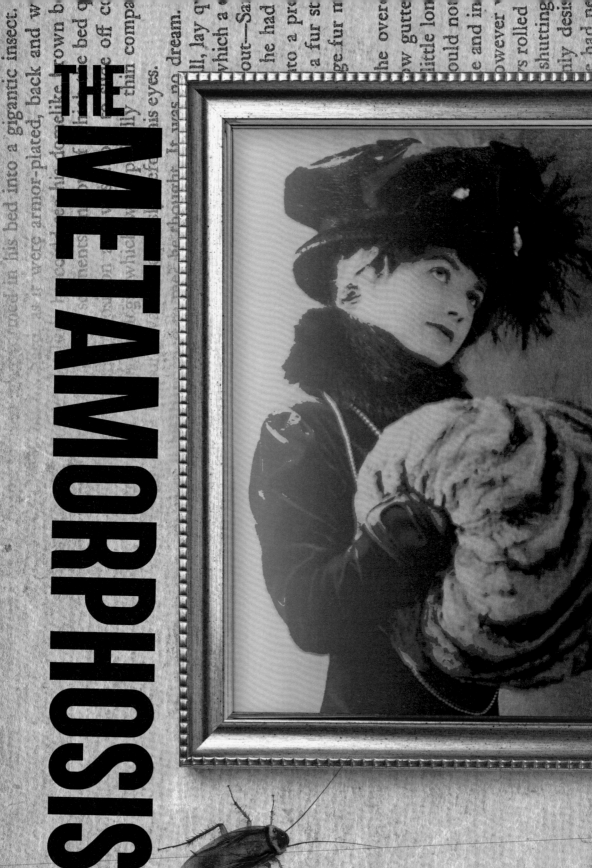

FRANZ KAFKA

July 3, 1883–June 3, 1924

BORN: Prague, Modern Czechia

OTHER NOTABLE WORKS:
The Trial (1925)
The Castle (1926)

Born in what is now Czechia in 1883, Franz Kafka never got to live the life of a literary giant—in fact, some of his most important works weren't even published until after his death at the age of forty. Instead, Kafka would spend his days toiling away at his job at an insurance agency, while working on his manuscripts for *The Metamorphosis* and *The Trial* at night. It's in these stories that Kafka crafted his signature absurdist style, often focusing on an anxiety-ridden protagonist squaring off against the convoluted machinery of modern society. These themes were so deeply ingrained in his work that today the term *Kafkaesque* is defined by the Merriam-Webster dictionary as anything that has "a nightmarishly complex, bizarre, or illogical quality."

"One morning, upon awakening from agitated dreams, Gregor Samsa found himself, in his bed, transformed into a monstrous vermin." That's how Franz Kafka introduced readers (in translation) to his 1915 novella *The Metamorphosis*, and the story only gets more bizarre from there. Though the plot is straightforward—a salesman struggles to adjust after transforming into a giant creature—the book has been provoking new questions and interpretations from readers since its debut.

THE FIRST SENTENCE STUMPED TRANSLATORS.

The Metamorphosis opens with one of the most famous first lines in all of literature. It also contains a tricky-to-translate phrase that's essential to the plot: *ungeheuren Ungeziefer*. This is what Gregor Samsa transforms into, and it has no direct translation outside the German language. *Ungeziefer* translates to something like "an unclean animal unfit for sacrifice," but the phrase is also used by German speakers to describe any kind of repulsive vermin. Kafka intentionally kept Gregor's true form vague, and even forbid his publisher from putting a clear illustration of the character on the cover. This hasn't stopped translators from applying more specific meanings to *ungeheuren Ungeziefer*, interpreting it as *gigantic insect*, *horrible vermin*, and *monstrous cockroach*.

THE BOOK INSPIRED GABRIEL GARCÍA MÁRQUEZ.

Before he introduced magical realism to generations of readers, Colombian author Gabriel García Márquez found inspiration in Kafka's most famous work. The first line of *The Metamorphosis* opened him up to new ways of writing and forever changed his life. "When I read the line I thought to myself that I didn't know anyone was allowed to write things like that," García Márquez told *The Paris Review*. "If I had known, I would have started writing a long time ago." Echoes of Kafka's style can be seen in García Márquez's magical realist epic *One Hundred Years of Solitude*.

IT WASN'T PUBLISHED RIGHT AWAY.

Immediately after writing the short story "The Judgement" in 1912, Franz Kafka penned *The Metamorphosis* over the course of three weeks. Despite the quick turnaround, it would take a while for the novella to get in front of readers. Difficult negotiations with publishers and the start of World War I meant that *The Metamorphosis* wasn't published until October 1915—three years after it was completed.

KAFKA WAS HIGHLY CRITICAL OF *THE METAMORPHOSIS*.

It may be his best-known work, but Kafka didn't view *The Metamorphosis* as his masterpiece—far from it. After finishing the novella, he wrote in his diary, "Great antipathy to *Metamorphosis*. Unreadable ending. Imperfect almost to its very marrow." But the author didn't take the full blame for his perceived failure. In the same diary entry, he noted, "It would have turned out much better if I had not been interrupted at the time by a business trip."

THE BOOK WAS BANNED UNDER NAZI AND SOVIET RULE.

The Nazis banned a lot of books, including *The Metamorphosis*. Kafka was starting to gain posthumous fame in the literary world when the regime took power in Czechoslovakia and banned his work. His writing was labeled as degenerate, and the fact that he was Jewish may have contributed to his censorship. His legacy didn't fare much better immediately after the war: His books were banned again under Stalin for being too "despairing." Following the Prague Spring in 1968, interest in Kafka's work experienced a brief resurgence in Czechoslovakia, only for it to be quickly suppressed again as a result of the Warsaw Pact invasion of Czechoslovakia.

IT'S REFERENCED ENDLESSLY IN POP CULTURE— EVEN TODAY.

Even if you've never read *The Metamorphosis*, you've likely been exposed to it through other media (whether you know it or not). In addition to direct adaptations like short films and plays, Kafka's novella has been nodded

FAMOUS AUTHORS' UNFINISHED MANUSCRIPTS

What do we do when an author dies with their work unfinished? Do we let it molder in vaults, stash it away in archives, or publish it for all the world to see—even if that's not what the author intended? The problem crops up more often than you might think, since most authors have many less-than-polished drafts hiding somewhere in their files. And while some authors have asked for unfinished work to be destroyed, doing so just might deprive the world of a treasure.

Take Franz Kafka: We would have very little of his works if it weren't for his rebellious friend and fellow writer Max Brod. Kafka didn't publish much during his life, and left his three big novels—*The Trial*, *The Castle*, and *Amerika*—unfinished when he died in 1924. He asked Brod, his literary executor, to destroy them, but Brod disobeyed, to our benefit. Here are other authors who left work unfinished, and the fates of those works.

to numerous times in pop culture. The cover art of the Rolling Stones's 1975 compilation album *Metamorphosis* featured the members of the band with their heads replaced by those of giant insects. Ovid Works turned the story into a video game. And some authors have even written books in direct response to *The Metamorphosis*.

Marc Estrin's 2002 novel *Insect Dreams: The Half Life of Gregor Samsa* is about Gregor's life after the events of the novella, and in Coleridge Cook's *The Meowmorphosis*, published in 2011, the character wakes up as a kitten instead of a hideous vermin.

VLADIMIR NABOKOV //
The Original of Laura
Before he died in 1977, Vladimir Nabokov left behind an unfinished manuscript for a book he tentatively titled *The Original of Laura*. In 138 index cards, the book told the story of an "unnamed 'man of letters' and a nubile twenty-four-year-old," as *The Guardian* put it. In 2008, Nabokov's son Dmitri revealed that his father had given him spectral permission to publish the book. According to Dmitri, his father appeared to him from beyond the grave and said: "You're stuck in a right old mess. Just go ahead and publish."

CHARLES DICKENS //
The Mystery of Edwin Drood
When he died in 1870, Dickens had completed only six of his planned dozen installments for *The Mystery of Edwin Drood*. Unfortunately, his death meant that the identity of the story's murderer was never revealed—but things might have been different, if Queen Victoria had been into spoilers. Three months before his death Dickens sent a letter to the Queen offering to tell her "a little more of it in advance of her subjects." She declined the offer, and now we'll never know what he might have told her. That hasn't stopped at least a dozen people from writing continuations and adaptations, including one from a Vermont printer who claimed to have channeled Dickens's ghost with his "spirit pen."

MARK TWAIN //
The Mysterious Stranger
At his death in 1910, Twain left behind three unfinished manuscripts of three different but related stories— "The Chronicle of Young Satan," "Schoolhouse Hill," and "No. 44, the Mysterious Stranger." All involved Satan, Satan's nephew, or "No. 44." Twain's biographer, Albert Bigelow Paine, cobbled the three together into a 1916 book called *The Mysterious Stranger*, based mostly on "The Chronicle of Young Satan" but with the ending from "No. 44." The extent to which the work was Paine's product, as opposed to Twain's, wasn't known until the 1960s, when editors published a second version that supposedly stuck closer to Twain's original intent. The dark, dreamlike story is now considered Twain's last great work.

ERNEST HEMINGWAY //
The Garden of Eden
Hemingway began *The Garden of Eden* in 1946 and worked on it intermittently until a few years before his death in 1961. The book was finally published in 1986, after a controversial editing process that cut it down by at least two-thirds and ripped out an entire subplot. Intriguingly, some scholars have argued that Hemingway was forging a new direction with the work, both in style and content, which the editing sacrificed and compressed.

TRUMAN CAPOTE //
Answered Prayers
During the last years of his life, Truman Capote frequently claimed to be working on a book called *Answered Prayers*. (He signed the contract just two weeks before *In Cold Blood* hit bookstores and became a spectacular success.) But despite repeatedly extended deadlines with his editors and a generous advance, *Answered Prayers* was never completed. In 1971, during an appearance on *The Dick Cavett Show*, Capote referred to it as his "posthumous novel," saying "either I'm going to kill it, or it's going to kill me."

A few chapters of the book were finally published in *Esquire* in 1975 and 1976, with disastrous results: The book was a thinly veiled account of the lifestyles of the rich and famous, many of whom were Capote's friends. Stunned after recognizing themselves in the chapters, most of Capote's friends abandoned him—sending the writer into a depressive spiral of drugs and alcohol from which some say he never recovered.

The book's remaining chapters are something of a mystery. They may still be languishing in a safe deposit box somewhere (some think they're in a locker at the Los Angeles Greyhound Bus Depot). Others think they may have never existed, despite all of Capote's talk. Nevertheless, three of the chapters from *Esquire* were published in book form in 1987 (three years after Capote died) under the title *Answered Prayers: The Unfinished Novel*. Critics weren't kind.

THE OLD MAN AND THE SEA

ERNEST HEMINGWAY

July 21, 1899–July 2, 1961

BORN: Oak Park, Illinois

OTHER NOTABLE WORKS:
The Sun Also Rises (1926)
A Farewell to Arms (1929)
For Whom the Bell Tolls (1940)

In their 1926 review of Ernest Hemingway's debut novel, *The Sun Also Rises*, *The New York Times* wrote that, "No amount of analysis can convey the quality of *The Sun Also Rises*. It is a truly gripping story, told in a lean, hard, athletic narrative prose that puts more literary English to shame." It was this distinctive economy of words that allowed Hemingway to stand apart from his contemporaries and become one of the literary giants of the twentieth century. Yet while his writing may have been understated, his real life was anything but: The Pulitzer Prize-winning author had a never-ending appetite for adventure, and a talent for converting his experiences into heroic tales like *A Farewell to Arms*, *For Whom the Bell Tolls*, and *The Old Man and the Sea*. But much like the characters he wrote about (many of whom were semi-autobiographical), the writer known as Papa was a tragic figure who spent his life fighting personal demons. In 1961, just shy of his sixty-second birthday, Hemingway took his own life.

The Old Man and the Sea was the last major work Ernest Hemingway published in his lifetime. The simple story is about an old man who catches a giant fish in the waters off Cuba, only to have it devoured by sharks. Defeated, he returns home with the fish's skeleton attached to the boat. Many consider this spare novel to be Hemingway's best work.

HEMINGWAY WROTE THE NOVEL TO PROVE HE WASN'T FINISHED AS A WRITER.

When *The Old Man and the Sea* was published in 1952, Hemingway hadn't written a significant literary work for over a decade. His last successful book, *For Whom the Bell Tolls*, had come out in 1940. To make matters worse, his 1950 novel *Across the River and Into the Trees* was panned by critics. People were saying that Hemingway was through as a writer. He began *The Old Man and the Sea* to prove that not only was he still in the writing game, he had yet to produce his best work.

THE STORY HAD BEEN IN HIS MIND FOR YEARS.

In 1936, Hemingway wrote an essay for *Esquire* that contained a paragraph describing an "old man fishing alone in a skiff out of Cabañas" who hooked a big marlin that dragged him eastward for two days. The man killed the fish and then fought off sharks attracted to its blood. When the man was finally picked up, "what was left of the fish, less than half, weighed eight hundred pounds." Two years later, Hemingway started writing *The Old Man and the Sea*, but then got sidetracked by *For Whom the Bell Tolls*. By the time he returned to the story, it had been percolating in his brain for at least sixteen years.

THE OLD MAN MIGHT HAVE BEEN BASED ON A BLUE-EYED CUBAN NAMED GREGORIO FUENTES.

Although Hemingway said the old man, Santiago, was based on "nobody in particular," he most likely used aspects of his fishing buddy Gregorio Fuentes when developing the character. Like Santiago, Fuentes was gaunt and thin, had blue eyes, came from the Canary Islands, and had a long, battle-scarred history as a fisherman. Fuentes was the captain of Hemingway's boat and the two frequently talked about the novel.

THE FISH WAS AN ATLANTIC BLUE MARLIN.

While living in Florida and Cuba, Hemingway frequently fished for marlin in his boat, the *Pilar*. Not to be confused with a swordfish, Atlantic Blue Marlin are large billfish that live in the temperate and tropical regions of the Atlantic Ocean. They can grow up to fourteen feet long and weigh as much as two thousand pounds. Like in the book, a common predator is sharks.

THE BOOK WAS DEDICATED TO RECENTLY DECEASED FRIENDS.

The dedication in *The Old Man and the Sea* reads "To Charlie Scribner and To Max Perkins," both friends who passed away before the book came out. Max Perkins, who also edited F. Scott Fitzgerald and Thomas Wolfe, died in 1947, and Scribner, who was president of Charles Scribner's Sons, died in 1952. They were among many of Hemingway's literary peers who had recently passed away, along with Fitzgerald, Gertrude Stein, Sherwood Anderson, and James Joyce.

HEMINGWAY CLAIMED THERE WAS NO SYMBOLISM IN THE BOOK.

The fable-like structure of the novel suggests that the story is symbolic, which is why many view *The Old Man and the Sea* as an allegory. But Hemingway thought all that was bunk—or at least, that's what he said. "There isn't any symbolism," he wrote to critic Bernard Berenson. "The sea is the sea. The old man is an old man . . . The sharks are all sharks no better and no worse. All the symbolism that people say is shit. What goes beyond is what you see beyond when you know."

HE BELIEVED THE NOVEL WAS HIS FINEST WORK.

When Hemingway sent the manuscript to his editor, Wallace Meyer, he said, "I know that it is the best I can write ever for all of my life, I think, and that it destroys good and able work by being placed alongside of it." Then he added that he hoped it would "get rid of the school of criticism that I am through as a writer."

THE *LIFE* MAGAZINE EXCERPT SOLD OUT IMMEDIATELY.

Life featured an excerpt of *The Old Man and the Sea* in its September 1952 issue. The five million copies of the magazine sold out in two days.

THE OLD MAN AND THE SEA MADE HEMINGWAY A CELEBRITY.

Of course, Hemingway was a known and respected author beforehand, but *The Old Man and the Sea* elevated his reputation to the literary giant we think of today. Critics loved the book. It won the 1953 Pulitzer Prize in Fiction and was cited as a reason Hemingway won the 1954 Nobel Prize. It was also a best seller and made Hemingway a fortune. In 1958, it was made into a movie starring Spencer Tracy.

EVEN HEMINGWAY'S LITERARY RIVAL, WILLIAM FAULKNER, LIKED IT.

The following is an excerpt from a one-paragraph review Faulkner wrote about *The Old Man and the Sea*, published in *Shenandoah*:

"His best. Time may show it to be the best single piece of any of us, I mean his and my contemporaries. This time, he discovered God, a Creator. Until now, his men and women had made themselves, shaped themselves out of their own clay; their victories and defeats were at the hands of each other, just to prove to themselves or one another how tough they could be. But this time, he wrote about pity: about something somewhere that made them all . . . "

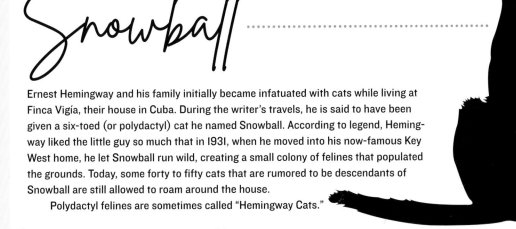

Snowball

Ernest Hemingway and his family initially became infatuated with cats while living at Finca Vigía, their house in Cuba. During the writer's travels, he is said to have been given a six-toed (or polydactyl) cat he named Snowball. According to legend, Hemingway liked the little guy so much that in 1931, when he moved into his now-famous Key West home, he let Snowball run wild, creating a small colony of felines that populated the grounds. Today, some forty to fifty cats that are rumored to be descendants of Snowball are still allowed to roam around the house.

Polydactyl felines are sometimes called "Hemingway Cats."

Fascinating Facts about Ernest Hemingway

Ernest Hemingway was a titan of twentieth-century literature, converting his lived experiences in multiple wars into rich, stirring tales like *A Farewell to Arms* and *For Whom the Bell Tolls*. The avid sportsman also called upon his love for the outdoors to craft bittersweet metaphorical works like *Big Two-Hearted River*. Here's what you should know about the writer also known as Papa.

1 HEMINGWAY EARNED THE ITALIAN SILVER MEDAL OF VALOR AND A BRONZE STAR.

Hemingway served as an ambulance driver in Italy during World War I, and on July 8, 1918, he was badly wounded by mortar fire—yet he managed to help an Italian soldier reach safety. The action earned him an Italian Silver Medal of Valor. That honor was paralleled almost thirty years later when the US awarded him a Bronze Star for courage displayed while covering the European theater in World War II as a journalist. His articles appeared in *Collier's* and other magazines.

2 HE WAS ALSO ACCUSED—AND CLEARED—OF WAR CRIMES.

Following D-Day on June 6, 1944, when Hemingway, a civilian, was not allowed to disembark on Omaha Beach, he led a band of Resistance fighters in the French town of Rambouillet on a mission to gather intelligence. The problem was, war correspondents aren't supposed to lead armed troops, according to the Geneva Convention. The Inspector General of the Third Army charged Hemingway with several serious offenses, including removing patches from his clothing that identified him as a journalist, stockpiling weapons in his hotel room, and commanding a faction of Resistance operatives. Eventually, he was cleared of wrongdoing.

Hemingway always maintained that he'd done nothing but act as an advisor. He wrote to *The New York Times* in 1951, stating he "had a certain amount of knowledge about guerilla warfare and irregular tactics as well as a grounding in more formal war, and I was willing and happy to work for or be of use to anybody who would give me anything to do within my capabilities."

3 HE WAS ALLEGEDLY A KGB SPY—BUT HE WASN'T VERY GOOD AT IT.

When *Collier's* sent the legendary war correspondent Martha Gellhorn to China for a story in 1941, Hemingway, her husband, accompanied her and filed dispatches for *PM*. Documentation from the Soviet Union (revealed in a 2009 book) shows that Hemingway was possibly recruited as a willing, clandestine source just prior to the trip and was given the codename "Argo." The documents also show that he didn't deliver any useful political intel, wasn't trained for espionage, and only stayed on their list of active sources until the end of the decade.

4 HEMINGWAY CHECKED OUT F. SCOTT FITZGERALD'S PENIS IN A PARIS MEN'S ROOM.

Hemingway chronicled his life in Paris in his 1964 memoir *A Moveable Feast*, in which he claimed he had one memorable encounter with F. Scott Fitzgerald. *The Great Gatsby* author shared that his wife Zelda had mocked his manhood by claiming he wouldn't be able to satisfy a lover. Hemingway offered to investigate the matter and render a verdict.

He took Fitzgerald to the bathroom at Michaud's, a popular restaurant in Paris, to examine the organ in question. Ultimately, Hemingway assured Fitzgerald that his physical endowment was of a totally normal size and suggested he check out some nude statues at the Louvre for confirmation.

5 ONE OF HIS BEST WORKS CAME ABOUT FROM HIM LEAVING SOME LUGGAGE AT THE RITZ HOTEL IN PARIS.

Speaking of *A Moveable Feast*, Hemingway wrote it later in life (it was published posthumously) after a 1956 stay at the Ritz Hotel in Paris wherein he was reminded that he'd left a steamer trunk (made for him by Louis Vuitton) in the hotel's basement in 1930. When he opened it, he rediscovered personal letters, menus, outdoor gear, and two stacks of notebooks that became the basis for the memoir of his youth in Paris's café culture.

6 THE FAMOUS "BABY SHOES" STORY IS A MYTH.

Oddly enough, a story many people associate with Hemingway has nothing to do with him. The legend goes that one night, while drinking, Hemingway bet some friends that he could write a six-word short story. Incredulous, they all put money on the table, and on a napkin Hemingway wrote the words "For Sale: Baby Shoes, Never Worn." He won the bet. Unfortunately, there's no evidence it ever happened. While some newspapers had printed versions of the general plotline in the 1910s, there's no record of Hemingway's link to the phrase until 1991—three decades after his death—when it popped up in a book about the publishing business.

7 HEMINGWAY ALMOST DIED IN BACK-TO-BACK PLANE CRASHES.

In 1954, Hemingway and his fourth wife, *Time* and *Life* correspondent Mary Welsh, were vacationing in Belgian Congo when their sightseeing charter flight clipped a pole and crashed. When attempting to reach medical care in Entebbe the following day, they boarded another plane, which crashed upon takeoff, leaving Hemingway with burns, a concussion, and his brain leaking cerebral fluid. When they finally got to Entebbe (by truck), they found journalists had already reported their deaths, so Hemingway got to read his own obituaries.

8 HE DEDICATED A BOOK TO EACH OF HIS FOUR WIVES.

Each time he got divorced, Hemingway was married again within the year—but he always left something behind in print. The dedication for *The Sun Also Rises* went to his first wife, Elizabeth Hadley Richardson; *Death in the Afternoon* was dedicated to second wife Pauline Pfeiffer; *For Whom the Bell Tolls* was for third wife Martha Gellhorn; and *Across the River and Into the Trees* went "To Mary with Love."

PAPA

HEMINGWAY'S GUIDE TO LIFE IN NINE QUOTES

Though he made his living as a writer, Ernest Hemingway was just as famous for his lust for adventure. Whether he was running with the bulls in Pamplona, fishing for marlin in Bimini, throwing back rum cocktails in Havana, or hanging out with his six-toed cats in Key West, the Nobel and Pulitzer Prize–winning author never did anything halfway. Here are nine memorable quotes that offer a keen perspective into Hemingway's way of life.

ON DECIDING WHAT TO WRITE ABOUT

"A dull subject I should say would be impotence. Murder is a good one so get a swell murder into [your] next book and sit back."

— *From a 1925 letter*

ON TRUST

"The way to make people trust-worthy is to trust them."

—*From a 1953 letter to Dorothy Connable*

ON TRAVEL "Never [go] on trips with anyone you do not love."

—*From* A Moveable Feast

ON THE DEFINITION OF COURAGE

"Grace under pressure."

— *As quoted in a 1929 article in* The New Yorker

ON GOOD VS. EVIL

"About morals, I know only that what is moral is what you feel good after and what is immoral is what you feel bad after."

—*From* Death in the Afternoon

ON TAKING ACTION

"Never confuse movement with action."

— *As recounted by A.E. Hotchner in* Papa Hemingway: A Personal Memoir

ON THE DOWNSIDE OF BEING SMART

"Happiness in intelligent people is the rarest thing I know."

— *From* The Garden of Eden

ON HAPPY ENDINGS

"There is no lonelier man in death, except the suicide, than that man who has lived many years with a good wife and then outlived her. If two people love each other there can be no happy end to it."

—*From* Death in the Afternoon

"Always do sober what you said you'd do drunk. That will teach you to keep your mouth shut."

—*As recounted by Charles Scribner in*
In the Company of Writers: A Life in Publishing

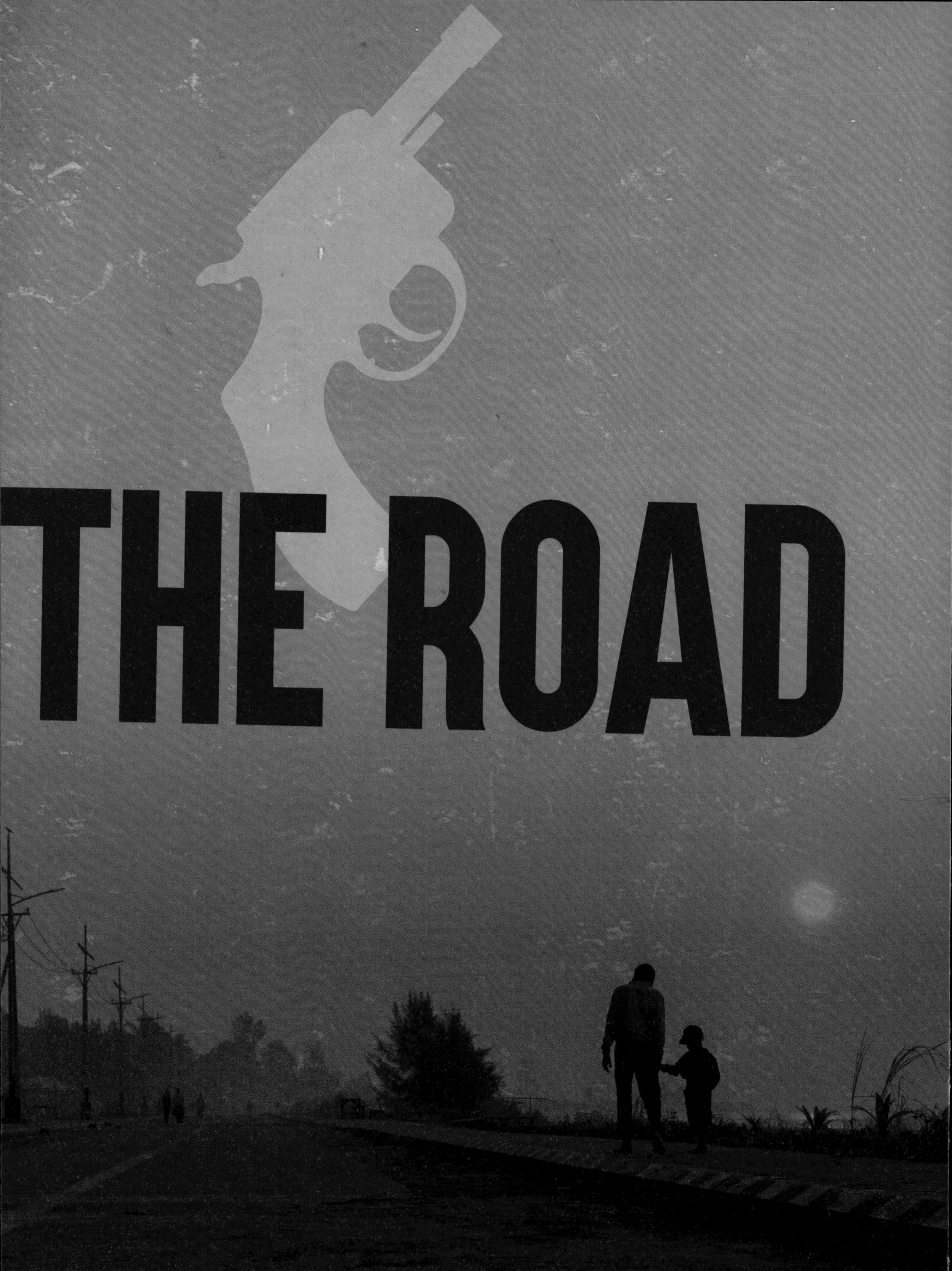
THE ROAD

CORMAC McCARTHY

July 20, 1933

BORN: Providence, Rhode Island

OTHER NOTABLE WORKS:
Blood Meridian, or the Evening Redness in the West (1985)
All the Pretty Horses (1992)
No Country for Old Men (2005)

Though Cormac McCarthy was born in Providence, Rhode Island, his distinctive Southern Gothic style was defined by his family's move to Knoxville, Tennessee, when he was still a child. His early works center around an overbearing feeling of despair in the region, with 1974's *Child of God* and 1979's semi-autobiographical *Suttree* pulling inspiration from the real-life stories of murder and tragedy. The themes of violence followed him as he moved his novels out west, starting with *Blood Meridian*, a nightmarish epic set on the Texas-Mexico border.

In 1992, McCarthy released his most successful novel up to that point, *All the Pretty Horses*, the first part of his Border Trilogy. The book sold more than 100,000 copies in its first year and took home the National Book Award. In the 2000s, McCarthy's popularity reached even greater heights with the release of novels like *No Country for Old Men,* which, along with *Pretty Horses,* was adapted into a feature film.

Thrown into a post-apocalyptic wasteland with little hope in sight, a father and son desperately search for salvation by making their way to the coast in Cormac McCarthy's ***The Road***. Along the way, though, they have to combat the elements, starvation, and the remnants of humanity driven mad by society's collapse after an unknown cataclysm. Here's what you should know about this brutal masterpiece.

THE INSPIRATION FOR THE BOOK CAME TO MCCARTHY DURING A TRIP WITH HIS SON.

It should come as no surprise that a book with such a strong father-son theme as *The Road* came about while Cormac McCarthy was on a trip with his own son in El Paso, Texas. One night, as his son slept, McCarthy gazed out the window of his hotel and thought about what the city might look like in fifty to one hundred years—he imagined fires off in the distance and the town in ruins. Immediately, his thoughts went to his son. He began writing these notes down, though he didn't quite know where the story was going at first. All he had in his mind was a father, a son, and the end of the world.

In an interview with *The Wall Street Journal*, McCarthy said he took further inspiration from conversations he had with his brother Dennis about hypothetical post-apocalyptic scenarios—namely the descent into cannibalism. "We talked about if there was a small percentage of the human population left, what would they do?" he said. "They'd probably divide up into little tribes and when everything's gone, the only thing left to eat is each other. We know that's true historically."

TO PROMOTE THE BOOK, MCCARTHY TOOK PART IN HIS FIRST-EVER TELEVISION INTERVIEW.

McCarthy's aversion to publicity has added to his mystique, but it's also made personal insight into his works nearly impossible to come by. But in June 2007, McCarthy ended up sitting across from Oprah Winfrey for his first-ever television interview to promote *The Road* after she chose it for her Book Club.

During the interview, McCarthy opened up to Winfrey about everything from the inspiration behind the novel to thoughts on his own writing process. Surprisingly, McCarthy admitted his stories aren't very structured as he works on them. "You can't plot things out," McCarthy told Winfrey. "You just have to trust in, you know, wherever it comes from."

The extra press Oprah brought to the book worked: The Oprah paperback version of *The Road*, advertising its place in her book club, wound up selling 1.4 million copies on its own by 2011. That's in comparison to the pre-Oprah numbers, which came in at under 200,000. Not even news of McCarthy winning the Pulitzer Prize in Fiction in 2007 could bump sales of *The Road* the way Oprah could.

MCCARTHY DOESN'T KNOW WHAT CAUSED THE DISASTER IN *THE ROAD*.

One of the most haunting aspects of *The Road* is that readers are simply thrown into a nightmarish vision of a world in chaos with no explanation. The exact nature of the world-ending calamity is never revealed—McCarthy, instead, focuses on the horrifying events in the moment as the unnamed father and son walk through barren forests and come into conflict with scattered camps of deranged survivors. So what happened? Was this a natural disaster that wiped out humanity, or did something manmade finally do us in?

"A lot of people ask me," McCarthy told *The Wall Street Journal*. "I don't have an opinion." He did, however, relay other people's opinions, saying some of his friends within the scientific community, namely geologists, have settled on a meteor as the trigger. McCarthy, though, stressed that it's not really important— what's important is what you do next.

PUNCTUATION MARKS DISLIKED BY FAMOUS AUTHORS

Punctuation marks aren't the most important tools in a writer's toolkit, but writers can develop some strong opinions about them. Here are a few punctuation marks that famous authors actually grew to disdain.

QUOTATION MARKS

Cormac McCarthy famously doesn't use quotation marks in his books. "If you write properly," he told Oprah Winfrey, "you shouldn't have to punctuate . . . I believe in periods, and capitals, and the occasional comma, and that's it." (He added that colons are fine to use, but only if what follows is a list.)

THE QUESTION MARK

Gertrude Stein found the question mark "positively revolting." There was no reason for it since "a question is a question, anybody can know that a question is a question and so why add to it the question mark when it is already there when the question is already there in the writing."

THE SEMICOLON

Kurt Vonnegut, in his essay "Here Is a Lesson in Creative Writing" (published in the book *A Man Without a Country*), came out forcefully against the semicolon in his first rule: "Do not use semicolons." He insults them as representing "absolutely nothing" and claims "all they do is show you've been to college." Semicolon lovers can take heart in the fact that he may have been kidding a little bit—after using a semicolon later in the book, Vonnegut noted, "Rules take us only so far, even good rules."

THE STAND

STEPHEN KING

September 21, 1947

BORN: Portland, Maine

Stephen King's fecundity for fiction is nearly unparalleled in literature. As a teen, he novelized the latest Roger Corman B-movie in a matter of days and sold mimeographed copies to his peers for twenty-five cents apiece. By the time he was in college he had completed a handful of original novels. If his immense prolificacy has been spurred by his father's early disappearance from his life or his mother's untimely death, King will leave it to armchair psychologists to declare. For his part, the author of more than seventy books says simply, "The goal is to do what God made you for and not hurt anyone if you can help it."

Widely considered King's magnum opus,

The Stand (1978) pits a cast of survivors

that are immune to a viral plague that's wiped out most of the population against the villainous Randall Flagg as they try to salvage what's left of an uncertain future. Even if you've read every unabridged word, there's a lot about the making of—and meaning behind—the book you may not have heard about.

KING HAD WRITTEN ABOUT "CAPTAIN TRIPS" BEFORE.

In *The Stand*, humanity is ravaged by a super-flu with the nickname of "Captain Trips" that leaves few survivors behind. "Captain Trips" actually made an appearance earlier in King's work. The short story "Night Surf," published in 1969, describes a virus originating in Southeast Asia that spreads throughout the world. King rewrote it in 1974 and again for his short story collection, *Night Shift*, in 1978.

RANDALL FLAGG WAS INSPIRED BY AN EARLY KING POEM.

In 1969, King wrote a poem, "The Dark Man," about a malevolent wanderer in cowboy boots hitching rides. That image came back to him while he was writing *The Stand*, and out of it came the book's villain, Randall Flagg. The character has since appeared in many of King's other works, which is fitting. Thanks to the poem, King said, Flagg has "always been around."

KING WAS PAYING TRIBUTE TO *THE LORD OF THE RINGS*.

With its sprawling cast and all-powerful antagonist, King has said that he set out to have *The Stand* resemble a fantasy epic like *The Lord of the Rings*, only in an American setting. Instead of a hobbit, King had a Texan named Stu Redman and Sauron was Flagg. The hedonistic city of Las Vegas was his Mordor.

THE BOOK WAS IN DANGER OF BECOMING UNGLUED—LITERALLY.

As massive as *The Stand* is, the 823-page tome was originally submitted to King's publisher, Doubleday, at 1153 pages. King was surprised to hear that the work was too long, but not for editorial reasons. The glue used in the book binding, his editors explained, wouldn't be able to handle such a massive page count without falling apart. King ended up cutting around 150,000 words, which amounted to 400 pages, from *The Stand*. He later released an unedited—and sturdy—version in 1990.

KING WROTE A NEW ENDING FOR A TELEVISION ADAPTATION.

Throughout the publication history of *The Stand*, King has continued tinkering with it, changing the setting from 1980 to 1985, rearranging chapters, and more. For the 2020 CBS All Access adaptation, King wrote a new conclusion that he said had been "in my mind for thirty years."

Fascinating Facts about Stephen King

In addition to being one of the world's most successful and prolific writers, Stephen King is also the toast of Hollywood with a seemingly never-ending stream of adaptations being made of his work. Here are a few things you might not have known about the modern-day horror master.

1 HE WAS HIT BY A VAN, THEN BOUGHT THE VAN THAT HIT HIM.

In 1999, King was hit by a van not far from his summer home in Maine. The incident left the author with a collapsed lung, multiple fractures to his hip and leg, and a gash to the head. Afterward, King and his lawyer bought the van for $1,500 with King announcing that, "Yes, we've got the van, and I'm going to take a sledgehammer and beat it!"

2 AS A KID, HIS FRIEND WAS STRUCK AND KILLED BY A TRAIN.

King's brain seems to be able to create chilling stories at such an amazing clip, yet he's seen his fair share of horror in real life. When King was just a kid, his friend was struck and killed by a train (a plot line that made it into his story "The Body," which was adapted into *Stand by Me*). While it would be easy to assume that this incident informed much of King's writing, the author claims to have no memory of the event. He would later write that about an hour after going to play at a neighbor's house, he returned "as white as a ghost" and didn't speak for the rest of the day. He wouldn't tell his mother why he hadn't called her to pick him up. "It turned out that the kid I had been playing with had been run over by a freight train while playing on or crossing the tracks (years later, my mother told me they had picked up the pieces in a wicker basket)," he wrote. "My mom never knew if I had been near him when it happened, if it had occurred before I even arrived, or if I had wandered away after it happened. Perhaps she had her own ideas on the subject. But as I've said, I have no memory of the incident at all; only of having been told about it some years after the fact."

3 HE PLAYED IN A BAND WITH OTHER SUCCESSFUL AUTHORS.

King played rhythm guitar for a band made up of successful writers called The Rock Bottom Remainders. From 1992 to 2012, the band "toured" about once a year. In addition to King, Amy Tan, Dave Barry, Mitch Albom, Barbara Kingsolver, Matt Groening, and Ridley Pearson were just some of its other members.

4 HE HAS BATTLED DRUG AND ALCOHOL PROBLEMS.

Throughout much of the 1980s, King struggled with drug and alcohol abuse. In discussing this time, he admitted that, "There's one novel, *Cujo*, that I barely remember writing at all. I don't say that with pride or shame, only with a vague sense of sorrow and loss. I like that book. I wish I could remember enjoying the good parts as I put them down on the page."

It came to a head when his family members staged an intervention and confronted him with drug paraphernalia they had collected from his trash can. It was the eye-opener King needed; he got help and has been sober ever since.

5 HE IS SURROUNDED BY WRITERS.

Stephen isn't the only writer in the King family: His wife, Tabitha King, has published several novels. Joe, their oldest son, followed in his dad's footsteps and is a bestselling horror writer (he writes under the pen name Joe Hill). Youngest child Owen has written a collection of short stories and one novella and he and his dad co-wrote *Sleeping Beauties*. Naomi, the only King daughter, is a minister and gay activist.

FIVE BOOKS THAT WILL (PROBABLY) NEVER BE PRINTED AGAIN

In an age where readers can get their book fix via downloads or overnight shipping, it can be easy to overlook the fact that not everything is available on demand. Thousands of titles remain off-limits in both digital and analog form for a variety of reasons—some controversial, others due to the author's wishes. Take a look at five titles you're unlikely to find on shelves anytime soon.

1 Rage // STEPHEN KING

Stephen King published seven books under the pseudonym Richard Bachman. One of them, *Rage*, was written while King was in his late teens and concerned a high school student who kills his teacher and takes his algebra class hostage. By 1997, at least three adolescents who had brought weapons to school and killed or injured classmates had admitted to reading the book or had it found in their possession; one said he modeled his behavior directly after the book's lead character. A distraught King convinced his publisher that the book was a "possible accelerant" and had no place on shelves. They complied; King has said that "I pulled it because in my judgment it might be hurting people, and that made it the responsible thing to do."

2 Fast Times at Ridgemont High // CAMERON CROWE

Screenwriter and director Crowe (*Say Anything, Almost Famous*) began contributing to *Rolling Stone* and other music publications when he was still a teenager. At the age of twenty-two, he convinced Clairemont High School in San Diego to let him enroll as a student so he could chronicle the experience of a senior class. *Fast Times*, which changed his classmates' names to maintain a semblance of privacy, was adapted into the 1982 film starring Sean Penn.

Despite the name recognition of both the title and its author, Crowe has resisted any attempt to put it back in print. Talking to *The Hollywood Reporter* in 2011, Crowe said that he "[likes] that there's one thing that's not readily available . . . I like it too much as a kind of bootleg."

3 Promise Me Tomorrow // NORA ROBERTS

Roberts's success in the romance genre is impressive by any measure. As of 2011, she had over four hundred million books in print. The lone exception: *Promise Me Tomorrow*, a title she wrote early on in her career. Though Roberts had already finished well over twenty books by the time *Promise Me Tomorrow* was released, it doesn't appear she's eager for people to revisit it. In 2009, Roberts told *The New Yorker* that it was full of clichés and committed the most egregious of romance-novel sins: an unhappy ending.

4 Sex // MADONNA

By the time Madonna committed to shooting a coffee table photography book of herself and models (including Vanilla Ice) in various compromising positions, the world had gotten fairly used to her provocative behavior. Nonetheless, when Warner Books released *Sex* in 1992, it promptly sold through half of its million-copy print run inside of a week. Intended as a limited-availability collector's item, the publisher has never expressed interest in returning to it; BookFinder, which, for years, released an annual list of the most sought-after out-of-print titles, regularly places the 132-page book at or near the top of the heap.

5 Encyclopaedia Britannica

The venerable reference volume taxed its last particle-board bookshelf in 2012, when Encyclopaedia Britannica, Inc. decided to cease publication of its analog information library. At 129 pounds, the $1,395 collection sold just eight thousand copies— a far cry from the 120,000 sets the company moved in 1990. The advent of online resources like Wikipedia and a prohibitive cost led Britannica to focus on online strategies. A total of fifteen editions were released through 2010.

THINGS FALL APART

CHINUA ACHEBE

November 16, 1930–March 21, 2013

BORN: Ogidi, Nigeria

OTHER NOTABLE WORKS:
A Man of the People (1966)
Girls at War and Other Stories (1973)
Anthills of the Savannah (1987)

Few authors have related the Nigerian experience more powerfully than Chinua Achebe, who made a splash in 1958 with his first novel, *Things Fall Apart*, setting the stage for a remarkable career. Through his work and university teachings, Achebe illustrated encroaching Western values in African culture and sought to demystify a place too often reduced to stereotypes. After enjoying further acclaim with novels like *No Longer at Ease* (1960) and *Anthills of the Savannah*, Achebe passed away at age eighty-two in 2013.

Describing the oppression of the Ibo (now called Igbo) people in Nigeria by British colonial administrators and following the life of Okonkwo, an Igbo leader and wrestling champion, *Things Fall Apart* has been called "the finest novel written about life in Nigeria at the end of the nineteenth century" and "a classic of world literature." Here's what you need to know about Chinua Achebe's debut novel.

THE BOOK WAS PARTLY A RESPONSE TO BOOKS LIKE JOSEPH CONRAD'S *HEART OF DARKNESS*.

One of Achebe's goals with *Things Fall Apart*, which takes its title from W.B. Yeats's poem *The Second Coming*, was to present a different picture of Africa—of a vibrant place with thriving culture—than had previously been painted in literature by European writers. Most famous is Achebe's criticism of Joseph Conrad's 1899 book *Heart of Darkness*. "*Heart of Darkness* projects the image of Africa as 'the other world,' the antithesis of Europe and therefore of civilization, a place where man's vaunted intelligence and refinement are finally mocked by triumphant bestiality," Achebe wrote in the essay "An Image of Africa," in which he declared Conrad "a thoroughgoing racist."

"If you don't like someone's story, you write your own," Achebe told *The Paris Review*. "If you don't like what somebody says, you say what it is you don't like." He explained that he wasn't saying people shouldn't read Conrad—in fact, he himself taught a course on *Heart of Darkness*. "What I'm saying is, Look at the way this man handles Africans. Do you recognize humanity there?"

THE MANUSCRIPT WAS NEARLY LOST.

In 1957, Achebe was studying at the BBC in London when he showed his manuscript for *Things Fall Apart* to Gilbert Phelps, an instructor at his school. Phelps wanted to give the book to his publishers, but Achebe still had revisions to make, so he took the manuscript back to Nigeria, and made the edits.

What he did next could have had dire consequences. He sent his handwritten manuscript, the only copy of *Things Fall Apart* in existence, to a London typing agency in the mail.

Thankfully, the manuscript made it to London. The agency responded that they'd received his manuscript and requested a payment of thirty-two pounds for two copies, which Achebe sent.

And then he waited . . . and waited . . . and waited. For months.

Achebe wrote the agency repeatedly, but got no answer. "I was getting thinner and thinner and thinner," he recalled. Eventually, his boss, who was heading back to London for vacation, went to the agency, demanded they find and type the book, and send it back, which they did—but only one copy, not the two Achebe had paid for. And he never got an explanation for what had happened.

INITIALLY, THE BOOK HAD A VERY SMALL PRINT RUN.

Things Fall Apart was bought by Heinemann, which initially printed a very small number of copies of the book. The publisher was taking a risk, Achebe told *The Paris Review*. "They had no idea if anybody would want to read it." *Things Fall Apart* quickly went out of print, and according to Achebe, it wouldn't have graced shelves again if not for Alan Hill, who decided to take a gamble and put out a paperback edition.

It was a gamble that paid off. In the years since, *Things Fall Apart* has sold more than ten million copies and has been translated into fifty different languages, and it remains one of the most taught and dissected novels about Africa. "It would be impossible to say how *Things Fall Apart* influenced African writing," scholar Kwame Anthony Appiah wrote. "It would be like asking how Shakespeare influenced English writers or Pushkin influenced Russians."

Fascinating Facts about Chinua Achebe

Chinua Achebe was just twenty-eight when he published *Things Fall Apart*. Here's what you should know about the author often referred to as "The Father of African Literature."

1 HE HAD PLANNED TO BE A DOCTOR.

Though he was always an avid reader and began learning English at the age of eight, Achebe hadn't always planned to become a beacon of the literary world. After studying at Nigeria's prestigious Government College, Achebe earned a scholarship to study medicine at University College in Ibadan. One year into the program he realized that writing was his true calling and switched majors, which meant giving up his scholarship. With financial help from his brother, Achebe was able to complete his studies.

2 JOYCE CARY'S *MISTER JOHNSON* INSPIRED HIM TO WRITE—BUT NOT IN THE WAY YOU MIGHT THINK.

While storytelling had long been a part of Achebe's Igbo upbringing in Nigeria, that was only part of what inspired him to write. While in college, he read *Mister Johnson*, Irish writer Joyce Cary's tragicomic novel about a young Nigerian clerk whose happy-go-lucky demeanor infects everyone around him. While *TIME* Magazine declared it the "best novel ever written about Africa," Achebe disagreed.

"My problem with Joyce Cary's book was not simply his infuriating principal character, Johnson," Achebe wrote in *Home and Exile*. "More importantly, there is a certain undertow of uncharitableness just below the surface on which his narrative moves and from where, at the slightest chance, a contagion of distaste, hatred, and mockery breaks through to poison his tale." The book led Achebe to realize that "there is such a thing as absolute power over narrative," and he was inspired to take control of it to tell a more realistic tale of his home.

3 ACHEBE DIDN'T THINK THAT WRITING COULD BE TAUGHT.

Though he studied writing, Achebe wasn't all too sure that he learned much about the art in college. He recalled to *The Paris Review* that the best piece of advice he had ever gotten was from one of his professors, James Welch, who told him, "We may not be able to teach you what you need or what you want. We can only teach you what we know."

"I didn't learn anything there that I really needed, except this kind of attitude," the author said. "I have had to go out on my own. . . . You really have to go out on your own and do it."

4 HE WAS WARY OF MACHINES.

Though typewriters, followed by computers, were ubiquitous, Achebe preferred writing in a more old-fashioned way: with pen and paper. He explained to *The Paris Review* that he wasn't a great typist, and that when he tried to write using a typewriter, "it's like having this machine between me and the words; what comes out is not quite what would come out if I were scribbling."

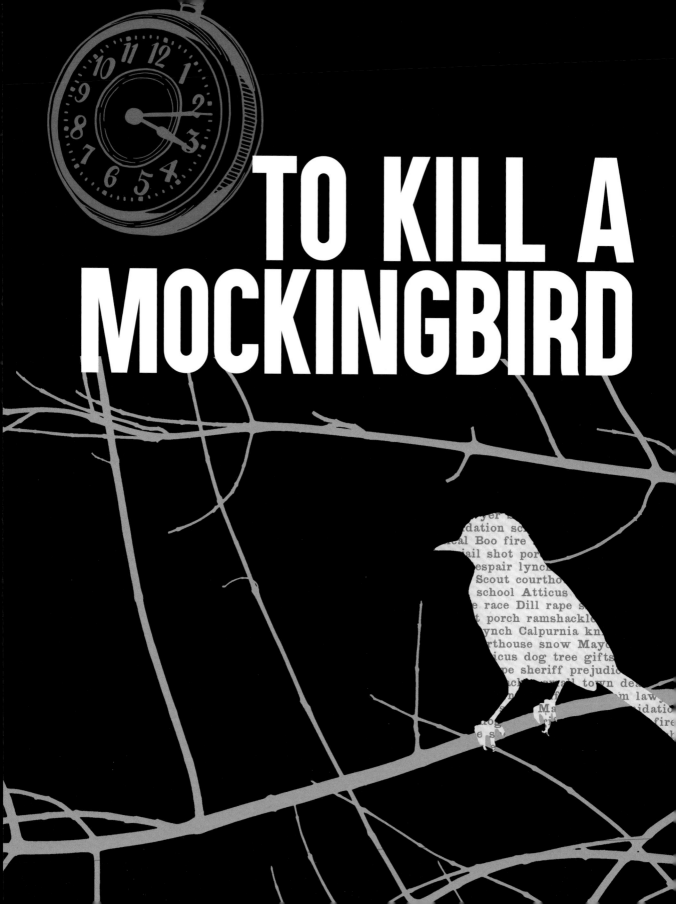

HARPER LEE

April 28, 1926–February 19, 2016
BORN: Monroeville, Alabama
OTHER NOTABLE WORKS:
Go Set a Watchman (2015)

arper Lee published only two novels, but the first—1960's *To Kill a Mockingbird*—became a touchstone of American literature. Lee lived most of her life in her hometown of Monroeville, Alabama, and pulled the novel's themes of racism, justice, and morality from her own backyard. *To Kill a Mockingbird* won the Pulitzer Prize for Fiction in 1961, but for decades afterwards, Lee wrote only a few essays and worked on a true crime book that would ultimately not be published. In 2007, Lee was the recipient of the Presidential Medal of Freedom, and three years later received the National Medal of Arts. She died in 2016 at the age of eighty-nine.

More than sixty years after its publication, Harper Lee's *To Kill a Mockingbird* still resonates with readers. The novel tells the Depression-era story of the Finch family in Maycomb, Alabama. While youngsters Scout and Jem investigate the local legend of Boo Radley, father Atticus agrees to represent a Black man named Tom Robinson who has been falsely accused of raping a white woman. The two stories dovetail as Scout receives a surprising and at times painful education in the realities of life in the American South. The coming-of-age tale was a phenomenal success from the start, and has only become more popular with time. Here's what you need to know.

THE NOVEL DREW ON LEE'S CHILDHOOD IN ALABAMA.

While *To Kill a Mockingbird* is not autobiographical, there are similarities between the novel and Lee's life. The book is set in Maycomb, Alabama, the fictional name for Monroeville, where Lee grew up. Like the main character Scout, Lee was a tomboy who was uncomfortable with traditional femininity. She and Scout would have been the same age and her brother Edwin was around four years older, just like Scout's brother Jem. She even gave the family her mother's maiden name, Finch.

DILL WAS BASED ON TRUMAN CAPOTE.

As a child, Capote—the author of *In Cold Blood* and *Breakfast at Tiffany's*—lived next door to Lee. They played together and even shared Lee's typewriter. Both children were outside the social circles of their close-knit Southern town. As Gerald Clarke wrote in *Capote: A Biography*, "Nelle was too rough for most other girls, and Truman was too soft for most other boys." Capote's first book, *Other Voices, Other Rooms*, has a tomboy character resembling Lee. Her name is Idabel Thompkins.

LEE GREW UP IN THE COURTROOM.

Like the character Atticus, Lee's father, A.C. Lee, was a lawyer. Soft-spoken and dignified, he defended two Black men accused of murder and lost the case. Lee spent much of her childhood in the Monroeville courthouse. "Her father was a lawyer, and she and I used to go to trials all the time as children," Capote said. "We went to the trials instead of going to the movies." Lee herself went to law school, but hated it and dropped out.

BOO RADLEY MAY HAVE BEEN MODELED AFTER A CHILDHOOD NEIGHBOR.

In the book, Boo Radley is a recluse who leaves presents for the children in a tree. Lee may have modeled him after a real man, Alfred "Son" Boulware, who lived in Monroeville when the author was a child. According to Capote, "He was a real man, and he lived just down the road from us. We used to go and get those things out of the trees. Everything [Lee] wrote about it is absolutely true."

GO SET A WATCHMAN WAS WRITTEN BEFORE *TO KILL A MOCKINGBIRD*.

Lee wrote *Go Set a Watchman* in the 1950s. Set twenty years after *To Kill a Mockingbird*, it contains many of the same characters and themes. An editor who read the manuscript loved a flashback about Scout's childhood and told Lee to write a book from the child's point of view. Lee then started *To Kill a Mockingbird*. *Go Set a Watchman* was thought to be lost until Tonja Carter, Lee's lawyer, found it in the author's archives in 2014. When HarperCollins published *Go Set a Watchman* in 2015, critics questioned Lee's approval of its publication.

LEE WAS ABLE TO WRITE BECAUSE OF A GIFT FROM HER FRIENDS.

After withdrawing from law school, Lee moved to New York and worked as an airline reservationist. One Christmas, her friends Joy and Michael Brown gave her a gift: enough money to write for one year. In an essay for *McCall's* in 1961, Lee wrote that they told her to quit her job and write whatever she wanted, no strings attached. "*Our faith in you* was really all I had heard them say. I would do my best not to fail them."

TO KILL A MOCKINGBIRD CHANGED CONSIDERABLY DURING EDITING.

Lee's agent sent *To Kill a Mockingbird* to ten publishers and all of them turned it down. Finally, the publisher Lippincott accepted the manuscript, even though it needed a lot of work. "There were dangling threads of a plot, there was a lack of unity—a beginning, a middle, and an end—that was inherent in the beginning," editor Tay Hohoff said. "It is an indication of how seriously we were impressed by the author that we signed a contract at that point."

There followed "a long and hopeless period of writing the book over and over again," Lee said. It was published in 1960.

LEE THOUGHT THE BOOK WOULD FAIL.

In 1964, Lee said she "never expected any sort of success with *Mockingbird*. I didn't expect the book to sell in the first place." But the novel was a massive success. Not only was it a best seller, it was followed up with an Oscar-winning movie starring Gregory Peck. It also won a Pulitzer Prize in 1961. Today, the book sells almost a million copies a year, more than fellow twentieth century classics *The Great Gatsby* or *The Catcher in the Rye*.

TRUMAN CAPOTE DID NOT WRITE *TO KILL A MOCKINGBIRD*.

At some point, a rumor started that Capote wrote *To Kill a Mockingbird*, or at least edited it. Aside from the fact that Lee's writing sounds nothing like Capote's, he only saw the manuscript once. In 1959, Lee accompanied Capote to Kansas to research *In Cold Blood*. During that trip, she showed him a finished version of *Mockingbird*, which was about to go to print. Since the book was done, it would have been impossible for Capote to edit it, let alone write it.

CAPOTE WAS JEALOUS OF THE BOOK'S SUCCESS.

While Capote initially seemed supportive, his friendship with Lee soured as her novel was increasingly lauded. According to Lee's sister Alice, "Truman became very jealous because Nelle Harper got a Pulitzer and he did not. He expected *In Cold Blood* to bring him one, and he got involved with the drugs and heavy drinking and all. And that was it. It was not Nelle Harper dropping him. It was Truman going away from her."

THE RISE OF PAPERBACK BOOKS HELPED TURN THE BOOK INTO A LITERARY CLASSIC.

After its publication in 1960, *To Kill a Mockingbird* was reviewed favorably in *The New York Times*, but it wasn't the bestselling novel that year. It was the evolution of paperbacks that helped put it into more hands.

Prior to the 1960s, paperbacks were often kind of trashy, and when literary novels were published in the format, they had sexy covers, like a softcover edition of *The Great Gatsby* that featured a shirtless Jay Gatsby on the cover. But then, the mass-market paperback for *To Kill a Mockingbird* came out in 1962. It was cheap, but had stellar credentials, which appealed to teachers. Suddenly, it was in virtually every school and, even half a century later, it still is.

LEE HATED THE SPOTLIGHT.

When asked about her success in 1964, Lee called it frightening, saying her reaction was "sheer numbness. It was like being hit over the head and knocked cold." While she never became the "Jane Austen of south Alabama" as she once hoped, she did work on a true crime novel in the 1970s. The book remains unfinished, though a 2019 book called *Furious Hours: Murder, Fraud, and the Last Trial of Harper Lee* covers her attempt to write it.

AMAZING THINGS HARPER LEE DID AFTER *TO KILL A MOCKINGBIRD*

Up until 2015's *Go Set a Watchman*, Harper Lee was often referred to as a literary one-hit wonder. But while the Pulitzer Prize-winning author of *To Kill a Mockingbird* only published two novels, she still accomplished some incredible things.

LEE ROASTED A SMALL-MINDED SCHOOL BOARD.

In 1966, a Virginia school board unanimously elected to ban all copies of *To Kill a Mockingbird* from its libraries, citing the book as "immoral." Outraged, Lee wrote a fiery letter to the *Richmond News Leader* condemning the group's actions. "Recently," she wrote, "I have received echoes down this way of the Hanover County School Board's activities, and what I've heard makes me wonder if any of its members can read." Lee went on to compare the officials' mental gymnastics with 1984's doublethink and capped off her epic beat-down by enclosing "a small contribution . . . that I hope will be used to enroll the Hanover County School Board in any first grade of its choice."

LEE HELPED TRUMAN CAPOTE WORK ON *IN COLD BLOOD*.

Capote asked Lee to accompany him on a trip to the small town of Holcomb, Kansas, in 1959 to investigate the recent murder of a wealthy family under mysterious circumstances. It didn't take long for Capote to discover that his companion had a much easier time talking to the locals, an ability that proved invaluable to his efforts. Lee was so dedicated to the case that she wrote 150 pages of notes for Capote (who reportedly ignored her suggestion to make the victims more complex). Capote's best-selling account of the incident, *In Cold Blood*, became an instant sensation.

LEE WROTE AN IMPASSIONED DEFENSE OF BOOKS AND LIBRARIES.

In 2006, Lee composed an open letter to Oprah Winfrey's *O* magazine that discussed her love of books: "Instant information is not for me," she wrote. "I prefer to search library stacks because when I work to learn something, I remember it. And, Oprah, can you imagine curling up in bed to read a computer? Weeping for Anna Karenina and being terrified by Hannibal Lecter, entering the heart of darkness with Mistah Kurtz, having Holden Caulfield ring you up—some things should happen on soft pages, not cold metal."

VIRGINIA WOOLF

January 25, 1882–March 28, 1941

BORN: London, England

OTHER NOTABLE WORKS:
The Voyage Out (1915)
Jacob's Room (1922)
Mrs. Dalloway (1925)

Best known for her highly imaginative and nonlinear novels like *Mrs. Dalloway, Orlando,* and *To the Lighthouse,* writer Virginia Woolf lived her life as unabashedly as many of the characters in her novels. The author helped pioneer modern literature and feminist theory by refusing to adhere to the status quo on just about anything, and often presented complex characters who struggle to escape the confines of certain societal expectations of them—especially women—and with flowing prose and a courageous pen, she dissected every topic from the idiocy of warfare to the joys of sex.

The plot of Virginia Woolf's fifth novel, *To the Lighthouse*, is thin: The Ramsey family and their guests are on vacation and decide to put off a trip to a nearby lighthouse until a later visit. The book has thrilled and frustrated readers since it was published in 1927. Today, it's considered a masterpiece, and frequently appears on lists of the best novels of the twentieth century.

IT'S LOOSELY BASED ON EVENTS FROM WOOLF'S LIFE.

To the Lighthouse is Woolf's most autobiographical novel, and, according to Shirley Panken in *Virginia Woolf and the Lust of Creation: A Psychoanalytic Exploration,* she wrote it "to grapple with the impingement of unresolved feelings concerning her parents." Like the Ramseys, Woolf's family had eight children. They also, like the Ramseys, spent summers vacationing on the coast—in this case, St. Ives in Cornwall, where her father, Leslie, rented a home every year until Woolf's mother, Julia, died when she was thirteen.

Woolf based Mr. and Mrs. Ramsey on her parents; as she wrote in her diary in 1925, "This is going to be fairly short: to have father's character done complete in it; and mother's; & St. Ives; & childhood; & all the usual things I try to put in – life, death & c." Mrs. Ramsey was so was similar to Julia that Woolf's sister, Vanessa, told her after reading the novel that "It is almost painful to have her so raised from the dead." Other characters have much in common with Vanessa and their brother Adrian, who—like James in the novel—was disappointed at not being able to take a trip to the lighthouse. The lighthouse had real-life inspiration, too: The Godrevy lighthouse, which also inspired the cover of the novel, designed by Vanessa, an artist, who did all of the covers for Woolf's novels (with the exception of her first).

WOOLF PURPOSEFULLY DEPARTED FROM CLASSIC NOVEL CONSTRUCTION.

Carefully structured in three sections ("The Window"; "Time Passes"; "The Lighthouse"), *To the Lighthouse* follows the shifting perspectives of each character—a narrative technique Woolf had experimented with in her previous books, *Jacob's Room* and *Mrs. Dalloway*—as they grapple with themes such as time, loss, gender roles, and the purpose of art. It wasn't even close to the construction of a classic novel, and it wasn't meant to be.

"Life is not a series of gig lamps symmetrically arranged," the author wrote in her essay "Modern Fiction." "Life is a luminous halo, a semi-transparent envelope surrounding us from the beginning of consciousness to the end. Is it not the task of the novelist to convey this varying, this unknown and uncircumscribed spirit, whatever aberration or complexity it may display, with as little mixture of the alien and external as possible?"

THE NOVEL PUZZLED CRITICS.

"My present opinion is that it is easily the best of my books," Woolf wrote of *To the Lighthouse*, but others weren't so sure. Some savaged the novel—"A group of people plan to sail in a small boat to a lighthouse," novelist Arnold Bennett wrote. "At the end some of them reach the lighthouse in a small boat. That is the externality of the plot"—while others were puzzled by it. "Dear Mrs. Woolf," wrote one, "do you wish to create an atmosphere? Is there a hidden meaning there? . . . All your characters go away . . . after having entered upon the scene unannounced. You assume that your readers are as intelligent as you and as accustomed to seeing into the obscurity and resolving mysteries." In the end, it didn't matter: *To the Lighthouse* outsold Woolf's previous novels.

THE LIGHTHOUSE DIDN'T SYMBOLIZE ANYTHING.

Since its publication, readers have said the lighthouse symbolizes things like desire, stability, and truth. Woolf, however, didn't assign any symbolism to the lighthouse herself.

"I meant *nothing* by The Lighthouse," Woolf wrote to a friend in 1927. "One has to have a central line down the middle of the book to draw the design together. I saw that all sorts of feelings would accrue to this, but I refused to think them out, & trusted that people would make it the deposit for their own emotions—which they have done, thinking it means one thing after another. I can't manage Symbolism except in this vague, generalised way. Whether it's right or wrong I don't know; but directly I'm told what a thing means, it becomes hateful to me."

MARGARET ATWOOD WASN'T A FAN— UNTIL SHE WAS.

In a piece for *The Guardian*, Atwood writes that she first read *To the Lighthouse* as part of a class. "Virginia Woolf was off on a siding as far as my nineteen-year-old self was concerned," she recalled. "Why go to the lighthouse at all, and why make such a fuss about going or not going? What was the book about? . . . In Woolfland, things were so tenuous. They were so elusive. They were so inconclusive. They were so deeply unfathomable."

Her reaction was much different when picked up the book again, forty-three years later, after she was older, wiser, and had experienced loss. "How was it that, this time, everything in the book fell so completely into place?" she wondered. "How could I have missed it—above all, the patterns, the artistry—the first time through? . . . Some books have to wait until you're ready for them. So much, in reading, is a matter of luck."

WOOLF'S WORDS OF WISDOM ON WRITING AND LIFE

ON FOOD
"One cannot think well, love well, sleep well, if one has not dined well."

— *From "A Room of One's Own"*

ON BEING AN HONEST WRITER
"If you do not tell the truth about yourself you cannot tell it about other people."

—*From* The Moment and Other Essays *(1947)*

ON PERSONAL GROWTH
"I am made and remade continually. Different people draw different words from me."

—From her 1931 novel *The Waves*

ON RECORDED HISTORY

"Nothing has really happened until it has been described."

— *Said to a young acquaintance, Nigel Nicholson, who later became a successful publisher, memoirist, and politician*

ON THE UNIVERSE
"When you consider things like the stars, our affairs don't seem to matter very much, do they?"

—*From the novel* Night and Day *(1919)*

ON WRITING FICTION
"Fiction is like a spider's web, attached ever so lightly perhaps, but still attached to life at all four corners."

—*From her seminal 1929 essay "A Room of One's Own"*

ON SEXISM
"As long as she thinks of a man, nobody objects to a woman thinking."

—*From* Orlando: A Biography

ON GETTING OLDER
"I don't believe in ageing. I believe in forever altering one's aspect to the sun."

—*From her diary (entry dated October 2, 1932)*

ON ARTISTIC INTEGRITY
"So long as you write what you wish to write, that is all that matters; and whether it matters for ages or only for hours, nobody can say. But to sacrifice a hair of the head of your vision, a shade of its colour, in deference to some Headmaster with a silver pot in his hand or to some professor with a measuring-rod up his sleeve, is the most abject treachery."

— *From "A Room of One's Own"*

ON WORDS
"Of course, you can catch them and sort them and place them in alphabetical order in dictionaries. But words do not live in dictionaries, they live in the mind."

—*From "Craftsmanship," a BBC radio address Woolf delivered on April 20, 1937*

ULYSSES

JAMES JOYCE

February 2, 1882–January 13, 1941

BORN: Rathgar, Dublin, Ireland

OTHER NOTABLE WORKS:
A Portrait of the Artist as a Young Man (1916)
Finnegans Wake (1939)

Born in Dublin, Ireland, in 1882, James Joyce became one of his country's most prominent literary greats. Despite his tumultuous education—Joyce was shuffled between boarding school, home school, grammar school, and finally college—he excelled, picking up new languages and earning praise for his writing at a young age. After graduating from University College, Dublin, he briefly planned to become a doctor, but ditched that idea and went to Paris instead. Though he traveled widely, his home city of Dublin remained at the heart of his stories and his life. "When I die," he is said to have remarked, "Dublin will be written in my heart."

Perhaps no book has triggered such strong and polarizing reactions as James Joyce's *Ulysses*. The gargantuan novel's 265,000 words have simultaneously enchanted, bewildered, and downright revolted readers and critics since the Irish novelist first published them about a century ago. Having endured despite being banned in the US and UK for years on moral grounds, *Ulysses* is today hailed as a masterpiece of the modernist movement, frequently ranking atop the various lists of the English language's greatest works—as well as the most difficult. The epic follows the travails and encounters of one Leopold Bloom through an ordinary day in Dublin, June 16, 1904. Joyce once commented that he had placed within *Ulysses* "so many enigmas and puzzles that it will keep the professors busy for centuries arguing over what I meant," and so far, so good. The book has become known as "the novel to end all novels" for the scope, complexity, and sheer volume of its pages, and reading it is a feat of endurance: It's made up of eighteen "Episodes," each adopting a separate form and reading completely differently. Chock-full of symbolism, experimentation, obscure references and historical allusions, the author's wit and mastery of language reward the most patient of students as forcefully as they can daunt the faint of heart. Following is some background on Joyce's life and epic work.

JOYCE WAS ONLY NINE WHEN HIS FIRST PIECE OF WRITING WAS PUBLISHED.

In 1891, shortly after he had to leave Clongowes Wood College when his father lost his job, nine-year-old Joyce wrote a poem called "Et Tu Healy?" It was published by his father John and distributed to friends; the elder Joyce thought so highly of it, he allegedly sent copies to the Pope.

As an adult, Joyce would publish his first book, a collection of poems called *Chamber Music*, in 1907. It was followed by *Dubliners*, a collection of short stories, in 1914, and the semi-autobiographical *A Portrait of the Artist as a Young Man* (in which Clongowes Wood College is prominently featured) in 1916.

HE CAUSED A CONTROVERSY AT HIS COLLEGE'S PAPER.

While attending University College, Dublin, Joyce attempted to publish a negative review—titled "The Day of the Rabblement"—of a new local playhouse called the Irish Literary Theatre in the school's paper, *St. Stephen's*. Joyce's condemnation of the theater's "parochialism" was allegedly so scathing that the paper's editors, after seeking consultation from one of the school's priests, refused to print it.

Incensed about possible censorship, Joyce appealed to the school's president, who sided with the editors—which prompted Joyce to put up his own money to publish eighty-five copies to be distributed across campus.

The pamphlet, published alongside a friend's essay

to beef up the page-count, came with the preface: "These two essays were commissioned by the editor of *St. Stephen's* for that paper, but were subsequently refused insertion by the censor." It wouldn't be the last time Joyce would fight censorship.

NORA BARNACLE GHOSTED HIM FOR THEIR PLANNED FIRST DATE.

By the time Nora Barnacle and Joyce finally married in 1931, they had lived together for twenty-seven years, traveled the continent, and had two children. The couple first met in Dublin in 1904 when Joyce struck up a conversation with her near the hotel where Nora worked as a chambermaid. She initially mistook him for a Swedish sailor because of his blue eyes and the yachting cap he wore that day, and he charmed her so much that they set a date for June 14—but she didn't show.

He then wrote her a letter, saying, "I looked for a long time at a head of reddish-brown hair and decided it was not yours. I went home quite dejected. I would like to make an appointment but it might not suit you. I hope you will be kind enough to make one with me—if you have not forgotten me!" This led to their first date, which supposedly took place on June 16, 1904.

She would continue to be his muse throughout their life together in both his published work (the character Molly Bloom in *Ulysses* is based on her) and their fruitful personal correspondence. Their notably dirty love letters to each other—featuring him saying their love-making reminded him of "a hog riding a sow" and signing off one by saying "Goodnight, my little farting Nora, my dirty little fuckbird!"—have highlighted the NSFW nature of their relationship. In fact, one of Joyce's signed erotic letters to Nora fetched a record £240,800 ($446,422) at a London auction in 2004.

JOYCE HAD REALLY BAD EYES.

While Joyce's persistent money problems caused him to lead a life of what could be categorized as creative discomfort, he had to deal with a near lifetime of medical discomfort as well. Joyce suffered from anterior uveitis, which led to a series of around twelve eye surgeries over his lifetime. (Due to the relatively unsophisticated state of ophthalmology at the time, and his decision not to listen to contemporary medical advice, scholars speculate that his iritis, glaucoma, and cataracts could have been caused by sarcoidosis, syphilis, tuberculosis, or any number of congenital problems.)

His vision issues caused Joyce to wear an eye patch for years and forced him to do his writing on large white sheets of paper using only red crayon. The persistent eye struggles even inspired him to name his daughter Lucia, after St. Lucia, patron saint of the blind.

HE WAS FLUENT IN MANY LANGUAGES.

English was one of seventeen languages Joyce could supposedly speak; others included Arabic, Sanskrit, Greek, and Italian, which eventually became his preferred language, and one that he exclusively spoke at home with his family. He also loved playwright Henrik Ibsen so much that he learned Norwegian so that he could read Ibsen's works in their original form—and send the writer a fan letter in his native tongue. (One of Joyce's friends, however, later said that Joyce's claim about speaking seventeen languages was a joke, and that while he was fluent in French, Italian, and English, his skill in other languages was "limited.")

JOYCE TURNED TO A COMPLETELY INEXPERIENCED PUBLISHER TO RELEASE HIS MOST WELL-KNOWN BOOK.

The publishing history of *Ulysses* is itself its own odyssey. Joyce began writing the work in 1914, and by 1918 he had begun serializing the novel in the American magazine *Little Review* with the help of poet Ezra Pound.

But by 1921, *Little Review* was in financial trouble. The published version of Episode Thirteen of *Ulysses*, "Nausicaa," resulted in a costly obscenity lawsuit against its publishers, Margaret Anderson and Jane Heap, and the book was banned in the United States. Joyce appealed to different publishers for help—including Leonard and Virginia Woolf's Hogarth Press—but none agreed to take on a project with such legal implications (and in the Woolfs' case, length), no matter how supposedly groundbreaking it was.

Joyce, then based in Paris, made friends with Sylvia Beach, whose bookstore, Shakespeare and Company, was a gathering hub for the post-war expatriate creative community. In her autobiography, Beach wrote that Joyce was in the store, lamenting his situation, when "it occurred to me that something might be done, and I asked: 'Would you let Shakespeare and Company have the honour of bringing out your *Ulysses*?" Joyce accepted right away. "I thought it rash of him to entrust his great *Ulysses* to such a funny little publisher. But he seemed delighted, and so was I," Beach wrote.

"Undeterred by lack of capital, experience, and all the other requisites of a publisher, I went right ahead with *Ulysses*."

Beach planned a first edition of one thousand copies (with one hundred signed by the author), while the book would continue to be banned in a number of countries throughout the 1920s and '30s. Eventually it was allowed to be published in the United States in 1933 after the case *United States v. One Book Called Ulysses* deemed the book not obscene.

ERNEST HEMINGWAY WAS HIS DRINKING BUDDY—AND SOMETIMES HIS BODYGUARD.

Hemingway—who was a major champion of *Ulysses*—met Joyce at Shakespeare and Company, and was later a frequent companion among the bars of Paris with writers like Wyndham Lewis and Valery Larbaud.

He recalled that the Irish writer would start to get into drunken fights and leave Hemingway to deal with the consequences. "Once, in one of those casual conversations you have when you're drinking," Hemingway said, "Joyce said to me he was afraid his writing was too suburban and that maybe he should get around a bit and see the world. He was afraid of some things, lightning and things, but a wonderful man. He was under great discipline—his wife, his work, and his bad eyes. His wife was there and she said, yes, his work was too suburban—'Jim could do with a spot of that lion hunting.' We would go out to drink and Joyce would fall into a fight. He couldn't even see the man so he'd say, 'Deal with him, Hemingway! Deal with him!'"

HE'S THOUGHT OF AS A LITERARY GENIUS, BUT NOT EVERYONE WAS A FAN.

In a letter, D.H. Lawrence said of Joyce: "My God, what a clumsy olla putrida James Joyce is! Nothing but old fags and cabbage stumps of quotations from the Bible and the rest stewed in the juice of deliberate, journalistic dirty-mindedness."

"Do I get much pleasure from this work? No," author H.G. Wells wrote regarding *Finnegans Wake*. "Who the hell is this Joyce who demands so many waking hours of the few thousand I have still to live for a proper appreciation of his quirks and fancies and flashes of rendering?"

Even his wife, Nora, had a difficult time with his work, asking, "Why don't you write sensible books that people can understand?"

JOYCE'S SUPPOSED FINAL WORDS WERE AS ABSTRACT AS HIS WRITING.

Joyce was admitted to a Zurich hospital in January 1941 for a perforated duodenal ulcer, but slipped into a coma after surgery and died on January 13. His last words were befitting his notoriously difficult works—they're said to have been,

"Does nobody understand?"

One of the most well-known book-based holidays, Bloomsday derives its name from Leopold Bloom, the protagonist of James Joyce's *Ulysses,* and is set on June 16, the day that the majority of the book takes place. Most popular in Joyce's Dublin, the Stateside celebration centers at Philadelphia's Rosenbach Museum & Library, home to the handwritten manuscript of *Ulysses.*

LITERARY FART JOKES

Bathroom humor has a proud literary tradition, with breaking wind having been a particularly popular scatological topic for millennia. Throughout history, the chance to make an occasional fart joke has often proven irresistible, even to such influential authors as Dante, Shakespeare, and Mark Twain. *Ulysses*'s protagonist, advertising canvasser Leopold Bloom, is described in a particularly unflattering scene as sitting "asquat the cuckstool . . . seated calm above his own rising smell." Here are seven references to cheese cutting made by some of the most esteemed writers of all time.

THE FIRST JOKE EVER RECORDED (1900 BCE)

Who says girls don't fart? According to University of Wolverhampton professor Paul McDonald, this ancient Sumerian one-liner is the oldest known joke in recorded history: "Something which has never occurred since time immemorial; a young woman did not fart in her husband's lap."

DANTE ALIGHIERI'S
The Inferno
(FOURTEENTH CENTURY CE)

This fourteenth-century masterpiece chronicles a fictional journey purportedly made by Dante himself through the circles of hell. At one point at the close of Chapter XXI, he witnesses a demon mobilizing his troops by using "his ass as a trumpet."

WILLIAM SHAKESPEARE'S
A Comedy of Errors (1594)

In Act 3, the Bard writes "A man may break a word with you, sir; and words are but wind; Ay, and break it in your face, so he break it not behind." (According to some, Shakespearean fart jokes are more common than one might expect.)

JONATHAN SWIFT'S
"The Benefit of Farting" (1722)

In this notorious essay, the author of *Gulliver's Travels,* writing under the pseudonym Don Fartinhando Puff-indorst, Professor of Bum bast in the University of Craccow, argues that women would be better off if they farted more.

MARK TWAIN'S *1601* (1880)

Never one to shy away from irreverent humor, Samuel Clemens's one-act show is set during a private gathering of Queen Elizabeth's court wherein somebody unexpectedly rips one, prompting the Queen to ask about its source. Lady Alice (a woman in attendance) quickly declares "Nay tis not I [who has] broughte forth this rich o'emastering [sic] fog, this fragrant gloom, so pray you seek ye further."

ARISTOPHANES'S
The Clouds (423 BCE)

At one point in the play, a simple-minded character named Strepsiades gives Socrates (yes, *that* Socrates) a bit too much information about his bowel movements: "I get colic, then the stew sets to rumbling like thunder and finally bursts forth with a terrific noise."

J.D. SALINGER'S
The Catcher in the Rye (1951)

Listening contemptuously to a "phony" minister's self-aggrandizing sermon, Holden Caulfield's scorn is temporarily interrupted when "this guy sitting in the row in front of me, Edgar Marsalla, laid this terrific fart. It was a very crude thing to do, in the chapel and all, but it was also quite amusing. Old Marsalla. He damn near blew the roof off."

UNCLE TOM'S CABIN

HARRIET BEECHER STOWE

June 14, 1811–July 1, 1896

BORN: Litchfield, Connecticut

OTHER NOTABLE WORKS:
Dred, A Tale of the Great Dismal Swamp (1856)

H arriet Beecher grew up in a family of well-educated ministers with strong opinions and no shortage of integrity, qualities that she emulated throughout her life and work. After teaching for several years, she married a professor named Calvin Ellis Stowe and quickly pivoted to writing full-time. *Uncle Tom's Cabin* earned her enough money and acclaim to probably justify an early retirement, but Stowe continued to publish stories, novels, essays, and more, cementing her legacy as one of the most influential authors of the nineteenth century.

Over forty-one issues, Harriet Beecher Stowe's novel *Uncle Tom's Cabin* was published as a serial in the abolitionist newspaper *The National Era*, beginning on June 5, 1851. Initially, it was followed by only a small group, but its audience steadily grew as the story unfolded. "Wherever I went among the friends of the *Era*, I found *Uncle Tom's Cabin* a theme for admiring remark," journalist and social critic Grace Greenwood wrote in a travelogue published in the *Era*. "Everywhere I saw it read with pleasant smiles and gushes of tears." The story was discussed in other abolitionist publications, such as *Frederick Douglass' Paper*, and helped sell $2 annual subscriptions to the *Era*.

The popularity of *Uncle Tom's Cabin* exploded once it was made available in a more accessible format. Some publishers claim the book edition is the second best-selling title of the nineteenth century, after the Bible. Stowe went on to write more than thirty books, both fiction and nonfiction, plus essays, poems, articles, and hymns.

STOWE'S FATHER AND ALL SEVEN OF HER BROTHERS WERE MINISTERS.

Harriet Elisabeth Beecher was born on June 14, 1811, in Litchfield, Connecticut. Her mother, Roxana Foote, died five years later. Over the course of two marriages, her father, Calvinist preacher Lyman Beecher, fathered thirteen children, eleven of whom survived into adulthood. He preached loudly against slavery. All seven of his sons followed him into the ministry, and Henry Ward Beecher carried on his father's abolitionist mission; according to legend sent rifles to anti-slavery settlers in Kansas and Nebraska in crates marked "Bibles."

The women of the Beecher family were also encouraged to rise to positions of influence and rally against injustice. Eldest child Catharine Beecher co-founded the Hartford Female Seminary and Isabella Beecher Hooker was a prominent suffragist.

THE FUGITIVE SLAVE ACT—AND A SURPRISE $100 GIFT—INSPIRED *UNCLE TOM'S CABIN*.

In 1832, Harriet Beecher moved to Cincinnati with her father, who assumed the presidency of Lane Theological Seminary. According to *Harriet Beecher Stowe: A Life* by Joan D. Hedrick, she met formerly enslaved and free African-Americans in the city, and it was there that she first practiced writing in a literary group called the Semi-Colon Club.

She married Calvin Ellis Stowe, a professor at Lane, and eventually relocated to Brunswick, Maine, when he went to work at Bowdoin College. By then, Stowe had published two books, *Primary Geography for Children* and the short story collection *New England Sketches*. She was also a contributor to newspapers supporting temperance and abolitionism, writing "sketches," brief descriptive stories meant to illustrate a political point.

Following a positive response to her *The Freeman's Dream: A Parable*, Gamaliel Bailey, editor of the anti-slavery paper *The National Era*, sent her $100 to encourage her to continue supplying the paper with material. The 1850 passage of the Fugitive Slave Act, obligating authorities in free states to re-enslave refugees, took the slavery fight northward. It also encouraged Stowe to step up her game.

"I am at present occupied upon a story which will be a much longer one than any I have ever written," Beecher Stowe wrote in a letter to Bailey, "embracing a series of sketches which give the lights and shadows of the 'patriarchal institution' [of slavery], written either from observation, incidents which have occurred in the sphere of my personal knowledge, or in the knowledge of my friends." For material, she scoured the written accounts relayed by escaped enslaved people.

UNCLE TOM'S CABIN MADE HER RICH AND FAMOUS.

According to Henry Louis Gates Jr.'s introduction to the annotated edition of *Uncle Tom's Cabin*, *The National Era* paid Stowe $300 for forty-three chapters. Before the serial's completion, Stowe signed a contract with John P. Jewett and Co. to publish a two-volume bound book edition, and that's when it really took off. Released on March 20, 1852, the book sold ten thousand copies in the US in its first week and three hundred thousand in the first year. In the UK, 1.5 million copies flew off the shelves. Stowe was paid ten cents for each one sold. According to a newspaper article published six months after the book's release, she had already amassed $10,000 in royalties. "We believe [that this is] the largest sum of money ever received by any author, either American or European, from the sales of a single work in so short a period of time," the newspaper stated.

SHE WENT TO COURT TO STOP AN UNAUTHORIZED TRANSLATION OF *UNCLE TOM'S CABIN* . . . AND LOST.

Immediately after *Uncle Tom's Cabin* became a literary sensation, a Philadelphia-based German-language paper, *Die Freie Presse*, began publishing an unauthorized translation. Stowe took the publisher, F.W. Thomas, to court. American copyright laws were notoriously weak at the time, irking British writers whose work was widely pirated. As someone who overnight became America's favorite author, Stowe had much at stake testing them.

The case put her in the Philadelphia courtroom of Justice Robert Grier, a notorious enforcer of the Fugitive Slave Act. "By the publication of [Mrs. Stowe's] book, the creations of the genius and imagination of the author have become as much public property as those of Homer or Cervantes," Grier ruled. The precedent set by *Stowe vs. Thomas* meant that authors had the right to prevent others from printing their exact words, but almost nothing else. "All her conceptions and inventions may be used and abused by imitators, play-rights and poet-asters," ruled Grier.

STOWE VISITED ABRAHAM LINCOLN.

Though Stowe had criticized what she saw as his slowness in emancipation and willingness to seek compromise to prevent succession, Stowe visited President Abraham Lincoln at the White House in 1862, during the early days of the Civil War. Reportedly, Lincoln greeted her with, "so this is the little woman who brought on this big Civil War," but scholars have dismissed the quote as Stowe family legend spread after her death.

Details of their conversation are limited to vague entries in their respective diaries. Lincoln may have bantered with her over his love of open fires ("I always had one to home," he reportedly said), while Stowe supposedly got down to business and quizzed him: "Mr. Lincoln, I want to ask you about your views on emancipation."

STOWE AND MARK TWAIN WERE NEIGHBORS.

The Stowes' primary residence, beginning in 1864, was a villa in the Nook Farm section of Hartford, Connecticut, a neighborhood populated by prominent citizens, including Mark Twain. The homes of Nook Farm had few fences, and doors stayed open in sunny weather, creating an air of gentility. That did not prevent Twain from writing a somewhat unflattering portrait of Stowe, as she gave way to what was probably Alzheimer's disease, in his autobiography:

"Mrs. Harriet Beecher Stowe who was a near neighbor of ours in Hartford, with no fences between. And in those days she made as much use of our grounds as of her own, in pleasant weather. Her mind had decayed, and she was a pathetic figure. She wandered about all the day long in the care of a muscular Irish-woman, assigned to her as a guardian."

BEECHER STOWE OUTLIVED FOUR OF HER SEVEN CHILDREN.

While continuing a lucrative and prolific writing career, Stowe gave birth to and raised seven children. When she passed away at eighty-five in 1896, she had outlived four of them, as bad fortune seemed to follow their offspring.

Her third child, Henry, drowned in a swimming accident in 1857. The fourth, Frederick, mysteriously disappeared in 1870. The fifth, Georgiana, died from septicemia, probably related to morphine in 1890. (She was an addict.) The sixth, Samuel, died from cholera in infancy in 1849. These losses informed several of Stowe's works.

THERE ARE SEVERAL HARRIET BEECHER STOWE HOUSES YOU CAN VISIT.

The Harriet Beecher Stowe House of Cincinnati is where she lived after following her father to Lane. The Harriet Beecher Stowe House on the campus of Bowdoin in Brunswick, Maine, is where she wrote *Uncle Tom's Cabin*. The site housed a restaurant from 1946 to 1998 and is now a faculty office building, but one room is open to the public and dedicated to Stowe. The Harriet Beecher Stowe Center preserves her home in Hartford. Stowe's home in Florida is gone, but the site where it was located is indicated by a marker.

WAITING

HA JIN

February 21, 1956

BORN: Jinzhou, Liaoning, China

OTHER NOTABLE WORKS:
In the Pond (1998)
A Map of Betrayal (2014)
The Boat Rocker (2016)

Ha Jin didn't think he'd become a writer. In the 1970s, he followed in his father's footsteps, enlisting in the People's Liberation Army; he was just fourteen, but lied about his age. After his time in the military, he worked at a railroad company, where he learned English, and three years later, he finally went to college. ("During the Cultural Revolution, no colleges were open," he once explained. "So for ten years we couldn't go to college—hence the big interruption.") Jin, whose real name is Xuefei Jin, studied American literature and got his master's, then came to the United States to study in 1985—and watched from afar four years later as the Chinese Army fired on student protestors in Tiananmen Square.

It was then that his life as a writer began. He decided to stay in America, and write only in English, publishing poetry and short story collections before releasing his first novel, *In the Pond*, in 1998, followed by *Waiting* in 1999. All the while, Tiananmen stayed with him. "To some Chinese, my choice of English is a kind of betrayal," he wrote in 2009. "But loyalty is a two-way street. I feel I have been betrayed by China, which has suppressed its people and made artistic freedom unavailable." Writing in English, he said, had been a struggle, but "literature can transcend language. If my work is good and significant, it should be valuable to the Chinese." Jin has yet to return to mainland China.

Waiting, Ha Jin's story of a doctor torn between two very different women in a changing China, won the National Book Award for Fiction in 1999. "With wisdom, restraint, and empathy for all his characters," the judges noted, "he vividly reveals the complexities and subtleties of a world and a people we desperately need to know." Here's how the book came to be.

HE GOT THE IDEA FOR *WAITING* FROM HIS WIFE.

Jin was visiting his in-laws for the first time when his wife told him the story that would inspire *Waiting*. As they were leaving the hospital where her parents worked, Jin saw a man from a distance. "My wife mentioned that guy waited eighteen years to get a divorce and now the second marriage is not working," he recalled in an interview with Asia Society. "Later, I joked, 'This would be good for a novel. I am going to write a novel based on this.'"

JIN WROTE THE BOOK TO KEEP HIS ACADEMIC JOB.

Though he tried to write *Waiting* at the time he first heard the story, Jin said he "didn't have the skills." He also didn't really have the interest: "I'd been writing, but not seriously. Even in the States I wasn't that serious," he said in an interview with Boston University's CAS News. "I published a book of poems in English, but I thought I'd return to China to teach American literature—that would be my profession. I was half-hearted."

That changed when he began teaching at Atlanta's Emory University. "I had to publish in order to keep my job," he told Asia Society. "So I think that's why I started writing *Waiting* in 1994." As he told CAS News in 2014, "I'm still in the process of becoming some kind of writer."

***WAITING* IS HIS ONLY BOOK THAT WAS PUBLISHED IN CHINA.**

In 2009, Jin reflected on the choice between writing in Chinese and writing in English. "If I wrote in Chinese, my audience would be in China and I would therefore have to publish there and be at the mercy of its censorship," he wrote. "To preserve the integrity of my work, I had no choice but to write in English." As a result, only one of his novels—*Waiting*—has been published in his home country (though he noted to *The Paris Review* that after publishing it "they suspended publication. And what they published, they edited"). "All the other books are banned," he told GRANTA. "But all my fiction books have been translated into Chinese and published in Taiwan. The readers in the Chinese diaspora can read them."

THE QUOTABLE JIN

"Imagine your books are banned—you can go back but your books are not allowed. I wouldn't feel comfortable accepting those terms."

—From an interview with *The Paris Review*, 2009

WAR AND PEACE

AND

PEACE

LEO TOLSTOY

September 9, 1828–November 20, 1910

BORN: Yasnaya Polyana, Russia

OTHER NOTABLE WORKS:
Anna Karenina (1877)
The Death of Ivan Ilyich (1886)

Widely considered one of the world's greatest novelists, Leo Tolstoy has written books that, more than a century after their publications, are still regarded as some of the best literary works ever put to paper. According to some estimates, more than 400 million copies of his works have been sold.

Tolstoy was born into wealth—his mother was a Russian princess and his father a count—and though both parents died when he was young (he was raised by an aunt), Tolstoy had a happy childhood. In 1851, four years after dropping out of law school, he joined the Army and fought in the Crimean War. The next year, he published his first novel, *Childhood*—a fictionalized account of his youth—and in the following years, he left the Army, gambled away all of his money in Paris, and started his own literary journal. In 1862, he married his wife, Sofia, and, with her support and help, began work on what would become his best known novels: *War and Peace* and *Anna Karenina*.

When he wrote that "all happy families are alike, but each unhappy family is unhappy in its own way," Tolstoy might have been speaking about his own home life. He and Sofia had thirteen children (eight of whom would survive to adulthood), and he often carried on affairs with local women while she was pregnant. Sofia did all of the housework, managed the estate, and cared for their children in addition to acting as his secretary and editor. At first their marriage was happy, but it began to sour after Tolstoy experienced a religious conversion in the 1880s. Their marriage grew increasingly bitter and, in 1910, Tolstoy fled his estate. He contracted pneumonia and died at a railroad station of heart failure just a few days later. He was eighty-two.

Leo Tolstoy spent years writing *War and Peace*, his masterful examination of Russian society in the early nineteenth century. Parts of the novel originally appeared in serial form in the journal *Russian Messenger*, but Tolstoy's wife Sofia convinced him that publishing the work in bound volumes would be more successful. Today, the 1,200-page epic remains a best seller.

WAR AND PEACE WAS NOT ITS FIRST TITLE.

The novel opens at a party in St. Petersburg at which many of the main characters are introduced. The year is 1805; Napoleon Bonaparte rules France and has recently executed a French duke whom he accused of treason, a killing that shocks Europe's ruling families. In Russia, Tsar Alexander I forms an alliance with Britain to restrain Napoleon's power. These real-life events set the characters' storylines in motion, which is why the original title of *War and Peace*, when it was serialized in the *Russian Messenger* in 1865, was *1805*.

TOLSTOY HAD ISSUES WRITING THE OPENING OF THE NOVEL.

Speaking of the book's opening scene: It did not come to Tolstoy in a flash. In fact, it took almost a full year for the author to write an introduction that he was happy with. During that time, according to Tolstoy scholar Kathryn B. Feuer, he wrote fifteen beginnings, elaborating on two of them, as well as four introductions and a preface to the novel.

It wouldn't be the only time Tolstoy struggled with a book: Nearly a decade later, while writing *Anna Karenina* (1878), Tolstoy ended up in a similar position. After outlining the entire story in just a few weeks, it then took him nearly four-and-a-half years to complete the book (though more than half that time was spent avoiding the manuscript, which he had deemed both "sickening" and "unbearably repulsive").

It didn't help that Tolstoy was experiencing major personal upheaval during that time, with three of his children passing away. Yet again, it was Sofia—whom he dubbed *Anna Karenina*'s "midwife"—who encouraged her husband to complete the book.

THE NOVEL IS SET DURING THE NAPOLEONIC WARS.

War and Peace takes place between 1805 and 1820, when Europe was transformed by Napoleon's military power and the aftermath of his defeat at the Battle of Waterloo. Over this period, Napoleon's Grande Armée crushed Russian, Spanish, and Austrian forces in several key battles, prompting Tsar Alexander to form alliances with France. But Russia wasn't a particularly keen ally, so Napoleon invaded in 1812; he was forced back after a series of extremely bloody fights. Tolstoy's three main protagonists— the Romantic intellectual Pierre Bezukhov, the patriotic Prince Andrei Bolkonsky, and Natasha Rostova, the charismatic woman they both love—experience these events and react to the changes they bring to Russia.

THE BOOK CONTAINS A MASSIVE CAST OF CHARACTERS.

For readers who have trouble keeping track of who's who in a book, it might be a good idea to keep a notebook handy while reading *War and Peace*. The novel introduces a total of 559 characters from beginning to end, with approximately two hundred of those names being real-life historical figures.

WAR AND PEACE EMPLOYED INNOVATIVE METHODS OF STORYTELLING.

Tolstoy used literary devices like stream of consciousness, an omniscient point of view, expository essays, and multiple perspectives in *War and Peace* to enhance the story's realism. The novel didn't fit into established literary categories when it was published as a novel in 1869, and that was by design. "It is not a novel, still less an epic poem, still less a historical chronicle," Tolstoy explained in 1868, before the last parts of the book were published. "*War and Peace* is what the author wanted and was able to express, in the form in which it is expressed."

IT'S NOT THE LONGEST NOVEL EVER WRITTEN— NOT EVEN CLOSE.

War and Peace is regularly used as a punch line when discussing the longest books ever written, but it doesn't even come close to earning that title. While its first published edition was 1,225 pages long, its English version (owing to translation changes) puts it at about 587,287 words total. Vikram Seth's 1993 novel *A Suitable Boy*, on the other hand, comes in at more than 590,000 words; Ayn Rand's *Atlas Shrugged* is about 645,000 words; Victor Hugo's *Les Misérables* is 655,478 words; and American author Madison Cooper's 1952 tome *Sironia, Texas* contains a whopping 840,000 words (albeit in two volumes).

IN 1918, *WAR AND PEACE* GOT A LITTLE BIT SHORTER.

In 1918, the Russian alphabet got a bit of a makeover in order to get rid of several underutilized letters, which included the letter Ѣ. Its removal from *War and Peace* supposedly led to the book becoming eleven pages shorter.

TOLSTOY VISITED BATTLEFIELDS TO ENSURE HIS NOVEL'S AUTHENTICITY.

At twenty-six, Tolstoy fought in the Crimean War's Sevastopol campaign, during which British, French, and other allied troops forced an eleven-month siege on the important Black Sea port and eventually captured it from Russia in 1855. The siege introduced trench warfare and other horrible forms of modern fighting. It also gave Tolstoy first-hand experience in the central themes of *War and Peace*: "that battles were a form of deliberate folly, that the only enduring nation was humanity, that ordinary Russians were always better than the rulers whom history seemed to give them," professor and historian Charles King wrote. When he was researching the Battle of Borodino, a key scene in *War and Peace*, Tolstoy visited the actual battlefield where 25,000 soldiers were killed and 55,000 wounded.

A MAJOR SCENE IN *WAR AND PEACE* HINGES ON A COMET.

At a turning point in the novel, Pierre reveals his longstanding romantic feelings for Natasha, though she is in love with another man. He steps outside to collect his thoughts and looks up in the starlit sky: "Surrounded on every side by stars, but distinguished from all the rest by its nearness to earth, and by its white light, and by its long, curling tail, stood the tremendous brilliant comet of 1812, the very comet which men thought presaged all manner of woes and the end of the world. But in Pierre, this brilliant luminary, with its long train of light, awoke no terror."

The comet's appearance was a real event in 1811 (and was visible with the naked eye into January 1812). Reportedly, the tail appeared as long as fifty full moons. It remained visible for 260 nights—enough time for people to assign all kinds of meaning to it. Napoleon saw it as a good omen for his invasion of Russia, which Tolstoy echoed in *War and Peace*.

WAR AND PEACE INSPIRED A MUSICAL.

Natasha, Pierre & The Great Comet of 1812 is based on seventy pages of *War and Peace*—specifically, Volume Two, Part Five (chapters three through five were omitted). Composer and lyricist Dave Malloy was working on a cruise ship when he read the novel; he told Radio Boston that he was "swept away" by how the section had the "perfect structure" for a musical, thanks to its narrative drive and elements like Natasha's fall from grace and Pierre's mid-life crisis. *The Great Comet of 1812* debuted on Broadway in 2016 with Josh Groban as Pierre and Denée Benton as Natasha; it won two Tony Awards.

TOLSTOY DIDN'T LOVE *WAR AND PEACE*.

War and Peace is arguably Tolstoy's most famous work, not to mention one of the most celebrated novels ever written. But it wasn't exactly what you'd describe as a "labor of love." Despite spending so much time with the book (or perhaps because of it), Tolstoy quickly grew disdainful of the novel once it was completed. In a 1908 entry in his own diary, he wrote, "People love me for the trifles—*War and Peace* and so on—that they think are so important."

TOLSTOY NEVER WON A NOBEL PRIZE.

While Tolstoy himself may have grown tired of all the accolades for *War and Peace*, its importance in the history of literature has never been disputed. Which is why, when the Nobel Prize in Literature debuted in 1901, many people assumed Tolstoy would be the obvious winner. In what's still considered one of the biggest snubs in the award's history, he was passed over in favor of French poet Sully Prudhomme. Forty-two Swedish writers and artists wrote Tolstoy to express their disagreement with the Nobel Prize committee, to which he responded, "I was very happy to know the Nobel Prize was not awarded to me. It deprived me of a big problem of how to use the money." He was nominated each subsequent year until 1906 (and was nominated for the Nobel Peace Prize in 1901, 1902, and 1909).

TOLSTOY IS ONE OF THE BEST-SELLING AUTHORS OF ALL TIME.

While it's difficult to come up with any exact sales numbers for books published prior to the twentieth century, it's safe to say that Leo Tolstoy's books are perennial bestsellers. In 2004 alone, *Anna Karenina* got a major boost from Oprah Winfrey when she chose the title for her Book Club, leading its publisher to increase that year's print run of the 1878 novel from twenty thousand to 800,000 copies. *War and Peace* also sold enough copies to make the UK Bookseller's top fifty list in 2016, the same year the BBC adapted it into a miniseries starring Paul Dano, Lily James, and James Norton. According to some estimates, more than 400 million copies of Tolstoy's works have been sold.

A 1965 FILM ADAPTATION WAS MORE THAN SEVEN HOURS LONG.

While a word-for-word version of *War and Peace* would be impossibly expensive—not to mention long—even the truncated 1965 film adaptation was its own epic. It had massive battle sequences, used 12,000 extras, and took approximately five years to make, during which time director Sergey Bondarchuk had two heart attacks. The film was originally released in four parts and had a total running time of seven hours and eleven minutes (down from Bondarchuk's original eight hours). It earned rave reviews from the likes of *New York* magazine's Judith Crist and Roger Ebert, who called it "the definitive epic of all time"; when a restored version of the film was released in 2019, *The New York Times* called the adaptation "a singular feat of filmmaking that can never be repeated."

Bondarchuk's *War and Peace* was nominated for two Academy Awards, and picked up the Oscar for Best Foreign Language Film at the 1969 ceremony.

TERMS EVERY BOOK LOVER SHOULD KNOW

7

Bibliophiles can use these words to spice up their literary vocabulary.

Librocubicularist: A person who reads in bed. The word was coined in 1919 by Christopher Morley in *The Haunted Bookshop*.

Bibliotaph: A word, dating to the nineteenth century, that refers to a person who keeps their books "under lock and key," according to the *Oxford English Dictionary. Mrs. Byrne's Dictionary of Unusual, Obscure and Preposterous Words* defines it as "one who hoards or hides books." A person who steals books, meanwhile, is a biblioklept (and someone who steals and destroys books is a book-ghoul).

Book-bosomed: The *OED* defines book-bosomed as "carrying a book concealed in the bosom"—in other words, having a book on you wherever you go.

Chaptique: Coined by Molly Schoemann-McCann on Barnes & Noble's blog in 2014, this portmanteau of "chapter" and "fatigue" is what you can use the morning after you've been up late reading.

Omnilegent: "Reading or having read everything," according to *Merriam-Webster.* Omnilegent dates back to 1828.

Bibliobibuli: In his 1956 book *Minority Report*, H.L. Mencken came up with this word—which combines the Greek *biblio* (books) with the Latin *bibulus* ("drinking freely")—for "people who read too much" and are "constantly drunk on books." Sorry, H.L.: In our opinion, there's no such thing as reading too much.

Abibliophobia: Those afflicted with abibliophobia fear running out of things to read.

OUR FAVORITE NOVELS THAT DIDN'T MAKE THE CUT

These novels may not have made our main list, but we love them nonetheless.

THE PICTURE OF DORIAN GRAY

BY OSCAR WILDE

RECOMMENDED BY:
KAT LONG, SCIENCE EDITOR

Wilde's novel is a morality tale—although Wilde himself said that books are neither moral nor immoral, just well or badly written. Dorian Gray, a beautiful and petulant young man, represents the flip side of Victorian values. He's decadent, spoiled, and lives only for pleasure, aided and abetted by the unctuous Lord Henry Wotton. Sybil Vane, an actress, has the misfortune to fall in love with Dorian, and her demise sets Dorian's complete surrender to depravity in motion. And yet, though it all, he remains as handsome as ever, thanks to that portrait stashed away upstairs. I love how Wilde's presentation of Victorian morality in a fun-house mirror makes readers re-evaluate their own ethics.

A LITTLE LIFE
BY HANYA YANAGIHARA

RECOMMENDED BY:
ELLEN GUTOSKEY, STAFF WRITER

Describing this novel with a plot summary is so reductive it almost seems irrelevant. *A Little Life* technically follows a group of four young men—an artist, an actor, an architect, and a lawyer—as they grapple with their pasts and stumble toward their futures in modern-day New York City. It's less about what happens to them (though a lot does, much of it tragic) and more about how those experiences mold their identities and sense of purpose. Yanagihara has created characters so uniquely human that it's hard to remember they're just characters. By the time you've finished reading their stories, you might find that Jude, Willem, Malcolm, and JB have seeped into the part of your brain occupied by your own real-life loved ones.

THE AMAZING ADVENTURES OF KAVALIER & CLAY
BY MICHAEL CHABON

RECOMMENDED BY:
JUSTIN DODD, VIDEO PRODUCER

If you're interested in the history and culture of America during World War II but don't really want another overly masculine or patriotic story of battle, this book is perfect. A totally unique, empathetic, heartbreaking, and genuinely funny novel about a Jewish refugee and his Brooklyn cousin trying to make it in the comic business.

CIRCE
BY MADELINE MILLER

RECOMMENDED BY: KERRY WOLFE, STAFF EDITOR

This isn't the Circe you met while poring over the *Odyssey*. Miller's version of the legendary sorceress offers a new perspective on the classic tales you learned in high school. In this novel, Circe's strangeness is her strength. Told from her point of view, the story offers an enchanting look into the witch's mind, letting modern readers discover that the unsavory antics she's known for—turning Odysseus's men into swine, for example—are rooted in unfailingly familiar, human instincts.

THE TIME TRAVELER'S WIFE
BY AUDREY NIFFENEGGER

RECOMMENDED BY:
JAKE ROSSEN, SENIOR STAFF WRITER

Time travel is a well-worn trope, but Niffenegger embraces its romanticism rather than its action potential in this irreverent love story. As Henry DeTamble bounces in and out of wife Clare's life, the victim of a genetic abnormality that causes him to bounce through time, Clare ponders the consequences of an absentee relationship. Funny and occasionally wrenching, it's that rarest of genre works—a study in the human effect of the fantastic.

BURIAL RITES
BY HANNAH KENT

RECOMMENDED BY:
ERIN MCCARTHY, EDITOR-IN-CHIEF

Hannah Kent's *Burial Rites* imagines the final days of Agnes Magnúsdóttir, a real Icelandic woman convicted of murder who was beheaded in 1830 in the country's last public execution. Researching the events surrounding Magnúsdóttir's life and death, Kent was unable to find details about what factors may have led her and her two co-conspirators to commit their heinous crime. In real life, Magnúsdóttir was demonized and painted simply as an evil monster—but in *Burial Rites*, Kent flips the script on those ugly stereotypes, portraying Magnúsdóttir as an complex person worthy of sympathy, in spite of her terrible crime.

A CONFEDERACY OF DUNCES
BY JOHN KENNEDY TOOLE

RECOMMENDED BY:
JENNIFER M. WOOD, MANAGING EDITOR

In the more than forty years it's been since *A Confederacy of Dunces* was published, the movie rights to John Kennedy Toole's Pulitzer Prize-winning novel have been passed around Hollywood with no finished product to speak of. In many ways, this might be the ultimate compliment to the perfectly absurd world that Toole created, and the singularly absurd character of Ignatius J. Reilly—a lazy and obnoxious glutton who hates everything about the modern world and considers himself better than most of it—in particular. To give life to the character via a living, breathing actor would undo too many of the brilliantly nuanced eccentricities the author crafted in creating Reilly, who serves as more of a caricature. Nor would any real-world setting be able to replicate the very specific version of New Orleans that Toole wrote about (nope, not even the real New Orleans). While the bulk of the book revolves around Reilly and his equally odd mother (with whom be lives, because of course he does) as Ignatius is forced to interact with his fellow New Orleanians while attempting to find a job, it also serves as a love letter to city's endless quirks—many of which only NOLA natives ever get to see. It's a sprawling story that is equal parts hilarious and tragic, and demands that every word of it be read.

REVOLUTIONARY ROAD
BY RICHARD YATES

RECOMMENDED BY:
JAY SERAFINO, SPECIAL PROJECTS EDITOR

You'd be hard-pressed to find a more compelling indictment of America's post-World War II boom than what Richard Yates achieved here. In this story, a quiet suburban life isn't a symbol of comfort and success—it's a source of stagnation where passion, personal connections, and creative fulfillment are put out to pasture. With unflinching realism, Yates details the erosion of idealism, as it gives way to the crushing maw of conformity.

MY STRUGGLE
BY KARL OVE KNAUSGÅRD

RECOMMENDED BY:
JOHN MAYER, SENIOR VIDEO PRODUCER

Knausgård's controversial title is at once a hyperbolic joke and a deeply empathetic view of existence. His "struggle" consists largely of ordinary activities like getting his children dressed, but his minute observation of these mundanities somehow elevates them. "This is life!" each page seems to scream. "This heartbreak!" "This herring sandwich. This, too, is life!" Vain and graceful, self-absorbed and searching, Knausgård creates a singular sketch of what it is to be alive.

THE OVERSTORY
BY RICHARD POWERS

RECOMMENDED BY:
MICHELE DEBCZAK, SENIOR STAFF WRITER

I thought I loved trees before reading *The Overstory*, but it turns out I had nothing on the book's author Richard Powers. His novel is an ambitious ode to a part of our ecosystem many of us take for granted. Following multiple, interconnected characters that have all been touched by trees in some way, *The Overstory* forever changed the way I view nature.

EVERYTHING I NEVER TOLD YOU
BY CELESTE NG

RECOMMENDED BY:
ANGELA TROTTI, SOCIAL MEDIA EDITOR

Opening with the line "Lydia is dead. But they don't know this yet," Celeste Ng's debut novel follows the story of a family in crisis after the mysterious death of their "favorite" child. Ng expertly captures the complexities of navigating familial relationships through grief. The novel will hit you where it hurts—but keep reading.

ACKNOWLEDGMENTS

You would not be holding *The Curious Reader* in your hands if not for the hard work of many people. First, thank you to our agent, Dinah Dunn, and our designer, Carol Bobolts, at Indelible Editions, and to our publisher, Weldon Owen, Inc., especially Roger Shaw, Mariah Bear, and Ian Cannon.

To the whole Mental Floss team—Michele Debczak, Justin Dodd, Ellen Gutoskey, Kat Long, Jon Mayer, Jake Rossen, Jason Serafino, Angela Trotti, Jenn Wood, and Kerry Wolfe—for their enthusiasm, support, and, of course, for contributing incredible work to *The Curious Reader*; and to the former Mental Floss staffers whose writing also appears in this book: Shaunacy Ferro, Anna Green, Nick Greene, Kate Horowitz, Hannah Keyser, Bess Lovejoy, Beth Anne Macaluso, Emily Petsko, Caitlin Schneider, Ethan Trex, and Sonia Weiser.

We could not have made this book without the support of our Minute Media family. Many thanks to Matan Har, Ze'ev Rozov, Chad Payne, Kimberly Holland, and everyone else who was so enthusiastic about this project.

Thank you to Austin Thompson for his meticulous fact checking of the manuscript; to Melanie Gold for proofreading; and to Bess Lovejoy for her work on the proposal for *The Curious Reader*.

Finally, thank you to the freelance writers who contributed: Mica Arbeiter (Facts About *1984*, *Brave New World*, *Catch-22*, *Don Quixote*, and *Lord of the Flies*); Scott Beggs (Facts About Ernest Hemingway); Alex Carter (contributed research to Ruthless Rejections Letters); Stacy Conradt (Facts About Ray Bradbury, Stephen King, and *The Great Gatsby*; Literary Characters Based on Real People; Mary Shelley's Favorite Keepsake; Things Mark Twain Didn't Really Say; Famous Author Feuds; Authors Who Hated Movie Versions of Their Books); Jill Harness (Novels Written in Under a Month); Sean Hutchinson (Writers Who Loved Cats; Harsh Reviews of Classic Novels; and Facts About *Ulysses*); Nick Keppler (Facts About *Uncle Tom's Cabin*); Joy Lanzendorfer (Facts About *Frankenstein*, *Jane Eyre*, *Little Women*, *Pride and Prejudice*, *The Adventures of Huckleberry Finn*, *The Bell Jar*, *The Call of the Wild*, *The Grapes of Wrath*, and *To Kill a Mockingbird*); Mark Mancini (Facts About *Dune*, *Moby-Dick*, and *The Jungle*; Literary Fart Jokes; Awesome Things Harper Lee Did After *To Kill a Mockingbird*; Virginia Woolf Quotes); Linda Rodriguez McRobbie (research for *Pride and Prejudice*'s Greatest Critics); Arika Okrent (Authors Who Disliked Punctuation Marks); Rebecca Pahle (entries in Differences Between *A Game of Thrones* Book and the Show); Garin Pirnia (The Real Mr. Darcy); Kristy Puchko (Facts About *Fahrenheit 451*); Suzanne Raga (Facts About Louisa May Alcott, Aldous Huxley, and Kurt Vonnegut); Austin Thompson (Best-Selling Books of All Time); and Natelegé Whaley (Amazing Books by Black Authors).

INDEX